KILL ME NO MORE

GAYLON DINGLER

KILL ME NO MORE

iUniverse books may be ordered through booksellers or by contacting:

iUniverse
1663 Liberty Drive
Bloomington, IN 47403
www.iuniverse.com
844-349-9409

ISBN: 978-1-6632-2517-7 (sc)
ISBN: 978-1-6632-2516-0 (hc)
ISBN: 978-1-6632-2518-4 (e)

Library of Congress Control Number: 2021918663

Print information available on the last page.

iUniverse rev. date: 09/10/2021

1

The slash of twigs and the splat of lead balls hitting tree trunks could be heard behind the Texas infantry as they waited to move forward into a withering fire from the Union 1st Corp approaching them from the South. The battle had raged since daylight and Union artillery was dropping exploding cannon balls on them, adding to the scene of horror.

The Texans were in a fighting mood after being rousted from morning breakfast. Except for a ration of beef, the men had not been fed in three days. The Texans had arrived the day before and had been placed in the West Woods, the far left of the Confederate defensive line north of Sharpsburg, Maryland, a mile from Antietam Creek. General John B. Hood pleaded with General Robert E. Lee to let his men be taken out of line and fed, knowing that a battle was near and his men needed all the strength they could muster. Lee decided that if Hood's commanding officer, General Stonewall Jackson agreed, the hungry soldiers could be taken out of their defensive position long enough to eat.

Arrangements were made, and at 10:00 p.m. Hood's men were withdrawn several hundred yards, behind the white Dunker Church, to rendezvous with the commissary wagons to be fed before the coming battle. The supply wagons caught up with them early the next morning, and they consumed their first good breakfast in days and received some mail.

At first, General Stonewall Jackson was reluctant to take Hood's 2400 men out of his defensive line. The evening before, the Union General "Fighting Joe" Hooker had sent part of his 1st Corps southward down the Hagerstown Pike toward Sharpsburg, but the battle fizzled out at dark. Jackson knew, however, the battle would most likely resume along the road at daylight, so Hood had orders to be ready to move forward, if needed, on an instant's notice.

During the night, sporadic fire between pickets alerted sleeping men to the impending fight. As expected, at daylight, Hooker's 1st Corps moved southward and was immediately engaged by Confederate cavalry leader, General Jeb Stuart and his horse artillery, which poured cannon fire into the advancing Union line. Infantry joined in and the deadliest single-day battle of the American Civil War began. The battlefield was shrouded with foggy, damp, misty weather with just enough moisture to make the soldiers uncomfortable. Gun smoke added to the fog, making it hard to see very far in front of them.

That morning, just as the Texans had started eating, the mail caught up with Hood's Division and was dispensed to the soldiers. The soldiers, were so hungry they gobbled down their food, but before they could eat all they wanted, an order came for the brigade to move forward immediately. The soldiers grabbed what food they could carry with them, moved rapidly to the front, and took their defensive positions again in the West Woods, behind a slope just west of the Hagerstown Pike.

They knew it was furious up front. Stretcher bearers hurried past them with their ghastly cargo of mangled bodies, many of which would never see, walk, or breathe again. This stream of destroyed humanity did not motivate a soldier to move forward, but these men were Hood's Texans, and they had seen many sights like this in the past year. Most were afraid, but they were too proud to reveal it. A few men read from small Bibles as they knelt behind the ledge, knowing there was a real chance they only had a few more minutes on earth. Men discarded decks of cards, thought by many to be instruments of the devil. Several men huddled and scribbled and exchanged notes, hoping if they were killed, their friends might pass them on to their loved ones.

The noise of the battle grew nearer, but the Hood's Brigade waited for the order that would send them ahead. A Confederate officer, protected by the steep bank rode up and ordered the men to "give the Yankees hell" when they went forward.

Marcus Mills, an eighteen-year-old soldier, also hidden behind the steep bank, prayed that he would not run and cower, but accept what triumphs or tragedies faced him this day. Earlier, the Texans had filled the cartridge boxes on their belts with as many Minie balls as they would hold. Each lead projectile was wrapped in paper that contained black powder inside. As a soldier reloaded he bit the end of the paper and tore it off, poured the powder down the barrel, inserted the bullet wrapped in paper, and pushed it down the barrel with his ramrod. After placing a percussion cap under the hammer, the bullet was ready to fire. A good soldier could get off three rounds per minute.

Although he was in Hood's Texas Division, Marcus belonged to the 18th Georgia Regiment that fought with the Texans. He had received a letter from his fiancé that morning before breakfast, but near starvation, he stuffed the letter in his pocket, and ate while he had the chance, knowing they would advance at any moment. As he waited against the bank, Marcus thought about home; his fiancé; Bonnie, his family; and his best friend, his dog Fetch. He wanted to open his letter, but a ferocious fire was coming in and he feared he might lose it.

Marcus was sixteen when he entered the war, too young to shave his handsome face, now covered with heavy peach fuzz and framed with shaggy blond hair sticking out of the bottom of his gray Confederate cap. He was a happy, friendly sort of young lad who made everyone who met him want to be his friend. Back home, all the young girls had wanted Marcus to choose them to go to a dance or be their special beau, but Marcus was in love and planned to marry Bonnie Staples, the girl who lived on the next farm over. He would read her letter when the woods were not filled with hot lead peeling bark away from the trees.

As the men came up out of their cover they could hear the large 59- caliber Minie balls snipping the leaves and smacking the trees. Instinctively the men leaned forward as if going into a heavy rain. As they tramped ahead through the West Woods in orderly ranks, they heard the music of battle: the steady hum of bullets, the loud crescendos' of cannon fire, the moans and screams of wounded men, officers yelling commands, bugles blowing, galloping artillery horses, all being conducted by generals they could not see.

Marcus could see they were near the edge of the woods and would soon be exposed to the full fury of the rifle and cannon with no protection from the trees. The black powder smoke from thousands of guns began to sting eyes and accumulate on white faces, giving the soldiers the appearance of players in a minstrel show. This new make-up along with the rebel yell, gave the soldiers a demon like appearance. Men in the line began to fall as they cleared the woods and tried to make it to the shelter of a split-rail fence on the edge of a corn field. Smoke from the rifles and cannon filled the landscape making vision almost impossible for any distance. The battle music was building. Suddenly, his best friend, slightly ahead of him in line, collapsed on his face as they crossed the Hagerstown Turnpike. The moment he collapsed Marcus noticed his hat flew off his head as if it had been tied to a string and someone had jerked it, causing it to fly in the air. Marcus fell to his knees by his fallen friend and rolled him over only to see his friend's forehead was shattered by a large lead ball.

Before he could say anything, a crusty old sergeant grabbed him by the back of the neck and pulled him forward and yelling in the din of battle, "You can't help him. He's looking at God right now."

Marcus had no time to think about what had just happened, a scene he had witnessed many times before; but this was his best friend. He did not have time to mourn as the men stopped for only moments behind the rail fence. Orders were given to move forward into the "cornfield" that was being cut down to the ground by the heavy volleys as if it had been mowed. The men leaped over the fence, formed a line, lifted their rifles, and fired into the smoke at advancing Union infantry. The Union ranks were blown away by the tremendous volley. The men reloaded and the command, "Forward," was heard above the noise. They moved a few yards into the smoky, loud landscape and started running forward, yelling like crazy people, planting fear in their enemy with the "rebel yell" that had proven so successful in past battles. Some said it was equivalent to an extra brigade.

It seemed things were going well, and then the entire line was struck by canister fire from the Union cannons, and the men fell in rows as if they had been carefully placed next to each other. Canister was the machine gun of the Civil War or the equivalent of a large shotgun. The artillery men fired tin cans filled with small steel balls and fired them at close quarters at the enemy. The steel balls cut down everyone in their path. Often the cannons would be loaded with double and triple canisters, to make the killing more effective.

Almost the entire line had been swept away by the vicious blast of canister. Marcus and a few other men next to him were fortunately still standing without a scratch. Apparently, his part of the line was not directly in front of one of the cannons belching its deadly shot, and they were missed by the awful discharge. Seeing their predicament they fell to the ground and tried to hide in the small furrows between the rows of corn. Their only protections from the fierce fire were the short stalks of corn, the dirt that made the row of corn, and the bodies of dead men who might shield them from the fire.

One of the men who had not been hit was in front of him, and Marcus huddled on the ground and looked at the bottom of his worn-out shoes. He could hear the cries of the wounded men next to him. The concussions of the nearby cannons shook the ground, like big bass drums added to the music of war. The sergeant who had jerked him forward was lying on his back unbuttoning his coat and shirt to see where he was hit. He knew a body wound was most often fatal, but he hoped it was only a flesh wound or a hit in the ribs where there were no major organs.

Marcus's clothes was soaked with blood that had been spilled by the earlier contestants in the morning battle. The "cornfield" had been won and lost by both armies before the Texans arrived. The entire 40- acre cornfield was nearly covered in bodies. General Hooker said later one could walk across the entire field without ever stepping on the ground. The smoke and noise continued, although the canister fire had been the crescendo of the morning conflict.

Marcus and the few survivors realized they needed to get out of there, but as they watched, a new Union-blue line emerged from the smoke and approached them. He knew if he stood up and ran away he would immediately be shot down. To surrender was no option either. He had heard rumors about the cruel conditions in Northern prisoner of war camps and knew he would most likely die of disease after enduring terrible miseries and privations before he died.

The firing died down somewhat and smoke again covered the approaching Union line. Thinking they were hidden, two of the men with Marcus stood up and ran, fear finally taking over their legs. At that moment, Marcus saw the new Union line beginning to appear out of the smoke. Although foggy earlier, the sky was clearing and the day was turning out to be sunny and hot. Marcus caught sight of the shiny bayonets reflecting the sun giving a crisp sparkle to the horrid landscape. One of the two men who ran was shot many times by the approaching line. The other man fell to his knees with his hands up, and fortunately, was spared.

Marcus decided to play dead. He hoped the Union line would pass over him and be forced back, and when the Confederate line came forward across the "cornfield," he could join his men again; or maybe if that didn't happen, he could crawl to safety after dark. He knew at night, battlefields quieted down, and an unwritten truce enabled sympathetic soldiers to render aid to the dying and wounded.

The blue Union line emerged clearly out of the smoke as they neared him. To appear dead, Marcus lay motionless between the rows of stalks and eyed the enemy through one eye as the line came forward. He could hear the sound of boots shuffling the broken stalks and the occasional command issued by the officers in the line, "Straight ahead, men. Look fit; be ready."

Marcus was awed by how well the men were equipped with their blue uniforms, boots, and weapons. His Rebel army looked like tattered scarecrows, with every kind of hat, ragged gray coat or a blue coat captured from Federal forces, and many of his comrades were unshod. How could they beat such a well-equipped army?

The rustle of leather packs and the clink of buckles and tin cups attached to their sides indicated the Union soldiers were nearly on him. He shut his eyes. Then the blue soldiers were on top of him. Most of the soldiers were having difficulty keeping the line straight as they marched through the fallen ranks; most tried not to step on the many who were only wounded, as they listened to their solos, "Help me," "Please, please, give me water," and a few pleading to be shot to end their miseries.

Whether on purpose or by accident, one of the soldiers in blue stepped right in the middle of his back. Expecting to be stepped on, Marcus held his breath, trying to conceal the fact he was alive, and did not move when the boot hit his back. He opened his eye and saw another line close behind the first. The second line passed over him without any contact or footprints on his body. He looked and saw a few stragglers coming up to catch the main battle line that had just passed.

He wanted to turn his head and watch the Union troops move forward, hoping there would be a major counterattack by his comrades. Finally, curiosity overcame his fear, and with no troops approaching, he quickly turned his head to see the Federal line disappearing in the smoke. The Federal attack seemed to make progress as the sound got farther away and muffled by the thick smoke. He could tell a raging fight was going on back toward Dunker Church, from where he had come. The sound turned into a roar so loud individual gunshots could no longer be heard.

Several minutes later, Marcus noticed the roar of battle was returning his way; louder and louder it came, like an approaching thunderstorm. He could hear the whine of the Minie ball overhead as the rifle fire increased from the Confederate lines. He could see Union forces retreating back toward him. Suddenly, a tremendous volley from the Confederate lines in the woods ripped into the Union brigade and many of the men melted into the ground at the edge of his vision. The survivors returned the volley and started walking backwards firing in the direction of the Confederate line. A bullet struck the ground four inches from the top of Marcus's head. He could hear more Minie balls coming in from the Confederates, hitting dead men with the sound all veterans remembered and never forgot, "thud."

The men in blue stopped, knelt, reloaded, and returned fire again. The hum of rifle bullets from both sides gave background music to the war being waged in front of him. Marcus wished he was smaller. Another salvo from the Rebels caused the Union line to turn and race for the protection of Union artillery at the north end of the "cornfield". The soldiers who had just passed over him a few moments ago in a neat straight line, now scrambled one by one back over his body to find safety. With his watchful eye, he saw a wounded man crawling toward him in the same row. The man had apparently been grazed in the head, but while bleeding, he still had the sense to keep low and get back to his lines any way he could. He got to Marcus and crawled over him trying to find relief from the fire that was increasing and getting closer. He crawled past Marcus and disappeared down the rows of broken cornstalks.

Marcus continued to play his part as a corpse to perfection. He opened his eyes and saw a few more Union stragglers coming his way. He squinted so he could see but not give away his masquerade. One of the lagging soldiers, obviously wounded, abandoned by his comrades, and using his rifle as a crutch, was also trying to make it home. Just as he reached Marcus, a bullet hit him in the back and he fell forward and landed on Marcus. The man winced in pain, slid off Marcus, and tried to push him aside to make more room in the cornrow. The man's face was next to Marcus's chest, and even though wounded, he kept trying to push him out of the row. Marcus looked at the man, struggling to make himself more protected, and whispered, "Be still! You're gonna get us both killed." Startled by the bloody, talking corpse, the soldier raised his head, and unfortunately for him, directly in front of a Confederate soldier. The Rebel, also surprised by the movement at his feet, reacted and stabbed the unlucky man in the back with his bayonet; and the poor man collapsed again on Marcus's back.

More Rebels appeared in the smoke coming his way, and Marcus became jubilant. He was safe now, but not saved. Just at the moment he decided to pick up his rifle and move forward, another round of canister tore into the Confederate soldiers as the remnants of the Union infantry disappeared behind the safety of their cannon. The dead man on top of him was riddled by the blast and his carcass most likely saved Marcus's life. He saw no Confederate soldiers retreat back to the woods.

The bloody body oozed warm blood on top of him but gave him protection from incoming fire from both sides. After a few moments, heavy Yankee artillery fire from the east, beyond Antietam Creek, started falling into the cornfield among the wounded men. As the cannon balls exploded, dirt was thrown up and fell on Marcus and his dead companion. He prayed one of the huge shells did not fall on him. His gray uniform was now dyed with the deep red blood of the dead man still on top of him.

The battle approached midmorning and the fighting died down to random shots taken by snipers and riflemen back in their main defensive line with an occasional boom from an artillery piece. Groans and pleas for help could be heard out in the "cornfield." Each side expected a new advance and kept alert and ready to fire on any enemy movement that might appear in their front. They saw the carnage and heard the cries, but it was too dangerous to help their fallen brave men. Anyone who had entered the "cornfield" that day was a hero. However, the Union soldiers were readying for one more attempt to try and take the "cornfield," and Marcus could sense by the shouting along the line another attack was imminent.

Marcus lay in his cramped row, protected by the dead man on top of him and other corpses next to him. He appreciated the fact that this body had saved his life from the canister, but his fears of the dead began to take over his senses; he was tired of looking at the man's face whose eyeballs were staring right back at him, as if he was watching and waiting for him to help but never saying anything. The warm blood began to cool and clot on his clothes and would soon be stinking in the hot sun. He had to find a way out of this predicament.

Marcus raised his head enough to see the soldiers in blue forming a column behind their artillery several hundred feet away; so he slid out from under his new friend, slowly, as not to draw attention to his locale. The cornfield was not like an unmoving, uncovered graveyard, but instead similar to a tangle of writhing snakes spread over the forty acres. It definitely was not still; arms moved and wounded soldiers raised up or attempted to sit up to draw attention to their dilemma, hoping they might attract someone to help them, or maybe shoot them, depending on their pain. Marcus felt it was safer now for him to try and get back to the Hagerstown Pike and the West Woods before the impending Union advance began.

He needed a drink of water. His canteen was still strapped around his shoulder and laid at his side. He pulled it up close to his mouth, but it was empty. He flipped it over and saw where a bullet had punctured it.

He pushed himself backward down the row slowly. He thought to himself, "I know how a snake feels now." He hugged the ground and carefully pushed carcasses out of the way. When he began this retreat on his belly he was near the top of a slight crest in the "cornfield" and was much exposed, but as he made his way back, he got lower and he noticed he couldn't see the Union soldiers anymore. That also meant they could not see him. He hoped his buddies in gray would eventually see what he was doing and try to help him.

As he crawled, he passed many dead soldiers, some with gold and silver jewelry, and many had taken out their leather wallets to look at photos of their loved ones before they died. Marcus noticed both Confederate and Federal paper money scattered in the rows which he collected and stuffed in his pocket; but Marcus would not permit himself to steal jewelry from a dead man's body. Raised a Christian, he feared God would punish him, and in his current situation, the only friend he had was his Lord and Savior.

When he had the chance, Marcus checked haversacks for food. He still had his rifle and an empty haversack. He had eaten all his morning's rations before he arrived on the battlefield, so now he needed food and a replacement canteen.

As Marcus pushed back down the row, he kept watch in the direction of the Union line expecting them to move forward at any moment. The smell blood was everywhere. As he slid back in his bloody uniform his nose suddenly sensed a strong odor of human excrement. He looked down at the ground at the coagulating blood in the row and noticed his body has just slid through the innards of a comrade who had been blown in two, his legs on one side and his upper body on the other, spilling his insides in the row. Marcus had been in terrible battles before, but nothing like this. This was the worst moment of his life. He wanted to jump up and run, but he gained control of his senses. He knew if he showed himself he would be killed instantly by riflemen watching the field. His gray Confederate uniform was so encrusted by battlefield wastes it was unrecognizable, and he might be shot by either side.

He accepted his plight and bore the stench as he crawfished his way down the row toward the Confederate line. He knew a strong odor wouldn't kill him. As he slowly pushed back down the row, he felt something under his legs, then his stomach, and when he got above it, he saw it was the wrist and hand of some poor soldier. On the hand he saw a beautiful gold ring. From the color and shine it had to be pure gold. Knowing the hand could never be attached to its carcass again, he easily removed the ring, as no swelling had occurred, and put it in his pocket. Surely God would forgive him for robbing a hand of a valuable possession. He pushed on, and then suddenly, he felt his feet hanging out over space. His toes felt no ground. He pulled his body into a tight ball so he could see his feet. They were hanging over a crater made by the artillery bombardment a few minutes before. He pushed into the deep crater and found an island of protection in this sea of horror. It was only two feet in depth and maybe six feet across, but he felt safer now.

At the back of the shell hole he saw a dead Union soldier whose body had fallen over the edge of the crater. Seeking water, he pulled the dead man into the crater. As he unstrapped the canteen and drank the precious water, he noticed the man's uniform was clean and pristine with no blood. He rolled the man over. Apparently, there were no wounds on his body. Then, he saw a large exit wound where his ear should have been attached and where the man's face had rested in the blood.

Marcus saw the opportunity, in the midst of this hell, to shed his stinking uniform and improve his condition, and even get a pair of good shoes. Lying low in the crater, he ripped off his awful clothes and tried to unbutton the dead man's jacket, but his bloody hands were slippery on the brass buttons. He took another swig of water and then tried to wash his hands and face, using a handkerchief he had found in the man's knapsack. With cleaner fingers and hugging the ground, Marcus was able to undress the soldier and put on his new garments.

Marcus wore high-top leather shoes that were all but gone, nonetheless, they had protected his feet during the long trek from Virginia. He pulled off the man's shoes and they seemed to fit fine. Union soldiers wore shoes made by the Shoddy Shoe Company. There were no left and right shoes, all made with a rather square toe that could fit either foot. The term "shoddy" came to be known for poor quality, but to Marcus, they felt great compared to what he had.

The man's forage cap was missing. Marcus looked over the edge of his new fort and saw a hat. He used a stalk of corn to pull the hat into the hole. The dead man must have recently enlisted. His uniform seemed brand new. Marcus looked in the dead man's haversack for food or identification. If he was questioned, he wanted to be able to tell them who he was and where he belonged. He searched the man's uniform and pulled out a little leather packet from the pocket with papers inside. He scanned them briefly and learned he was in the

1st Corps, a soldier in an Indiana brigade. Even though he was in an awful place, Marcus felt much better and believed things were now going his way.

Before he cast away his old coat, he reached in the pocket and retrieved his pocketknife, the money, the newly-found ring, and his letter from Bonnie, now stained by the dead man's blood. He inserted the moist red letter in his new coat. Before he could read more about his new identity from the dead man's papers, boom, boom, boom, the Union cannon roared on the other side of the "cornfield." From his new location, Marcus could not see the Union line, but he sensed that the attack had begun. The Union artillery started firing over his head in the direction of his friends, a sign the Rebel infantry was coming or the Yankees were softening the Confederate line for another Union attack. Marcus curled up in his new nest and prayed for his safety. It dawned on him now, he could not continue toward the Confederate lines in his new uniform. He would be shot by his own army.

The Federal artillery stopped firing and the Confederate guns spoke up, indicating they were firing at the new Yankee procession coming toward them again. Marcus peeked out of his hole and saw the tops of battle flags, then bayonets, and finally the heads of men coming over the crest of the high ground marching toward him. He pulled his head back down and pondered whether he should play dead again.

Marcus hugged the ground and trying to amuse himself in his agony, he pondered, "The price of corn must have gone up. It seemed both sides want that corn awfully bad."

As he waited, he thought of a plan that might save his life. He grabbed the dead man's papers he had discarded a few minutes before and again scanned them quickly. He was going to be this new man. As the soldiers approached, he reviewed quickly who he was and learned enough to be ready to answer questions if captured. His new name would be Jacob Stone in Hooker's 1st Corps. However, he did not want to get killed attacking his own line, so he became a corpse again and would retreat back to Union lines, if the Yankees were pushed back again. He lay on his stomach and waited for the Union line to pass over him.

As before, the soldiers paraded over him and headed out of the "cornfield." Another raucous battle ensued beyond his sight, and after a quarter of an hour, the retreating Union forces appeared, running in his direction. Before they arrived, Marcus jumped up and high-tailed it toward the Union guns, hoping he wouldn't be shot in the back.

For all practical purposes, the battle at the far left of the Confederate line was over. Both sides had been beaten to a standstill like two boxers who had fought so long they were out of breath and did not have the strength to give or take another blow. The two armies settled down and faced each other for the rest of the day, each hoping the other did not move forward.

Marcus ran past the Union cannon that had belched death in his direction all morning, and ran into a chaotic camp of wounded soldiers, stretcher bearers, screaming officers, wagons, caissons, and limbers. Soldiers, like disturbed ants, hurried everywhere in all directions, not going anywhere but everywhere, with no common goal in mind. He could see in the distance new brigades of men approaching from the east to reinforce the exhausted line. Marcus continued past men loading empty limbers, the two-wheeled carts that carried artillery ammunition from larger ammunition wagons to the individual cannons that were spewing their deadly iron over the bloody landscape.

Dead and wounded men were sorted; the wounded were then separated by the severity of their injuries. They waited in agony to be tended by the butchers that were called doctors. Hundreds of soldiers huddled in small groups; some hid behind trees; some lay prone on the ground, while others tried to make coffee and cook, as if this activity would make the war go away. The soldiers who fought that day wore the familiar black mask of battle from the burned gunpowder. Many mouths and lips were black from tearing the cartridges with their teeth. All had completely spent their energy and could not wage any more war that day.

2

Marcus did not know where to go. He wanted to get out of this cauldron of activity and find a peaceful place to rest and make plans to escape from his new situation. He saw a young boy sitting against a tree mumbling to himself, his face blackened with the soot of battle, shivering with fear, and reading a Bible. He apparently was trying to thank God for his survival Marcus realized he had to fit in to pull off his guise as a Yankee soldier and needed to form a friendship. He hoped this would be temporary and, maybe, after dark, he could somehow make his way back to the Confederate Army.

Marcus walked up and slumped down close to a lonely lad, leaning his rifle against a tree. The boy didn't look up, just continued reading quietly, almost mumbling, "Yea, though I walk through the valley of the shadow of death," at that point Marcus interrupted him, "I shall fear no evil, for thou art with me; thou rod and thy staff, they comfort me," at which time the boy looked up. "We have definitely been in the valley of death today," Marcus grinned at the boy, trying to comfort him and at the same time, possibly find a friend. "I have never been in a scrape like that before."

"No, I haven't either, and I don't know if I can take it anymore," he said as he looked back down at his Bible. Then he looked up again at

Marcus's washed face and questioned whether he had been in battle. "You didn't fight this morning; your face and hands are clean!"

"Oh, I can explain that. I got caught in the middle of the 'cornfield' this morning and I was out there until I escaped a few moments ago. I found a shell crater and climbed in it to get out of a swarm of bullets. I was pinned down all morning until that last attack. While I was out there, I took my canteen and washed my face." He reached in his pocket and showed the lad his blackened handkerchief. "I just hate that stuff when it gets on me." He also showed the young soldier small blood stains on his uniform.

Marcus continued, "What outfit are you in? I got lost from my bunch early this morning and I haven't seen any of my squad since. Like I said, I've been huddled down out there all morning."

"I am in General Hooker's 1st Corps, 124th Brigade, Company B of the Pennsylvania Infantry." The young boy looked up and stared at Marcus with a questioning look, "You talk kind of funny. Matter of fact, if you were not in that uniform I would swear you're a Johnny Reb. What corps and division did you say you were in?"

Marcus did some quick thinking. Before he got started this kid was going to unmask him. Marcus knew if he was discovered he would be shot as a spy right on the spot; and if not that, he would be taken prisoner and have to endure the rest of the war in a Union jail, and then be shot. "I guess I do talk different from you, but I'm a member of the 18th Indiana under General Smith, not remembering the dead man's papers he had in his pocket, but creating army ranks that most likely didn't exist.

"Before the war I grew up in Indiana, but my parents died and I was left an orphan. I got a job on a riverboat and ended up in Nashville for the last few years. When the war broke out, I came back home and enlisted with my former friends in Indianapolis."

"Yeah, while, you were down in Nashville, you sure picked up their speaking. You don't sound like you're from Indiana," the young lad replied. Accepting him now as a Union soldier, he reached out and shook his hand in friendship, "My name is Edward Brewster; most people call me Ed."

"Good to meet you, my name is Mar..," then he coughed intentionally, remembering he was now a new person. "Excuse me; I guess I got too much smoke this morning. My name is Jacob Stone." Just as he reached out to shake his hand, a lone cannon ball crashed into the tops of the trees nearby making a terrible crash. Both men leaned over and hugged the ground. "That was close. Must have been solid shot," Marcus said when he rose back up.

Edward leaned over and shook Marcus's hand. Edward's hand was quaking from the fear still in control of his nerves. "I don't know if I can take it much more. Do you ever want to run?"

"I'm glad I think with my brain instead of my legs, or I would have run this morning. I've never had that feeling before, but I almost got up and ran a while ago in that 'cornfield'," Marcus answered.

Ed reached in his haversack and took out two large thick crackers, a food called hard bread, also known as hardtack, and offered one to Marcus. "I don't think I can walk into a field of fire again. The generals need to rethink this tactic of sending men into the valley of death without any protection. Let those Rebels attack us and we can stay down and stay protected while we shoot at them. It would save lots of lives."

"I agree. As we went forward this morning I heard my friends being hit on both sides of me. You know that 'thunk' you hear when some guy is hit; a noise in battle I will never forget. It's like the smell of burning flesh. There's no stink like that, and you will never forget it either."

Ed put his Bible in his knapsack and looked at Marcus's new blue uniform. "Yes, back in Virginia, a friend of mine was hit as we attacked through some dense woods. He went down next to me. I wanted to stop and help him, but there were two more lines coming up behind me so I went on. The rifle fire became loud and artillery started exploding above us, the bits of iron tearing falling down on us. We all hunkered down." Ed stopped to recall the awful event and took a drink from his canteen. Looking up at Marcus, he continued, "We all tried to find protection behind large trees, but there weren't any, only vines and brush. Then the woods caught fire and the leaves and brush began to burn. The fire spread through the fallen wounded catching them on fire. Many of them were paralyzed and couldn't move and burned to death. Their cartridge boxes ignited and the gunpowder began to explode. I could distinctly hear my friend calling to me; another sound I will never forget. He kept calling my name, but I could not go. The brush fire was too intense and the bullets were still coming in, and if I had tried, I would have only killed myself. I, also, will never forget that smell of burning flesh."

The two men continued their conversation, sipping water and eating the tough cracker ration. Off to the east, beyond Antietam Creek, they could hear the artillery beginning to talk again, and they understood new waves of Union soldiers were preparing to attack the Confederate center. It remained rather quiet in their front, with only a stray cannon shot occasionally falling into their midst. Stragglers continued to come from the front line and settle in the woods and tend to their minor wounds and compose themselves after facing the sickle of death.

Marcus remembered the letter inside his pocket and thought he would read it while he rested with Ed. "I got a letter from my girl back home in Buckhead……..," he almost said Georgia, but caught his mistake in time and said, "Indiana. I got this letter this morning before breakfast and haven't had time to read it." Marcus looked at the bloodstained envelope, but he saw the postmarks that revealed it had come from Georgia, and slid it back in his coat."

"Aren't you going to read it?" Ed questioned.

"No, on second thought, I want to be alone with my girl when I read her letter. I get pretty down-hearted. I haven't heard from her in a good while. I'll just wait 'till I'm alone somewhere." Marcus looked up at Edward, "I love her so much, and I don't want you to see me crying. We were going to get married, but a brass band came along and convinced me it was the right thing to do, you know, defend your country and all. All my buddies joined, so like a dumb fool, I joined the army. We were going to build a cabin down by Sandy Creek, a place near where I was born." Marcus was quickly weaving a web that could be difficult to explain if Edward inquired further into his past.

But instead, Edward quickly replied, "I worked in the post office back home and sorted letters to everywhere, but I never heard of Buckhead, Indiana."

Again, realizing he was getting on thin ice again, "Oh, you wouldn't. Buckhead is just a small village south of Indianapolis but maybe a dozen or so miles north of the Ohio River."

"I see. However, I sent a letter or two to a place in Georgia called Buckhead," Ed informed.

Knowing now, more prying on this subject could spill the beans that Marcus was hiding, "No, I never heard of Buckhead, Georgia. I guess there could be towns with the same name, but in different states."

"Oh, you bet. I don't know how many states have Salems and New Hopes in them."

Marcus wanted to end this conversation now and focus on something else. "Where did you work in that post office? Where are you from?"

"You wouldn't believe it, but I grew up," he hesitated like he was getting his bearings, "I guess about five or ten miles southwest of here, north of Shepherdstown."

"Well how about that! You know, I thought you talked a little southern, too. Why, this battle nearly was in your back yard! Shepherdstown is in Virginia. Why didn't you fight for our side?"

"I did fight for our side! You see this blue uniform?"

Marcus suddenly realized he had let the chicken out of the bag. Pretending to be confused, he said, "You know what I mean. I don't know why I said it that way. What I meant was, why did you fight for our side, you being a southerner an' all?"

Edward thought a long time, as if he wanted to avoid talking about times that brought back bad memories. "I guess it was over a family feud. I grew up different from my folks and wanted to be more than a farmer. I wanted to read and think about things and make a living without breaking my back. While I worked in the post office, a lawyer in town encouraged me to go to law school, so with his help, I went north of here a few miles to study law. While I was there, I made new friends and they convinced me to take up the Union cause. When it appeared the war was about to break out, I went home and told my family I was going to fight to save the Union. One night I got drunk, and being a hot head, I got mad and got in a fight with my brother. I don't remember much about it, but when I came to my senses, I was on a horse heading north in the middle of the night. The next morning I remembered I had hit my brother in the head with a stick of firewood, and I couldn't go back home." When the war broke out, I quit school and joined the 124th Pennsylvania volunteers and went to war. I haven't been home in almost two years."

He continued to think, "When we retreated from Virginia, I kept telling everybody it looked like we were going to have a fight in my backyard." He hesitated and then looked Marcus straight in the eye, "You know how odd that would be to fight all over Virginia and then come and get killed in your own back yard?" He picked up his rifle and pointed to a deep dent in the wooden stock where a Minie ball came close to killing him. "You know, that happened today."

Marcus could see Ed was sensitive over the trouble with his family. He looked at Marcus again, "When I'm on the firing line, I often wonder if I am shooting at my father or brother."

"Yeah, that would bother me, too. I'm sorry to hear about your family. I hope you can work that out after the war."

"I never got along well with my father or brother, but I didn't want to kill them. I loved my mother. She was the kindest and sweetest mother a boy could have." He paused and thought about his days at home. "She was the best cook, too. Oh, I loved my mother and I am missing her comfort so much. I would do anything for her, but under the present conditions I cannot go home." He stopped talking and lay back on the ground with his forearm over his forehead.

Marcus could see Ed didn't want to talk about it anymore as he put his rifle down and rubbed his face with his hands. Marcus realized he was in a good and bad situation. He was thankful he was out of the "cornfield", but he was in the enemy's nest and another wrong move could reveal he was an imposter. He also understood he had penetrated enemy lines and possibly could do some damage to the Union cause.

After an hour of rest, a Union captain rode up to the men hidden away from the front line and urged the soldiers, in no uncertain terms, to get their tails back in line and join their ranks. Edward asked the captain where the 124th Pennsylvanians could be found. The officer replied, I don't think there is a 124th Pennsylvania anymore. "Then where should I go sir?" Edward asked.

"For now you men return back to the front up there," pointing in the direction of the main army. "Right now, I don't think anybody cares what brigade or division you are in, just get to the front with your rifle, and get yourselves ready to fight. It looks like the Johnnies may strike us again at any moment. Replenish your ammunition, too."

The officer looked at Marcus's washed face. He was so young. His beard was still peach fuzz and gave him an innocent look. "Boy, have you been in battle today, or are you a skulker hiding down here in the woods? You need to grow up and become a man. Your mama can't help you here."

Marcus jumped up and saluted, "Sir, I am no coward. I was in the 'cornfield' all morning and just got out of there about an hour ago. I washed my face, sir."

Edward spoke up in his defense, "He's telling the truth captain, he was with me all morning, and I saw him wash his face. Show the captain your handkerchief."

Marcus, surprised by his new friend's help, pulled out the dark gray cloth and showed the captain the evidence. "I see," and trying to save face changed the subject, "You guys hurry and get back to the front; they are going to need you soon," and trotted away to push more foot-draggers back to the lines.

Marcus turned to Edward, "Thank you for backing me up. I appreciate that. I'll try to help you out one day."

"Think nothing of it. He just seemed like the kind of chap who sold ribbons in a flower shop before the war, but now with those captain's bars, he thinks he's the cock of the walk and tries to make the world respect him by making it harder for everyone else. He was looking for someone he could pull his rank on and give him a bad time. I have seen his kind before." Edward stood up and looked down at Marcus, "You noticed *he* didn't wear the mask of war. Let's get back to the front."

The two young men picked up their gear and rifles and made their way through the maze of trees to the battle front. They walked by a doctor trying to assess whether a man should be treated or left to die. It was standard procedure to diagnose a wound and decide whether to put a man in the "dying pile," so to speak, or if the doctors thought life was possible and try to treat him. Most often the men died alone waiting for help.

Edward kept asking people about the location of his Pennsylvanian Brigade. It seemed from their answers, his brigade had been blasted into eternity, but he kept searching for any men that might be left. Marcus did not want to find Jacob's Indiana brigade. Being an imposter, his false portrayal would be detected when the roll call was made. Even the soldiers who survived would know he was an outsider. Marcus definitely wanted to avoid an Indiana roll call.

Officers and veteran soldiers who had been in previous battles began to organize the chaos, and by afternoon, men were back in a semblance of order waiting for a new attack that was expected at any moment. Wounded men were loaded on carts and hauled behind the lines to a temporary hospital in a house or barn for attention; the living were replenished with food, water, and ammunition.

By midafternoon, Edward noticed Marcus seemed uninterested in finding his Indiana boys. It was apparent that Marcus seemed apathetic and Edward wondered why. Maybe, Edward thought, Marcus saw most of his friends killed beside him in the "cornfield" and was still in a state of shock; or possibly he had run away under fire and the survivors would accuse him of being a coward. "Aren't you the least bit concerned about the condition of your squad and company?" Edward waited for an answer.

Seeming to be in deep thought or possibly ashamed, Marcus finally replied, "Yes, I care, but I fear most of them are splattered all over that field out there. I don't want to know if I lost my best friends, and I guess I don't want to face the truth." Those were his honest thoughts, but they were not Union "friends" that he remembered, but Georgians and Texans that had fallen in the Hagerstown Pike and the "cornfield".

Edward stared at Marcus, understanding him now, "Yes, this has been a hard day on me also. I know I have lost many friends."

At that time, a soldier passed by dragging his rifle, completely spent, and looked as if he might collapse at any moment. Edward noticed on his forage cap that he had the same corps, brigade, and company insignia as Marcus. He stopped, ran over to the man and asked him where his Indiana boys were assembling.

"I don't know, and frankly, I don't care. They can shoot me, but I am going home." Before Edward could ask him more, the soldier turned and disappeared into the turmoil of confusion that was slowly being organized back into an army corps.

Edward turned to Marcus, "That guy was in your company. Do you know him?" A company was roughly a hundred soldiers, and luckily for Marcus, the man was in a mental stupor and had no interest in comradeship.

"No, I didn't see him that well."

The officers were trying to make heads and tails of the situation, reading division and brigade numbers and directing groups of soldiers here and there to regroup with their people. Suddenly, an officer saw Marcus and told him to get back to the Indiana brigade trying to muster under a large oak back to the northeast of the Union artillery. Edward saw two of his friends and stopped them and learned his brigade had taken a beating that day, but what was left was rallying behind the caissons and supply wagons a few hundred yards to the rear. Marcus wanted to follow Edward and trailed after him, but the officer yelled again for him to rendezvous at the oak tree, then rode up and pulled on the back of his army jacket and pushed him forward. "Now, do what I said!" Marcus could see the Captain was angry, so he turned toward the oak tree and obeyed the order, hoping not to draw more attention to himself. He and Edward parted ways, each saying nothing, but wishing each other well with a glance.

The officer sat on his horse and watched Marcus for a time, but as soon as the mounted captain was out of sight, Marcus stopped and took his knife and carefully cut the threads that held the patches on his uniform. That would give him anonymity while the battle raged. If questioned, Marcus could always think of an excuse why his insignias were torn off. He realized in all the chaos, he could stay independent and move between the brigades, all the time pretending to be lost. He then had no peers that could recognize him as a Rebel. While he had the opportunity behind enemy lines he wanted to damage the Army of the Potomac as much as possible.

After departing from his new friend, Marcus spent the rest of the day moving through the army pretending to look for friends and brigades. He did more looking than talking, fearing his extreme southern accent might bring suspicion on him. The Confederate army had been known to place spies behind the Union lines and in the Union army, but when caught, spies were immediately executed. Marcus knew he was walking a thin line between being shot or a hero.

As the day wore on, Marcus saw more organization in the Union ranks. The battle of Antietam had started in the "cornfield," moved to the center, later known as "Bloody Lane," and finally, by evening to the far Union left, and concluded at "Burnside's Bridge." Except for flurries of rifle fire and the occasional boom of cannon, it remained quiet in front of Marcus.

3

As he wandered behind the lines, Marcus noticed the ammunition trains were parked far to the rear. They appeared to go for miles. Some carried powder and various kinds of projectiles for the artillery, including canister, grape shot, cannon balls, fuses, and solid shot. Other wagons carried thousands of rounds of paper cartridges, while others were filled with piles of provisions for humans, mules, and horses. The Union army lacked for nothing. As he observed the "wagons of plenty," it dawned on him again, the Confederacy could not win this war. Any lives lost now would be wasted and just victims in an unknown cemetery far from home.

Nevertheless, he was patriotic and loved his home and was willing to die for his cause, even though a lost one. As Marcus watched the goings on, he stewed up an idea. If he could get into one of those wagons and kindle a fire inside to ignite the black powder, thousands of Confederate soldiers would not have to face that hail of steel tomorrow, if the battle continued.

He started watching the wagons closely to see how they were guarded, and if they were vulnerable to attack. While he leaned against a tree, he noticed an officer gallop by and discard a lit cigar near his feet. Marcus studied the smoldering stub for a moment.

"That's it," he thought. "There's my fire. If I can get that lit cigar into the wagon train of ammunition, I can damage the entire right wing of the Union Army."

An hour before dark Marcus had worked out a plan of attack. He had wandered close by the wagons; no one had confronted him about being near the ammunition. He observed the wagons were scarcely guarded at all, only watched by the teamsters and artillerymen loading their limbers and caissons.

Night fell over a horrible scene of carnage and bloodshed. Hundreds of voices cried out for help from the thousands of men wounded that day. Occasionally a shot was heard from the ghastly plain indicating a hero couldn't endure the pain any longer and had taken his own life. Paralyzed men pleaded for someone to kill them to end their intense pain. Some could not accept the fact they would be confined to a bed the rest of their lives. When total darkness arrived, soldiers on both sides observed dim lights beginning to appear on the field of slaughter moving through the many wounded. Some were sympathetic comrades trying to give a drink of cold water to a thirsty mouth; others were thieves picking the carcasses of valuables they found on the helpless and the dead. The soldiers watched, but did not fire on the angels of mercy nor the devil's disciples.

Men lay quietly recalling the day of slaughter. The single bloodiest day of American warfare had just ended. Seventeen thousand men had been killed; although the men did not know it at the time. They just knew what had happened in their vicinity, and they all were aware the fighting had been ghastly as the soldiers tried to find their companies and brigades. Some had lost eighty percent and would never be an effective fighting force again, even with new recruits. The cream of the crop from both sides had been badly mauled that day.

Marcus watched the stage where he hoped a great act would take place that he would direct. He studied how the wagons had been parked. By now, most of the limbers that had been loaded with the cloth bags of gunpowder and projectiles that had been rammed down the hungry mouths of the cannons that day had returned to their guns. The ammunition wagons were now kept isolated. Now, the artillerymen were ready for day two. Marcus reckoned his friends would still face a new barrage of cannon fire in the morning no matter what he did, but he still wanted to do as much damage to the Union forces as possible.

By midnight the firing ended except for an accidental gun going off that caused the sleeping men to wake and fire, creating a crescendo of shots to come forth for a few moments and then die down. The nervous soldiers fired at unseen enemies in the dark, everyone on edge, fearing a new attack would resume at dawn.

Marcus had picked up the lost cigar and saved it in his pocket. It was time now for him to seek what damage he could cause to the Union artillery. Out of the dark, he approached a group of soldiers huddled around a small fire boiling coffee and sharing a ham donated by a local farmer, trying to do his part to rid the Southern invaders. Marcus neared the men as if he were on guard duty with correct posture and saluted. He said nothing but motioned he needed to light his cigar in the camp fire. One of the men scooted back indicating acceptance of his request. Marcus picked up a burning twig and lit his cigar, nodded thanks, and disappeared toward the wagons as if he had guard duty. Nobody paid him any mind-just a soldier doing his duty. He noticed several men lying on their blankets nearby trying to get some rest, not wanting to be interrupted after such a day's trauma.

"This is easier than I thought," Marcus contemplated the situation. Everyone was spent physically and mentally. He continued toward the selected wagon at the edge of the wagon park. Then he heard footsteps crackle in the fallen leaves as they approached from behind him. He immediately turned and confronted the man emerging out of the dark using his best military display, pretending to be stationed with the parked wagons. "Who goes there?"

"Private Brewster with the 124th Pennsylvania Brigade, Company B." Marcus recognized the voice as the soldier he had met earlier in the day. At the same time, Edward recognized Jacob's southern drawl and whispered back at him so not to disturb the surrounding soldiers, "What are you doing down here? I figured you were with your Indiana boys over there someplace," pointing in the dark where he thought they had gathered.

"Yeah, I found my squad," Marcus said, bowing his head, trying to cover up his seeming lack of concern toward his fellow compatriots earlier in the day. "As I feared, there a re only a few of us left. Our only surviving officer, Captain Newton, knew we couldn't be of use on the line, so he sent us back here to guard the wagons. He felt we would be safe, but at the same time be of use to the army." Marcus lied, making up a story as he talked.

As he chatted, Marcus took his lit cigar and rubbed the ashes against the wheel of a wagon. He did not want to lose his detonator.

"Be careful with that cigar. These wagons are loaded with a ton of black powder," Edward cautioned.

Marcus jerked the cigar back as if forgetting what was in the wagon. "Oh, you're right. I forgot about that. I'll watch myself. Thanks for warning me."

"Where is the rest of your squad?" Edward inquired.

"Like I said, there weren't many of us left, maybe a dozen men, and we just spread out through the wagons. I imagine most of them are standing around licking their wounds. By the way, why are you back here?"

"Like your brigade, my bunch was torn up badly today also. One of our surviving officers led us down here to guard the wagons too. He spread us out up and down the rows of wagons and told us to rest, but keep an eye on things."

Agreeing with Edward's assessment of things, "Yes, it seems that way, but I've been down here a while and I don't think anything will happen tonight. The Rebel army appears to have been defeated, or at least, stopped in their tracks. Tomorrow will tell the tale."

Edward looked around in the dark, "The only worry tonight would be a rebel spy who might try to penetrate our lines, maybe from the rear, and blow up our supply trains." Little did Edward know he was talking to the man that had that aim in mind. "Keep alert. I am going over there by that large tree and stand guard." Edward grinned, "Don't shoot in that direction."

"Alright, I won't shoot down there," Marcus replied with a hint of humor in his voice. "Instead, of shooting you, I think I'll climb in an empty wagon and take a nap. This has been a long day."

The two men parted, each seeking a place to hide and watch. However, Marcus wasn't guarding; he was seeking a place to plant his cheap detonator in a bag of black powder. He watched Edward disappear in the dark heading toward the large tree. It was a dark night, but the shapes of men and wagons were silhouetted by the small fires set by tired men scattered throughout the woods. The scene was tranquil, maybe too still, although sounds of moans and screams still pierced the night and muffled voices could be heard in the distance.

If Marcus was going to make his move, now was the time. He looked in the direction of Edward but could not see anyone. He deduced if he couldn't see Edward, there was a good chance Edward couldn't see him. Marcus picked up his rifle, held it in front of his chest, and walked to the back of the nearest wagon as if on guard duty. He unlatched and eased the back of the wagon down. As the back came down, the hinge suddenly squeaked in the night. To Marcus, nervous now, the squeak sounded as if someone had banged on a tin bucket; but in actuality, it was not loud. He froze and watched to see if the noise had stirred any attention. He looked in the direction of Edward, but the scene remained quiet. If Edward was watching him climb in the wagon, he wouldn't be suspicious of his behavior; he just told Edward he was going to do that. He slowly eased the back of the wagon on down and climbed into the dark. Once inside he could not be seen under the white canvas top with a big US stenciled on the sides. It was very dark inside the wagon, and he had to sit there a few minutes to let his eyes adjust to the darker environment. When he could see a little, he noticed the wagon was nearly empty. Unable to see much and feeling his way, he found a crate and slid his knife under the top and pried it up. He reached inside and felt the canvas bags. He pulled out one of the bags that was destined to be rammed down the barrels of the cannons that were to spew out projectiles of death in the face of his friends.

Black powder was very explosive. Many artillerymen had been killed in the midst of battle by pushing a bag of powder down a hot cannon that still had sparks inside, resulting in an explosion in the face of the rammer. Between each blast, a wet sponge on a long wooden rod was rammed in and out of the barrel to extinguish any sparks before a new bag of powder went in. The cannon could be made more powerful by putting two or three bags down the barrel. Marcus was very aware of the danger of being around black powder.

Marcus kept watching out the back of the wagon, hoping not to see a guard looking in. He was very anxious now, a spy handling explosives behind enemy lines. He knew steel hitting steel would cause a spark. He took his knife and very slowly pressed the point into the bag causing the black granules to pour out like sand in an hour glass. Then he reached for his cigar.

Marcus realized that in his nervous apprehension, he had forgotten to light the detonator after he rubbed it out on the wagon wheel. He would have to go light the cigar again and come back and plant it in the hole he had cut in the bag. He crawled out of the wagon unnoticed. Most of the fires he had seen earlier had died down to glowing embers and the men around them were trying to get some sleep. However, he saw some silhouettes around an orange glow about a hundred yards from him. He took out the cigar again and approached the fire, nearly stepping on a sleeping man. Again, without saying a word, he approached the soldiers holding his cigar out indicating to them he needed a light. One of the men picked up a small stick with a flame and held it out for Marcus to light his cigar. He nodded thanks and disappeared back from where he came. The soldiers understood he was just a guard doing his duty.

Marcus came near the wagon and stopped. He puffed on the cigar to get it hot and studied the surroundings to see if anything had changed since he had left. After he was sure all was the same, he went back to the wagon and crawled inside. He was in a very perilous situation now, holding a lit cigar in a wagon partially filled with bags of gunpowder, some of which had fallen from small punctured holes to the floor. If a piece of cigar ash fell on the loose powder, he would instantly be torn into a thousand pieces. He held the cigar over the edge of the wagon, tapped off the ashes, and put the cigar in his mouth. He had to wait a minute so his eyes could adjust to the dark again. When he could see, he carefully pulled the bag away from the spilled powder and leaned it back so no more powder would leak out. His hands trembled from fear. He pondered his danger and got an idea. He took his blackened handkerchief, folded it up and soaked it with water from his canteen and stuck the wet cloth under the slit he had cut in the bag. He tapped the ashes off one last time and using his finger pushed a hole into the black powder and eased the moistened end of the cigar inside. Any ashes that might fall off as the cigar burned would fall on the damp cloth. This would insure he would be far away when the simmering spark reached the powder.

Satisfied his plan would work, he slipped out of the wagon and turned around to leave; but instead, stood face to face with a guard. In his intense concentration Marcus had not heard the guard approach. The guard stood in a confrontational stance with his bayonet six inches from Marcus's stomach. "Sir, May I ask what you are doing in that wagon?" the guard asked.

Marcus was startled, but he thought quickly. "Lying down, just resting. I was in the "cornfield" today. When we retreated, I fell and my back was stepped on. I fear I have severely hurt it." Marcus bent back seeming to wince in pain. "Captain Newton sent me down here to guard these wagons, but my back hurt me so bad I couldn't stand up anymore. I found this wagon was nearly empty, so I just climbed inside to lie down on something flat and try to get some relief. I heard your footsteps and crawled out to see who you were. I was hoping it wasn't an officer who might think I was sleeping on duty."

"Were you sleeping?"

"No, like I said, I heard your feet in the leaves, and I was fixing to crawl out and see who you were."

"You talk like a Southerner. We never say 'fixing' around here."

"Funny you said that, "Marcus replied pretending to grimace in pain. "That's the second time today somebody asked me that. No, I'm not a Rebel. I was born in Indiana, but when I was a young boy my family moved to Nashville." Remembering his supposed back trouble, Marcus stopped, "Just a minute, my back is killing me again. Oh, ohhh, let me lie down for a minute or two." Marcus dropped to the ground and stretched out as if he was in severe pain.

Marcus did not want to start a conversation now with a lonely soldier while a cigar smoldered in a sack of black powder less than six feet away, but wanted to get away from the danger.

"No, like I said, I am no Rebel. I fought in the 'cornfield' this morning. Come with me and I can prove it." Marcus got off the ground and walked toward the tree where Edward had gone, trying to put as much distance as he could between the wagon and himself. The guard had taken Marcus's gun, still suspicious of this man and wanted to see some proof he was who he said he was. When Marcus neared the tree, he quietly called to his friend, "Edward, Edward are you here." At first there was no response, but on a second call, they heard Edward respond from behind the tree. He apparently had dozed off.

"What is it Jacob?"

"Stand up and tell this guard who I am. He thinks I am a Rebel."

Edward laughed, "If I didn't know any better I would think so too by the way you speak."

The guard inquired, "You know this man?"

"Yes, he is 'Jacob Stone'. We fought together this morning and we have been sent down here to rest and guard those wagons. You can be rest assured he is one of us."

With that, the guard apologized to Marcus, turned and walked away mumbling, "If you weren't in that blue uniform, I'd swear you were a Rebel."

Marcus thanked Edward for backing his story again, but expected a loud explosion at any moment. Edward teased Marcus, "I'm like that guard there; if I didn't know for sure, I would think you were a Johnny Reb also." With that statement, he rolled over on his side to go back to sleep.

Marcus looked down and thought, "It's too bad you don't know the truth." Then speaking aloud he said, "See you in the morning;

I'll get back to my duty," but instead of walking toward the wagon Marcus hurried away from the anticipated explosion. He wanted to warn his friend, but he was behind a huge oak tree and would be safe.

Marcus had no idea what the explosion would look like. He found a secure spot behind another large oak farther away and knelt on his knees peeking around the tree at the wagon and waited, and waited, and waited. After an hour, he wondered what went wrong. Recalling his past associations with cigars, it dawned on him how stupid he had been. "Cigars go out if they are not puffed on. That's what probably occurred," he reasoned.

Knowing what most likely happened, Marcus cautiously returned to the rear of the wagon. He looked around and climbed inside for the third time. He found the cigar had gone out. He had to find something else. He looked and felt around in another box and luckily found a long length of fuse used to insert in hollow projectiles that made them explode. He pulled out his old cigar and inserted one end of the long fuse deep inside the bag of black powder. He uncoiled the fuse as he crawled to the back of the wagon, constantly looking over his shoulder. He would have a hard time explaining what he was doing if another guard came up. He then realized he had no fire to light the fuse. The events of the night had taken a toll on his nerves, and he was very uneasy.

He felt around on the floor of the wagon and found his old cigar again. He went back to another campfire finding all but one soldier asleep, the one soldier poking the coals and keeping it alive. He only had a small stub of a cigar left which under normal conditions would have been thrown in the fire, but he was able to retrieve an ember on the end of a small limb and relight his cigar.

The soldier made a comment to Marcus about the size of his cigar. "You just don't know how I like cigars," Marcus remarked as he returned to the wagon puffing on the cigar to keep it lit. He raised the back of the wagon up so anyone looking could not see the floor of the wagon and the fuse burning. He took one big puff making the cigar glow its brightest and stuck it to the end of the fuse. In a second the sparks began to fly and the sparks headed down the fuse toward the bags of black powder. Marcus turned and ran as fast as he dared without drawing attention to himself.

He was making his way through trees, getting farther away from the potential blast. As he walked he noticed a soldier walking toward him, apparently another guard. As he neared, the guard stopped and put his rifle across his chest, "Identify yourself."

Marcus replied, "1ˢᵗ Corps, Company B," but before he could say more he heard that familiar voice again, "Is that you 'Jacob'?" the soldier called out, also recognizing the southern accent he had heard during the day. It was Edward again.

"Yes, it's me. How are things going?" Marcus replied, apprehensive about what was imminent, seeming to forget he had talked to Edward a half hour before.

"Fine. After I talked to you, I got up and walked around and found an old sergeant brewing tea. He offered me some which woke me up. I feel pretty good now so I thought I would do what they sent me down here for, to guard the wagons.

"Yeah, I am doing the same thing. Time just stops when you are on guard duty. I believe this is the longest night I've ever lived. I also have a touch of dysentery and need to find a latrine. You know what I mean?"

"Yes, but go where you can. I don't think officers are worried about sanitation right now. I just came from down there," Edward said as he pointed back in the dark. "It seems sparsely populated compared to the rest of the woods. I'll probably see you later when I come around again. At dawn, maybe we can eat some grub together."

"Yeah, let's do that!" Marcus saw him turn and walk in the direction of the burning fuse. Even though Edward was a Yankee and a hated enemy, Marcus had gotten to know him, and he seemed not to be such a bad fellow. Twice during the day Edward had come to his rescue when the officers questioned him. He wanted to kill all the Yankees now, but not Edward. He yelled back at Edward, "Don't go down there. It's dangerous. Those wagons could explode. They are filled with gunpowder."

"Yes, I know. I will be safe. There's no shooting going on now."

"No, Edward, stay away; get out of there."

"Don't worry, I'll be all right," Edward replied and continued directly for the wagon that might explode at any moment. Marcus had warned him all he could, without revealing his conspiracy.

Marcus watched as Edward paraded closer to the wagon, and hurried behind his tree again. Dawn was just beginning to light the eastern sky when the fuse arrived at the black powder. A huge explosion burst forth, and for a split second he saw Edward silhouetted against the explosion and his body thrown back toward Marcus.

Marcus was excited as the blast lit the woods. In another second another wagon went up and then another as the sparks and flames spread from wagon to wagon. Over the next five minutes, seven wagons exploded sending pieces of iron and wood raining down on the surroundings. He feared Edward had been lost, but hoped that he might have survived somehow. Fuses on cannon balls ignited and there were more, smaller explosions. Before all the wagons could blow, Marcus knew it was time for him to get out of there, and he started running to the rear, ducking down when another wagon blew. Marcus realized if Edward lived he could identify him; but from what he saw, Edward was most likely killed. He hated that though. The unknown guard had not seen him well enough in the dark to identify him but might recognize his southern voice. One thing was sure, there had been an explosion in the powder wagons and soon the Army of the Potomac might be hunting a Southern boy in a blue uniform.

The Union army came alive. Again the scene was filled with cowards and heroes. Some men ran toward the explosions, and some sped away running side by side with Marcus not knowing what had happened nor caring, just trying to save their own lives. As Marcus ran, he was proud of what he did. He hoped if Lee attacked today, his army would not face the blasts that had killed so many of his comrades the day before.

For the first time though, the war had become personal. He wished he had not killed Edward. Shooting at Yankees across a field was war, but killing someone you have met, talked to, and even befriended, concerned Marcus. "Was it murder? I tried to warn him," Marcus thought and tried to justify his deadly deed as he raced through the fields and woods north of the Antietam battlefield, trying to escape and find repentance for what he did to Edward.

Suddenly, Marcus realized his escapade had been successful and he had hurt the Union army, but he had failed to think about his escape. It was getting light now and he could see where he was going, but he didn't know where he was going. He felt his only chance was to get back to Lee's army camped north of Sharpsburg with their back to the Potomac River. He knew the river was off to the west, within a mile he hoped. If he could get to the river without being spotted, he could cross over and go south and be behind Lee's army.

He had to change clothes. He couldn't walk into the Army of Northern Virginia in a blue uniform. He was getting tired and slowed down to a walk. If spotted by someone, he could justify his retreat by saying he was next to the large explosion and was addled and his mind hadn't settled down yet. He figured it would be better to stay in the blue uniform until he crossed the river. Then he would try to steal some clothes. That was his plan.

4

Back in the Union camp, chaos reigned. Many officers thought it was the launch of a cannonade by the Rebel forces to soften the Federal line before a new infantry attack. Soldiers rallied behind the Union artillery expecting to see the red, white, and blue battle flags of the Confederate Army appear across the cornfield again. Reserves were brought up to repair any breaks in the Union line that might occur.

Across the "cornfield" General Lee's army did not have the men or munitions to renew an attack, but since daybreak, to make his enemy think otherwise, he ordered ranks of soldiers here and there to look as if another all-out attack was imminent. What ammunition the Confederates had, they needed to repel a Union attack if it occurred. They hoped the Union Army was hurt as bad as they were and did not resume the battle that day. Lee was pretending to play a hand he did not have, and the Union general nicknamed "Cautious McClellan" fell for it.

Everyone was nervous, but news spread back to the generals that only sporadic shots had been fired from the Confederate side, and soon they decided a stray cannon shot had landed in an ammo wagon causing the explosions that spread through the wagon park.

As the scene settled down around the remnants of the wagons, soldiers eased forward, hoping a smoldering spark did not ignite more explosions. Miraculously, only five wagons had been destroyed. Since the wagons had been lightly guarded only a few men were wounded or killed. The wounded and dead men were pulled back and given attention, either moved to the surgeons or stacked with the other dead from the battlefield.

The searchers soon found Edward's body several yards from the initial explosion. They expected he was dead, but when they pulled his body away from the smoking debris, they noticed he was still alive and was coming to. The soldiers helped him sit up and gave him water.

Edward, in a dazed state of mind, began to talk. "What happened? Where am I?" he asked, rubbing his eyes and face and trying to get things together.

"Are you hurt? Where are you hurting?"

He could barely hear the voices talking to him as he came to his senses, his hearing damaged by the loud blast and concussion. In his mind, he tried to put together what had happened. He wiggled a finger in each ear, trying to remove what seemed like cotton that had been stuffed in his ears. "I don't think I'm hurt. That's the loudest noise I ever heard. Let me stand up." He wobbled to his feet and stamped the ground to see how solid he was.

One of the soldiers asked him, "Did you see what happened?"

Edward stared down at the ground trying to remember the events before the big blast. He looked up with an expression on his face as if he had solved a riddle. "Jacob, Jacob!" he yelled. He looked at the senior officer present and said, "It had to be Jacob."

"Who's Jacob?" they inquired intensely interested in his answer.

Edward took another swig of water, "You know…. there was something wrong with that guy. He seemed like a good soldier, but, you know, he just didn't act right." Seeming to talk to himself now, more than to his listeners, "It's my fault; I should have checked him out more closely. He must have been planted by the Rebels to carry out this plot." Edward stopped talking and thought a minute; slowly he raised his head, "You know though, he tried to save my life."

"What do you mean, he tried to save your life?" one of the soldiers demanded.

"I met the guy yesterday shortly after I came out of the 'cornfield.' I spent most of the day with him until we were ordered to go back and guard the wagons, and we got separated." He drank some more water. "Last night I happened on to him again down by the wagons." Edward's eyes brightened and he rose up slightly, "And he had a lit cigar, and I warned him about smoking and having fire around those wagons. Just before the explosions, I was walking toward the wagons and met him again walking away from them. He warned me not to go down by the wagons; it was dangerous around all that black powder. You know I guess he wanted to save my life since I had met him and befriended him."

A group of soldiers had gathered around Edward and listened to what he said. One of the listeners was the other guard who had also confronted Marcus. When Edward finished he spoke up. "What he said is true. I caught the same southern-talking guy crawling out of a wagon."

An officer demanded, "Why didn't you arrest him?"

"He told me his back had been hurt in the 'cornfield'. He said someone had stepped in the middle of his back, and he was in agony and had climbed in the wagon to lie down to ease his pain. He told me he was on guard duty and climbed out of the wagon to check me out when he heard me approaching. I had no reason to doubt his story. He was very believable."

"Do you remember his rank or squad numbers?"

"No, it was too dark, but that had to be the guy. I remember that southern drawl. He said he was raised in Indiana but had moved to Nashville and came back North when the war started."

Edward spoke up again, "That's right. He told me he was in the 18th Indiana Brigade, but as a matter of fact, when I was hunting my friends, it seemed he had no interest in finding his squad. I even asked him about it, but being a good actor, he gave me a story that sounded true."

"Well, what did he look like?" the officer demanded, removing a small hardback notebook from his coat pocket to record the infiltrator's description.

Both Edward and the guard agreed he was dressed in a Union uniform; about five and a half feet tall with light brown hair; still with the voice of a young boy; a profile that would never fit a saboteur. Edward added that his face was covered in peach fuzz and needed shaving.

The Union officers were concerned now that a saboteur might still be behind their lines. The description of Marcus fit thousands of young men, and he would be impossible to find without calling together all the brigades and doing a roll call, now impossible after the killing and scattering of troops throughout the battlefield. They were expecting another attack at any moment and chasing down one enemy was beyond their capacity. When the matter of a saboteur finally reached the major generals they sent out orders for soldiers on guard duty to be extra cautious and check out all suspicious people.

5

Within the mile behind the battlefield, Marcus saw stragglers and cowards who had or were fleeing from the heat of battle. He passed civilians who had gathered to rubberneck the great event. The woods were full of people. As he passed the farmers, several questioned why he was running away from the fight, and one even threatened to shoot him for being a coward. He pointed a rifle at Marcus and told him to turn around and go back toward the battlefield. To convince the man he wasn't a skulker, Marcus reached in his pocket and held up the bloody letter and said that he was on a mission to deliver an important message to the 12th Corps. He informed the man he was a trained messenger working for General Hooker. He also showed the man that his uniform had no corps or brigade numbers which signified he was a messenger. Again, his acting seemed to satisfy the patriot and he let Marcus pass.

Marcus kept going northwest until the people and stragglers thinned out and he was alone. He knew the river was off to his left somewhere, more or less a mile away he reasoned. His courier story had worked so well, he continued this ruse as he asked people for directions to the river. People apparently thought he was on an important mission and wanting to be of service to their country, pointed out his way to the river. However, he wanted to get off the roads as he neared the waterway, fearing the fords on the river would be guarded by Union or Confederate cavalry. He felt safer now. The morning had gone well for him, but he was getting hungry.

He left the road and crossed a field that had grown corn that summer. He diligently searched among the dry stalks to find a few inferior ears of dried corn missed by the pickers and placed them in his shoulder bag. He continued across a stone fence into a secluded field that had not been plowed that year. As he walked, he noticed horse tracks had trampled down the grass, signifying many horses had been there. He saw a pistol and picked it up. Several chambers had not been fired, so he stuck it in his belt and moved on. He noticed hats that had been lost and then two dead horses. This must have been a site where cavalries had sparred with each other. He checked out the saddle bags and found pistol cartridges and a large knife, similar to the one made famous by James Bowie at the Alamo, which he also secured. He wished he could take the saddles with him, but that was out of the question. He gathered up what valuable gear he could use and packed it tightly in a haversack.

In front of him, the field gently sloped down to a creek hidden by dense trees. He hurried forward spreading the tall grass as he walked. Near the creek his eyes caught a glimpse of red in the grass off to his right, an unnatural color for the locale. He approached cautiously and soon saw it was the collar of a uniformed man lying in the grass, possibly sleeping. As he neared, he saw it was a Confederate cavalryman. He may have been one of the owners of one of the dead horses. If he was still alive, he feared the Confederate might kill him if he surprised him, so he drew his pistol and aimed at the man as he approached. Marcus sensed he might be wounded and hiding from the authorities. However, when he got close, he saw clotted blood covering his face from a gunshot wound to the forehead. He bent down and examined the body. It was stiff, but had not bloated.

Marcus saw his chance to turn into a Confederate cavalryman. He quickly stripped the man of his coat and pants, held them up against his body to see if they would fit, then folded them up and packed them in his knapsack. The man also had a pistol in a scabbard that was fully loaded. The cavalryman also wore a long scabbard, but the sword was gone. Marcus added the pistol to his small armory. He found a wad of US currency along with Confederate paper money stuffed in the soldier's pockets. He knew this man would never need it again, so he confiscated the money for future use. Again, he did not think God would punish him for stealing under the circumstances.

The corpse also wore new cavalry boots that came up to his knees, but they would be difficult to walk in over a long distance, so he let them be. For a Confederate, the uniform was not ragged, but in good condition, only dirty. With his new loot, Marcus went down to the creek and found water gurgling up from a sandy spring, drank the cold water, and filled his canteen. He felt for sure this little creek would lead him to the Potomac.

He reached in his haversack and pulled out a piece of hardtack that Edward had given him and tried to eat the hard bread. He poured water on it to soften it a bit so he could chew it up; then he headed down the creek toward what he hoped was the Potomac River. He felt safer now with each step and reflected on what had happened to him since yesterday. His hell had now been replaced with a beautiful creek bank. He saw squirrels that he wanted to kill for food, but he did not want to reveal his location to others, fearing the shot would bring unwanted guests who might be lurking in the woods. By late afternoon the creek ran faster and rapidly descended down a steep slope to the river. He was on a wooded bluff above the river, but he could see Virginia now. All he had to do was cross the river, and he would soon be safe.

He scrambled down the steep rocky bank to the river's edge and looked around for any activity. All was calm. He sought and found a secluded hiding place along the shore and settled down to wait until dark before he crossed the river. He ate more hardtack and crunched on the dry corn just to give him energy.

He searched his confiscated haversack and found some coffee, but he had no way of making a fire. Coffee would sure taste good, however. Then he remembered he had a fire maker leaning against the rock, his rifle. He gathered some dry fuzzy weed tops to make some tender, and then gathered some sticks together in case his plan worked. He took a percussion cap from his cartridge belt and placed it on a rock surrounded by the soft tender. He slammed a rock down on the cap amidst the fuzz; there was a sharp bang, and as he expected, the fuzz started burning. He quickly added more fluff and sticks and soon he had a small fire. He used dry wood, and the smoke was hardly visible. He took a tin cup from his possessions and boiled a little coffee over the open fire, holding the cup with the bayonet off of his rifle. Compared to where he was the day before, he was in "hog heaven," a quote he had heard from his father when life was going right. Now he had everything ready to enjoy the letter from Bonnie, something he had been looking forward to since he had retrieved it the morning before; but he had been quite busy and unable to read it until now.

He pulled the letter from his pocket, very wrinkled now and partially blood- stained. He sniffed it to see if he could smell the familiar perfume that she often sprinkled on the letter. Time in transit and the odor of dried blood, however, compromised all but the slightest scent of Bonnie. He looked at the beautiful writing on the outside of the envelope. The stamped date indicated that it had been ten weeks in transit.

He slipped his small pocket knife out and gently sliced the end of the envelope and tilted it up and tapped it to ease out the letter; as he did, grains of sand sifted out of the envelope. He quickly turned the envelope to save the rest. He poured some of the sand in his palm and stirred it with his finger. Then he recognized a familiar piece of home. The sand was from Sandy Creek, a place where they had spent much of their leisure time growing up. He had a piece of home in his hand that made him yearn to be there. The scent he thought he smelled was more obvious now as he read.

My dearest Marcus, I pray this letter finds you safe and your battles won, and that you will be coming home soon and the war is over. I hope you got my last letter as I worry now, that I have not received one from you since June. Please write me soon and relieve my fear. As you read these words I hope you think of me waiting for you down by Sandy Creek where we shared so many good times. I am there now as I pen this letter. Did you find the grains of sand I put inside the envelope to remind you of home?

I was so lonesome today. I wanted to be near you the best way I knew how. I hitched our horse, Blaze, to the buggy, fried some chicken like we used to do, got old Fetch from your house, and came down to our rock by the creek to write you. I feel your presence and I can see you as if you were here, wrestling with Fetch, you grinning at me with the sun pouring through the hole in your hat spilling sunlight on your face. Oh, how I wish this war had never started.

As Marcus read, the words on the page turned into familiar images that he knew so well. He pictured the big rock on which they had picnicked so many times, and he saw Bonnie's beautiful face and friendly smile embraced by her beautiful flowing hair with her two shiny silver combs. Old Fetch always went with them and enjoyed the fun fetching sticks Marcus threw in the creek. Marcus was so far away from this person and place he loved. The letter made him homesick. His eyes began to water as he read on.

I am enclosing a picture of me standing by the tree in front of our house. Since I can't be with you I sent you this picture. I hope you will look at it every day and my face will be a reminder to you that I am waiting for you.

Marcus, I have some bad news though. Times here in Georgia are hard. You know it was even before the war, ever since our house burned down. As mentioned in my last letter, everything seemed to be against us. Father tried to save his cotton, but the drought ended any hope of making it profitable. As a result, he has decided to take our possessions and go to Texas. Rumor has it there is plenty of cheap fertile land there. We are leaving sometime next week after he takes care of all his obligations. I do not know where we are going, but he heard there was land available around Fincastle in Texas. His brother, Uncle James, is already there. That's all I know about where I will be. I will write my Aunt Ethel over at Buckhead and tell her my new whereabouts when I know them.

I am beginning to worry, Marcus, that you are captured or killed since it's been so long since I got a letter. Please write me, and please, please Marcus, if you are alive, come and find me. Don't ever fail to remember me. I will always be waiting for you. Until we can be together again, please know all my love is with you.

Bonnie

He looked back in the envelope and saw a small rectangular piece of paper, much thicker than the letter and slightly smaller than the width of the envelope. It fit snugly and was difficult to slip out. When he got it out, he saw the most beautiful photograph he had ever seen. It was a clear picture taken of her face, but with enough background to see the tree in her front yard they had climbed as children. He was mesmerized by her extreme beauty. He saw her long light-brown hair with the two silver combs that seemed to create a crown on his lovely princess. He couldn't take his eyes from the picture. He was so proud. Now, in a way, he would have Bonnie with him forever. He seemed so attracted by her image he did not want to put it away. He lay back on the river bank thrilled with the photograph. There seemed to be something magical about the picture. He had never seen a photograph that came alive and spoke to him with such feeling and emotion, as if she had cast a magical spell on him that would never be broken.

He continued staring at her picture, wishing so much she was with him. Her family was poor and he questioned how she got the picture. She was the most beautiful girl in his county, and any man with a camera would have loved to take her picture.

Yet, the thought of her being gone when he came home saddened him deeply. What if she never wrote a letter to her Aunt Ethel? How would he ever find her? The worry of war, how he was going to get back south and now, the fact that Bonnie would no longer be there deeply depressed Marcus. He rolled over in his hiding place and looked again at her picture. Then suddenly, his entire being changed; he wasn't sad anymore. He quickly sat up and looked Bonnie in the eye "No matter what I have to do, I will survive, I will get home, and I will find you, Bonnie Staples!" They will "kill me no more!" In that moment he made up his mind and determined he was going home for sure. No river, no Yankee, no nothing could stop him now!

The war was over for Marcus Mills. At that moment he was calling it "quits." After what he saw behind the Union lines, he knew the Confederate cause could not be won. The Yankees were too strong. It seemed for every Yankee killed; there were two more to replace him. Lee had demolished the Union Army in four major battles and still they came forth, stronger than before. He remembered the well-stocked supply wagons and the hundreds of mules that kept their army so well supplied. He knew for sure he was backing a losing cause. It was time for him to head south.

As he lay hidden in the rocks elated with the photograph, and determined now he was going home, he suddenly realized something incredible. He stood up and listened. It dawned on him; he had not heard the sound of battle today. He reasoned there had not been a battle. Artillery could be heard as far as fifty miles when the wind was right, but he was only five miles, at most, from the battlefield, yet it had been quiet all day. He hoped his act of sabotage had helped his brothers in arms and had saved many of their lives.

He continued to think about Bonnie and pondered why he had left such a beautiful girl to take a chance on being killed or the chance she might be snatched away by some rich planter wooing her with his wealth while he was gone.

When the war broke out and the bands played and the politicians urged all red-blooded Georgians to come forth and defend their state, he forgot about his love for Bonnie and went prancing off with the other guys to prove their manhood. He was only sixteen, a time in life when logical thinking is not a priority. Since he left Bonnie, the "hurrah, hurrah" thing quickly wore off, and he had been miserable ever since, having to sleep in horrible places, endure rainstorms, hot and cold weather, worn-out clothes and shoes, dirty latrines, cursing, terrible food and, most of the time, nearly starving, and had marched himself nearly to death. He reckoned he had lost twenty pounds. He had endured and survived all of the battles since defeating General McClellan on the peninsula. However, what he saw and experienced yesterday was the worst. Marcus was not a coward, but common sense told him now his cause was lost, and it was senseless to keep on killing each other. All he wanted to see was Bonnie, but "Here she is," he thought. "She joined me the only way she knew how."

Bonnie's letter had cheered Marcus up. He felt events now were going his way since being in the bloody pit the day before. He had discovered earlier a piece of soap in the Union haversack and decided to ease into the river and take a bath, something he hadn't done in quite a while. The river was cold, but bearable, and soon he was dry again. He had even used the soap to wash his hair. He felt like a new man now, and he would cross the river when it got dark.

He kept looking at Bonnie's picture and sniffing the letter. He knew this wonderful moment would soon be a memory, and he would soon be seeing the real Bonnie. As he waited for dark, to his surprise, he saw a small rowboat drifting along the edge of the river, bumping into the rocks in front of him, being pushed to his side by the current. He jumped up and pulled his shoes off, rolled up his pants, waded out, and pulled the boat against the bank before it got away.

Marcus couldn't believe this. He would not have to swim the river tonight; he could row across. This was a gift from God. He knelt down and thanked God for his new blessing. Being a small rowboat, he was able to pull it ashore and hide it in the rocks. As he examined his new prize, he discovered five bullet holes in the side above the water line and a few drops of blood on one of the seats and floor. There was only one oar leaning across the seats, and there were bloody hand prints smeared on the handle. He decided whoever was in the boat was shot, fell out, and the boat drifted down the river to Marcus. According to his experience with blood, the event had occurred in the last two hours, but far enough away he did not hear the shots.

It was almost dark; Marcus crunched on the dried corn and drank some water. He thought about the small treasure he had accumulated in the last twenty-four hours and with the boat he would be able to row all of it across the river. He suddenly realized, the boat would enable him, not to just cross the river, but float on down the river in total darkness until he found Lee's Army. There were fords that led into Sharpsburg, and he could pull in there, get out and be back with the troops. If he did that, he needed to change uniforms and turn into a trooper of the Southern cavalry. He peeled out of his blue disguise, folded it up for possible use again if necessary, and donned the gray wool outfit. His new suit was a bit large, but comfortable. He secured his most valuable treasure, Bonnie's letter and photograph and he secured it in an inner pocket above his heart; he thought at the time, an appropriate place. The boat had caused him to change his plans. His life was getting easier.

6

Marcus had not slept for thirty-six hours. It was mid-afternoon and his surroundings were quiet and peaceful and seemed to be an eternity from a war. Marcus crawled back in the tall dry grass above the river to get on softer ground hoping he could get a good nap before dark. He situated his haversack on the ground to make a comfortable pillow and in a few moments fast asleep.

Shortly before dark, his eyes abruptly opened. Although sound asleep, his brain was awake and alert for possible danger. Why did he awaken? Then he heard a distant noise he was familiar with back home. He froze and listened intently. He thought he heard a dog's bark; yes, it was hound dogs far away. He rose up in the high grass and listened again. The sound of the faraway dogs seemed to ebb and flow with the wind, sometimes louder and then almost gone. He crawled back to his possessions and smothered the fire, now almost dead, but still weeping a little white smoke into the air. He did not move, seeming to be listening with his eyes. After a few minutes he realized the dogs were coming down the river, apparently following the shoreline probably followed by authorities rounding up possible skulkers, cowards, Rebels, and maybe looking for him, waiting to cross the river. He knew all the fords were guarded.

The day was almost gone, but not dark enough to hide a boat crossing the river, but soon, it would be hard to see the brown boat on the river. Marcus wondered if the dogs would arrive and force him out before dark settled in. It was going to be a race against time. He pushed his loaded boat to the edge of the river, ready to launch with just a push of the paddle. From his experience coon hunting back home, it sounded like there were six to eight dogs and they were definitely coming toward him, each bark seeming closer than before. It was evident they were following a scent. Suddenly, like a clap of thunder, the approaching dark was pierced by a rifle shot, closer than he expected. "Should he push off?" Marcus worried, "or be patient and wait for more dark."

However, the rifle shot bought Marcus time by causing the dogs to come in and bunch around their owners, the dogs hoping to see the prey that was shot. Marcus calculated by the sound they were less than a quarter mile away. "Why did they shoot? Who did they shoot? It must have been someone. Could it be he was worrying for nothing, and it was really just some guys hunting coons? No, not on the edge of one the greatest battles in history; they were after men. Coon hunting began at night when the animals were stirring the most, not in the afternoon."

He continued to sit on the edge of the boat and pay close attention. If he could get another fifteen minutes, he would be hard to see in the brown wooden boat. Another five minutes passed, and the dogs were closer now. He began to hear the commands of the hunters to their dogs, but now the hounds seemed to be going past him.

A good hunter listened to his dogs and by their howls, knew what the dogs were broadcasting back to their owners. The man could tell when the dogs hunted for a scent, when they found a scent, when they were chasing a scent, and when their prey had been found.

Marcus read the same howls that he also knew so well. From what he heard, he felt safe for the moment. He wondered if they went by him now, would they spot him farther down the river. He looked out at the darkening landscape, "Could they see me if I left now?" He kept pondering the question as one of the dogs, from its sounds, had turned and appeared to be coming right for him. Indicated by his howl, he was on a strong scent, probably his. The lone barker got closer and closer.

Marcus tested the paddle against the sand to make sure he could move the boat. He pushed against the shore and the boat easily moved closer to the flowing water. The dog now seemed to be less than fifty yards away and he heard the howl changing as the dog picked up his stronger scent. Marcus heard the dog brushing the weeds. He pushed the boat off just as the dog emerged out of the grass along the river and ran into the water as if he were going to jump into the boat. But Marcus had pushed away from the rocky shore and the boat had caught the strong current on his side of the river and began to pick up speed, just as a horseman broke out of the trees on top of the bluff and emptied his pistol in Marcus's direction, two of the projectiles hitting the boat, the others splashing the water beside him. Then the rider jerked his rifle from his saddle holster and tried to put a bead on Marcus who was now about fifty yards away. Marcus hunkered down between the seats and let the current push him along as the man fired. He knew it was difficult to line the sights up in the dark on a moving target while on horseback. Instead of hitting Marcus, the side of the boat near the bow splintered. He knew it would take his pursuer another thirty seconds before he could fire again and by then he would be hidden on the dark river.

While Marcus rode his ark down the river he heard the commotion behind him as the horsemen gathered to devise a plan to catch their prey before he got too far. They knew the Rebel Army was downstream and they were likely to run into Confederate cavalry guarding the left flank of the army that was anchored against the Potomac River. Marcus hoped he could get behind Confederate lines before they caught up with him. He had no idea how far he had to go before he would be safe. It might only be a mile to the Confederate army, but by the twisting river, it could be many more.

The horseman's silhouette disappeared behind the dark rim of the river, but soon reappeared again against the fading evening sky with more riders alongside. The riders disappeared again on the wooded bluff, but Marcus knew where they were by the sounds of the howling dogs, their presence like a bell clanging in the distance. It seemed the riders were trying to get ahead of him now as if they knew a place where they could cut him off or at least have a chance to kill him.

The men with the dogs appeared to be civilians numbering only five or six, but more riders joined the group. That many horsemen indicated the Union cavalry may have joined in the chase. In the dark he could barely make out the silhouettes galloping down the river with the dogs howling and leading the way. He felt for sure now they were going to cut him off or stop him at a ford.

As the riders and dogs disappeared in the dark, Marcus rowed hard to get the boat to the other side of the river where he found a place to stop between two large boulders. He used the oar to stop his forward progress and felt for the bottom of the river as he bumped onto the rocky shore. He listened and could barely hear the dogs in the far distance ahead of him. He felt sheltered for the time being. He got out and pulled the boat on shore to be safe from floating away, but still in the water so he could make a quick escape if he needed to. There wasn't a steep bluff on this side of the river and the terrain that disappeared into the woods seemed level.

Marcus waited silently in full darkness now. The sounds of dogs had faded out. He wondered why the hunters had not collided with Confederate Cavalry guarding the far left flank of Lee's Army. Maybe he had traveled farther than he imagined that day. He also reasoned Lee's Army may have retreated or surrendered after the battle. Forbid that last thought, but if Lee had, the good side meant the war was over and he would be going home; but for now, he had to keep himself safe. In time, he would find out if Lee had left or given up.

Marcus looked at the cards played on his table of life before him. He could take his chances and push off down the river hoping to avoid his predators and their dogs, leave the boat and travel down the Virginia side of the river until he found Lee's army, or just stay put. He was hidden here and he had a piece or two of hardtack left and some corn kernels to keep him fed. He decided the best hand he could play was to stay hidden and see what happened.

He secured the boat and took the blanket from the top of the knapsack and spread it on the ground and he lay down, and although not a feather bed, he was comfortable using his Union haversack for a pillow.

No sooner than he was comfortable, he jerked up, leaned back on his elbows with his head up, and intensely listened. He turned his head so one of his ears faced the direction he thought he had heard the faint bark of a dog again. Could they be coming back? That should be no trouble for Marcus now; he was on the other side of the river and safe. Those guys probably ran into the Confederate Cavalry and were running for their lives, trying to get back to safety as fast as their horses could run. He laughed to himself, "They are probably leaving the dogs behind."

But no matter how he tried to imagine he was safe, the dogs' barking indicated a different story. They were getting closer and as they came back down the river he suddenly realized, the group had split into two groups, and one of them was on his side of the river. He knew they were hunting for him along the river banks. It sounded like the dogs were now about a half-mile away but coming fast.

Marcus stepped out on one of the large boulders hiding his boat. He looked down the river and saw a scene he did not like. As he reckoned, there were two groups coming along next to the river holding lanterns and torches making the edge of the river bright as daylight. There was no place for Marcus to hide. Again he looked at the cards on the table. He could jump in the boat and try to pass between the groups, but the torches lit the river far enough out he could easily be seen. A second card he could play to save his life, was to jump in the river and hide along the rocky shore; or he could run, trying to stay ahead of the dogs.

Being familiar with how dogs hunted, Marcus decided to use some tricks he had learned from the coons he hunted back home. He knew ways to lose the dogs or at least slow them down so he could buy enough time to eventually find safety and get away. Back home he never figured one day he would be the coon the people were hunting.

He quickly took what gear he needed and could carry out of the boat. He eased the boat off of the river edge and pushed it as hard as he could out into the current, hoping his hunters would see it and think he was trying to slip by them in the dark, chase it, and give him time to use his plan to escape the dogs. He watched a moment as the boat disappeared into the night. He grabbed his gear and entered the river wading along the edge, staying in the water as far as he could go. He figured after they secured the boat and discovered he was gone, they would continue their search along the river bank. Eventually the dogs would find where he had landed the boat. Since the scent did not go anywhere, the dogs would be confused for a while until the riders caught up, realized what Marcus had done, and then lead the dogs on up the river to find where he came out of the water and cause the chase to be hot again.

Marcus, now using his plan to fool the hounds, came back on shore and ran a hundred yards into the woods, twisting and turning, trying to paint his odor on the ground. When he reached the end of his path he ran around a large tree several times, holding his hands on the tree, making the dogs think he had climbed the tree. Then Marcus ran back down the same path back to the river, now having only enough visibility to see the lighter colored bark on the trees. He then entered the river to stop the scent and wade upstream again, and then do the same procedure again. He repeated this ruse of leaving false scent trails that only ended in the woods again and again. These false trails should not only confuse the hounds, but frustrate them as well.

Apparently the boat drifting down the river had caught the attention of his pursuers when sounds of rifle shots echoed back to Marcus, and the horsemen would waste time catching it. The howls of the dogs that seemed to be approaching, now seemed to be going back down the river, but he was sure it would not be long until they returned.

Now, Marcus played the last card in his scheme, maybe not an ace, but at least his best card. He entered the river and waded upstream and came ashore one last time. He pulled out his blue uniform and dropped it on the ground as if he had taken it off. He took off his shoes and left them on top of the clothes along with his hat, a pistol, and one of his rifles.

Although he had tough feet, he would miss his shoes, but to save his life, he had to leave them next to the water to convince his foe he had jumped in the river to swim back across. That should send his predators back across the river to continue the chase there. Most of the soldiers in the Confederate army were barefoot, so he reasoned if necessary, he could join many of his comrades and go barefoot too. He would rather have cold feet than to freeze to death in a Yankee prison.

He waded back down the river until and entered the dark forest again to make a new track for the dogs to follow. His eyes had adjusted to the dark, and the starlight filtering through the trees gave him enough vision to walk through the dark woods. Like all the other scent trails, after reaching the end, he walked about half way back toward the river and found a tall tree and ascended to near the top lugging all his gear and guns. That was a trick called "back tracking," a ploy wise old raccoons had played on him many times. This coon trick had saved many of their lives, and he hoped it would save his; it was his only chance. The tired and frustrated dogs should pass under his tree with their noses to the ground, discover a dead end, and then hurry back to the river leaving Marcus high in the still leafy tree.

Marcus also knew his trackers would soon learn what he was doing and probably call all the dogs out of the woods and hurry on up the river farther, and farther away from him in the tree. In time, they would find the bundle of clothes and shoes at the edge of the river, meaning their prey had crossed back over the river.

Not hearing the dogs now, Marcus knew his pursuers were still faraway. Apparently the boat ruse had worked and for the moment called off the dogs and bought him time to enact his escape plan. For the moment he was safe and climbed lower in the tree to find a more comfortable place to wait and listen. It would take his chasers a while to come back up the river and sniff out the empty trails he had made.

As he had anticipated, he soon heard the dogs faintly coming toward him again. After a short wait, he heard the barks and howls change pitch when the dogs found where the boat had been. The trail was hot again. As he continued to listen, the dogs discovered his odor going into the woods and the howls changed again. They had taken his bait and the dogs were running into the woods away from the river expecting to find their prey at any moment with the mounted men behind them. At the end of the first trail all the dogs surrounded the tree and bayed, some with their paws scratching on the tree. Their prey had been treed.

7

Back at Antietam, the information Edward told his officer's eventually came to the attention of a General in the 1st Corp. A known saboteur could cause havoc behind the lines and efforts were ordered to catch him. The general dispatched a messenger to the local constable with instructions to help the military gather up stragglers from the army and to be extra aware of a young man with a noticeable southern drawl who fit Marcus' description. He also urged his officers to check out unknown soldiers who may have drifted into their squads and brigades and seemed to be lost. If Lee attacked again, they feared they would need every soldier they could scrounge up. Soon, many young, blond, youngsters had been rounded up for Edward to look at. Edward found one suspect, but when he was asked to speak, his New York accent dismissed the case against him. The officer ordered, "This scoundrel has to be attached to the earth somewhere; catch him!"

The local constable gathered up all the local raccoon hunters he could muster and by midafternoon with his force of dogs, horses and men, he was on the hunt for stragglers, cowards, and Confederates behind the Union lines. He quickly discovered the backwash from the huge battle; a variety of souls were hiding in the woods, some wounded physically and many wounded mentally, all trying to find cures for their misfortunes.

Many of the folks he met were civilians getting out of the way of the army. Many soldiers were wounded, but didn't need a surgeon, and were seeking a safe place to mend for a while. By the time the dogs flushed out Marcus; they had killed three soldiers who had resisted their detention, and had rounded up a dozen or so of what most people called cowards, but in modern times they would be considered "shell shocked."

When the searchers saw Marcus floating away, they proceeded down river to a shallow ford to wait for him, but when he didn't show up, the posse divided and came up each side of the river looking for him. They saw the boat float by, chased it, and eventually brought it to shore where they found it empty. Eventually, they came up the river and discovered where he had landed. The constable knew they had him now; it was just a matter of time and patience. One of the men shot three holes in the bottom of boat with his pistol, preventing Marcus from circling back and using the boat again.

All Marcus could do now was wait and hope his plan would trick the dogs. A wise old veteran dog was hard to fool, however, and Marcus knew that. An old dog often used his own knowledge gained from years of experience and hunted on his own, not going with the flow of the other dogs. He hoped, if his foe had one; that dog had died.

Marcus listened to the yowls coming up the river and soon heard the men's voices and saw the glow of their torches through the trees. He climbed back to the top of the tree. The men were working the dogs slowly, not rushing them, letting the dogs sniff out every interesting smell that told a story that only a dog could interpret. After they had found their third false corridor, and as Marcus predicted, he heard one of the men say he was going to take Buster and go on up the river and see if he found new scents so they could determine what this guy was up to and possibly save time. He suspected they were being duped.

The dog and rider hurried on up the river and soon discovered a new scent trail. The constable yelled back, "There's another trail up here. He's trying to throw us off track sending us down these dead ends." That was what Marcus wanted to hear. His plan was working perfectly. Marcus heard the other dogs and riders obeying orders staying close to the river.

Marcus saw the glow of the torches through the trees. The riders passed by without checking the path where Marcus was hidden. He was within fifty yards of the men as he watched the torches and heard the men talking as they came up the river, staying close to the shore. It appeared all of them would pass his trail and he would be a free man, but at the last moment one of the young dogs, Barker, turned and followed the secret path that only a dog could detect. One of the riders called to the dog to follow but Barker kept his nose to the ground and came toward Marcus's tree. This would be the first test to see if he was going to be a free man. He was in the top of a tall tree and was hidden by the leaves that had changed colors, but he could be seen if they looked up from underneath. Fortunately for Marcus, he had selected a tree full of mistletoe. Earlier, while he waited, he had taken out the large knife he had confiscated from the dead Confederate and cut some mistletoe to reinforce his disguise and block the view from below.

All the dogs headed on up the river with their owners, all of the time broadcasting to their keepers what was happening. One of the riders stayed back to watch and follow Barker. In a moment or two, Marcus heard the pat of a dogs paw on the forest floor. The rider kept hollering to his dog to come out of there, but Barker was concentrating on what he sensed was a fresher odor. Marcus listened as the dog came under his tree. Barker sniffed rapidly, his nose never leaving the ground, his head moving back and forth to pick up the direction of the scent. Marcus watched intently from above. He heard the owner call his dog again, then turn his horse and follow where his dog had gone into the woods. Soon, the rider saw his dog in the light of his lantern. He watched the dog slowly approach Marcus's refuge, walk around it, stop, then put his feet on the side of the tree, look up and gave a loud bellow. He knew something had climbed that tree and continued to whine as if he was bothered by something he wasn't sure of. Barker's owner knew his dog was a young and an inexperienced hunter; often baying up the wrong tree, but just in case the dog might have something, the rider rode up next to the tree trunk, hollering at the dog to move on. The dog obeyed and continued on into the woods following the false scent.

The rider pondered a moment what had gotten the dog's attention. He held the torch up high and looked up. Marcus did not breathe or move fearing he might knock a piece of bark or dust off that would draw attention to his hiding place. The man could see dark clumps of mistletoe all through the tree, and one large clump near the top large enough to hide a man. The rider stared up at the mistletoe. He thought a moment; if there was a man up there hiding; he figured a little serious bluff would bring him down. Pretending he had seen Marcus he yelled, "Hey, I see you. Whoever you are, reveal yourself."

Marcus did not move. How could he see him high in the tree? He was trying to get Marcus to show his hand.

"All right, I guess you want to get shot?"

Marcus remained quiet. He even kept his eyes shut hoping a reflection from a wet eye might reveal his location in the dark tree.

The man studied the clump of mistletoe. He didn't want to waste a bullet and attract all the other riders back down the river. After all, they had discovered another scent track up the river. As a last resort to get his prey to move, the man took out his pistol and aimed it at the dark mass, pulled the hammer back with a loud click. "Come on out, this is your last chance."

Marcus had played the game this far. "Might as well call his bluff and see if the guy had a good hand," Marcus reasoned, "And even if he shoots, Marcus had odds in his favor of being missed with a pistol shot at that distance."

The man held the gun in the air waiting for a response, but none came. He lowered the pistol and returned it to the holster. He reined the horse back toward the dog now deeper in the woods. "Come on, Barker, let's get out of here. They're waitin' for us up river." The dog obeyed this time, believing he was on a cold trail, but when he came back by Marcus' tree, he stopped, raised his leg and marked his territory. He knew something was in that tree. With that final gesture the horse, rider, and dog cut through the woods to join the pack. Soon Marcus heard the lead man up the river yell, "He's not down there, there's another hot trail up here. Bring your dog on up!"

That was music to Marcus's ears. He saw the glow from the torches cut through the woods going toward the constable. He relaxed and breathed easier. How close could he get to being captured? He had nearly dodged a bullet. He had been sitting on a limb holding the mistletoe below him not moving a muscle. With the threat over he stood up on the limb to relax and the mistletoe fell to the ground, bouncing off the lower limbs as it descended. Marcus was glad that had not happened when the man or the dog was under the tree.

When the lone rider joined the constable, Barker's owner told him, "I thought I had our man a while ago when Barker bayed. He was interested in a large oak full of mistletoe. It was large enough to hide a man, but I checked it out with the lantern and even pretended I saw him up there and told him to climb down. I even threatened to shoot him, but no response. If it was anything, it was probably a raccoon or a possum. My dog, Barker, just needs to get a little older and he will quit that lying."

The constable studied a moment. "Did you check the bark on the tree to see if a man had knocked it off when he climbed it?"

"No, I didn't. You think I should go back and be sure?'"

Before the constable could answer, they heard a holler from up the river. "You guys, come up here. I think I found what's left of our man." The dogs, men and horses hurried through the woods lighting up the surroundings with their torches. "Look at that," he said pointing at the ground. I believe he has given us the slip." He pointed at a pile of clothing now being pulled and tugged on by some of the dogs. They found a rifle and a pistol and two new shoes worn by the Union soldiers.

The man who had shot at Marcus on the other side of the river looked down at the blue clothes. "You know that's kind of odd. I would have sworn the man in the boat had on a gray uniform."

"That rascal has jumped in the river and crossed to the other side. He's probably watching us now. Get that gear, I need a new squirrel rifle and a pistol," the constable said. "Before we go back down to the ford, why don't two of you men go on up the river a half mile with the dogs and see if he really crossed the river. Whoever this guy is, he's a cunning old bird. We'll wait here for you. If you don't find anything, we'll try and pick up his scent on the other side of the river. Maybe, if we are lucky, we can find where he came ashore."

When no more trails were found they concluded their prey had swum the river. The constable and his party returned to the ford and crossed the river back into Maryland and reunited with the hunters who had stayed in Maryland. The constable made a final statement to his men, "You know that guy we were chasing today acted like a raccoon. He must be an old coon hunter!" They all agreed. "You don't think he acted like a smart coon and "back tracked" us did he?" He thought a moment, "Naw! He wouldn't have done that."

Marcus had watched the glow from the torches pass by and disappear in the dark and taking his fear of capture with them. "That was close," Marcus thought. He had been uncomfortable in the tree and he had no shoes, but he would gladly accept the temporary pain to be free rather than spending several years in a prison or being shot.

He could not hear the dogs any more. He had hated to sacrifice his rifle and a pistol, but he had to make his disappearance in the river seem real. It felt good to be out of that tree. He was so high the limb he sat on was small and made his position uncomfortable. He still had a rifle, pistol, haversack, knapsack and his basic supplies. He gathered up his gear and eased back over to the river.

He felt for sure, the men took his guns. His feet were very tough, but he needed his shoes and he hoped they had left the wet shoes. He found the place of his supposed departure into the river and searched for his shoes. The men got his guns and the dogs had fought over his shoes and clothes, and had apparently carried them off. It was dark and trying to find two shoes was nearly impossible. Realizing their importance, however, Marcus decided to wait until morning and see if he could locate them. He went back in the woods and kicked up some leaves to insulate him from the cold ground, took out his new army blanket, and wrapped up tightly, being sure to cover his feet. He used his haversack for a pillow, and at this moment totally spent, he was soon asleep.

8

"Wake up boy, your running days is over." Marcus looked up and faced the business end of a double barrel shotgun aimed right at his nose. A large man with a gruff voice was grinning at him. Behind the large man were several more men with rifles all pointing at him, all grinning like devils. He had never seen such a filthy group of men. As he looked, hundreds of gray clad soldiers all connected by ropes tied tightly around their necks, were marching up a trail by the river. He could not see the end of the line. "Lee must have surrendered," Marcus thought. He was relieved somewhat, knowing the war would be over soon and he would be going home to Bonnie. Then a man came forward with a star pinned to his coat. "We're gonna shoot this guy. He gave us all kinds of trouble last night and I ain't gonna take a chance that he will get away." As he spoke, he drew his pistol out and aimed it at Marcus and fired.

Suddenly, Marcus's body jerked from the pain and he sat up. Gaining his senses, he looked around and found he was not hurt but alone in the woods. The sun had been up an hour and he realized he had been dreaming, a nightmare, possibly exposing a hidden fear that he had suppressed. He rolled over on his blanket and gave a sigh of relief.

His leafy bed had flattened during the night from his weight and was no longer comfortable. He sat up and rubbed his eyes. He gained his senses and gave a morning prayer that he had not been captured and his dream was not real. He was hungry and had only hard corn to eat. He had eaten his last big cracker while he sat in the tree. He had some coffee that would taste good in the chilly air, but, his nightmare reminded him the hunters might still be alert for his presence.

His feet were cold and he needed his shoes so he returned to the river, scanning for any activity. Seeing none, he came out in the open and started hunting from the spot he had left his shoes. He soon found one shoe in pretty good shape and he went down the river in the direction the men had retreated and found his other shoe. The sole was almost torn from the shoe by the two tugging dogs, each trying to retrieve the prize. He put his shoes on and noticed the ragged shoe sole flopped on the ground as he walked and the good shoe had lost its laces, but under the conditions, it was better than being unshod.

Marcus shelled a small ear of dried corn to give him some nourishment as he pondered his situation. He knew Lee was down the river holding his line or had retreated back into Virginia. He decided if Lee had gone, the Union army would be in control of the battlefield now. The country would be filled with Union Cavalry to harass Lee's retreat and capture straggling Confederates, so he decided to go farther west and try to flank the Union army and get back to Virginia.

He turned his back on the river and headed west. The trees quickly ended and he crossed farmed fields with split rail fences, the same that he had hid behind during many battles. After a mile he came to a wooded bluff that looked down on a large river. Did he walk a big circle and didn't realize it? No, he could see the sun behind him and he knew if he walked in the direction of his shadow he would be going in a westerly direction. The river must have had a loop and he had walked across it. Even though he was east of the river he figured he was still west of the river. He had seen no people, but needless to say, he was trying to avoid any human contact.

He stayed on the edge of the bluff and followed the river south and before long the river turned west again. At this point he went south. He walked along grown up fence rows, skirted around small villages and people's houses. Marcus felt the farther south he went the more kindly the people would be. At noon, in a heavily wooded bottom, he wandered up on a squirrel and shot it for lunch. He immediately found some heavy brush to hide under to see if the shot attracted any unwanted visitors to his table. It seemed that he was alone.

The woods seemed isolated and he felt safe, safe enough now to build a fire. Using his percussion cap he made another fire and roasted his skinned delicacy on a stick. Marcus was so hungry; he couldn't believe anything could taste so good. He devoured every bit and morsel of the animal. He even polished the bones with his teeth to get all the nourishment he could. An old veteran soldier once told him to break the bones and suck the marrow from inside and he did. He drank some water and lay back and rested a moment. He was in General Stonewall Jackson's Confederate corps, known as Jackson's "foot cavalry" because they moved so fast. Jackson marched his men hard, but let them take a short rest every hour. Remembering that, Marcus was soon back on his feet, using the sun for guidance, and walking south. He calculated by late afternoon he had to be below and to the west of Sharpsburg. He should have encountered parts of Lee's army now. He had found the Potomac River again, and deduced he was now below the place the dogs had almost caught him; but where was Lee's army?

All of a sudden he heard the thunder of hooves approaching. Cavalry! Probably Yankee cavalry. Marcus scurried into the dried grass near the road and watched the Union horsemen pass. He was definitely in Union territory and would have to be alert now. He moved away from the river to search for empty fields and forests in which to travel. It would be dark in another hour so Marcus found a secluded spot in a grove of trees, made his bed, crunched some corn, drank lots of water to try and stave off hunger hoping the water would swell the corn inside him, made his bed, and was fast asleep again.

The next morning he was hungry. The risk of being captured seemed less hazardous than starving to death. He set out again, hoping to find a rabbit or squirrel, or someone's loose chicken to kill. He walked through some thick forest and came out on the edge of a large field that had left fallow the year before. Beyond the field he saw smoke rising up from behind a row of trees. That meant people were there, but he was in Virginia now; that meant southerners that could give him aid or hide him if necessary. He approached with caution and saw an elderly lady sitting beside a large black pot of boiling water plucking feathers from a chicken she had killed and was preparing to fry. Marcus carefully watched to see if any other danger might be in the vicinity. She seemed to be alone and hoping she would be proud to help a southern patriot and the lure of a piece of fried chicken helped Marcus decide to take his chances.

He came out of the woods and "hollered up" the lady, giving her the courtesy to know his presence, a common custom when approaching a stranger's home. She stood up and quickly ran inside her house and immediately appeared in the doorway holding a rifle.

Marcus gently laid down his rifle on the ground and raised his arms in the air, indicating to her, he meant no harm, although he had his pistol stuck in his belt behind him under his coat.

"What do you want?" the lady yelled in an unwelcoming voice.

"I'm just passing through. I was in the battle the other day and got cut off from my men and trying to find my way back home to Georgia. Can you spare something to eat?"

"Come forward where I can see you better."

Marcus looked rather comical walking forward in his cavalry uniform, now hatless, and his dog chewed shoes with one of the soles flopping on the ground. The lady seemed a little relieved as she observed the young boy with the peach fuzz on his face approaching her.

Marcus smiled as he came closer, "I don't mean you no harm. I was just following the river and saw the smoke from your fire there and hoped I could find somebody that could help me and tell me how to get home."

"What's your name boy?" she asked, still pointing the gun at him, suspicious about what he might be up to.

"Marcus, ma'm, Marcus Mills from Georgia, ma'm."

The old woman lowered her rifle and leaned it against the wall inside the door. "You know how to finish plucking this chicken?"

"Yes ma'm, I helped my mama lots of times do that. I also know how to skin a rabbit or a squirrel, and I have scraped a many a hog, too."

She pitched the half plucked chicken to Marcus. "Finish this then and I'll get you something to eat."

Marcus sat down in the old lady's chair and started pulling feathers. As he cleaned up the chicken, Marcus noticed there were no other chickens in the yard. He thought that unusual since most homes, inside and outside of towns had a chicken yard for meat and eggs. He saw the hen house and chicken yard were empty. He wondered if this was her last chicken. He knew both the Union and Southern Armies, as they passed through farms and towns, confiscated food and left the owners a voucher indicating the value of what they took. Supposedly the vouchers could be redeemed later at a Confederate or Federal bank. Marcus took his pocket knife and degutted the chicken and cut the feet and head off.

As he finished washing the chicken in a bucket of water beside the chair, she came out the door with a piece of ham stuck inside a soft biscuit and a cup of coffee. "This is all I got right now, but I'll soon have that chicken fried and I have some tater's baking in the stove. I'll fix some cornbread and cut an onion up and maybe that will get you by."

Then the elderly woman noticed the head and feet of the chicken on the ground, "What did you do that for?" she asked as she pointed at the remains beside his chair.

"You don't eat those do you? Only black folks eat heads and chicken feet." She reached down and snatched them up and wiped the dirt away, "Where I come from, times were hard, and we never wasted any part of a chicken. Pickled chicken feet were all we had some time." Marcus apologized and thanked her for his ham and biscuit. As he chewed, he felt as if he was back home at his mother's table. She turned to go back in the house and Marcus, wanting to pay for her for her kindness and food asked, "While I'm waiting, is there anything I could do for you that might help pay for my meal?"

She stopped and looked back at Marcus and thought a minute. "Yes there is. I have a feather bed that needs to be hung out on the fence a few hours in the sun to air out before winter. Could you do that for me?"

"Yes ma'm that would be no problem at all."

"Come in the house then, and I'll show you where it is when you finish that biscuit." She stopped and pointed at the front fence. "Just lay it out there and take the broom and give it a few whacks. If you are still around later, I'll get you to turn it over and whack it again." Marcus followed her up on the porch and into the three room house. It wasn't a large house, but neatly kept. There was a large stone fireplace built in the wall opposite the front door and was the first thing Marcus saw when he entered. The lady shuffled over to her cooking area to the right of the fireplace and lay the feet and head on a table. He noticed an iron stove that not only cooked food, but also helped warm the room in winter. On either side of the fireplace room were two smaller sleeping spaces attached on the side of the structure with beds inside. She went in the side room and pulled her bedding and quilts from the feather bed and stepped back for Marcus to gather the mattress up. Marcus pulled on the rather heavy feather bed and tried to roll it up so he could get his arms around it. He then realized how weak he was from lack of hearty food over the last few weeks. The lady noticed his struggle and came up to help him, but he shooed her back, "No, I can get this. I just haven't eaten in a while and I'm a little weak." Marcus felt embarrassed at his inability to move the mattress at first.

He got hold of himself and heaved the bundle on his shoulder and took it outside and laid it in the sun as she had instructed. He saw a large stout staff on the porch, probably used to herd animals, fetched it and starting beating the mattress causing the dust to fly. After a few minutes he turned it over and beat the other side. When he finished he walked up on the porch and asked the lady if he could do anything else. "No, that will be all." He watched her fry the chicken and poke a fork in the potatoes baking in a Dutch oven hung over the fire in the fireplace. When she opened her pantry cabinet, he saw it was empty of any dried food or staples. It was obvious she had nothing stored for the coming winter. She turned to him, "Have a seat there at the table. I'll have this done in another moment or two."

As Marcus watched, he became curious about this elderly lady. "Do you have a family?"

She turned and smiled as she grabbed a pot holder and lifted the lid on the iron skilled to move the frying chicken with a fork, "Yes, I have a son in the Union Army and a daughter that's married to a Confederate Colonel in Richmond."

When she mentioned "Union Army" a fright ran through him that she is probably a Unionist and didn't appreciate him being in her company, but felt easier when he heard about her daughter.

"Where is your husband?"

"Out there under that oak tree; he died last year."

Her answer puzzled Marcus. Since he had seen so much dying in the past year, the word "died" made him wonder if he had been killed in the war or died of natural causes. "Was he killed in the war?"

"No, he died of a broken heart, a heart that broke into three pieces. My heart was broken too, but I didn't die. It was the children. Right before the war Anna, my daughter, was going to marry Colonel Bridges, a soldier she had met while she was visiting her cousin down at Charlestown. One of my two boys, Edward, had gone up to Harrisburg to study law. Growing up he was different in a way from the other kids. He didn't like farming or hunting, but enjoyed reading books and writing stories. He tinkered with things." Looking up and for a second sparked by an idea she recalled, "He got an idea one time that he thought would make him rich. Ohhh, he got excited and drew pictures and whittled out some wooden parts: wheels and stuff. He even worked for the blacksmith for a little while to get him to make iron pieces he needed for that thing he made."

"What did it do?"

"Well, it worked pretty well." Turning and looking at Marcus, "It planted seeds. It wasn't much bigger than a large pistol with a wheel on the end, but you could bend over and push the wheel down the row and it would drop a seed on the ground with the same space between each seed. It worked pretty well, but it sometimes clogged up and he would have to take it apart and clean it. He showed folks in the village his gadget hoping he could make some money on it, but after they looked at it, they went home and made one of their own. Edward was hot headed and it made him mad that people would steal his idea. That's why he wanted to study law, so he could get a paper on it that said it was his idea so nobody could steal it." Edward would work on the farm when his father made him, but he didn't like it. For a while, he worked down at the post office in Shepherdstown. He wanted to be somebody; somebody that worked with his mind and not his back. He was hot headed though, like a lot of young'uns, and thought he knew more than his ignorant father."

She pushed the skillet off the hot burner to the side of the stove the grease still popping, and put the chicken in a serving dish and put it on the table. The potatoes were given a final look and served with butter and fresh cornbread she had stirred up and cooked while the chicken was frying. As she was gathering the tableware and dishes she continued her story.

"While he was up there at school, he was taught by the Northerners that the South was run by the disciples of the devil and would reap the whirlwind if they 'ceded from the Union. When it finally looked like war was imminent, he came home and told us he was going to fight for the Union cause."

"Yes, he was different from his other brother alright. Matt was just the opposite of Edward. He wanted to stay on the farm and help his father and someday take over the place." She poured Marcus a glass of water from a stoneware pitcher and sat down to eat. "He loved the soil and enjoyed the abundance of his labor. Unlike Edward, he was always calm and hard to bother, but if you did arouse him, you had a bear by the tail. He and his father favored Virginia and had decided to go with whomever Virginia backed in the war, North or South, you know, like Gen'l Lee."

Edward and Matt were downtown waiting on the news whether Virginia would go Union or Confederate. A lot of people were downtown that night and when the news came up from Richmond that Virginia had gone with the South, a big celebration broke out, but some were Unionists, like Edward, and got into fist fights around the town square. Edward, being hot headed, bought some liquor and got in a fight with a "sesh." By the time Matt found him, Edward had been hurt bad, but he was too proud to admit it. People hollered that Edward couldn't fight like a man and was being saved by his little baby brother, you know, insulting his manhood. Matt picked him up and put him on the horse, like a big doll." The old lady seemed to grin in a sad way. "That embarrassed Edward even more. By the time my boys got home Edward was out of his head. I don't know whether the liquor caused him to do what he did or if he was touched in the head from a hit on his noggin' during the fight, but when they got home, Edward was hollering and wouldn't get off the horse and was trying to get the reins out of Matt's hands so he could go back to town and show them he was no coward."

"We were inside here; Carl, my husband, was sitting in the rocker when we heard the commotion outside. He knew the boys were fighting. When he went outside, he saw Matt pull Edward off the horse, so he couldn't go back to town. Edward tried to stand, but being drunk stumbled to the ground. Matt turned away to lead his horse to the barn." The elderly lady's eyes started to glisten in the light from the open door. "When he had turned away and wasn't looking, Edward got up from the ground holding a piece of firewood and came up behind Matt and clubbed him in the head. Carl yelled to Matt, but it was too late. Matt fell to the ground and was stunned, but fought back. Edward was able to strike him again and again before Carl got to him and jerked the log away and backhanded him to the ground. Edward somehow climbed back on the horse and disappeared in the dark and we haven't seen him since."

She stopped and looked out the window at the place where it happened as if she had forgotten the story and was trying to remember again. "Carl went to Matt and tried to wake him up, but he was unconscious. My husband picked him up and brought him in and put him in that bed right there," pointing to one of the beds in the side room. "He lay there six days wasting away and never woke up. The doctor did everything he knew to get him up, but he never came to. I'm sure, not intending to and not knowing, Edward killed his brother. We buried him out there under the tree."

"My husband never got over what happened that night. We nursed Matt until he died and we never heard from Edward again."

Still wondering, Marcus asked, "How did your husband die?"

She scooted her chair closer to the table, "Let's give thanks to the Lord for what we have." Marcus bowed his head and listened as she prayed, "My Holy Father, thank you for what we are to receive. Place your blessings on my visitor as he passes by and may his road be easy, and Father, help me make it through the long cold winter ahead. Please bless Edward where ever he is and let him come home one day. In Jesus's name I pray, Amen."

Marcus looked at the chicken and potatoes. The entire chicken had been cut up and fried, to be eaten either for dinner and supper since there was no refrigeration. What was not finished at noon was usually left on the dining table, covered with a cloth to keep the flies off and eaten later.

Although Marcus was extremely hungry, he waited for her to pass him the chicken. He reached out with his fork and speared a piece of breast and a drumstick. "Now get you a tater or two and here's a slice of onion," as she pushed the small platter toward him.

The little lady took the platter of chicken and raked a wing on her plate. Then she remembered she had the rest of the biscuits she had baked that morning. As she returned to the table, she said she had some peach preserves they could top the biscuits off with, and the two began to eat.

Marcus could not remember when hot food tasted so good. He cut his potato in half and took a swath of butter from the dish she had previously placed on the table and spread it over his steaming hot potato. Marcus put the bites of the delicious fare in his mouth and chewed slowly trying to squeeze every morsel of enjoyment from each bite.

Marcus spoke up, "Mrs., uh, uh, you know, I don't know your name?"

"Genia, Genia Brewster, and your name is Marcus as I recall."

"Yes ma'm," he said, shaking his fork up and down emphasizing a point, "And you know, Mrs. Brewster, this is the best food I ever put in my mouth."

"No, my boy, you are just the hungriest you have ever been in your life. How long has it been since you had a meal?"

Marcus thought a second, "I guess about a week ago. The morning before the battle we were supposed to be fed, but just when we were about to eat we were called to the front line. Everybody grabbed what they could eat and placed the rest in their haversack and took it with them as we ran to the front. I found some hard bread in some dead folk's haversacks out on the battlefield and some dry corn I gathered out in a field a while back and, oh yes, I killed a squirrel yesterday."

"I should say then, my cooking is pretty good to you then if you hadn't eaten in that long a time."

About that time, a calico cat came in the door crying for something to eat, but shy at first recognizing a new person was in her house. "Come here, Buckles, and I will give you a little chicken." The cat hurried over to the table and the lady pulled off a piece of meat along with the skin and gave it to her as the cat placed her paws on the side of her lap. Thinking she had retrieved a treasure, Buckles jerked it to the floor, tilted her head, and started chewing the warm morsel.

"Even though the cat is a she, we named her Buckles because she loved to play with anything shiny like the buckles on our shoes or harnesses or belts. She almost ate my sewing thimble once."

"Mrs. Brewster, could I have another piece of chicken? This is the best chicken I ever ate." When Marcus said "Brewster" a small light came on in his head. Thinking to himself, "Brewster, Brewster, where have I heard that name Brewster. I know that name and I have heard it lately," and then Genia interrupted his thought.

"I have seen lots of traffic down my road the last few days. Day before yesterday, or was it the day before that? Anyway, whatever day it was, I heard great boomings off to the northwest nearly all day. There must have been a terrible battle up there around Sharpsburg. I heard there was. I even heard a few booms yesterday and last night."

"Yes, there was a terrible slaughter up there. I am lucky to be here." Marcus went into telling her his story of the last few days and the terrible killing he had seen. He related how he had got caught between the lines and switched sides. He told her about meeting a Union soldier reading the Bible, and later how he blew up the wagons. Marcus told how he had outwitted the coon hunters, making Mrs. Brewster laugh. The two talked on even after they had finished their meal.

Marcus was about to tell her about the Union soldier he befriended shortly before the big explosion. "Mrs. Brewster you wouldn't believe what I have seen." All of a sudden Marcus stopped and threw his head back in sudden shock. "Mrs. Brewster! Mrs. Brewster! Do you have a son named Edward?"

"Yes, I told you I did."

Marcus put down his fork with a noticeable transition on his face and put his elbows on the table to cradle the side of his face with his hands. It seemed for a moment he couldn't speak; then he looked up in a rueful stare back at Genia, "I think I killed your son the other night."

"What are you talking about?" she replied in a high voice.

"In the battle the other day; remember I told you about meeting a union soldier reading his Bible, remember me telling you about blowing up the powder wagons that night?"

Very interested now she replied, "Yes, I do, but what about my son?"

"That young soldier I met had to be your son. Your story didn't have much meaning until you mentioned your name was Brewster.

His name was Brewster and his first name was Edward, but he wanted to be called Ed."

"Yes, Edward wanted to be called Ed."

"When I first talked to him he thought I was a Rebel soldier because of the way I talked and he mentioned he was from Virginia. I asked him why he fought for the Yankees and he told me almost the same story you did. He even mentioned he had worked in a post office."

All the pieces fit perfectly to tell the story unraveling in his mind. "He mentioned he had a fight with his brother, but he didn't know he killed him. He also said he didn't get along well with his father or brother, but he loved you very much."

The elderly lady was touched by what Marcus told her. "Why did you kill him?"

"Oh, Mrs. Brewster, you have to believe me. I did not intend to kill him. That night after I lit the fuse to blow up the wagons, I saw a lone soldier walking toward me. When he got close, I recognized him as the young man I had met earlier in the day. I stopped him and told him not to go down to the wagons." Marcus cleared his throat, "In war, shooting at a crowd of soldiers trying to kill you was, I guess, acceptable, but to kill somebody you had talked to and befriended was different. "I warned him several times not to go down there. I even yelled at him one last time. If I had told him what I had done he would have taken me prisoner and I would have been shot." Genia could tell he was upset and was telling the truth. "When the explosion went off I saw his body blown back, even though he was several yards from the wagons. I will never forget his silhouette against the bright light. He just kept walking into danger, and I couldn't do anything about it."

Thinking about the death of her son and the love he apparently had for his mother began to affect her sentiment as her old eyes filled with tears again. They had stopped nibbling on the food, both visibly moved by what Marcus had said and uncovered.

Trying to keep her composure she asked, "Are you sure he died? He might have only been injured."

Marcus looked up, "I don't know. If nothing hit him from the explosion except the concussion, he might be only injured. I wondered about that after my escape. I knew, if he survived, he would be the only one who could identify me if I was captured. I hope now, for your sake, he survived knowing he is probably your son."

Feeling there was a chance Edward could be alive, she gathered her feelings up trying to make something out of the sad news she had heard, "Marcus, finish off that chicken; I know you're still hungry. I know now you didn't try to kill him nor was it a personal thing. You had to do what you thought would help your army. I blame Edward for going north. He was just a hot-headed kid who couldn't live with his heritage." She stopped talking and looked down at her hands as if they were her only friends now, and then looked up at Marcus and began to cry, "I am alone in this world. I have nobody to help me now, nor the hope I ever will. I was hoping Edward would come back some day and stay here."

Kind-hearted Marcus was absolutely distraught. The old lady's last sentence tore into Marcus's heart. He reached out and gently took her hand and rubbed it. "Don't fret or worry ma'm. I will stay here until we work things out. Shucks, if nothing else I will take you to Georgia with me and you can live on my farm."

"You are so kind, Marcus, but I will have to die here." She started to sob again, "The only family I have now is out there under that tree. I want to be buried there too."

Marcus leaned back a bit and shook his head back and forth. "I cannot believe what has happened. Of all the soldiers in the Union Army I had to meet," Marcus stopped and picked his words, "I met your son and by...." he stopped and hesitated and thought, "And by only a miracle I meet you. I remember when he told me about living near the battlefield, 'how odd it would be, after fighting all over Virginia, to be killed in his own back yard.' There must be a reason for this that only God understands."

"Yes, there are situations that occur in our lives that we don't understand at the time, but in the end we see God's purpose and see His ways. Since I was a little girl, I always heard say, "The Lord works in mysterious ways." Yes, indeed, He works in mysterious ways," as she thought back over her life.

"I remember when I was a young girl; I fell in love with a young lad who grew up over there across the river. I thought he was the most handsome man I ever saw. All the young people would meet downtown on Saturday while their parents did their business. After we met, he started coming around the house and courting me. He was always well dressed and had a fine horse and buggy. I thought he was such a gentleman, but my father and brothers knew otherwise. They told me he came from a rough background and made money illegally selling whiskey he cooked, but didn't pay the taxes on it. I wouldn't believe what they said because I thought I knew better. Finally my father put his foot down and told him never to set foot on our place and he was never to see me again." She looked up at the ceiling and paused a few seconds. "When I learned of this, I hated my father and brothers. I was so mad I was going to leave my family and go marry that man, no matter what they said about him. You know, I guess maybe, if I had been a man, I would have fought my father like Edward did, but when I threw a fit, they tied me to a chair for a day or so and watched me closely. I was crazy. As I cooled down over the next few days, a young man came to work for my father. It was Carl and I soon fell in love with him and a few months later I married him. What a blessing! He didn't have much money, but he worked hard. Before we were married my family built us a cabin on the place and in five years he had saved enough to have some horses and a cow, and we bought this land we are on now."

She continued, "The man I had been in love with soon married another woman. The rumor in town said he beat her and made her life miserable. The law finally caught up with his misdeeds and he was put in jail for several years. His wife nearly starved to death. When he got out, his reputation was ruined and he couldn't get a good job; therefore he ran away somewhere and no one has seen him since. I often think how wrong I was and how right my father was, and that abandoned woman could have been me. The Lord does work in mysterious way for people who love Him."

Marcus started eating again and pondered what the old lady had said. "Now that I think about it, God sent me here for some reason. I know that because I should have been killed in the battle. It was a miracle that I was not killed or wounded. I should have been captured the other night, but He gave me the ability to avoid the hounds and get away. Now I'm here for some purpose. I wonder for what reason?" The two continued to talk as they finished eating. Marcus then helped the kind lady gather and wash the dishes. When they finished, the elderly lady told Marcus she needed to rest a bit and take a nap and suggested Marcus do the same. Marcus agreed that a good nap after such a fine meal would suit him just fine.

9

Marcus lay on a small but comfortable cot she had invited him to use in one of the side rooms. Having slept on the ground for the past several months, the stuffed cotton mattress felt like heaven to him. He took his picture of Bonnie out and adored her beautiful face for a moment or two, but after the warm meal, his escape, and lack of slumber, he immediately fell asleep with a full stomach. He dreamed he was in battle again and was trying to kill a Union general, but no matter how hard he tried his rifle would not point at his target. He strained and pulled on the gun to aim at the general. Soldiers behind yelled for him to kill the general and the war would be over. The general was right in front of him now and he was directing fire into his men behind him as they screamed, "Kill him, kill him!" As the nightmare continued, he could not function, loading his gun again and again, but unable to shoot and kill the general. Suddenly a buggy came up in the midst of battle with an elderly woman whipping the two horses forward, her gray hair blowing in the wind. She motioned for him to run toward her and get in the buggy. "Come quickly," she yelled, "We have to find Edward." He jumped in the back of the buggy and he was shaken by the rough ride. Suddenly he woke up and found Genia shaking him, "Wake up, Marcus, wake up. You are dreaming."

He opened his eyes and saw her face above him. At first he was confused whether or not he was still dreaming. After a moment his surroundings came into memory, and he knew where he was. He rose up and told her, "I was fighting in the war, trying to kill a general, and you came up driving a buggy and saved him. He looked at her with a puzzled stare, "Do you own a buggy?"

"Yes, it's out there beside the barn under a shed. Didn't you see it when you came up this morning?"

"I don't remember it, but I guess my mind did. How else would I know you had a buggy in my dream?"

She went out the back door and came back in with a dipper of cold water and a wet rag. "Here, drink this and wipe your face. You'll feel better now."

Marcus, remembering Bonnie's photograph, reached in his coat pocket and showed her his picture of his love. "Isn't she pretty? She is what kept me alive these past few months."

"She is indeed, a beautiful girl. Look at those beautiful combs. You are a very fortunate man."

Marcus drank the cold well water and wiped his sweaty face. "I feel much better now. Thank you for your care." Marcus had not been treated like this since he left home over a year ago. "I hope I have not been a burden to you, but I feel I need to get back home. I wouldn't mind giving my life if I thought we had one pea pod out of a bushel of a chance to win, but we can't. After I saw what we were fighting against the other night, I know now the South will lose the war. I don't want to die for a losing cause. Every Southern soldier who now dies is a waste and our cause is doomed. It's just common sense."

"I don't blame you Marcus. I would do the same thing."

Unexpectedly their conversation was interrupted by the sound of many horses' hooves approaching the house. Marcus jumped up and looked out the door and noticed a large Union cavalry brigade coming toward the house. "Yankee cavalry; I've got to run. Is there any place I can hide?"

"No, I've got a better idea. Go in my room and look in the trunk over in the corner. My husband's clothes are in there. You are about his size. Put on his clothes and if they come in the house, pretend you were taking a nap, and I will tell them you are my sister's boy that came over from Shepherdstown to bring me a chicken to eat. Hurry change quickly, they are almost here." He turned and started for the room when she added, "And get rid of those shoes. They would give you away. There's some old boots under the bed. Put them on. His straw hat is hanging on the wall. Put that on too."

The Union horsemen rode up in front of the house and hollered for whoever was inside to come out now. Genia walked to the door and put her hand above her eye as if trying to see who the visitors were. "Woman, come out here." Genia eased out on the porch as two soldiers dismounted while several others rode around to the back of the house, insuring if anyone was inside, they could not escape. "Old woman, come out here in the yard and talk to me."

Genia delicately descended the steps and slowly walked toward the mounted officer taking her time, giving Marcus time to change into his new clothes. "If you are here to get my food you are too late. The Rebels cleaned me out last week. I have nothing to give you."

"I'll see about that later, but we are here searching for renegades from both Union and Confederate armies. Is there anyone else in your house?

"Why yes, yes, there is my nephew."

"How old is he?"

"Old enough, I guess," she answered as if she didn't want to answer the question.

"Is he old enough to be in the Army?"

"Yes, I think he might be that old."

"Go get him, so I can see him. I might conscript him right here on the spot."

"I don't think you want him now. He's sick"

"What do you mean sick. Bring him out here so I can make up my own mind whether he is sick or not," the captain yelled getting irritated with the old lady's answers.

"Oh, you'll see he's sick alright," she answered as she turned to make her way back inside to fetch Marcus. She disappeared inside and shut the door.

Marcus was pulling on the old man's shoes as he heard the lady hurriedly go to her cooking area and rush into his room grasping the bloody chicken head. "Listen, I've got an idea that will make them leave you alone, but you must do what I tell you as fast as you can." She showed Marcus the chicken head with the clotted blood around the neck. "Take my hand mirror over there on my dresser and use this damp chicken blood to put red splotches all over your face and the back of your hands. I am going to tell them I think you have a pox when I get outside. Now hurry and do that. I will stall them off as long as I can." She turned to go outside, but remembered something and turned to Marcus and said, "Your name is William Brewster," and disappeared.

Marcus quickly found the mirror and squeezed some drying blood from the chicken head on to her dresser. He carefully put the tip of his finger in the dark red, almost black blood, and started dabbing dots around on his face and neck and on the back of his hands. He remembered what his younger brother had looked like when he had chicken pox.

The old lady opened the door and started outside, then raised her hand and finger, indicating to the captain she had forgotten something. She went back inside, closed the door again, and whispered over at Marcus, "Hurry, boy, I can't keep them out of here forever." While inside she took her time to don her bonnet, trying to slow time so Marcus could put on his makeup. She opened the door, stopped, shielded her eyes again as if she had just come outside of a cave, and then slowly sauntered across the walk taking tiny steps.

"You sure are slow old woman. Now where's your nephew?"

"He's coming. He's sick you know."

The captain was losing his patience. He kept asking why her nephew did not come outside. "He's sick I tell you. I had to wake the poor boy up. He'll be out here when he's able. After a minute, the captain motioned for two of his lieutenants to come forward. "He ain't coming out; he's had plenty of time to get his pants on. Go in there and drag him out here. He's probably a slacker hiding under his mother's bed."

Two soldiers dismounted and started inside just as Marcus came to the door, but his presence stopped them in their tracks as Genia added at the right time, "I meant to tell you, I think he has a pox." The two soldiers knew what they saw and what those words meant, and they turned and ran over each other as they tried to get through the front gate to rejoin their captain.

The Union soldiers had seen all of Marcus they wanted and the captain said nothing more than "good day" as he turned his horse from the house and galloped away. Genia and Marcus watched as the hundred or so horsemen passed in front of them. They both smiled and waved goodbye.

10

As the soldiers rode away, the two pals now turned to face each other, stared a moment, and then died laughing. "I don't think they'll be back soon," Genia laughed.

Marcus bent over and slapped his knee in happiness, "You know, you are not an old woman, you are a sly old fox. How did you think of the idea of small pox?"

"The captain made me think of it when he said to bring you out so he could see you. I wanted him to see something that would scare him away and I immediately thought of small pox. That scares all of us including a whole army. As I walked in the house to get you I wondered what I could use to make red spots on your face and as I walked in the house I saw where I had killed the chicken. I saw the red dots of blood on the ground and I remembered where I put that chicken head. I figured if you could paint your face I could stall them long enough for you to get that done. Everything worked out perfect. If you hadn't cut the head off and if I hadn't brought it inside our trick wouldn't have worked. Yes, as I mentioned, the Lord works in mysterious ways!"

"Yes indeed He does. Now I owe you for my life as well as the good dinner."

"You don't owe me for anything. I need to sit down; I'm getting tired. Let's sit in the swing." Marcus, still showing the red dots on his face, helped her up the stairs and escorted her to the front porch swing, a wide seat suspended from the rafters by small chains.

After Marcus sat down he noticed the buggy he had seen her drive in his dream. "Mrs. Brewster, after today, I know I was sent here for some reason to help you. It all adds up for me now. I survived a horrible battle, met a soldier who happens to be your son, pulled off a huge explosion behind enemy lines, escaped capture, outsmarted the constable and his coon dogs, escaped again, and fortunately today, escaped capture again, thanks to your fast thinking. I'm beginning to think I am invincible."

"Well, what do you think that purpose would be?"

"I don't know, but I see your buggy over there under the shed, the same one you came in and saved me in my bad dream. That had to be a message from God."

"I thought the days of prophesy were over."

"I guess you're right, but all of this couldn't be a coincidence. I noticed this morning you have no chickens or fowl in your hen house or cattle or pigs. Your cupboards were empty. It seems to me you ate your last chicken and tater. Where's your food?"

"Like I told that Yankee man a while ago, the Confederates came through before they crossed the river into Maryland before the battle and cleaned me out. They took everything, but left me a piece of paper that said it would pay for everything. I can't read so I don't know what it means." Her voice began to squeak and break up, "winter's coming on," she hesitated and looked at Marcus with moist eyes on the verge of crying, "and for the first time since I was a little girl, I have nobody to help me. I have nothing but a lonely house. It once was a warm home, but now it is just a cold house. Without love in a home you only have a house."

"Don't say that. As long as you're there it will always be a place of warmth."

"Thank you Marcus." She took a small white handkerchief out of her pocket and with old wrinkled hands wiped a tear that had rolled down her face. "Marcus, maybe God did send you here to help me."

"After my dream, I know He did, and for some strange reason, I don't think Edward is dead. He is alive." He turned and looked at her, "I will help you. Let's start now. What will you need?"

"Nearly everything; I don't have any food. There's a few hens and a rooster or two that's still in the woods that the Confederates scared off, but that is just about all there is. I was so hungry I killed my last chicken I could catch this morning."

"What's in your smokehouse?"

"Nothing to speak of; the Confederate army took everything. My neighbor came by yesterday to check on me, and he said he saved most of his food. Before the Confederates got to his house a rider came through warning of their approach. He and his boys put his chickens in coops and took them way back in the woods along with his cows. He covered the floor of his tater cellar up with dirt so it looked empty and hid his smoked sausages and meat in boxes and stacked his firewood over it. "When the Rebel foragers came through and couldn't find anything, they asked my neighbor where he hid his food; he told them they were too late. A foraging party had been there early that morning and took everything. He said he demanded they bring his food back so his family could survive the coming winter. He said Confederates didn't give me any stuff back but I guess he believed me and left." Genia looked sadly at Marcus, "Since I don't eat much, I was praying he could help me survive this year."

"That's good to hear. I feel sure he will help you this winter. I know where I can get plenty of food, but I'll have to steal it."

"No, Marcus, don't do that. Don't stoop to being a thief to help me."

He smiled at her. "I should have used the word confiscate rather than steal. I'll rest up a day or two and then I am going to Maryland and see what I can find. I know they have chickens and grain I can confiscate."

"I'm afraid you will get caught and you won't come back. I need somebody here. I've lost everything."

Marcus assured her everything would be just fine. He knew it would be chancy to make a raid into Maryland, but if he could reinforce her neighbor's help with a few chickens and flour she could make it. Marcus began to assess what she needed and realized she was nearly out of firewood, both stove and fireplace wood. Her two horses that her husband had plowed with and used to pull the wagon fortunately had been in a bottom close to the river and far away from the house when the foragers came. She told him where they should be and he soon appeared back at the house with the two large horses. He also discovered a wagon behind her barn not taken by the Rebels because of a broken wagon tongue. Marcus gathered some tools and soon had it repaired and ready to roll.

Marcus hooked up the horses to the wagon and told her he would be back at dark. After a few hours with dark nearing, she heard the wagon pulling up to her house. He had taken axes, saws, and wedges down to the bottom and by dark had cut and split nearly a half cord of good oak, along with dead limbs that had naturally fallen out of the trees. "At least this is a start," he said as he showed the elderly lady her new load of wood.

"Oh thank you, come in. I have the rest of the chicken, made some gravy and I baked a dozen biscuits for supper. I know you're hungry." The two went inside and ate supper lit by a candle. After eating, she showed Marcus his new room that she had cleaned and arranged while he was gone.

They spent another hour talking and making plans to solve their problems. Marcus decided he would take Genia to her neighbor's and see if they could give her some staples that could help her cope for a while. Then he came up with an idea that could permanently save Genia, but possibly take his life.

11

The next morning began at sunrise. Two of the roosters and three of the hens came home and dependable as an alarm clock, invited one of the sleepers to wake up and begin the day. Genia had gotten up as always before daylight before the cock crowed, and had a fire going in the stove and fireplace. She carved a few slices of pork from the ham she had hidden from the foragers. When Marcus entered, they dined on biscuits, water, and fried ham.

Buckles had waited patiently for a morsel of ham. Genia looked down at Buckles and picked her up and started stroking her back. "I guess you're all the family I have left now, but I can't afford to give you ham every day. You need to earn your keep by catching mice."

Marcus looked over at the woman petting her calico. "Oh, Mrs. Brewster, we can get some more ham, go ahead… give her a piece." I noticed she slept on the foot of your bed last night. She needs to be nourished so she can keep you warm at night."

Genia took her knife and whittled off a small piece of ham.

After breakfast, Marcus hooked up the buggy and the two rode over to the kind neighbor's house to plead for help. Genia introduced Marcus to her neighbor and told him the reason why they were there. Marcus explained Genia's needs for the winter and what she considered necessary to get for the moment. "She has nothing to eat right now. When we return to her kitchen, there's a few biscuits and a little ham hanging on the bone to feed her the rest of the winter. Can you help us?"

Being somewhat proud, Genia had not revealed how empty her cupboards were, but Marcus made it clear to him how poor his neighbor was. The neighbor, Tom Wolfe, a sincere Christian and supporting only his wife now, had plenty and told Marcus to follow him. His wife came out and invited Genia inside while her husband dealt with Marcus.

As the two men walked back to Tom's barns and smokehouse, Tom mentioned, "I was really lucky. A rider came through, similar to Paul Revere I guess, warning us the Confederates were coming and taking everything. I sent for my four boys who live on farms around me, and we hid all our food and herded the animals down into a thicket and tied them to trees way off the road, and by the end of the day we had hidden everything. One of my boys lost some stuff, but saved everything else. I told Genia I would help her the other day. Matter of fact I owe her. Her husband saved my life when we were kids by pulling me out of that frozen river down there. I will give her as much as I can."

"I cut her some firewood and plan to cut more before I leave, but please give her all you can part with, and visit her often. She is a wonderful old lady. I have only been there a short time, but her sharp thinking saved my life. He told him how she had fooled the Yankees. "As I mentioned, they took everything she had. Fortunately her horses were down in the bottom and were saved."

"When we heard the Confederates were gone and most of the Union forces were over at Sharpsburg, my family got together and brought some of our food and animals back yesterday. There's still some work to do, but we feel we saved most of our food and animals. There's still several sows we let loose in the bottom, but we can call them up when we need them."

Marcus added, "And they'll get fat off them oak acorns, too." Tom grinned, "I 'spect if I took a stick and started beating on my metal bucket we'd have all the hogs we wanted in a few minutes. They know what that means."

After they saw what Tom was giving Genia, Marcus knew he needed the wagon to carry everything. He also knew Genia would survive the winter. Marcus went back and unloaded the wood, and brought the wagon while Genia stayed and visited Mrs. Wolfe. While he was gone, Tom gathered up the cache of food that he was giving Genia and the women cooked up a hot meal. Marcus was eating well now.

When they returned home later, they had fifty pound sacks of beans, flour, cornmeal, and sugar. Tom had also given them several sugar-cured hams, sausages, slabs of bacon, coffee, tea, three coops of chickens, and a milk cow tied to the back of the wagon. There were also sacks of corn for feeding the chickens. There were also large bags of oats for the horses, but that would have to be picked up later since the wagon was filled above the side panels. Tom told Marcus to bring the wagon back and they would fill it with hay and he would help Marcus put it in Genia's barn. In a day Genia's problems were solved. Marcus started a fire in the smokehouse, and hung up the meat. The chickens were released in the hen yard and their clucking brought in about a dozen more chickens from the surrounding woods. Marcus milked the cow that evening and they had milk again. By evening, all the food was stored, animals fed, and Buckles got a warm bowl of milk and a large piece of ham.

As they ate that night, feasting on eggs, bacon, and milk, they both praised the kindness of Mr. Tom. "I can never repay this man," Genia said.

"From what Tom said, you already have."

"What did I do," she questioned.

"Mr. Wolfe told me your husband had saved his life when they were growing up and he had always felt indebted and tried to pay him back many times, but Carl would never hear of it. He said your gift was actually a reward from Carl for what he had done fifty years before."

"Carl never told me that story. Again, it's just God watching over us and caring for his children," she said. "This story has been in the making for forty years and I didn't even know it."

"Just imagine if all people were not greedy and followed our Christian values, what a wonderful place this world would be. Everyone would eat and there would be no wars."

Genia looked up at Marcus, "I feel guilty for having taken all this food."

"Don't feel that way. Mr. Tom said when I left with that last wagon load of hay, he felt better in his head and heart than he had in years. As I departed he said it was true, 'it is better to give than to receive.' So don't worry your heart. The Lord fixes it so He is happy and you are happy. That is the way it is when you believe in Him."

"Two nights ago, I knelt beside my bed and prayed to God for Him to help me. It looked bleak for me, but the next day you came, and today my cupboards are full and my future is looking better. Who says the days of miracles are over? My prayer was answered. It was indeed a miracle."

12

The next morning at breakfast, Marcus told Genia that he felt she was safe now for him to leave. Immediately, before he could add more, she pleaded, "No, Marcus, don't leave just yet. Stay longer and rest up so you will be strong whenever you decide to go. I hoped you would stay all winter."

"No, Mrs. Brewster, you didn't let me finish. I want to leave for a short while. I thought about it last night, but I got the idea yesterday. Mr. Wolfe said the Union Amy was still camped at Sharpsburg. Except for the cavalry the large force has not moved." He looked at her straight in the eye, "I have to go find Edward for you."

"No, don't risk that. You will be captured."

"Hear me out. Let me explain what I want to do. The Union generals know for sure now that Lee has gone up the Shenandoah Valley and has abandoned his invasion plans. As bad as that battle was the other day, I am sure he is out of ammunition, men, and supplies. He will not be coming back anytime soon and the Yankees know this."

"How can you find him?"

"I know what corps and brigade he's in. That huge Army took a bad beating like we did; that's why they haven't moved. They are sitting there licking their wounds. I was looking at your buggy and thinking I could ride over to the Union camp and ask around, pretending I was looking for my brother. That would be believable since he did grow up so close to this battlefield. I have seen civilians on the battlefield amongst our soldiers when we had won the battle. It happens all the time. I can do this for you. Wearing your husband's clothes I will look like a civilian."

"What if they ask why you aren't in one of the armies?"

"I'll tell them I was wounded earlier. Matter of fact I have a scar to prove I was shot."

"Oooh, are you healed now?" she recoiled in surprise.

"Oh, yes, it's not really a bullet wound; it just looks like one. It's just a scar I got back on the farm. I will tell them I am nearly well and will be joining the army again soon and I am there to find my brother to see if he is still alive. Remember, Edward doesn't know he killed his brother, what was his name?"

"Matt."

"Matt, yes, I remember now. With what he's been through, he will be glad to see somebody from home."

"But when he sees you he will turn you in. He's the only one that knows what you did that night."

Marcus thought a moment and then looked her straight in the eye again, "I'll just have to take my chances. I feel now this is why I am here, to bring Edward back home to you. When he understands my mission he won't turn me in. I'll get him to come home with me for a few days."

"But he doesn't want to come home. Can't you see that?"

"No, Mrs. Brewster, what I heard him say and how he looked, he wants to come home. As I said before, he loves you very much. I am going to bet my life on it."

Following a hearty breakfast, Marcus took the wagon and spent the day cutting and gathering more firewood, taking time only to come to the house to eat and later coming in at dark. The next day he would begin his trip to find Edward.

Genia, reluctant at first, finally agreed to Marcus going to Antietam to find out about Edward. She still feared he might be captured or shot. She had gotten Carl's finest clothes out and ironed them, using the heavy irons heated on the stove. Carl's suit was not a conservative black or brown color, but instead rather garish. She convinced him though it was time for him to get rid of his ragged peach fuzz and shave his face. She had shaved her husband many times and had mastered the art. She put the hot towels on his face and lathered him up good, and soon, he had lost his shaggy peach fuzz and looked like a young man instead of a boy. She brushed and cut his hair. Proud of her accomplishments she looked at Marcus, "Mr. Mills, if I was sixty years younger I would let you sit on my porch."

"I sit on your porch now."

"Now Marcus, you know what I mean."

He put on Carl's shiniest brown shoes and a new looking hat and he was ready for his journey. Genia walked him to the wagon, asking him one more time not to take the chance, but he insisted and climbed upon the wagon seat and took the horse's reins. "If I don't come back, Mr. Tom assured me he would take care of you. You will do well this winter. Don't worry though, I'm invincible. I have God on my side; I am doing what I feel He wants me to do and best of all, I will be back." With that, he clicked his tongue, and the horses moved forward. After a ways he looked back at Genia who had her hand up, slowly waving, like she would never see him again.

13

Marcus drove the wagon south to Tom's place. He asked Tom how to get to Sharpsburg. Tom told him to follow the road he was on to Shepherdstown and turn left on the Sharpsburg Pike and within a few miles he would be in there. He told him again the Union Army was camped near there and it might be dangerous.

"Do you remember Edward?" Marcus asked. Tom nodded yes.

Marcus continued, "I am not for sure but there's a chance he is still alive. I must try and see if I can find out for sure. If he's alive, I am going to convince him to come home and help his mother. You are a good neighbor and I thank you for your help. If I don't see you again, I want to wish you the best. Have a good day now." He clicked his tongue and the horses jerked forward and the two departed.

It wasn't long until Marcus arrived in Shepherdstown. He saw Union soldiers and cavalry occupying the town. Not to appear suspicious he drove up to a group of soldiers apparently guarding a crossroads and asked if the road to Sharpsburg was open. They asked him what business he might have there. Marcus told them he was going there to find his brother who was in the 124th Pennsylvania and ascertain his status, and if possible, bring his body home if he had been killed. They told him the battlefield was in the process of being cleaned up and it was a horrible place. They questioned why he wasn't in uniform. Marcus unbuttoned his shirt and showed them an ugly scar, a wound he said he had received at Bull Run, the first battle in the war. It wasn't a battle wound, however, but a scar obtained when he was running back to the barn when he was younger and fell on the sharp end of broken hoe handle he was carrying.

The soldiers, seeing no reason to stop him, let him travel the 3½ miles to Sharpsburg. He passed through town and headed north on the Hagerstown Pike, passing burial parties continuing to bury the dead. On the way he saw many broke-down wagons and dead horses. As he got closer to the battlefield, the stench from unburied horses and soldiers filled the air, but soon, the scenes from the carnage filled his eyes, competing with the stench to dominate his senses.

He passed the Dunker Church behind which he had eaten breakfast on the first morning of the battle before being called to the front. Hundreds of soldiers and civilians were scattered throughout the field of battle burying the dead and searching for identities. Trees, fences, and corpses, were scattered about by the destruction. He approached the "cornfield" and saw the place his friend had fallen in the road. Most of the bodies had been removed; he saw large mounds of fresh dirt where Confederate soldiers were buried in mass graves and years later would be honored with a monument. He stopped the wagon and walked out on the field of death where he had seen so much horror. He saw scraps of dried flesh and bone that had been torn to small pieces by the intense canister fire. His eye caught a glimpse of sunlight coming out of the ground and stooped to see the source. He scratched the dark soil and saw a gold oval locket on a gold chain. He opened it up and saw a "Bonnie" that would never see her man again. Marcus dropped it back on the soil and covered it again with his shoe, letting it stay with the spirit of its owner.

He searched for the cannon crater he had hid in at the height of the battle and eventually found it. It was shallower than he thought and he couldn't imagine that he had changed clothes in such a small space, but there was his old uniform, stained with blood and feces.

He wanted to pick it up and save it for future conversations after the war, but it reeked with the odors of an outhouse. He let it be.

There were many civilians picking through the debris, looking for whatever might be of value. The Union soldiers were picking up the remaining bloated bodies in blue uniforms and trying to identify them and give them a proper burial. Marcus approached one of the officers overseeing the work and asked if he knew where he might find the 124th Pennsylvania. He pointed north and told him he thought the 1st Corps was farther north and he should go and inquire over there.

Marcus took another look from the "cornfield" and saw smoke from the funeral pyres of horses and mules. It also added to the horrible odors that filled the landscape. He could not believe he had survived the carnage. It could have been him they were burying that day.

He walked back to the buggy and rode farther north. He was passing people, both soldiers and civilians, on the crowded road. When he got to the wooded area where he first saw Edward, he saw hospital tents filled with wounded men on army cots. He noticed a man with a wheel barrow pushing a load of human limbs away from one tent to be buried in their own unmarked grave. He went on and found where he had blown up the wagons. Except for several craters, broken trees, charred ground, and pieces of splintered wood, most of the damage would have gone unnoticed. He saw the tree he had stood behind when he saw Ed's body silhouetted against the light. He still wasn't sure if he could have survived such a blast.

The entire smelly smoky scenario seemed unreal as if he was in one of his dreams and he expected to wake up from this awful place. There was no order, just people coming and going, toting, digging and covering up, walking and running, like a cast of characters in a play with no one directing. He wanted to ask a question but the characters never stopped to give him a chance.

A bugle sounded back to the northeast and the clear brassy sound caught his attention. That meant there were troops over there. He headed the horse in that direction following ruts through the woods made by ambulance wagons and artillery pieces. He soon saw hundreds of white tents arranged in rows with colorful banners waving in the breeze above them. When he emerged from the woods he could clearly see more tents with large areas nearby where soldiers were being drilled. There were several blacksmiths shoeing horses and men getting haircuts and shaving, all seeming to be getting ready for a big parade. Again, Marcus realized the South could not withstand such an enemy.

Everyone seemed busy; if not actually busy, at least acting busy to keep a strict army officer off their back. Soon, a young soldier walked by and said good morning. Marcus asked him, "By any chance do you know where the 1st Corps is camped, in particular the 124th Pennsylvania.

"Yes, they're down there past those woods," he said pointing at a small forest. "When you get down there you can see their camp." Marcus went off in the direction the man had pointed and saw a group of men standing in line filling their canteens from a large barrel at the side of a wagon. He stopped his wagon and approached the men who turned and seemed curious about a civilian so deep in their lines. After a minute of conversation he was informed the 124th was over the hill, camping in a flat valley.

Marcus thought several times about turning around and abandoning his mission, but he had to know for Genia and himself if Edward survived. He got in the buggy and followed the wagon ruts over the hill and saw the flag of the 124th outside a large headquarters tent. Officers sat around the table tending to paper work and smoking their pipes. He approached a captain at the table who looked up rather surprised to see a man not clad in blue. "Young man, what can I do for you?"

"I'm Matt Brewster from Shepherdstown…actually a few miles north of Shepherdstown. I am looking for my brother, Edward. He is a member of the 124th and I am trying to find out if he was killed or not." The captain leaned his chair back and mumbled something to an aid who got up and went to a covered wagon parked nearby and quickly returned with some folders. He shuffled through the papers and soon found what he was seeking. "Yes, the 124th lost many men, but according to this, he made roll call yesterday and you can probably find him down there around the mess tents this time of day. They should be starting to eat shortly.

"Where did you say their mess was?"

He pointed in the general direction, "Right over there at the edge of the woods."

"Thank you sir, that relieves my mind a great deal. Mother will be happy too." He started to walk away, but Marcus turned back, "If I may ask, would it be possible for him to get a pass to go home. He grew up less than six miles from here as the crow flies."

The officer tapped the ends of the papers on the table to straighten them and looked up at Marcus. "I think I can arrange that. It seems we are going to be here for another week or so before we move out."

"Oh, I think he would like that; thank you sir." Marcus reached out and shook his hand."

Now the question Marcus faced was whether Edward would turn him in immediately when he saw him or wait and listen to what he had to say. With his haircut and a close shave, Marcus hoped Edward would not recognize him at first, giving him time to explain why he was there. He knew he was "walking on thin ice." Soldiers were everywhere and as he neared the cooking wagons it became even more crowded. Marcus saw a line where beans were being served with a slice of bread. Each man held his tin plate in one hand, stuck out to get the beans, in the other hand, a tin cup for his coffee.

Marcus bumped into men getting in line and swerved around others making his way through the throng hunting for Edward. He stood and watched the soldiers go down the line. As he watched he saw the men go and sit under some shade trees after they secured their food. He thought Ed might be over there. He went over and walked through the squatting or sitting men on the ground. He saw several men that he thought were Edward, but on closer inspection saw him not. Then, just before going back to the serving line, he saw a soldier leaning up against a tree, similar to the sight he had seen when he first saw Edward. He slowly walked up to the soldier who stared down at his beans as he scooped them up, not aware of the man who had walked up beside him. Marcus saw for sure now, it was Edward. He had survived. Marcus squatted now beside him and Edward looked up. Marcus had his finger in front of his lips meaning to listen and not say anything.

At first Edward did not recognize him. Then he realized he had seen his face, but could not remember where. Marcus spoke. "Hush, don't say anything. I have come from your mother's house." Marcus wanted him to be focused on what he heard before he recognized him and started screaming.

Before he could tell him more he asked, "How is she?"

"She is fine for now, but you need to come home. The Confederate foragers took nearly everything she had for winter, but I have provided for her. Your neighbor, Tom Wolfe, replenished her needs, but you must go see her."

Ed looked down at his plate again and shoveled in another bite of beans. "I can't. I had a fight with my father and brother and left home to fight for the Union cause. They might kill me."

"No they won't kill you though I have some sad news."

Before Marcus could reply Edward noticed the colorful suit Marcus wore. "Hey, that looks like the suit my father wore to church. I always thought it was too colorful for the church."

"It is your father's suit. Your mother loaned it to me so I could come over here and see if you were alive."

He looked back at his beans with questions pondering in his head. "Sad, news, what is it?"

"I hate to be the one to tell you this, but you killed Matt the night you hit him in the head and your mother said your father died a few months later from a broken heart from losing both of his boys."

Edward looked up surprised, "What! I killed Matt? I just knocked him out."

"You probably don't remember, but you hit him many times with the stick of wood until your father pulled you away. Matt didn't die immediately, but died a week later. He never woke up from the beating you gave him."

"And father died?"

"Yes, your mother Genia told me all this."

"How do you know my mother? Who are you?" He looked Marcus over again, "I know I have seen you somewhere before, but I can't remember."

Marcus had not spoken loudly, but only whispered to Edward. Now he leaned forward and spoke in a normal voice, "Don't go down by that wagon, it's not safe."

Then, like a bolt of lightning, Edward remembered his face, and almost screamed out, but Marcus put his hand over his mouth, "Shhhh, don't yell until you hear me out." Marcus uncovered his mouth, wiping some bean juice from his hand on the back of his pants.

Edward stared intently, then spoke in a whisper, "You're the Rebel, your voice, you…you…you're the Rebel who blew up the wagons that night and almost killed me."

"Hush up! Listen to me. God has sent me here to tell you about your mother." Marcus looked around and noticed some of the soldiers were looking their way. Marcus smiled back at them and responded, "He's my brother." Apparently not hearing the remark about being a Rebel or talk of the explosion, they turned back to eating their beans.

Continuing, Marcus said, "Yes, I'm the Rebel soldier, and I did blow up the wagons, but if you remember, I told you not to go down toward those wagons and you ignored me. Remember, I even yelled at you, but you marched right on down there. I wanted to pull you back, but I didn't know when it would explode. I saw your body blown back and I thought you were dead. I did what any good soldier would do, I tried to destroy the enemy and those wagons were the enemy. I'm sorry you got involved."

Calmed down now somewhat, "How did you find my mother?" Marcus told him how he dressed in a Union uniform and ended up behind the Union lines, his escape after the explosion, being chased by the dogs, and finally ending up at his mother's house. "You see, it is a miracle. This is a mission God sent me on. Can't you see that? Think of all the houses I could have gone to, but God directed me to your mother's. Think what a miracle that was! I have your mother's buggy parked over by the headquarters tent. I even talked to the captain and told him I was your brother, and he agreed to give you a furlough so you could go home since you lived so close."

"That is amazing." He smiled slightly and looked down at the ground, "It is a miracle. I think I will go home. I love my mother. It is indeed a wonder that you found her after all that happened that night."

"Come on, get up, get your stuff and let's get out of here. Your mother needs you. Maybe you can work it so you won't have to come back. Edward, I am so glad you are alive. You don't know how I've worried about your well-being."

The two young men stood up and started walking toward headquarters. Marcus could see the news about his father and brother hit him hard. Edward kept thinking about his fight with Matt and repeating, "I am a murderer, I am a murderer, I am a murderer." Then he stopped, I can't go back, now. They'll hang me for murder."

"No, your mother is the only living soul, besides me, who knows you killed him. People around there think he was kicked in the head by a horse and died. You know it was an accident caused by too much whiskey, and you didn't mean to do it."

They arrived at headquarters and Edward saw his Mother's buggy and hurried to the horses he knew so well and patted them. The horses seemed to remember him and moved their heads up and down in recognition. Marcus approached the captain, "I finally found him and he agreed to go home for a spell and stay as long as you would let him." The captain prepared furlough papers while Edward went back to his pup tent and got his personal gear and rifle. When he returned the captain gave him his papers and Marcus led him back to the buggy. "Let me drive this wagon," Edward said. I know the way home. Edward's personality had changed, even after hearing the news of the family tragedy; just the thought of going home and getting out of the quagmire of war had lifted his spirits.

14

Edward steered the horses back through the remains of the deadliest single day battle in American history. The stench from uncovered corpses and the fires consuming dead animals choked them as they made their way toward the Potomac River and the ford that lead them back home to Virginia.

Edward turned toward Marcus, "You know, you almost killed me the other night."

"Yes, like I said, I worried about that. I told your mother I didn't know whether you were alive or dead, but I knew you were knocked down by the blast."

"Oh was I! It hurt my hearing pretty bad. I haven't heard much out of my right ear since."

"Did you fight in the "cornfield" like you said or were you planted as a saboteur before the battle?"

"No, I changed uniforms in the cornfield. I am in, or I should say, was in Hood's Texas Brigade."

"That's a mean bunch."

"Yeah, we did our share of damage to you folks." Continuing, "The only way I figured out I could get out of that field was to walk out on your side. Your cannons wouldn't let a man in gray retreat out of there."

"So you weren't a saboteur?"

"No, when I left you that afternoon, I saw those wagons filled with powder and I had seen what those cannons did to us. I just felt it was my duty to do as much harm as I could while I was behind your lines."

"So you worked alone?"

"Yes, it was just a moment's decision. I felt I had to do what I had to do. You would have done the same."

"Yes, I guess I would, too." The two rode on toward the ford.

About a half mile from the river Marcus noticed a squad of cavalry was coming up behind them rapidly. Marcus turned back watching, wondering why they seemed to be interested in a wagon. The horsemen rode up closely behind them and just trotted along.

Marcus tried to imagine why they would be following them so closely. "Maybe they wanted to know why a uniformed soldier would be driving such a nice carriage," he thought. "That's it, they think the buggy is stolen, or they might assume he was a deserter escaping." They continued to follow but did not stop them. Shortly before the river, the squad split and a line of horsemen passed on either side of the carriage, seeming to pay them no attention at all. Marcus was relieved as the men and horses grew smaller as the horsemen sped up.

When they reached the river, the mounted soldiers were stopped on the road at the edge of the river and appeared to be waiting for something. As soon as the buggy started through the crowd of mounted men, all at once they drew their pistols and aimed at Marcus and yelled, "Raise your hands!" Marcus looked at Edward and saw the face of a traitor.

"Why did you do this to me? I came here to get you and take you home to your mother. Why, Edward, Why?" Marcus screamed.

Edward looked Marcus in the eye, "I had to do what I had to do. That's what you told me a few moments ago. Like you, I had to do what I had to do as a soldier and turn in the saboteur who killed many of my comrades and nearly killed me." He turned toward the soldiers aiming their pistols at Marcus. "This is the man I told the sergeant about before I left camp. Tell them not to worry about other saboteurs. He was working alone and took the opportunity to do us some damage when it presented itself. "Don't hang him though as a spy; he was wearing a gray uniform. He had been captured and took advantage of a situation, and under the rules of war should not be shot as a spy. He did what any good soldier would do." Edward hoped they would not go back and check what he really said about Marcus, the man in a blue uniform with a southern accent. He then might find himself in trouble. He sighed, I've done my duty."

The soldiers told Marcus to get down from the wagon. One of the soldiers searched him for weapons, but missed the photograph of Bonnie concealed in his inner coat pocket. One of the troopers took a small rope from his saddlebag, dismounted, and took Marcus's hands and bound them tightly. Another rider removed a larger rope and tied a hangman's noose and placed it around Marcus's neck and also pulled it tight, so tight Marcus could hardly breathe. Seeing his mistake, the soldier loosened it slightly. Marcus thanked him.

Edward took one last look at Marcus, "I do want to thank you for helping my mother," then turned away, clucked his tongue and the carriage jumped forward.

Marcus yelled back, "Be sure and tell your mother what you did to me! Why did you betray me?" The buggy rolled on; Edward did not look back. Marcus kept yelling, "You will be sorry. Me or the Lord will get you for this. I can't believe you did this to me. I am going to kill you one day."

One of the officers also yelled to Edward. "I wouldn't worry about what he said. We will probably hang him before dark!"

The horsemen surrounded Marcus and made him walk behind, between, and in front of the horses, completely boxed in with his hands tied and a noose around his neck. As he walked back to the Union camp, he stumbled several times due to the fast pace and the abrasive rope strangled him and rubbed against his neck. Several times the cavalry would stop and let Marcus catch his breath or retrieve his hat, then move on, even forcing Marcus to run at times. By the time he arrived at 1st Corps headquarters his neck was red and chaffed with open sores that oozed blood and stained his shirt that Genia so carefully ironed for him early that morning. Proud of their capture, the captain requested that the commander of the corps come and see their prize.

Marcus was in bad shape, bloody around his neck and could hardly stand after his hard march between the horses. He needed water. When General Meade, the new corps commander who had replaced General Hooker during the battle arrived and saw Marcus's horrible condition. "What did this man do to deserve this kind of treatment? Is he a civilian?

"Sir, he is the one who blew up the artillery wagons the other night. He came back into camp to find his brother, a Southerner fighting for the Union, but his brother turned him in and we caught him trying to cross the Potomac River."

The general looked at Marcus, "Soldier, is this true?"

"Yes sir, it is true. I saw a chance to stop the guns killing my friends and since they weren't closely guarded; I lit a fuse and ran."

"How did you get into our camp that night? Were you dressed like this?"

Marcus had heard Edward tell his captors that he was captured in a Confederate uniform and was an escaped prisoner when he blew up the wagons. He knew Edward was trying to save his life, creating an opportunity for his life to be spared. Now, his life depended on how he told his story.

"I was captured during the battle but escaped that night. I saw a chance to do what I did, so I lit a fuse and ran away. As I was running, I saw my brother walking toward the wagons. I stopped and hid behind a tree long enough to see he was knocked down by the blast, but I didn't know if he had been killed. In all the confusion after that, I took off running and eventually made it back home to Shepherdstown. That's why I had to come back, to see if I had killed my brother that night. We grew up just north of Shepherdstown, so I just circled around your army and went home. You see, we fought on two different sides."

"Yes, I see." General Meade looked at Marcus and then at his men. "Does this story match what you know about the event?"

"Yes sir, as far as we know."

Another young officer added, "He did a cowardly act that night and should be hanged to the nearest tree."

A veteran soldier who admired gallantry, the General firmly replied, "I would have expected each one of you to do the same thing if the opportunity had presented itself. This boy is a good soldier; unfortunately he's on the other side."

General Mead told the men to remove the ropes, rub some salve on his neck to soothe his pain, and take him to the temporary stockade for prisoners. He also added, "It is a disgrace to treat a prisoner like this. All of you should be reprimanded for this kind of cruelty. We aren't living in the Middle Ages anymore. Dismissed!"

The soldiers followed their orders, removed the ropes and gave Marcus medical attention. They marched him to a make-do prison for the many captured Confederates from the battle. It was nothing more than a large field with a rectangular shape defined with a string pulled tightly between many stakes driven in the ground. The string represented imaginary walls of a make-believe prison, but any prisoner who stepped over that string would be shot. They escorted Marcus to the 300 by 300-foot imaginary stockade, told him the rules, and released him to his comrades. Marcus had dodged another bullet. The Yankees had observed the rules of war; he would not be hung or shot that day for being a saboteur or a spy.

15

Marcus stepped over the trip wire and entered the confinement of his new home. Due to the lack of a real prison, the field would have to do until the captured Confederates could be sent away to prison camps or be swapped for captured Union soldiers, a practice quite common early in the war.

Many of his comrades came forward welcoming him to their midst, shaking his hand and slapping him on the back. They all were curious why he was dressed like a civilian. His dark, burnt-orange coat, light- yellow trousers, fancy brown shoes, and a tall felt hat made him stand out like a rose in a weed garden. Marcus told his story and after his newness died down he and his comrades sat or lay on the ground in the open field. A few of the men still had their tent halves and blankets they shared with others. Marcus found a place in the crowd padded by a little grass and lay down.

What he had feared more than anything, being put in a Northern prison camp, had come true. He was placed in a prison where starvation, disease, and extreme cold would be his fate and most likely, his life would end there. Marcus mused over his condition. At that moment he decided he would escape and take advantage of any opportunity to do so, risking his life if necessary. The instant pain and death of a bullet would be better than months of torture. He propped up on one elbow, put a straw in his mouth, and looked around at his surroundings, trying to figure a way to escape, if not now, later.

There were two wagons parked inside the perimeter containing barrels of water with dippers hanging on nails driven in the side of the wagon. A corner of the large rectangle was used for a latrine without any privacy. He estimated there were 200 to 300 men in his group surrounded by the trip wire. Each man appeared to have a tin pan and cup he kept up with. There were twenty guards on each side of the invisible prison and many other soldiers camped beyond them who appeared to reinforce the perimeter. It would be difficult to escape, but possibly after dark his chances would be better. Marcus also knew these conditions were temporary and they would soon be shipped to a Yankee prison camp. But Marcus had an advantage; he knew he was invincible.

After a while, a cooking wagon came up to the corner of the stringed prison opposite the corner from the latrine. When the men saw the wagon coming they grabbed their tin pans and cups and hurried toward the wagon. Marcus had no plate or cup, but one of prisoners told him to get in line and the cooks would give him a plate and cup when they dished out his beans. The veteran soldier added, "You'll only get beans and water, but it's better than what we ate on our side. Two times they gave us bread." Marcus, was given a cup and tin plate, did what he was told and sat down on the ground, folded his legs up and ate the beans and drank the water.

After he was finished he became depressed. "Why did Edward betray his trust? Recognizing his father's suit and seeing his mother's wagon and horses proved he was telling the truth. I will find him after this war if I survive, and I will make him wish he had never been born. He is going to suffer like I will have to suffer. An eye for an eye, a tooth for a tooth." Revenge was beginning to enter Marcus's mind, a sin he should, instead, let the Lord handle.

He reached in his pocket and pulled out his letter from Bonnie and read it in the late evening light and admired the girl who was waiting for him although he had no idea where. She might already be in Texas by now. He wondered if he would ever see her again.

Marcus needed to use the latrine, but being a modest man, he decided to wait until dark. For sanitary purposes, shovels were provided to bury whatever he deposited there. For the first time in his life he felt like a cat as he covered his remains. When he finished, he stabbed the shovel in the ground and returned to his flat abode in the field.

He flopped down on the ground and leaned back on his side, and in so doing, he saw a rectangle form between the wrinkles in his coat. He leaned up and felt the part of the coat that did not crumple. He grabbed the coat and bent it back and forth. There was something sewn inside behind the side pocket. He took the jacket off and examined it closely. It seemed to be paper. Having no knife, Marcus took his fingernails and pulled at some threads that had carefully been sewn to make a hidden pocket. He bit on the threads and finally managed to make a hole large enough to peek inside. To his surprise he saw there were paper dollars inside. He carefully unraveled the threads so he could read the denominations. Marcus looked around to see if anyone was watching what he was doing. This would not be a good place to pull out a handful of currency. In all, there was fifty dollars in five dollar bills.

Apparently, when Carl heard the war was imminent, Carl had Genia sew the money in the coat for safe-keeping. Marcus had heard rumors growing up that older people did that sort of thing. He pushed the ends of the currency back inside and put his coat back on and tried to hide the surprise he was sure was written all over his face. He wondered if Genia had had a lapse of memory or just wanted him to have it for his kindness to her. In any case, he figured he might use the money to bribe a prison guard.

Marcus lay back and grinned to himself. Was this the beginning of God's plan to get him out of his predicament? Was this a message from his Creator to forget about revenge, and instead, use his new found money and go home if he could escape? Time would tell he thought, but it was a definite miracle that he found fifty dollars in the middle of a Union prison camp.

He knew it would be cold that night and he had no blanket or ground cover. It would be a miserable night. He lay on his back and looked up at the stars as they began to appear in the evening sky. He wondered if Bonnie might be out and looking at the same stars. He couldn't believe he had been captured.

Two hours into the cold, uncomfortable night a commotion over by the feeding area occurred. Two large freight wagons had pulled up, but instead of food, they contained blankets-hundreds of blankets. An officer came up and told the Rebel officers to line up their men and seek out those poor souls who did not have cover that night. Marcus was issued a blanket, and although not extremely warm, it improved his situation for the night.

The next morning was cold and Marcus appreciated his new gift. He sat up and was almost able to wrap the wool blanket around him twice. He felt warmer now as he watched the sun appear over the horizon. It too seemed to warm him inside, but he chilled at the thought of his captivity.

A good cup of hot coffee would taste good now. He looked up at the man who stood next to him and asked, "When do they serve breakfast around here?"

Seeing he was the new prisoner, the man answered, "They'll feed us after they feed their army. It's usually around nine to ten o'clock. You might not know this yet; they feed us only twice a day, but they give us a reasonable amount to make do. Keep yourself full by drinking lots of water."

Marcus could see many prisoners going to the latrine. Hoping to be hidden by the many men rather than be stuck out alone, he went and took care of his business and returned to the small homestead that he had claimed in the open field. He was getting quite wealthy; he now owned a tin cup, a tin pan, and a blanket along with fifty dollars in his pocket.

As the captive mentioned, about ten o'clock two cook wagons appeared and the prisoners formed a line before the wagons had stopped. As he went through the line Marcus was given a piece of salt pork, a large spoon full of porridge, and a piece of hardtack, finished off with a cup of water. Marcus asked the man pouring water if he had any sugar and coffee to go with his water. He gruffly replied in a deep raspy voice, "This ain't no fancy restaurant. Like it or starve."

Marcus knew they had no sugar; he just wanted to joke with him and maybe over time, make a friend who might appreciate his humor and put a little extra food on his plate. Unfortunately, he chose a veteran cook who had spent a lifetime in the army, and had heard all the "wit" before.

After the warm breakfast Marcus felt much better. The day was warming and he folded his blanket and sat down on it to watch the "going ons" and to see what awaited him that day. After an hour, two prisoners came along seeming to be on the prowl for picking a fight. From his blanket he had watched them come in his direction, purposely bumping into people, usually smaller than themselves, then pushing them back with a vicious harangue about "watch what you're doing," or, "Mister you've picked on the wrong guy this time. I'm gonna teach you a 'lesson.'" Most of the soldiers, not wanting to add an injury to their dire circumstances, turned and walked away, as the two bullies pointed and laughed, calling them cowards.

Not wanting to confront these men if they came near him, Marcus lay down, curled up, and put his head on his folded blanket, and pretended to be asleep. When they got to him, one of the thugs looked down at Marcus in his civilian clothes. "What do we have here? He must be a dandy from New Orleans. I've never seen a uniform like this. I wonder what side he was fighting on?" The two hooligans laughed, and then one of them kicked Marcus in the chest to arouse him to stand up. Marcus felt the man's shoe mash and bend the cardboard-backed photograph in his coat pocket. Marcus rolled over and pulled out his photograph of Bonnie. He immediately saw a deep wrinkle that marred the beauty of her face. Marcus became enraged. He carefully placed his Bonnie back in his coat pocket as the tough guy waited to see what Marcus would do next. Marcus started to stand up but the ruffian kicked him in the side and knocked him away, rolling him on the ground. Marcus kept rolling until he put some distance between them so he could stand up without being kicked again.

Once on his feet, Marcus rushed the man and buried his head in his stomach forcing the clumsy lout to the ground. Keeping his balance, he twisted backward and with the force of his fist gaining speed in a wide arc smashed the other assailant in the face crushing his cheekbone. As the man fell back, Marcus sensed from the pain in his hand that he had done a job on him. Still spinning on his left foot, he planted his right foot in the groin of the other attacker before he could get up. The downed hooligan instantly grabbed the source of his intense pain, while Marcus straddled him pinning his arms under his knees, making him unable to fight Marcus. Marcus took his fist and began pounding him until his foe passed out. Marcus stopped and looked at his bloody hands. They looked awful, but not as cut up as the man's distorted, bloody face.

The brawl was over before a crowd could even gather, but many of the soldiers saw what had happened and ran toward Marcus. As Marcus stood up the soldiers cheered him for taking care of a situation that others had avoided. Some of the men who had been intimidated by the two ruffians came up and started kicking the downed men, breaking ribs and giving them a "lesson" they would not forget. In the weeks ahead, they would be so sore, they wouldn't cause any more problems.

The men slapped Marcus on the back, thanking him for ending a problem. As Marcus came back down from his fit of anger he couldn't believe what he had done. He liked to wrestle other boys growing up but he never wanted to fight. When he was fourteen, he saw one of his friends get his two front teeth knocked out, making the boy forever after, embarrassed to smile at anyone.

A Confederate officer came up and investigated the commotion. The officer had dealt with these two bullies before, and he too, praised Marcus's victory. The soldiers ceased kicking the two men when the officer arrived. Slowly the ruffians gained their senses and sat up. The first man's cheek looked horrible and was swelling rapidly. He had other injuries to his face where other men had kicked him; many of his ribs were broken. The other guy stood up, still bent over, holding his knees together from the injury to his groin. His face was bloody from the pounding Marcus gave him. He raised his hand up and spit a tooth in it.

The officer looked at the two damaged men, "It looks like you guys sowed the wind, then reaped the whirlwind. I think if I was you, I would be careful who I picked on." The men standing around laughed as the officer took them off to another part of the camp; the two agitators limped away in disgrace. Later, one of the men was examined by a Union doctor.

One of Marcus's new friends asked, "Where did you learn to fight like that?"

Marcus looked up and gave him a cold glaze, "I don't know. That was really the first fight I ever had. It was so easy; I think God was in charge of that struggle. He was the whirlwind." From that moment on, Marcus was looked on with respect and fear by the other prisoners. New arrivals in camp were warned to leave that guy in the fancy suit alone.

Marcus came out of the fight with two injuries, one to his fist that would soon feel better, and the other, the damage to his most treasured and prized possession in life, Bonnie's photograph. Marcus was a hero now and the men followed him around. If the members of the prison camp had an election for a leader, Marcus would have won it with no opposition. This new popularity made it difficult now for him to be alone with Bonnie.

Marcus lived in the camp five more days and on the fifth day, a Union officer came out and gathered the prisoners around him and announced that some of the men would be exchanged for Union prisoners while others would be sent to a Union prison camp farther north. They would be marched several miles to the east starting the next morning and either take a train south to be paroled at Washington or be sent north to a prison camp.

The next morning they started a march that took two days. At least Marcus didn't have a rope chaffing his neck. His neck was nearly healed now and the reliable food source twice a day had brought his energy back. As they marched, Marcus talked to a cadre of friends that he had brought together, all with an intense interest in escaping at the first possible chance.

As they marched, Marcus thought of possible assets he might have that might give him an advantage at escape. He imagined he was a good runner as well as climber, remembering how he eluded the coon dogs by climbing a tall tree. If given the chance with his boy-like looks, he could talk and sometimes lie his way out of any situation. He had used that skill once or twice since the day of the battle. He wished he had a Confederate or a seized Union uniform. In his civilian suit he stuck out like a sore thumb.

As the soldiers plodded down the dusty road, Marcus had an idea hatching in his mind. As he trudged along he stitched together an idea that just might work. If he could get a gray uniform he could be like the lizards he played with a boy that could change colors from green to brown. If the right situation presented itself, he might be able to change colors from burnt orange to a Confederate gray in a matter of seconds and be a way for him to escape.

The prisoners were guarded by mounted infantry led and trailed by wagons of provisions. The men walked for an hour, then rested and got water for five minutes. During one of the rests, Marcus asked his friends if they could find and loan him a large gray Confederate field jacket and a pair of large gray pants. He told them he also needed a knapsack to carry it. His friends spread the word that Marcus needed those items. It wasn't long until a man marched up next to Marcus and told him he could use his coat; he had a warm shirt that he could make do with until it got real cold. Marcus declined his offer, expecting out of the 400 men there would be an extra pair of pants and a jacket somewhere. At the next rest stop, the soldiers spread the word what he needed. When they arrived at the next rest stop, some way, somehow, Marcus was given a knapsack containing a large Confederate uniform. His plan was about to hatch.

He asked his new friend, Stephen, to carry the clothes for him until he could find a place to change. A plan was continuing to develop in his mind as they got closer to the train depot. He told his closest friends to crowd close around him at the next rest stop, so he could put on the gray uniform over his loud colored coat and pants without being seen by the guards. As they marched his trusted comrades, now aware of Marcus's plan, closed in around him. Within the hour the Confederate prisoners were led into a grassy field to rest and water. While the men milled around looking for a place to collapse and rest, Marcus, now hidden by his curtain of friends in the center of the crowded soldiers donned the gray uniform over his colorful attire. After five minutes or so, the men were aroused out of the field to continue their march.

After the prisoners had marched for a half hour, Marcus told Stephen to walk up beside one of the guards on horseback walking beside them and start talking to him. After further instructions Stephen knew what to do to carry out Marcus's plan. Stephen hurried up beside a guard and started a casual conversation with him. Most of the guards just looked at him and told him to get back in line or "beat it Johnny," but soon he discovered a talkative young soldier from Indiana who let him march beside him. Stephen asked him where he was from and how he liked the army.

After several minutes of questions and answers, Stephen posed a question. "If I told you something that your army would like to know, would you do me a favor later, like maybe at the next food stop, get me some extra food. This marching is killing me and I am starving and need something sweet, like a piece of pie or cake, huh; could you do that for me?" Stephen marched along trying to get a head of him a little and walk sideways so he could look up at the mounted soldier. Continuing his plea, "If not something sweet, how about some chewing tobacco?"

"What are you going to tell me the army would like to know?"

"Promise me first you will get me something sweet to eat."

The soldier marched on not saying anything but obviously thinking about what Stephen said. "It depends on how important the information is."

"Oh, it's very important to you Yankees, but not me."

"Alright, if I think it is important enough I will get you something sweet to eat. Due to the war, we can't get your tobacco anymore. How about a biscuit instead; now what is it you want to tell me?" They continued walking along, Stephen on foot, the guard on horseback, the guard still not too interested in what Stephen was saying.

Stephen walked closer to the guard, "You know that guy in the civilian clothes who's been marching along with us? You know the one who stands out in that orange coat and yellow pants?"

"Yes, what about him."

"At the last rest stop, you noticed how deep the grass and leaves were where we rested?"

"No, what about it?"

"Well, while we were resting he found a slight impression in the ground and told his friends around him to bury him in the leaves. He's not with us anymore. He stayed back there. If you don't believe me run up there to the front of our column and see if you see him walk past you."

"Was he the only one?" he asked with a concerned look on his face.

"Yeah, he was the only one. I wouldn't have told you if there had been more."

"If this is true, I'll get your cake and pie. What's your name?"

"Stephen Jones, sir, Stephen Jones!"

The soldier spurred his horse forward, passing the long line of prisoners and sped to the front of the column and found an officer sauntering along on his horse thinking how well the day had gone thus far. His thought was broken, however, by the sound of a galloping horse approaching from the rear. He turned to see the guard come up alongside, "Sir, sir, I have to talk to you. I have some important information."

The officer reined his horse out of line. "What is it private?"

"Have you noticed the prisoner in the bright civilian clothes?"

"Yes, what about him?"

"A prisoner told me the man escaped back at our last stop. When I rode up here to you, I watched for him but did not see him. You might ride back through the column and see if you find him."

"No, we'll wait here and see if he passes. Go to the other side of the road and help me watch for him. If neither of us see him, he must have escaped." The two horsemen watched as the men trod by. Finally Stephen came by and yelled at the guard, "You hadn't seen him have you?

"No, not yet!" he replied.

That's 'cause he's back down in that pile of leaves; but he's long gone by now." When all of the prisoners passed, including the stragglers riding in two wagons, the horsemen knew the man in the bright colored clothes was gone.

The officer thanked the guard for the information and dismissed him back to his guard duty. He then immediately set about capturing the missing man, knowing, like Stephen had said, he was "long gone." Marcus and Stephen carefully watched as their scheme unfolded. They soon noticed ten mounted soldiers race by them returning rapidly to the last rest stop. Marcus looked at Stephen, "It seems I have disappeared. Now, all I have to do is reappear again at the right place and time."

They stopped for one more rest. Marcus feared if their guards lined up and counted all the prisoners they would find there was no one missing. But when it became obvious that one of their prisoners was missing, and according to the Rebel, no others, there was no need to waste time counting them. Marcus knew that some of the guards had picked up straggling prisoners who couldn't walk any longer and placed them in the trailing wagons. It would have taken more time than they wanted to spend. They had to meet a train at sundown.

The caravan of prisoners marched into a small town somewhere east of Sharpsburg. As they came up to the depot, they noticed two trains hissing steam, one facing north and one facing south. The soldiers were told to sit down in the open street. An officer walked out and said he was going to pick out 100 men who would be going to Washington to be paroled. He added, "I am going to walk among all of you and choose the ones to be paroled. If I touch you on the head, get up and walk over there and sit down in the street by those guards and that train," pointing to the train heading south. If you're not chosen, stay put and when the selection is over, you men will get on the train going north; that one over there by those guards."

Marcus whispered to Stephen. I hope we are not separated here. If we are, I want to thank you for your help. Tell all the others in our group I appreciated their effort, too." Stephen nodded.

After the selection started, it was obvious the only soldiers to be paroled were the older men along with all the stragglers who had ridden in the wagons. The Yankees wanted to keep the younger men from reenlisting in another southern army after they promised not to fight again.

As the process sorted the men, they were counted to make sure Stephen had told the guard the truth. To their surprise they had the same number they started with, but they knew one of the men was obviously gone. The officers discussed the matter, looked at their roll calls and figured they must have miscounted their prisoners back at Antietam.

Before the prisoners boarded their trains to head off in different directions, they were fed. As they sat on the ground eating their beans, Marcus noticed something that caught his attention. The Union Army was changing guards, and these new guards had not seen the prisoner in the burnt orange coat and ochre pants. This would help him when the chameleon changed back to his original color. He could not believe his plan was working as if it were a play on a stage with a director following a carefully written script. Then he sensed the director of his play was his Heavenly Father, making sure all the actors played their part to perfection.

The prisoners going south were loaded in boxcars and departed immediately. The locomotive going north pulled two boxcars, four flat cars, and a caboose, but was not scheduled to leave until after daylight the next morning. Instead of boarding, the prisoners were herded into a nearby park to camp overnight. An officer told them they would not leave until it was daylight for fear it would be too easy for a prisoner to jump off the train and not be seen in the dark. Marcus curled up in his two suits of clothes on his new blanket and went to sleep satisfied that his plan was working perfectly. He said a longer prayer that night.

The guards woke the men early. Marcus had had a good night's sleep and did not suffer from the chill. He felt very refreshed. The commissary wagon doled out extra food that morning for the long train ride ahead and the men climbed on the flat cars to be sent somewhere up north. Stephen asked a guard where they were going, but for security reasons, the soldiers had been given orders to stay mute.

Marcus and Stephen sat on the side of the car with their legs hanging over the side. A few soldiers decided to curl up in the middle and try to get more sleep. All prisoners understood that orders had been given to the guards to shoot any prisoner who jumped from the flat car during transit or at a standstill. Guards rode on flat cars in front of and behind the prisoners. It seemed there was nearly one guard for every prisoner.

Marcus told Stephen, "When they stop the train, I need to find a place where I can be hidden for thirty seconds, long enough for me to change out of this uniform and appear to be a civilian again. I don't know where or when that will be, but I'll know it and just do it on a moment's notice."

After several hours in a twenty-mile-an-hour wind, the prisoners began to snuggle together for mutual warmth. The men wrapped in blankets with their backs toward the front of the train. The countryside was beautiful and the trees were clad in their beautiful fall colors. Marcus commented, "If we weren't going to prison, this would be a pretty nice ride." His friends around him agreed. The trains stopped for water and coal, but the prisoners were not allowed to get off. Several guards climbed up on the car or stood on the ground with buckets and dippers filling cups with water. Soon they were underway again; the train followed tracks that curved through the hills and beautiful valleys, country that made the men want to get off and start farms. They commented to each other how plentiful the crops must have been.

Another water stop came up and the men were allowed to jump off the left side of the car and stretch. They were refreshed with water, water that seemed extra clean and pure. They expected to be fed since it was past noon now and it had been a long time since sunup. Sounds of dissatisfaction came from men who couldn't be seen, but an officer quelled the minor complaints by promising them they would be fed at their next stop. After a bit, the soldiers were loaded back on board unfed after the train was sated with coal and water.

As the train picked up speed, Stephen asked Marcus if he had seen any chances to make an escape. Marcus shook his head, "No, I looked for a place back there, but we were watched too well. I need to be hidden when I shed this gray hide." The sound of the tracks gave a rhythm to their ride. Marcus got another idea. "Stephen, do you still have that small pocket knife hidden in your shoe?"

"Yeah."

"Then let me borrow it for a moment." Marcus took the knife and started cutting parts of the seam in the crotch of his gray pants and down the inseam until it was only held together by a few stitches.

"What are you doing, Marcus?" Stephen asked.

Marcus handed the knife back to Stephen, "Now take this knife and cut some of the stitches holding the seams together in the back. When I decide to shed this thing, I need to be able to jerk it off in the blink of eye." Stephen understood what he wanted him to do. He pulled his blanket up over his head as if he were cold and then lifted Marcus's blanket up so he could see the seams to be cut. The bright sun penetrated the blanket and gave him enough light to get the stitches cut. Now, when the opportunity presented itself, Marcus could jerk the pants and shirt off, and in an instant, be civilian again. He had flattened his hat and had carried it inside his shirt. When his shirt was gone he could pop the hat back up, put it on his head and become a civilian again.

The train chugged on into the afternoon; ashes from the coal-fired boiler speckled the men's faces and clothes with small grains of black grit. The wind was blowing and leaves were raining on the scene. The time seemed to be about four o'clock to Marcus as the train entered a town. This time the train did not stop in the country, but came to rest at a respectable depot with many civilians around.

Apparently word had spread that a trainload of Confederates, recently captured at Sharpsburg, would be stopping for a short visit. All the locals had heard and read how the Southern soldiers had been invincible until the Antietam battle, and everyone wanted to see the beasts that had defeated their fine young men. The guards surrounded the flat cars and formed a hallway that allowed the prisoners to walk to an open park next to the depot to be fed and watered. The crowd pushed up closely behind the guards, almost shoving them forward to get a better look at the captured supermen. Some of the men jeered and called the Confederates dirty names, while others looked on with awe.

All of a sudden the gaggle of prisoners near the front slowed down and stopped when a man in the crowd lunged forward, accusing them of killing his son at Antietam, pointing his hand at an individual and calling him a bastard. That remark was an insult to the man's southern pride, causing the Rebel to lunge back at the man, managing to plant a fist in the accuser's face. The prisoners, outraged at what they saw, briefly lost their fear of the guards and pushed forward forcing the Union guards back. For a moment there was chaos with prisoners, guards, and civilians fighting briefly, until the bayonets went from vertical to horizontal and forced the prisoners back. Two Confederates broke through the line and started running into the crowd. The guards could not shoot because of the crowd; instead they gave chase on foot.

It was now time for Marcus to enter the stage and give the performance he had envisioned in his mind. When the riot began, he raced into the back of the mob, jerking off his gray lizard skin, and instantly turning into a colorfully clad civilian in the midst of the commotion; screaming for the guards to save him. Marcus gave Stephen one last look filled with a thank you, gave him one last grin, and pushed his way through the prisoners toward the front of quite a melee by now. He yelled to a guard, "Help me, they are trying to kill me! Please!" Immediately, a guard turned and saw a civilian at the edge of the fray, reached out, and pulled him to safety.

"Thank you soldier," Marcus said as he reshaped his fine felt hat, dusted off his coat, and stamped his feet to get the dust off of his brown shoes, now not so shiny. "I was standing on the other side and my hat blew off into the middle of that mob. The guard let me through so I could retrieve my hat, but I was soon part of the quagmire. Thank you for your service."

"Glad I could help," the guard replied as he turned back to corralling the calming disturbance.

Marcus quickly disappeared in the crowd and soon was walking the streets of this little "burg." He didn't know where he was and he didn't know where he was going, but he didn't care. He was free. He knew he could fend for himself now.

16

Marcus was a free man. He rapidly strolled through the small town elated and confident that he had pulled off the perfect escape. He had on a nice suit, but after a week of sleeping on the ground, his clothes were filthy. He had some money and when he could he would buy some new comfortable clothes. He was so excited to be free, but rued the fate of his Confederate comrades on the train. Marcus could move about freely now, not having to watch over his shoulder and wonder who was chasing him. It was now up to him to avoid being captured again.

Marcus remembered the money sewn in his suit. He sat down on a bench in front of a small shop and pulled the hidden pocket around and tore the lining of the jacket, just large enough to secure one of the five dollars bills, pretending to check a possible tear in his coat. He secretly slid one of the bills into his hand and put it in the side pocket. Five dollars should last him a while.

He needed to find out the name of this town before he made further plans; however, Marcus felt it would appear strange to ask a passerby to tell him where he was. He got up from the bench, confident now no one was chasing him and decided to ease back toward the center of town and the crowds that had come to see the Confederate prisoners.

He noticed a man standing, watching the affair from afar, with a newspaper in his coat pocket. Marcus approached and asked if he might look at the man's newspaper. The man pulled it out and gave it to him and told him to keep it; he had finished reading it earlier.

The name of the town was not in the newspaper name, so Marcus was still at a loss. Educated through the eighth grade, Marcus could read well and soon understood from the articles he was in Greensburg, Pennsylvania. "But where is that?" he thought. "I need to see a map." Recalling the train ride, he sensed he had gone west.

As he stood reading the newspaper, he noticed a middle-aged man in a wooden covered wagon rattling down the street. As he approached, it was obvious from the clanging and banging he was carrying tin pots and pans. He went past Marcus and pulled his two mules and the wagon to a stop in front of a hardware store. He dismounted, brushed himself off, and went inside. Marcus suspected if anyone knew where he was, where he had been, and where he was going it was a peddler. Marcus walked down and took a seat on the steps of the hardware store and gawked at the peddler's wagon. Much of the wares hung on the side of the wagon including pots and pans, mops, hoes, pitchforks, scythes, and axes, all covering posters about elixirs and medicines he had inside.

Shortly, the peddler and the store owner came out to the wagon and the peddler unlocked the back door and went inside and brought out three hammers, two crowbars, and a wooden box of an unidentifiable product. He handed the goods to the owner and went back inside his wagon and fetched an assortment of tin cups and returned inside the store with the shop owner.

When the peddler had finished he walked back to his wagon folding the money up and placing it in a leather purse and stuffed the purse inside a pocket of his pants behind his belt. Marcus thought that was a clever place to hide his money.

As the man came down the stairs Marcus stood up and put his hand out to shake hands and introduce himself. My name is Marcus Mills and I wondered if you could help me sir?"

"I will if I can. My name is Bruce Brown, The Pan Handler Man," he hesitated a second, "Get it, boy? I handle pans; I sell pans," he laughed expecting Marcus to get the humor in his name. I am a tinker, you know, I sell and fix pots and pans."

Not getting the humor, Marcus replied, "I thought a panhandler was a beggar."

"It is my boy, don't you see, I beg you to buy my pans."

"Oh, I catch on now. I see what you mean, there's your name written right up there," pointing to the old peeling black letters near the top of the wagon.

"What can I do for you?" the tinker said speaking faster than Marcus was used to hearing in Georgia.

"Well, you see sir, it's hard for a man like you to understand this, but I am lost. I am trying to make my way to Kentucky to see my folks. I have been back East studying to be a lawyer, recalling the story Edward had told him, and due to the war and hard times back home, they need me there." Looking down and pretending to be very humble Marcus added, "Mother said my father was in a bad way after a horse kicked him and she needs me back home to help her make it through the winter."

"Uh, huh, I see, and what else? How did you get lost?"

"Well sir, you might say I have been lost since I left Harrisburg. I have been more or less following the sun west, but yesterday, my horse started limping and when I got to town this morning, the stable owner looked her over and said she would probably be alright, but I needed to rest her for a while."

"Yes, I see, but why are your clothes so dirty?"

Marcus looked down at his dirty pants and looked back at the tinker with sadness on his face. "I have no money and have to sleep on the side of the road; I don't have time to wait around for my horse, Jessie, to get well so I sold him for five dollars; he's worth more than that," as he reached in his pocket and showed him the five dollar bill. "That won't buy me a new horse but I need to get on home."

"Well, what do you want to know?"

"I'm sure you travel all over these parts and know your way around. What I need to know is how you would get to Louisville, Kentucky from here?"

"Boy, that's easy," then he thought a second, "Maybe not if you don't have a horse." He hesitated again, "Is five dollars all you got?"

"No, I've got a few dollars more, but I needed that to travel on."

"Well, if you had more money you could ride the train down to Pittsburgh and then catch a coal barge down the river to Louisville. They're a rough bunch, but for a dollar or two I imagine they'd let you ride along." He removed his hat and scratched the top of his head, "On second thought, if they thought you had any money they might knock you in the head and throw you in the river. Have you ever lived around a river?"

"No sir, I grew up in Buckhead, Georgia."

"Are you a Johnny Reb? I noticed you talked kind of funny."

Marcus realized he had leaked some information that might cause problems and quickly amended what he said. "I grew up in Buckhead, but my family moved to Kentucky before I was grown. Shortly before the war, I went to Harrisburg to study law," again remembering Edward's story. "My family didn't own any slaves and my father always said, 'Slavery was alright as long as you weren't one. He taught me it wasn't right for one man to benefit from another man's labor. My new friends at the college convinced me to stay up north and go to school. That's what I was doing until my mother wrote me to come home."

The tinker climbed on the wagon seat. "I'll tell you what I'll do. I wasn't going to McKeesport, but I have a brother there I haven't seen in a year or two."

"Where's McKeesport?" Marcus inquired.

"It's twenty-five to thirty miles to the west. It's on the Monongahela River and that will take you down to Pittsburgh, and then you will be on the Ohio River and that will take you to Louisville. You can probably get a job on a barge and float down there."

"Thank you sir for your kindness; I can pay you a dollar for my ride."

"No, keep your money. I'll enjoy your company, particularly a future lawyer. I'll take you over there but it may take a while. I need to stop and sell my wares at the stores in the area."

Marcus knew nothing about law and wondered if his lie would be exposed through conversation. "Sir, I'm not a lawyer yet, matter of fact, I haven't taken any law yet, only grammar, math, and government."

"Well, in any case, pick up your gear and I will meet you back here in an hour or so. I have a few stores I need to call on before we set out." He looked around, "By the way, where's your stuff?"

Marcus stuck his arms out with his palms up, "Sir, this is all I have."

"Didn't you have any saddlebags on your horse? What about your saddle?"

"I let the livery stable have that too for an extra two dollars."

"You mean you let him have your saddle and horse for seven dollars?"

Marcus realized his lies were catching up with him and he had dug a hole that was going to be hard to get out of. His fancy talking and lying was failing him now.

"Boy, I don't know if you are a fool or trying to rob me, but get out of here before I call the sheriff and find out who you really are." He clucked his tongue, the mules moved forward, and he left Marcus standing in the street.

Marcus was afraid he had opened himself up for discovery, especially if the tinker contacted the sheriff. He did know where he was and where he needed to go to get to Kentucky, but he also knew he had to change from his Sunday clothes to something gray or tan, colors that would not draw attention.

When the peddler had gone around the corner, Marcus turned and went in the general store and browsed through the stock of clothes inside. Winter was coming on and he needed a warm coat, boots, gloves, wool shirts and under clothes, along with several pairs of wool socks, which necessitated him to acquire a canvas bag to carry it as he gathered up what he had and took it to the clerk. His bill came to twenty two dollars and a few cents. Having only five dollars, he asked the clerk if he might go outside and retrieve enough money to pay for his bill. He went outside and sat down on a bench, took his jacket off and removed twenty more dollars from his secret pouch. He returned inside and paid the man.

Before leaving he asked the owner if he had a place where he could change into his new clothes. The clerk pointed to a room under the stairs and soon, Marcus was a new man. He stuffed his old clothes along with his new in the canvas bag and walked out feeling like he had a new identity. He had changed his colors again.

Outside he pondered about the trip ahead and what additional items he might need. He wished he could afford a firearm for his safety and shooting game, and maybe a fishing line. He anticipated traveling on a river later and that might come in handy. He also needed a warm blanket and a rubber-coated canvas large enough to sleep under if he was caught outside in the rain. He returned inside and bought what he needed including matches, a tin plate and cup including eating utensils, a canteen, a good pocket knife and a small hatchet, and a heavy warm woolen blanket. After looking at the new gear on the table, he traded his canvas bag for a larger backpack. He now only had two five dollar bills left, plus four ones, a total of fourteen dollars.

It was afternoon now and he was hungry. He saw an eatery down the street and he went inside. He was aware he had to control his spending and could not order expensive food. He ordered a bowl of stew and a cup of water and sat down next to the front window. Although he had been fed well by his Union captors, he was tired of beans. In contrast, the stew with all the meat and vegetables was delicious. For six cents more he added a half dozen large sugar cookies in a paper bag. He could not remember when he had last tasted sweets. He polished off the stew and three large sugar cookies and stored the rest to eat later.

As he was crunching a cookie, he noticed the tinker coming back down the street accompanied by the sheriff. Marcus pushed his chair behind the restaurant curtain and saw the peddler pointing at the general store saying, "You can't miss him; he has on a reddish coat and dull yellow pants. I think he was going to rob me."

Marcus grasped the situation immediately, his time in Greensburg was over and he must get out of town. When they passed he hustled out and disappeared among the passer bys. With his new clothes on, he would be hard to find, since the tinker was the only man in town who could recognize him and he was looking for a man in a colorful suit.

About that time Marcus heard the train he had ridden on as a prisoner blow its whistle, indicating for everyone to be alert; the train would be moving soon. Aware the sheriff and the peddler were down the street, Marcus ran back to the depot to watch his friends depart. The guards had formed a corridor for the soldiers to pass through again to return to the flatcars. Marcus came up close and stood behind the soldiers hoping Stephen would see him. He wished he could talk to him a second or two. Maybe together they could plot a quick escape. He watched the men pass by, strung out in single file and a guard was counting them as they passed him. Finally, he saw Stephen, one of the last prisoners to come through. Just before he was to be counted he saw Marcus, and almost spoke, but gave him a short grin, acknowledging now he knew Marcus was free. Marcus wanted to do something, but instead, he had to watch Stephen get on the train and take his place on the flatcar.

One of the guards remarked to his superior officer, holding an official- looking folder up to prove his point, "It appears we are short one prisoner since our last stop,"

"You must have miscounted. We have watched all of these men closely. There is no way anyone got away. Just disregard and record all present."

Marcus watched Stephen roll out of town, as the train's dark gray smoke entwined the prisoners. Marcus raised his hand above his eye and gave Stephen a salute. Stephen saluted back. Marcus watched the train gather speed and disappear behind the buildings and smoke of the small town. Marcus regretted he could not come up with a plan to free his comrades. He never forgot that morning's memory of his friend most likely going to his death.

17

As the train chugged out of town, the crowd broke up and returned to the normal routines that make a small town so unique: blacksmith fires, bakeries, women washing, and burning leaves. A few men stayed in small groups and discussed what they just witnessed; some could not speak without using their hands to put more emotion in what they said while others listened. Marcus vaguely knew the direction of north by eyeing the sun as it went in and out between the clouds. He turned to a large fat man, well dressed, probably a lawyer, walking beside him returning to town and asked if he possibly knew the route to Pittsburgh. The man laughed, "You are definitely not from around here are you? Everybody knows the way to Pittsburgh."

"Not me sir, I'm just passing through."

"Then go to the depot and catch the train down there, or go over to McKeesport and get on a steamboat heading that way. Those are the easiest ways to go, or just follow the most horse and wagon tracks going out of town. Sounds like you are from the South."

"Yes sir, I'm from Kentucky; been going to school up north." Marcus was getting tired of explaining his biography because of the way he talked. The fact a war was going on, his southern drawl, and Northern mistrust of a southern brogue had nearly caused his capture more than once. If this man would tell him how to get to Pittsburgh, he would choose his conversations very carefully until he was back in Dixieland.

Obviously irritated, but still respectful, Marcus continued, "Sir, I can't help the way I talk. I was born in Kentucky and just trying to get back home to my sick mother. If you will just point the direction I need to go to find those tracks I'll get out of your town and will never come back."

"Now don't get riled, boy, I'll show you the road to take when we get close."

"Thank you sir, I'd appreciate that."

The two continued down the street, the large man walking rather fast Marcus thought for his size. "I see you bought a new coat."

"How'd you know that?" Marcus questioned.

The man reached over and pulled up a price tag dangling on a string stitched to the back of his collar. "Looks like all your gear is new. You didn't steal it did you?"

"No sir, my horse went lame just outside of town. I got off and walked into town. When I got to the livery stable, the owner told me he was indeed lame and would probably recover. I told him I didn't have time to wait, I needed to be gettin' on so I asked him what he would give me for old Jesse. He studied a minute or two, looked my horse over again and said he would gamble five dollars on his prognosis so I took him up on it; took the money and bought a new coat and all this other stuff I needed to walk on home. Why would you suspect I was a thief?"

The man stopped walking and turned toward Marcus, in the process, throwing his coat back to reveal a big belly and a silver star pinned over his heart.

"Well boy, I am the sheriff of this county and I need to know about what goes on in my town. Who knows, you might be one of those Rebels yonder leaving town and somehow got away. You talk like one of them. Just to be sure come with me and confirm your story about your horse. If the livery man confirms your story you can go on your way." With that he reached out and grabbed Marcus under the arm to hold him from running while they walked to the livery stable.

Marcus couldn't believe what was happening. Of all the people in town, it seemed he had the ability to find the person who made his life difficult. When his story didn't pan out and the encounter with the peddler was made known, he knew he would be in deep trouble, and might yet be on another train to a northern prison camp.

Realizing the sheriff was heavy and overweight Marcus was aware outrunning this lawman would be no problem, but in the crowd, the sheriff would yell for help, and he would soon be apprehended. He hoped a better escape route might present itself before they got to the livery stable.

Marcus begged him to turn him loose. "I am just a college-boy going home to help my mother during this war." Then he saw an opportunity that would at least give him a short lead on a chase he knew would have to occur; if he got caught, he would face criminal charges.

The livery stable was off of downtown and the crowd was gone, just a few people going about their business. Marcus begged again, "I have a letter in my pocket that will prove I am going home," and stopped walking forcing the sheriff to stop also.

"Let me see it," he said gruffly, disappointed that his prey might be telling the truth.

Marcus had chosen the spot to stop and reveal his letter. He reached inside his pocket and pulled the wrinkled letter out. "Here is my proof. I can even show you the picture of the girl I am going to marry when I get home." He slid the bent photograph out of the envelope and held it up for the sheriff to see, higher than his eyes so the sheriff would have to hold his head back slightly to be able to look up and view the beautiful girl.

Before the sheriff could react, Marcus lunged forward and pushed the fat man backward over a wooden crate, causing him to fall down several steps to the ground, severely stunned for a few moments. Marcus hesitated a second, wondering if he had killed the man, but his plan worked perfectly. He had seen the box at the top of the stairs as they approached, and he knew it would be a perfect place to perform an act he had done many times as a kid, pushing a friend over another friend in the school yard.

Marcus immediately disappeared down an alley between the buildings, carrying all his new goods as he ran. Growing up, Marcus had always been a great runner and could run several miles without stopping. He soon learned the lack of food and hard living during the war had taken the edge off of his speed and endurance, but he had to endure the pain and keep running, knowing the consequences of being captured would be much more agonizing.

He ran past homes and was soon at the edge of broken woods and fields, similar to what he had seen in Maryland. He knew he was a man on the run and they would soon have hounds and lawmen searching for him. At that moment the sun came out from behind a cloud, low in the sky, and showed he was running west, not the direction he wanted to go. He was exhausted and stopped a minute to take a break and listen for the hounds that he knew were behind him, probably coming on fast. Most of the people that time of day were coming in from their daily chores and readying themselves for supper. The woods he had stopped in were quiet; still no dogs. He held his hand up and counted the number of palm widths between the sun and the horizon, each width indicating an hour of time. He determined it would be dark in two hours and his chances of escape would be good.

His load was getting heavy and his arms and legs ached, but he pushed himself on. He kept looking back fearing who might be chasing him. He would continue farther west, then turn south, hoping the sheriff would turn south sooner expecting his prey had gone toward Pittsburg. The thought of capture and having to face a sheriff who had to eat dirt kept him going. He knew he was in for a good whipping if he not killed by the irate sheriff. He knew in Georgia, the sheriff handled his county as he saw fit with little accountability to any higher authority.

The stunned sheriff had fallen down the stairs backward and put his arm out to break his fall. His body slapped the hard ground like a sack of slop pitched down to feed the pigs as his head hit the brick street. No one had seen Marcus push the heavy man, but a shopkeeper saw the sheriff passed out at the bottom of the stairs and yelled across the street. The owner of the store where he fell heard the splat on the ground and came out to see the source of the sound and found the injured sheriff.

The two shopkeepers tried to move the heavy man and lift him up into a sitting position, but being passed out and fat made him difficult to grasp. They thought he might be dead at first, but after a few minutes he began to moan and come to. One of the shop owners yelled to his wife to bring out some water.

"Where am I?" the sheriff asked sitting up, "What happened?" He put his arm down to push himself up to stand, but suffered extreme pain and immediately grabbed his arm. "I think I broke my arm. Go get the doctor. What happened?" he asked again, still addled by the fall. "What am I doing down here?"

They informed him they had found him lying at the bottom of the stairs. The lady arrived with a dipper of water. He sipped at first but then swigged it down, trying to figure out what happened. "The last thing I remember was watching the train leaving town." He sat there in a daze, "Then I started back into town and I was talking to somebody......I guess I walked on down here, but who was I talking to?" then winced in pain from his broken arm. "Try to help me up; be careful with my arm." Having no handles to grab and finding him very difficult to lift, the several townspeople that had gathered finally got him to his feet. "I must have fallen down those stairs. I've never been knocked out like this before." The townspeople helped the sheriff get to the doctor's office where the physician set his arm. Marcus was not remembered by the sheriff and would not be identified. There would be no dogs or a chase. Unfortunately for Marcus, he did not know this.

Since leaving Greenburg, Marcus found the land to be quite hilly with fields and valleys filling the landscape. When nature gave him the chance, he removed his new shoes and rolled his pants up and waded down creeks to hide his odor in case the hounds were called out to track him down. He kept one ear alerted for the familiar bay of pursuing hounds. One of the creeks ran under a split rail fence. Without stepping on land, he climbed the fence and walked along the top rail for several hundred feet until the fence turned off in a direction Marcus wasn't going, never leaving a scent on the ground for the dogs to follow. Just before dark, Marcus came upon an isolated place to camp next to a tall hill and out of the wind. A clean creek flowed nearby. Thirsty now after the long run, he filled his new canteen and took a long drink. He had no food except for three sugar cookies now broken from the afternoon's ordeal, and he could feel the air was colder than it had been since the previous evening.

18

The sun disappeared beyond the western horizon creating beautiful arrangements of oranges and yellows above the tree line. Marcus calculated he had put three or four miles between Greenburg and himself. Although night was coming on and it was getting colder, he was free and had three broken cookies to eat.

He had chosen a good place to camp, too. It was up against the south side of a steep hill that he estimated was a hundred feet high. The site was shielded from view by green bushes similar to his native myrtle bushes that grew along the creeks of Georgia. The entire site was covered with a canopy of large oaks and other types of trees he had not seen before.

In the fading light, feeling secure from bloodhounds, he decided to build a fire between two large rocks protruding out of the side of the hill. The rocks were as big as wagons and the space between was only a couple of feet, creating a natural chimney. He gathered up some dead wood that was easily broken with his hands. Larger dry limbs could be broken by putting one end on a rock and jumping on them, instantly snapping them in two. He found his matches and used the leaves for kindling, soon a fire crackled between the rocks.

The light from the fire made it possible for him to take his hatchet and cut two forked sticks and a six foot pole to support his waterproof canvas. He expected rain that night and his make-do tent would hopefully keep him dry. He had been lucky and had been at Genia's house when it had last rained for two days. He drove the forked sticks in the ground and laid the long pole across the forks, creating a spine for his canvas. He aligned the center of the canvas on the pole and tied each corner to a driven stake. The fresh crispy leaves were so plentiful he gathered up enough to make a soft mattress on which to spread his blanket. To make his bed more comfortable, he cut some small vines to tie around a wad of rolled up leaves to form a pillow under his blanket. He got his three broken cookies and canteen and prepared to feast. He was learning to adapt to his new environment and what nature provided.

Just at the moment he was about to eat the first piece of cookie he heard a sound that made his hair stand up. It was the long howl of a hound dog very far away. "No, no, no, this can't be happening," he thought. Like Job he wondered why God was punishing him now. "What had he done to deserve His wrath?" He jumped to his feet so he could better hear. He listened and listened. He turned and faced a new direction and listened and listened, but he did not hear it again. As he listened he was thinking of a contingency plan to gather his stuff and make a getaway in the dark, but he did not hear the howl again. It must have been an old dog on somebody's farm that just let the world know he was alive and ready to hunt if anybody wanted to go.

God may not have been punishing him after all, but instead, reminding him to stay alert. He lay back down and ate the rest of his cookies and drank a lot of water to stave off hunger pangs. Considering what had occurred that day and what could have happened, he said a prayer and thanked the Lord he was still safe and free.

He pulled Bonnie's bent photograph out of his coat pocket and looked at her beautiful, yet broken face lit by the orange light from the fire. He hoped she had written letters concerning her new location to the people back home. He admired her a few moments longer and secured his most valuable treasure back in his pocket.

For him, the war was over. He had a touch of homesickness now; he was lonesome. His strong desire was to get home and see Bonnie, his mother, his father, and his dog Fetch. He imagined walking up to his house and seeing the glow from a lamp or candle his mother always lit after dark. A light in her front window meant to all her friends who passed her house, all was well.

During the night, he was awakened by a hoot owl, the sound of a prowling animal, most probably a raccoon going about his business, and a crawly thing that walked across his neck which he quickly swatted away. Occasionally the baying dog caught his attention, but he reasoned the dog was not on the hunt. Before long, the lengthy sprint escaping from the sheriff took its toll, and he was out. He slept well, even though the temperature dropped during the night.

Marcus woke at dawn and sat up, forgetting he was inside, and bumped his head on the spine of the tent. "Why did I do a fool thing like that?" he asked himself as he rubbed the small red spot on his forehead. He lay back down, pulling his blanket around him, and tried to stay warm on this chilly morning. He felt safe under his tent, but the reality of where he was and the ordeals ahead brought him out of his blanket of security. At least, if the fat sheriff was hunting him, he apparently had gone in the wrong direction; but he wanted to put more space between him and Greenburg.

His first concern was to find something to eat. The three cookies had worn off and his fat reserves had been used up months before in the war. He was painfully hungry again. His fire had died, but he didn't need it now. As he looked at the ashes, he wished he had bought some coffee and sugar back at the general store. That would warm him up and taste good on this cold morning.

He carefully untied his tent, leaving the strings attached to the corners, packed his gear and headed out. He hated to leave this little haven that had given him protection during the night. He went down to the small creek below his camp and followed the stream downhill, knowing eventually it would lead him to a bigger stream or river.

As he walked through the bottom land he saw fields that had been harvested of various vegetables. He was able to glean a few left morsels of food that had been overlooked. By the time he left the potato field, he had picked up three medium-sized potatoes and a dozen small ones of various sizes. He went down to the creek and washed two of the taters and ate them raw, wishing they had a sprinkling of salt. He also found some broken ears of dried corn. By noon his old cookie sack contained various edible bits of food.

He saw several villages, but aware that he was a hunted man and word had been spread about his presence, he decided to use trails and lanes that bypassed the towns trying to stay hidden as much as possible. The weather was turning colder and he expected it could rain at any moment; there would be frost that night. Shortly after noon, he discovered a pear orchard and he gathered as many as he could carry in his backpack while he feasted on one. They were yellow, soft, and ripe. If he were back in Georgia, he would ask his mother to cook some pear preserves. He took his pears and nestled in some high native grass by the creek he was following and ate three more, hoping he wouldn't get sick from eating too much fruit on an empty stomach.

As he sat in the grass, he felt like he was back home, hunting ducks and geese, hiding in the tall grass waiting for them to fly by or light on a slough off Sandy Creek. He liked this place; it reminded him of home. If it had been later in the day, he would have gotten closer to the creek and built a fire and camped, but he knew every step he took toward home now, would be better than one later. Winter would be on him soon and he feared the steps would be much harder then. After a few minutes rest, he gathered himself up and moved on down the creek, staying hidden as much as possible.

During the day, Marcus saw farmers going about their work, a man leading a milk cow and another butchering a hog, but each time he only waved from afar not getting close, acting like a traveler hiking through the land with nothing to hide, never getting close enough for them to hear his southern brogue.

Late in the afternoon he came upon a high bluff that overlooked a river that appeared to be flowing west; he deduced his direction by observing the moss that only grew on the north side of the trees. He struggled down the steep, wooded bank holding on to trees and saplings to slow him down. At the bottom he came upon a rock-strewn river bordered by flat bottom land. It wasn't far from the cliff to the edge of the river. The many crisscrossing trails and stony paths indicated folks had used these passageways for centuries. He estimated it was an hour before dark, and this seemed to be a good sheltered spot.

He went back next to the cliff and walked along its base looking for a good campsite away from the traveled paths. He saw where people had built fires, some since the last rain. After a quarter mile of hiking he saw a natural cleft in the rocks that provided an overhang he could get under. In the past many travelers had sought its protection, indicated by the soot that darkened the roof of the shallow cave.

He dropped his pack and started gathering wood. Although not as plentiful as before, there were many limbs that he soon stockpiled for the night's cold. He had carried his two forked sticks by tying them to the bottom of his pack and all he needed was a pole which he quickly found and cut to hang his tent on. The overhang was not deep enough to give him complete protection from the rain, but it provided a place for the fire to be safe except from the heaviest downpours. He used a match and got his fire going, and he pitched his tent so one of the open ends faced the fire. He removed some uncomfortable stones from his future bed and padded the ground with leaves to give him as much insulation as possible from the cold, rocky soil and make it more comfortable.

He still had a little daylight, and remembering his fishing line, he decided to see if he could have something other than pears for supper. A large fish of any kind would taste good tonight. He found and hacked a long slender limb, cleaned the small branches off, attached his line and hook, and he was ready. He got close to the river and turned over rocks to try to find some insect that had not gone into winter quarters and was waiting to be fish bait.

Marcus finally turned over enough rocks to discover a crawly-looking bug that he could use for bait. He held it down with a stick wondering if it would bite or sting him. He concluded it did not have a stinger; the bug was soon looking at the bottom of the stream on Marcus's hook. Marcus threw his line up stream and let the bug flow downstream several feet from shore until his bait reached the end of his line, and then he would repeat the throw again.

On the sixth cast Marcus heard some voices approaching. He could tell the two men had seen him and it would look suspicious for him to run and hide so he prepared to look as normal as possible and say little. As the two got closer he could see they were elderly men coming in from a day of fishing. Each one had his pole in one hand and a stringer of fish in the other.

When they came near one of the old men asked, "Having any luck today?"

Marcus hoped he could hide his southern heritage by speaking rapidly and purposely duplicating the northern accent, "No, I just got here and could only find a bug for bait," spitting the words out as fast as he could.

The other man replied, "You're not from around here are you?"

Marcus angrily thought, "How could he tell I wasn't from around here; I didn't talk like a Georgian," but understanding his secret was discovered, he disgustedly said, "No, I'm not!"

"I didn't mean to make you mad. We knew you didn't live around here because, if you did, you'd go down to that deep hole down there about a quarter mile. Nobody fishes up here."

Realizing it wasn't his twang that disclosed the truth, but where he was fishing, he quickly replied speaking rapidly again. "Oh, no sir, I am not mad. I am just disgusted that these fish won't eat my bait," as he pulled his bug out of the water."

One of the men looked with kindness at the young lad away from home, "If it wasn't getting dark and we didn't have another mile or so back to town, we'd take you up there and show you that hole. But here, we got plenty of fish; take a couple of ours. That should make you a good meal tonight." Both men laid down their stringers and removed a large fish. Marcus couldn't believe what he saw as he watched the two large fish twist back and forth on the sand, their gills moving back and forth gasping for air. He was going to eat like a king tonight.

"Oh, thank you so much. I figured I was going to eat pears tonight," Marcus replied, forgetting about his rapid speech, just happy to get the gift. "I cannot thank you enough."

"We'd give you some more, but we have some others that depend on us for their fish when we can find time to go." Not seeming to notice Marcus's change in speech, they wished him well, said good day and moseyed off down the river's edge.

Before they had gone far, Marcus yelled to them, "Did you say there is a town down there?"

They stopped and yelled back, "Yes, follow the creek on down two miles and you'll be in West Newton."

Marcus thanked them again for the fish. He got his knife and in a few minutes had the fish cleaned and stuck on a stick roasting above the fire. The fish cooked fast and he was soon eating big chunks of white meat. He picked every morsel of the white flesh he could scrape off of the bones and washed it all down with a cup full of water. He got a pear from his pack, got his picture of Bonnie out and sat on top of his world for a while.

However, it couldn't last long out there in the wilderness. The cold wind picked up, so he stoked his fire with more logs, took out his coat and hung it over the end of the tent away from the fire to keep the cold wind out and crawled in his tent; he was soon asleep in his warm blanket. Not long after he had dozed off he was awakened by the snort of a horse and the clop of a horse's hoofs as a lone rider passed during the night, not knowing Marcus was there only a few yards away.

19

Marcus slept soundly in his tent next to the rocky overhang. During the night it started to drizzle, but the ledge above him protected his fire and his wood and the ashes were still dry the next morning. The larger logs had faint glowing embers and by blowing on them Marcus lit the leaves and small kindling that he had kept dry under the rock. He wished for a cup of coffee, but at least he had a pear, which he ate with a cup of water. He lay back down on his now compressed bed of leaves and pondered what lay ahead that day. Was the sheriff still hunting him? Would he be captured or killed? He felt confident the sheriff had gone in another direction not expecting him to go the direction Marcus had asked about. His plan today would be to keep low and pass through the town unnoticed and find out where West Newton led him.

After he was packed, Marcus saw a real straight sapling about two inches in diameter that he thought would make a good walking stick. It could also be used to defend himself, if necessary, since he had no weapons other than his hatchet and a large pocket knife.

He was proud of his new stick as he headed down the well-worn trail he saw the fisherman use. It had stopped drizzling, but it was cold, overcast, and dreary. He soon passed several people fishing in a wide spot in the large creek-apparently the big fishing hole the men had told him about. To Marcus's surprise, after a mile from the fishing spot, the creek spilled into a large river.

Marcus came into the edge of the small town and scouted his situation. The town was on the edge of the river surrounded by large hills and could not be skirted easily, unless he made a large circle back to the east. He watched the "comers" and "goers" and he decided he looked like a "comer" and "goer" and proceeded into town. As he passed through, he noticed many people working with wood, shaping boards and beams; boat building seemed to be a significant operation in the town, employing many people, many of them older, since most of the young men were in the Union Army.

Marcus walked on the dirt road above the river. He spotted a building that had many horses and wagons tethered around it. Men stood among the horses and wagons carrying on conversations. The war seemed to be the major talk among the men. As he came closer he smelled the aroma of fried bacon and he became aware he could buy the cup of coffee he craved earlier. A good cup of coffee would taste good and lift his spirits for the day ahead.

He nodded at folks and went inside. It was warm and he could hear eggs and bacon frying. He sat down at an empty table and a young lady came up, gave him a big smile and asked him whether he wanted ham, bacon or sausage with his eggs. It had been months since he had been that close to a beautiful girl and she reminded him of Bonnie.

She waited a moment and then asked Marcus, "You aren't from around here are you?" Marcus looked up at her beautiful face, but a little irritated and thought, "I haven't said a word, how would she know I was a stranger."

Then she answered his thought, "Haven't seen you before. Cute young men are hard to find around here with the war and all. Why aren't you away in the war?"

He smiled back at her, "I was, but I am going home... yes indeed I was," he sighed emphasizing the point he had endured hell. "But I'm going home now for the winter. I got a furlough so I could go help my mother during the winter. The armies won't be fighting 'til next spring so they let me go home for a while. I promised them I would be back before the war started again." He laughed, "If I go home the army don't have to feed me."

"Where are you from? You talk like you're from down south."

"I am… I am from Kentucky; I grew up down there." She never questioned him what army he was from, assuming since he was in Pennsylvania he was in the Union Army.

"Have you been in any battles?" I hear there was a bad one over in Maryland about two weeks ago."

Marcus looked up sadly and said, "I have been in all of them, and yes, I was in the last one. It was terrible. I nearly got killed."

"What can I get you?"

"Just a cup of coffee. I can't afford anything more than that. I have to save the little money I have so I can make it home."

She hesitated a moment, "I'll be right back." She turned and walked to an older man working over the hot stove. In an instant he looked at her, then at Marcus, flipped an egg, said something back to her, and she turned with a smile on her face and hurried back to Marcus's table.

"That's my father. He owns the place. I told him you were a soldier going home for the winter, but didn't have any money. My father supports our soldiers. He said he would cook whatever you wanted."

Surprised, but humbled, Marcus shook his head, "No, I can't accept that. I just need a cup of coffee which I can pay for."

"You don't understand. My father does this all the time. Now what do you want, we insist."

"Well, If you don't mind," Marcus grinned as he scooted himself higher in the chair, "a good breakfast would taste good."

"Do you want ham, bacon, or sausage, and do you want your eggs fried or scrambled?"

Marcus was awed by their kindness and ordered scrambled eggs and sausage. When his order came, there were also two large slices of bread in addition to fried potatoes. As he ate, the young waitress kept his cup filled with hot coffee and stopped often to talk with Marcus.

Before he finished, she brought him a dish of butter and a small pitcher of maple syrup. Marcus finished off his eggs by pouring the syrup in his plate, stirring it with butter, then sopping the bread in his concoction. It tasted so good. Before he finished, the owner came over to his table to meet the soldier he was feeding.

He walked up, wiped his hands on his apron, reached out and shook hands with Marcus. Welcome to West Newton. My daughter tells me you fought in the war." He pulled a chair out and sat down to ask how the war was going. "She tells me you've been in all the major battles."

Everything was going so good. Why does he have to ruin it all by prying into Marcus's false façade? If he has been helping soldiers, he knows a lot about the war. Marcus had to be careful what he said, not to reveal a falsehood nor dig himself into a hole he couldn't get out of like he did with the sheriff back in Greensburg.

Swigging the coffee down while the question was asked, Marcus put the cup down, and wiped his mouth with his sleeve, preparing to talk, but choosing his words carefully. "Yes sir, I have been in all of them except the first battle or two. We have gotten beaten in every battle. We almost took Richmond, but Lee, is a genius, and he "out "generaled" McClellan down in Virginia, until three or four weeks ago at Sharpsburg." Marcus had learned that Lee had not been defeated at Antietam, but was forced to retreat back into Virginia to wait for the next Union advance, probably the next spring.

Marcus took another swig of coffee and looked directly in the owner's eyes, "Sir, you have never seen anything like the killing that took place in a cornfield over there at Sharpsburg," recalling how his fellow Texans and the Georgians had been mowed down by the artillery fire. "Our artillery cut the Rebels to pieces. We would go forward and be shot down by the hundreds, then they would push back and we would slaughter them again, and we would go forward again, and the same thing would happen again and again. Of course we won the battle and I walked over that "cornfield" afterward and I could have crossed that entire forty-acre field and never stepped on the ground because of the dead."

The man listened intensely, taking in every word Marcus told him. "Rumor had it we nearly won the war that day, but we were exhausted, and those Confederates were too. They were beat though. It is just a matter of time before they are defeated. Our prisoners and dead men were poorly clad and starving to death. I don't see how they had lasted that long under those terrible conditions."

"What corps were you in?"

"Oh, no, Marcus thought. I need to end this conversation now before I say something I shouldn't". He was proud of the performance he had just displayed, but it could all collapse with a careless remark.

"I fought with General Hooker. They don't call him "Fighting Joe" for nothing. To answer your question, sir, I was in the 1st Corp under General Hooker. We hung around Sharpsburg after the battle licking our wounds. It's October now and winter will be blowing in soon, and most likely the fighting is over for this year. I got a furlough to go home for the winter to help my mother. Before the war starts up again next spring, "I'll rejoin my outfit; it's just a matter of time before those Rebels are done."

"Speaking of Rebels, you sound a little Southern yourself." The remark caused Marcus to boil inside, but he had to handle the inquiry without showing any emotion.

"Yeah, I know, I'm asked that all the time. Marcus went on to tell him the Edward Brewster lie about being called home from law school.

About then, four blue-clad Union cavalry walked in the front door. The owner pointed, "Look there's four of your comrades." Suddenly, the eatery was getting too crowded for Marcus. He needed to end this conversation and get back on the road before the wheels came off the situation and he was discovered to be a fraud. The owner yelled to the soldiers to come over and meet Marcus, a survivor of Antietam.

The men walked over and took their hats and gloves off and shook hands with Marcus. Marcus quickly found out they were just local guards that patrolled the river and had not been in any confrontation. They had heard about the butchery at Antietam and seemed honored to meet a veteran of such a conflict. Marcus wondered what the owner and the soldiers would have done to him if they knew his true identity, but before he could be discovered, Marcus stood up to depart this predicament that was entangling him. "I hate to leave such good company, but I have a long way to go before I get home." He reached out and shook hands with the cook who had been so kind to him, thanking him over and over for his generosity. Then he shook hands with the four young men again, and then he turned to the beautiful girl who was also in line to get her goodbye. "And I have to thank you too. Without your consideration I would have left with only a cup of coffee. He bent over and whispered close to her ear, "Thank you. You are very beautiful."

Marcus picked up his gear from the floor, turned and walked out the door. It was beginning to drizzle again. He needed to purchase a rubberized cape with a hood if he could find one. As he stood adjusting his load, he heard footsteps approach him from the back and he turned to find the young lady running toward him. "You forgot your walking stick," she said, as she held out the stick for him to grasp. They looked at each other with a feeling that only young people can send and receive on a moment's notice. The sensation may be real or be a fleeting moment of anticipation. To tempt Marcus, whether his feeling was true or false she said, "The weather is sure bad today. Why don't you stay here? I can find you a place to sleep." The emotion on her face wasn't asking, but pleading that he stay there.

For the first time in his life, his feelings strayed from Bonnie and were drawn in a new direction. He was tempted by the plea and it didn't have to be written out for Marcus what awaited him if he stayed. His mind was suddenly filled with turmoil. He was looking at a beautiful girl, a warm place to stay, an approaching rain storm; all the signs pointed for him to stay, but then he thought of Bonnie, the girl that he loved, waiting for him to come home. He remembered the last words of her letter, "Please Marcus, come and find me. Please don't ever forget me. Whatever it takes, find me Marcus. I will always be waiting for you. Until we can be together again, please know my love is with you."

Marcus looked in the young girl's eyes and reached in his pocket and pulled out Bonnie's letter. "I have to go. I want to stay. You don't know how bad I want to stay, but I have a girl waiting now for me to come home," as he slowly eased Bonnie's picture up between them. "I cannot betray her trust and I must go back to her. My honor would be damaged if I did otherwise." He bent over and gave her a soft kiss on her cheek, turned and walked away in the rain, only turning back once to see if she was still there. She was.

The rain began to pepper down harder and he got his mind back on his journey. He needed a hooded cloak that could keep him dry. He saw a stretch of shops that made do for a downtown in the small village and he headed there. He looked back one more time to see if she had followed him, but she was gone and now she was only a memory that might haunt him the rest of his life, especially, if he never found Bonnie.

He stopped and stood in the rain. He fought the urge to go back, but he remembered something his father had told him, "When the road forks between right and wrong, follow your conscience; if you start down the chosen path and you feel guilty, stop, and take the other path. If you feel good, you made the right decision." Marcus felt guilty. He remembered Bonnie's lovely face, paused a moment, smiled, then he walked on in the rain.

20

After his father's reminder, he tried to forget about the girl and made his way across the street through the rain to the general store. The merchant had a long waterproof coat for three dollars, leaving him only fifteen dollars. He bought some coffee and sugar as well. Over the past three days, he had spent his money fast, but he still possessed the gold ring he had removed from the severed hand. He had kept it hidden in his shoe, worn on his toe.

The rain came down harder, but only the bottoms of his pants were getting wet under his new rubber rain protection. All of his gear was dry in his backpack that he now wore on his chest under his new large rubberized garment as he went down to the road that followed the river, to Pittsburgh he hoped. The rain forced the busy boat builders under sheds or inside small barn-like structures. He passed a small rowboat that had recently been finished and displayed outside one of the barns. He wished he could afford one. Riding down the river would be easier than walking. After assessing the price, he ambled on out of town.

He passed men on horses going toward West Newton and other men passed him riding toward Pittsburgh. At noon he stopped to rest beside the river. Although he wasn't hungry, he took another pear and bit down on it. It was beginning to rain hard now and Marcus thought about seeking shelter next to the steep hills that ascended from the river rather than waiting until dark to make a shelter. He hoped he could find dry wood to start a fire.

He left the river and entered the woods next to the river hoping the thick grove of pine trees he saw might provide some dry wood; the woods were so thick the rain was only beginning to soak through the many boughs above and dampen the ground. He found a level spot protected by several medium-size pines spaced close together and tied his canvas tightly to four trees making a flat cover over his selected campsite. He purposely slanted the tarp so the water would run off.

He swept the damp needles away and prepared a place for a fire under his cover. He built a small fire slightly under the high edge of the tent so the rain and smoke would blow away from the site of his future bed. He worked fast to gather dry pine needles for kindling and insulation for his bed. He broke off dead limbs from the bottom of the tree trunks. Since the wind blew from the north, needles and limbs on the south side of the tree were reasonably dry. He wanted to hoard as many limbs as possible before the rain soaked through the thick pine canopy and eventually wet everything.

Marcus knew if he could get a small fire going he could sustain his fire by adding damp logs since the flames vaporize the water and dried the wood and soon caught fire. He was pleased to find some pine knots from rotted trees, known by all fire builders as one of the hottest fuels found in the woods. His father kept pine knots by the fireplace at home to help start fires. Using his matches, he quickly had a fire giving him a little warmth, but more than warmth; it gave him a feeling of security against the approaching frigid night.

With some time left before dark, Marcus decided to make his temporary house cozier. He cut pine boughs and made a wall to slow the wind entering his abode. At last, he spread his blanket out, formed his pine-needle pillow and thought about supper.

He remembered the fish from the night before. He cut a new fishing pole and pulled some bark off the trees looking for a sleeping bug underneath. It was winter and most bugs were eggs and hibernating. Instead he took a piece of string he had picked up off the road and tied it to emulate a worm and walked back to the river. It appeared the river was higher than it had been earlier in the day, but maybe he was farther down the river. He hoped there would be a "hole" of water that contained a big fish, but after an hour he was discouraged. He kept telling himself, I will try one more time; no fish, but I will try one more time; no fish; but for sure, this will be the last time, as if he were telling God, He had one more chance to let him catch his supper and answer Marcus's prayer. On one of these last times, he got a bite and the line tightened and the pole bent. He actually had a fish, a large fish. He hoped the line wouldn't break or the hook straighten out. He eased the pressure off the pole and line by following the fish up stream. It was hard to watch the fish and his steps at the same time, but he still had the fish. The fish was testing Marcus's primitive tackle to its ultimate strength. The fish turned and ran down stream, Marcus trying to control his turns and pull him in. "Don't you ever get tired?" he yelled at the fish. Suddenly Marcus slipped and he fell in the river dropping his pole. He jumped up and leaped for his pole as it began to be pulled downstream. At the last possible moment it seemed, he grasped the end of the pole and made his way back to shore. The fish was tired and his fight was gone. Marcus came out of the water pulling the fish behind him on shore away from the river so he couldn't flop back in the water. Marcus lifted the fish up and felt his weight. "I think you weigh about five pounds and you are going to taste good tonight."

The cape had protected him from the rain, but it had not helped him when he fell in the river. Cold and wet now, he walked back to camp with his prize. He needed to get out of those wet clothes and put on his old suit he had gotten at the Brewster's. As he was getting out of his coat he remembered Bonnie's letter and photograph. He jerked them out and blotted them with one of his dry shirts. The ink had run but the words were still readable and his wrinkled picture looked the same. He secured them in a dry place, hung up his wet clothes high up under the tent on a make-do clothesline, dug out and dressed in his old colorful, wrinkled, stinky suit and prepared to clean the fish, all the time shivering in the cold. He got on his knees and scaled the large fish. He knew the guts would draw in every varmint going down the river, so after cleaning the fish, he placed his cape over his head and ran the short distance to the river and threw the remains in the flowing water and then washed his fish. He saved some internal parts to be used the next morning for bait if it was raining and he was forced to stay there another day. That night he feasted on fish again, a meat he never tired of eating, and for the first time, he made a cup of hot coffee with lots of sugar.

He thought again of the girl he had left behind, not Bonnie, but his new attraction. He wanted to go back and he wrestled with whether he should or not. He didn't know this girl or what kind of family history came with her beautiful smile. If he went back he might do something that would ruin his life forever. He concluded the Devil was tempting his faithfulness to Bonnie. Finally, remembering his father's advice, he rolled over and yelled out, "Get behind me Satan. Leave me alone!" Soon after, he dozed off with a clean conscience, but as he slept he kept an ear alert for the sound of a baying bloodhound.

21

The next morning the drizzle had been replaced with dry crispy air and a blue sky; although quite cold, it was not freezing. Marcus was eager to get on the road, but did not want to leave his warm abode. He stirred his fire back to life and added some more wood. He remembered his bait under the rock and rather than let it go to waste, decided to try his luck in the river again. Maybe there was another scaly beast to be caught this morning. He secured his pole and bait and walked over to the river. He wanted to fish a few minutes before he started on his day's trek. If he was lucky he would take the time to cook what he caught.

As he threw a piece of fish liver in the water and watched it flow past him, he looked up stream and saw a white rowboat floating down the river, the occupant occasionally putting the oar in the water to paddle or slow the boat to keep it aligned with the flow. Marcus watched him approach; he seemed to use no effort guiding the boat, and it seemed, except for the cold, a great day to be out on the river, but Marcus knew it would be difficult rowing back upstream against the flow.

Suddenly, he felt the jerk on his line; the liver had worked, and he had another large fish. Wiser this time, and less hungry, he was not going to fall in the river again landing the fish. The young man watched Marcus as he fought the fish and started paddling hard to bring his boat over to help. He landed upstream and ran toward Marcus who was pulling the large fish out on the bank.

"That's a good haul," the man yelled as he came up to Marcus. This river is full of fish like that. I caught "hun'erds" of em in my lifetime on this here river." By his choice of words, the man seemed ignorant and uneducated, and appeared to be too old for the army with only a few snaggle teeth left. He was one of the skinniest men Marcus had ever seen. He stuck his hand out, "My name is 'Bones' Jones. My real name is Jeter Jones but my friends call me 'Bones.'"

That figures, Marcus thought as he held out his hand and shook the emaciated hand. The fellow had no visible firearms and appeared too feeble to do him harm. "This is only my second fish. I caught one last night for supper so I thought I would try it again before I broke camp this morning. Guess I'll have to clean and cook it now. Would you want some of it?" Marcus cheerfully offered his new friend. "It looks big enough for both of us."

"Shore would; I hadn't eaten no good stuff in a day or two. Been on the run down this river; want to get to Pittsburgh as soon as I can."

"If you're hungry, why didn't you stop in West Newton and get something to eat?"

"Ain't got no money."

"Here, clean this fish while I build up my fire." Marcus unhooked the flopping fish and handed it to him. "Got a knife?"

"Shore, a man can't live without a knife."

The men set about their chores and they soon had the fish cut in two and each man cooked the meat to his own satisfaction. Marcus noticed the chap held his fish close to the fire so it would burn and blacken the surface.

As they cooked, Marcus commented about the man's boat. "That's a good looking boat; looks brand new."

"It is. That's why I've got to get to Pittsburgh. There's a man down there waiting to buy this here boat. This is what I do to make a little money. I row boats down to Pittsburgh. There are several companies that make them up river thar but they sell most of 'em in Pittsburgh. They go on down the Ohio River from there."

"Yes, I saw them being built at West Newton."

"Yeah, but this uns' from higher up the river. I'm 'spose to meet a guy in Pittsburgh where the two rivers come together, you know'd, right thar where they meet. He's gonna pay me for the boat then." He hesitated to chew his fish, and looked up to see if Marcus was listening, "He's already bought the boat, but he's gonna pay me ten dollars to row it down there."

"Ten dollars!" Marcus replied raising his voice, "That's great pay for you floating down a river."

"Well, you know, it ain't that easy. You got to know the river; where the rapids are and all. In the summer I have to pull the boat over not too deep places. It's more work than you thank."

"How far is it to Pittsburgh? That's where I want to go? I need to get down to Kentucky."

"Ohhh, I figure it's about ten to twelve miles down to McKeesport and maybe another fifteen down to Pittsburgh. If you could flutter like a bird, I 'magine it wouldn't be more than fifteen mile' or more; the river turns back and forth, but it's shore easier to float the river than walk."

"Well, if you're going down there to Pittsburgh, would you let me ride along?"

The old man thought a minute, figuring some way he could make an extra dollar in the deal. "I guess you could ride along, but I would take two dollars for my trouble."

"I guess that sounds fair since I wouldn't be any trouble on the trip, but two dollars is too high, but since you owe me a dollar for eating my fish; that means I just owe you a dollar?" That irritated Marcus that the fellow would charge him anything after he fed him the fish.

The old geezer rolled his eyes up in his head, seriously thinking about the proposition, then looked Marcus straight in the eye. "That's the highest priced fish I ever ate, but I tell you what, young buck; would you like to make five dollars?"

"Why yes I would. What do you want me to do?"

"You see I wouldn't normally offer you a deal like this, 'cause I need the money myself, but I almost didn't agree to take this trip. Shortly before I left home, my wife got sick and she wanted me to stay thar. We argued whether I should go or not. I didn't thank she was that sick, but since I have been on the river coming down here, I begun to worry and feel bad about leaving her." He stopped talking and looked intently at Marcus again, "If you will give me five dollars to pay me for my time on the river coming down this far, I'll let you take the boat on down to Pittsburgh. You can meet the feller and get ten dollars, making a profit of five dollars. That's a good deal for both of us."

"How will I find the buyer?"

"See that number thar on the boat, number eighty-seven. Just go and tie up where the two rivers meet and he will find you. He is expecting me tomorrow or the next day so 'spect he will be down thar about noon. Just tie up and he knows what the boat looks like and the number. You won't have any trouble. I've dealt with him many times. He's an honest man."

"If I do this, are there any waterfalls or dangerous places in the river between here and Pittsburgh?"

"Naw, like I said, there's a few rough places upstream, but you'll have a smooth river from here on down."

"Then I'll do it." Marcus was excited over his good fortune. He could float the river and avoid sheriffs and soldiers, lessening the likelihood he would be discovered as a Rebel soldier. "Let's shake on it then," Marcus replied as he threw down the last fish bone he was nibbling on, bent over and shook hands with "Bones."

Marcus stood up, brushed the fish crumbs from his lap, kicked dirt on the fire, grabbed up his gear and walked toward the boat with "Bones" behind him. "I've never been in a boat this big where you use two paddles at the same time. Show me how you work the paddles."

"If you got common sense, you'll figure it out by the time you've gone down the river a 'hunerd' yards. Most of the time, you let the river do the work and you just ride."

Marcus broke camp, threw his stuff in the back seat of the boat and climbed inside and sat between the two oars in the middle seat. He took the paddles and pretended to row. "Is this how I do it?"

"That's it. I think you got it already, but turn around and face backward and row by pulling back on the oars; makes it easier on yo're back. Hadn't you ever seen a man row a boat?"

"Yeah, but back home most of the boats were small; we just sit at the front of the boat so we can paddle with one oar on either side of the boat." Marcus rearranged himself and fanned the oars in the air. "I think I got it now. Push me off and let me get underway."

"I need five dollars, and then I'll push you off."

So excited, anticipating his new toy, Marcus had forgotten about paying the man. "Oh, I'm sorry. I am so anxious to get gone I forgot about the five dollars." He was wearing the red coat that had the money inside, but not completely trusting his new friend, he didn't want him to see where he hid his money. Marcus jumped out of the boat, "I'll be right back. Before I get on the river I need to tend to some business." He ran into the woods a short ways until he was hidden, took his jacket off, and secured a five dollar bill. He counted his money; he was down to eight dollars now with a long ways yet to travel. He returned, "I thought I had better go do that before I got out in that boat." He reached in his pocket and handed "Bones" a five dollar bill like it had been in there all along.

"Thank you sir," Bones replied as he pocketed the money.

"How are you going to get back up the river?"

"Walk; it's not that far. The road is purdy straight. Everybody knows me around here and I can usually find a ride in a wagon or help somebody row back up the river. Don't worry, son; I'll get home. Get in; I'll push you away."

The two scooted the large heavy boat back in the water and Marcus got in and took his position between the oars and "Bones" pushed him into the flow of the river. "So long, thanks for the boat."

"You're welcome. Enjoy the trip." With that the two men departed and Marcus slowly floated down the river. He wanted to get used to the boat and started paddling downstream. He found he could turn the front of the boat to the left by using only the right oar and to the right by using the left oar. He could increase his speed by rowing with both oars, but when he did that, it was hard to see where he was going. Over time, Marcuse preferred facing the direction he was floating, and he discovered he could easily turn the boat by dragging one of the oars in the water; drag right oar or paddle backward to turn right; drag the left oar to turn left.

The river was wide and he soon mastered the steering and for the most part, stayed in the center flow of the river. Once in a while, when a slow eddy pulled the boat out of the main flow, Marcus had to paddle to correct his direction. He remembered what "Bones" told him about letting the river do the work. As the river worked and he relaxed he decided to try to catch another meal for supper. Marcus had saved a piece of raw fish for this very thing. He put a piece of juicy raw fish on his hook and wondered how any fish could resist a meal like that. He hung his pole out of the back and trolled down the river. He hoped he would cross over one of those "holes" and he would catch a whopper for supper.

The river followed a twisted waterway that it had cut through the mountains over thousands of years. Around noon he came to McKeesport, a town where the Youghiogheny joins the Monongahela River. McKeesport was a city bustling with industry founded on coal and steel. A mill with a tall smoke stack that the town was centered around belched forth smoke. Many barges and steamers were tied next to the river. The war had increased the demand for steel and other metals and the air was full of sooty, black, coal smoke. A gray glaze was in the air that coated everything. Marcus pulled in his pole and decided to fish again later. He noticed the water was changing colors and had a muddy-gray appearance on the McKeesport side of the river that slowly dirtied the entire river.

The river was also busy with water craft. Marcus took full command of his ship from the flow of the river and paddled through the town avoiding another vessel here and there. When he was past the growing city, he put the oars down and let the river take over again, pushing his boat through the river valley. A half mile out of town, he noticed two men on dark brown horses who seemed to take interest in his presence. As he went by, they turned their horses down river, riding along at the same speed as his boat.

Was it a coincidence that they turned and started down river as he passed or were they following him? After a mile, Marcus feared the latter and steered the boat to the other side of the river away from the riders. Could they possibly be deputies from Greensburg and had they finally caught up with him?

The two men mixed in with more and more people as he descended toward Pittsburgh. He passed people working in small villages and men on horseback and wagons traveling the shoreline. As he got closer to Pittsburgh he passed vessels of all sizes and descriptions going up and down the river. Some were being poled by several men; some were small steamers carrying cargoes. But there were the two men, staying right with him.

Marcus became frightened at what these men wanted. He concluded two possibilities; one it was the man who was going to pay him, or secondly, they were deputies who had somehow discovered his escape route and had caught up with him.

Pittsburgh was much bigger than McKeesport with steel mills filling the sky with dark ugly smoke. The smell of burning coal and hot iron saturated the air. It was obvious he was entering an industrial area. Foundries and steel mills were everywhere. The sound of hammers striking hot steel could be heard in all directions echoing over the river.

Marcus saw a bridge crossing the river ahead of him. Before he went under the span, one of the riders had ridden ahead and waited above him as he approached and yelled out while pointing at Marcus, "Sir, you in the white skiff; land immediately, I want to talk to you."

"What about?" Marcus yelled back, but staying on course.

"Your boat, it's about your boat."

Marcus was relieved. It was the boat owner after all. Marcus yelled back, "I'll meet you where you were to meet "Bones." He noticed the rider did not join his friend, but crossed on over the river and continued to stay up with him. Now, there was a rider on both sides of the river. Marcus could only conclude they didn't trust him and must fear he might try to steal it. Marcus steered his ship to the middle of the wide river making each of the horsemen look small. At that point, Marcus estimated the river was a thousand feet wide.

Marcus started paddling hard to reach the Pittsburgh side of the river before he passed the town and got caught in the Allegheny River merging with the Monongahela. The meeting place was to be at the confluence of these rivers. He slowed down and let the river float him close to shore. He could see the different color of the other river water coming in from the right. He paddled toward a small pier. The rider who had spoken to him from the bridge ran out on the pier to help him dock the boat. As Marcus neared the dock, another rider rode up and hurried to help.

Marcus paddled backward with his oars to slow the wooden boat as he approached the pier. Marcus went to the front and grabbed a rope and threw it to one of the men who pulled the boat in, almost causing Marcus to lose his balance and sit down. The middle aged man tied the rope to the pier and mentioned to his partner, "Yeah, this is number eighty-seven, the one we're hunting." Marcus stood up to step out and saw he was looking at the business end of two revolvers.

"Sir, you are under arrest for theft," one of the men said as he pushed his coat back to reveal the star of a lawman.

"Theft? Theft? What did I steal?"

"Raise your hands and step out of the boat."

"What have I done?" Marcus pleaded.

"This boat; you stole this boat from West Newton."

"No sir! I am delivering this boat to a man who is going to buy it down here where the rivers meet."

"Where did you get this boat?"

"From a man I met on the river when I was walking down here. He said his name was 'Bones' Jones. I met him south of West Newton. I was fishing and he saw me catch a large fish. He looked like he was starving to death so I offered him half of my fish which we cleaned and cooked."

Marcus noticed one of the lawmen had put his gun away and the other had lowered his waiting to hear Marcus's entire story.

"We started talking and I asked him if he would let me ride with him down here to Pittsburgh since he was going this way."

The lawman started to smile, "Go ahead, I'm listening."

"He told me he would for two dollars, and I told him that price was too high and I didn't have much money. We decided on a dollar, but then he offered me a better deal."

The sheriff, holding the gun, also placed it in his holster, and said, "Let me finish your story. He was going to get ten dollars from a man down here when he brought him the boat."

"That's right! How did you know?"

"We know who 'Bones' Jones is. He's a thief who steals boats and offers young men like you an opportunity to make five dollars; am I not right?"

"Yes, that's right."

"And you paid him five dollars for his half of the trip?"

"Yes, you've got it exactly."

"Well, son, we are going to have to confiscate this skiff and get it back upstream or sell it here and send the builders their money." He hesitated a moment, then added, "I hate to tell you this, but you lost your five dollars."

Marcus smiled back, "That's all right. I got to ride in a boat, rather than having to walk; so maybe it was a little expensive, but I got here safe and no harm."

Then Marcus heard a question that put a chill down his spine, "By the way, where are you going. It looks like you ought to be in the army."

"I was in the army, sir. I fought at Sharpsburg about three or four weeks ago and all the battles before it. Sir, I was completely wore out, and my captain told me to go home for the winter, that I had been a good soldier. He figured the fighting was over for the winter and I wouldn't be needed 'till next spring."

"Where are you headed?"

"Kentucky, sir, south of Louisville."

The two lawmen looked at each other and smiled, "That's why he talks like a southerner…. Kentucky." Then asked, "Do you have your furlough papers?"

"I did, but I lost them in the river when I fell in catching a big fish. I had them sticking right here in my coat pocket and when I hit the water they floated away, but I can show you something just as good."

"What's that?"

Marcus took his coat off and unbuttoned his shirt. He pulled the shirt back so the two lawmen could see an awful scar in his shoulder where he had been wounded at Fair Oaks. "This is my proof I am a soldier."

The two lawmen looked at each other and one of them said, "Put your shirt on boy. I believe you. Gather your stuff up and go on home." One of the deputies reached in his back pocket and pulled out his leather wallet and pulled out a dollar bill and handed it out to Marcus, "This isn't your five but at least it might help you a little. I admire boys like you fighting for our country."

The other officer, seeing what his partner did, and also having sympathy for the lad, offered him another dollar. "This will give you two dollars; I'd like to give you more, but I have a family at home I have to feed."

Marcus at first refused the money, feeling guilty for the lie he was portraying in front of these kind men. They insisted so Marcus took the money and thanked them several times while he shook their hands. The two men secured the boat, and then one turned to Marcus again, "So you're going to Louisville?"

"Yes sir."

"Are you gonna walk down there?"

"I planned to, but after finding it so it easy floatin' down the river I'd like to get another boat someway. I think that boat spoiled me about walking. Would you know where I might buy an old boat for two dollars?" Marcus grinned as he held up his new money.

"To tell you the truth, boats are much sought around here, there's always somebody needing a cheap way to go down the river so they don't stay around long." He hesitated and thought a minute. "Come to think of it, there's an old boat builder up the Allegheny there about two miles. He sells old boats and if he likes you sometimes he'll nearly give you one, but he can be awfully ornery sometimes, and, by the way, if you manage to find one, be careful going down the river, there are a lot of pirates who prey on loners like you." He looked up and down at Marcus and his gear on the pier, "And you aren't armed are you?"

"I've got a large knife, hatchet, and this walking stick."

"You need a firearm. These hooligans leave people alone if they see they are armed." He thought a minute more, "Get your stuff and get on the back of the horse with me. Back in the office I have several guns we have taken off people breaking the law. I wouldn't do this for anybody, but I want to reward you for your bravery and give you a pistol. I'll also find you a rifle that should help you get home safely."

"I can shoot me some food too," Marcus added. "I had several chances from the boat to shoot something to eat if I had a rifle."

The head lawman told the other deputy to stay with the boat until he sent someone to row it to a safe locale. Marcus and the lawman left and approached the downtown area not far from the river. Because the war business was booming, business men were scurrying between tall brick buildings, crossing crowded streets, avoiding the throngs of horses, mules, and wagons. Marcus had never seen such a busy place.

The deputy stopped in front of a large three-story brick building. The two dismounted and Marcus followed the deputy up a flight of stone stairs into a large room. The lawman led Marcus down a hall and into a room with several desks. "This is where I work when I'm not out on a job. Hubert, the deputy you met earlier and I handle crimes committed along the river for the most part. Have a seat."

The deputy called for a man in the next office to stick his head in the door, "What you need boss?"

"Go back there to the armory and get me a pistol in good condition and a rifle with a shoulder strap. Bring me some paper cartridges for both. No, instead bring me a powder horn and a box of prepared cartridges. This man here is a soldier who needs some protection so he can get home for the winter. I want to help him if I can."

"Be right back boss. I'll see what we got." In a few minutes the man returned with two arms that looked new along with a cartridge box that could be carried on a man's belt. "These should perform well. I have checked them out and they seemed to work fine."

The deputy handed Marcus his guns and wished him good luck. Marcus thanked him and told the deputy how nice people had been to him in these parts. Marcus turned to leave the room but turned back and asked the deputy one more question, "Where does that man stay that sells the boats you told me about?" The deputy grabbed two sheets of paper and scribbled a note on one piece of paper and a map on the other and handed it to Marcus. "It's not far across the river and maybe this note will put him in a friendlier mood. Marcus bid him goodbye and thanked him one more time.

Marcus returned to the busy street and followed the directions. After he got out of sight of the sheriff's office he opened the letter and read, "Dear Mr. Dunigan, The young man who gives you this letter is a soldier who has been wounded in the war and is trying to get home on winter furlough. He is trying to get to Louisville and wants to purchase a small boat. As a favor to me, please try to help him if you see fit, Sincerely, Deputy Alvin Allen." Marcus folded the short letter and placed it in his coat pocket.

He only had five dollars and a few coins. He knew he needed a boat to make his trek easier, so he decided to play his last card. He stopped near the river and took his shoe off and untied the ring around his toe. Marcus pitched the ring up and down trying to estimate whether he had an ounce of gold or not. From his location he could see a boat shop across the river, but he needed to sell the ring in case he had to fork up some cash. He did not expect the grumpy old man he was going to meet to give him much of a break. Marcus turned and walked back to the busier part of town and looked for a jeweler. He soon found three stores on the same crowded street, selected one, and went in.

The owner was out, but his wife asked if she might help him. A young man in a jeweler's store meant he wanted to purchase a ring for his future wife, buy a watch, or sell something. Marcus had on his old red coat and ochre pants, both wrinkled and dirty, and did not look like a person fit to be in a jewelry store. "Yes, I 'spect you can," Marcus said as he reached deep in his pants pocket and pulled out the gold ring. "You're probably going to figure I stole this ring, so will you read this letter from the deputy sheriff?"

She walked closer to Marcus to retrieve the letter, "Are you in trouble with the law."

"Oh, no ma'am; read the letter and you'll know what I need." She looked down and read, her lips moving slightly as her eyes scanned over the letter. She stopped and folded the letter and gave it back to Marcus.

"Where did you get this ring?" the lady asked.

"I found it on the battlefield over at Sharpsburg."

"Were you there in that horrible battle?" she asked.

"Yes ma'am, I was in the middle of it and I am lucky to be in your presence, but that's where I found the ring," he said as he handed her the large gold ring. She took it and rolled it between her fingers examining all the surfaces. After a few moments of silence, he added, "It was on a hand." The morbid image shocked the lady and she dropped the ring on the glass counter. "It was on a hand; the hand of a dead soldier?"

I don't know if the man was dead, but I knew his hand was. Actually, it was just on a finger attached to a bloody hand lying on the ground. Matter of fact, I saw lots of jewelry on the dead soldiers, but to take it was too much like stealing and against my upbringing to steal from the dead, but in the middle of the battle, when I was crawling across the ground I saw this ring on just a hand; I didn't figure the hand would need it and I might be able to use it later so I pulled it off. As you see I want to sell it now and buy a boat to go down river if I can afford it."

The lady had been shaken by his words, but this time she took her handkerchief out and picked up the ring again, using her handkerchief to polish it and remove any dull blemishes that might be traces of dried blood. If she was repulsed by the hand, he didn't want to tell her it had been tied between his dirty toes.

She took a magnifying glass and looked at it closely, "Oh look, there is a date inside. Hmmm, it looks like 1814."

"Could I see," Marcus asked. After looking, "I didn't see that. Will that make the ring more valuable?"

"Not for the gold value, but possibly, if we knew its history, it might be real valuable."

"I just need as much as I can get. Like the letter said, I need to get home."

"Let me weigh it," she said as she turned and walked to another table as a man entered the store. "Good morning, dear," she said as her husband came in. "Did he buy the ring?"

"Yes, he did," answering her question about a previous customer.

He noticed the shabbily dressed young man standing in front of his wife as she examined the gold ring. "What are you looking at?"

"Come and look. This ring is a survivor of the battle at Antietam Creek. This young man survived the battle and found this ring on the hand of a dead person."

The man seriously looked at Marcus, "You mean you took this ring off of a corpse?"

"No sir, I told your wife I took it off of a hand I crawled over during the battle. There was no corpse, just a hand."

"I'll explain later, dear. He wants to sell it so he can get home for winter." She looked at Marcus, "Let him read your letter, he might give you more money."

The owner read the letter. "That's interesting. I know Deputy Allen. He's a good man." He focused back on the ring. "Let me see it dear."

After a quick examination, he looked up, "I'll give you twenty-five dollars for the ring, plus five dollars to help you get home, a gift from my wife and me. Is that a deal?

"I don't know what gold sells for, but thirty dollars is more than I have now." Marcus thought a second, "Yes, I'll take it."

The jeweler assured him it was a fair price, opened his wallet and paid Marcus the agreed amount. He then asked Marcus to write down a brief account concerning where he found the ring and sign the document.

Marcus agreed, but said he didn't write very well, but if the jeweler would write out what he said Marcus would sign it. The lady volunteered to write what Marcus dictated, then Marcus picked up the pen, dipped in the ink well, then hesitated and thought a moment, then signed his name. He started to write Jacob Stone, his Yankee name, but he realized he told the sheriff his name was Marcus. He didn't want to get caught in one of his lies again.

"You write very nicely," the lady complimented Marcus. Marcus thanked them for their generosity and stepped out the front door but stopped so he could listen inside. He hoped he might hear a comment on the deal he had just made. It was hard to hear a voice from inside, but he heard the lady say, "You overpaid that boy. That ring was only half gold."

"I know, but he needed the money. Someday this may be worth something for its historical value. Antietam will be a famous battlefield one day."

Marcus smiled, feeling secure that he had gotten a good price for his ring.

22

Marcus strolled proudly down the sidewalk, having renewed his monetary resources, and confident that he might purchase a craft that could carry him down the river, and avoid the long trek overland. He was beginning to appreciate this river style of traveling. He returned to the bridge and saw the place that matched the spot on the map. As he crossed the bridge he saw many barges driven by steam plowing the river below him. In the south, he had never seen so many factories and shops producing iron and wooden products.

Marcus walked up in front of the boat yard and read an old sign that needed to be refreshed with new paint. In large letters it read, "The River Rider;" in small letters under the title it continued, "If it floats we make it here." Marcus definitely wanted something that would float him to Louisville.

As he walked up the worn rocky path to the shop, Marcus heard hammering inside and although it looked deserted, when he peeked through the window, he saw numerous people going about their trade, shaping wood and assembling boats. Some of the boats were small, but he noticed outside under a tall shed, a large river steamer was being assembled. He entered and stood in the doorway watching the workers who seemed to have no interest in him being there. After five minutes he saw an old man, rather stoop-shouldered, showing many years in a bent over-occupation, come in the back door and finally notice Marcus. He approached with a scowl on his face; not seeming to appreciate Marcus being in his shop, looked up at Marcus and asked in a gruff, loud voice, "Well, don't just stand there, tell me what you want. I got work to do." Marcus remembered the deputy said he wasn't the friendliest person in the world, but if he liked you, you would be fine.

The old man looked as if he had not smiled in years; his lips created a perfect arc, not smiling, but frowning, and acted as though everyone he talked to was a foreigner trespassing on his time and property.

Marcus handed him the deputy's letter which brought a gruff reply, "What's this for," he yelled as if he was angry with Marcus as he reached out and jerked it from Marcus's hand. He mumbled something as he gave Marcus a stern stare and reached in his top pocket to retrieve a pair of spectacles. He pulled the spectacles over his ears and read the letter, much faster than he appeared capable of doing. Marcus didn't think his first encounter with the old boat builder was going well, expecting to be thrown out of his shop at any moment.

He stopped reading and lowered the letter and spoke softly and respectfully to Marcus. "So you fought at Antietam Creek. I have been reading about that in the newspaper." All of a sudden, the man had a complete change in his demeanor. He stuck his hand out to shake Marcus's hand, "Good afternoon, my name is Henry Dunigan, "Come in here and talk with me about this boat you need," as he put his hand on Marcus's back and steered him into his office. Marcus didn't know whether to reply or not, but finally said, "Yes sir, I was there. I have been at all the battles except the first one."

"Sit down; you are a brave boy; make yourself comfortable." Eager to get first-hand knowledge about the terrible battle, he said, "Tell me more about the Antietam skirmish. I am a veteran of the Mexican War myself, and I enjoy stories about that business. Tell me about where you fought." Marcus began by describing the awful carnage at Antietam and what he had seen during the battle, always remembering to tell it from the Union side. He combined his images from earlier battles and soon wove a tale that created a tapestry of heroic proportions. As he talked, the old man would lean over and tilt his head so he wouldn't miss hearing each word Marcus spoke. Every now and then he would smile when Marcus described a small Union victory on the battlefield; Marcus knew he was excited with what he was saying. After half an hour, Marcus ended up, "And that's how I got here. Deputy Allen said you might be able to help me." Marcus hoped his story had softened the old man's heart and help him get a boat.

"That's remarkable young man. You are lucky to be alive. Thank you for telling me your story."

The old man leaned back in his rocking chair and looked up at the ceiling as if he was pondering how to solve a problem. He then pulled a small bag of chewing tobacco out of a drawer and offered Marcus a wad. "No, thank you. My father gave me a chaw and told me to try it before I went in the war." Marcus grinned, "I can honestly say, nothing in this war has made me as sick as that chaw of tobacco."

The old man laughed and pinched off a chaw and put it in his mouth and began to chew and talk, occasionally leaning over and spitting in a spittoon beside his desk. "Deputy Allen says here in your letter that you want to go down the river to Louisville." All of a sudden Marcus was looking at a new man; the hard exterior had been replaced by a gentle soul. "Let's see, Cincinnati as I recall, is about 375 miles from here as the river flows, and I think, Louisville is a little farther, maybe 525 miles, give or take a few miles. Riding with the flow I imagine you could make twenty to thirty miles a day. The river flows about three mile an hour on an average, sometimes faster and sometimes slower depending on the rain and the width of the river. Have you got any idea what kind of boat you want?"

"No sir, I paddled a stolen boat down here from below West Newton though." Before Marcus could continue the old man interrupted him and even laughed to Marcus's amazement.

"Ohhh, I see now how you met Deputy Allen. He caught you didn't he."

"Yes sir, but I didn't steal the boat. An old man named 'Bones' Jones came down the river when I was fishing and," the old man butted in again, "Tell me no more. I know what he did. I know all about old 'Bones.'" He clipped me once and I never got my boat back. He ought to be hung. I thought he had gone on down the river to work his scams, but he must have come back now."

"He clipped me out of five dollars," Marcus added. After I told the deputies my story, they felt sorry for me and they each gave me a dollar to help me get home."

"Speaking of money, how much can you spend on a boat? That will give me idea what kind of boat to look for. Matter of fact, I have an old canoe out there I'd let you have for only a few dollars. It leaks a little, but it'll get you down the river."

"I never paddled a canoe. I understand you can get dumped in the river if you're not careful."

"Yes, you must be careful in one, but they are light, and you can pull them over log jams and rocks, even portage them overland if you need to, but I have a better idea." Marcus could not believe this was the same grouchy old man he had met a half hour earlier. After hearing that, Marcus sensed the old man appreciated his predicament and was going to help him. Then he suggested they go out in the boat yard and see what they might find.

The two men began to look at the boats. Marcus pointed to one that was similar to the boat he had brought down stream. "I really enjoyed this kind of boat. It was stable on the water, easy to row and steer and I had plenty of room. When I was floating down here I imagined how comfortable it would be to have a canvas top you could get under, you know," Marcus said excitedly, "Like a covered wagon, but only smaller."

"A tent would be a good idea, but in the wind it could be dangerous. It would also act like a sail that at times you didn't want."

"Then maybe just use it to sleep under and erect it when the wind was right. Might even help push you along. It's just an idea I had."

"Well, I'll think about it and see what I can come up with."

Marcus laughed, "It would also be handy to bring an old iron wash pot on board so you could build a fire, too. The legs would keep it off the bottom of the boat so it wouldn't catch on fire."

The old man added, "How about a bed? Maybe I could figure a way to build the seats so you could have a large flat place to lie on…. yes that would be perfect for traveling the river." The old man got excited about the idea. "Let's go inside and let me put some ideas down on paper. I think we have an idea here. If this works out, I might sell these one-of-a-kind boats for people traveling downstream. However, it's pretty cheap now to buy a ticket down to New Orleans on a river steamer."

Marcus watched the old man sketch out his new ideas. He would stop and go outside and take measurements from the boat Marcus was familiar with. It was getting dark and Marcus saw the men hang up their tools and go home for the evening, all stopping by the office and checking out with, "I'll see you in the morning."

Marcus stepped outside a moment to use the outhouse, and one of Dunigan's workers told Marcus, that is the way the boss behaves when he focuses on a new boat. He added, "He appears to be a bitter old man, but deep inside he is very kind, and if he likes you he will do anything for you," repeating what he had heard earlier from the deputy. "My house burned down last Christmas and we had no place to stay. We lost everything, but when he heard about my tragedy the next day, he stopped all the work here at the boat yard and brought all his workers out to my house. We cleaned up the site and in three days we had a new house, better than the one that burned. He said I could pay him back by working an extra half hour a day for a year. I might add this too, he is also a genius. I might warn you, I have seen him stay up all night working on an idea." The worker said good night and departed in the evening light.

Marcus returned inside. The old man only stopped long enough to light two lamps so he could see in the fading daylight, seemingly oblivious now to his surroundings. He continued to work into the night on his new idea. He had all but forgotten about Marcus, but about nine o'clock he eased back from his drawing table and gave a long sigh. "I think that will do it." He turned and looked at Marcus, "I'll pull some men off other jobs tomorrow, and I'll give them these plans. We'll pull that old boat in the shed here and check it out for cracks and leaks; seal it again, and add the changes. I didn't want to make the canvas top too high and let it catch too much wind and blow you over." He scratched his head, "But if you get caught in high winds with the tent up, I would head for shore and tie up until the wind died down. However, if it is blowing you forward, it may act as a sail and speed you up as you mentioned. It's got a wide flat bottom, but it doesn't have a keel."

After watching the man labor over his plans and talk about this new boat, Marcus spoke up, "Mr. Dunigan, I think you have put more into this boat than I can afford to pay for. At the most I can only pay you twenty-five dollars."

"Forget it son. I am going to loan you this boat for your duty in the war. If I could, I would give you two boats for every one of those Rebels you killed. I'm getting old and have no children. My workers are my children and people like you who come by needing help. I hope the good Lord remembers my good deeds when I am gone."

"If this man knew who I really was, he would kill me himself," Marcus thought. He felt guilty taking advantage of people's kindness, but it was war, and he had been thrust into a situation he didn't appreciate either. He just wanted to go home and see Bonnie.

Finally the old man took his spectacles off and stared at Marcus and asked the question Marcus had expected all day, "Before I build this boat, I need to know one thing, where did you get that heavy southern drawl. You said your home was in Louisville, but you sound like you come from farther south?"

Marcus had rehearsed his answer many times in his head and was ready to explain. "Yes sir, I do have quite a twang. When I was a young'un we lived below Nashville several miles. My father would bring his crop of cotton to Nashville to sell. While he was there, he met a man who offered him a job in Louisville to help him purchase cotton. I was too young to remember moving, but I got my twang from my mother and father. When I got older, my father's boss sent me north to begin schooling. That's when the war broke out so I just joined the Union Army with my school friends. Believe me, my accent has nearly gotten me killed several times; people think I am a Rebel spy."

"I see. I understand where you come from." He stood up and pulled his watch out of his pocket, "My, my, it's getting late. Come with me Marcus; you can stay with us tonight. I would like for you to meet my wife. I often come home late and she will have super ready for us. She'll have plenty." With that, he blew the lanterns out and they walked next door to a two-story house.

When Mrs. Dunigan saw Marcus's filthy condition she insisted he take a bath after supper and let her wash those filthy clothes. While they ate, she filled the tub in their indoor bathroom with water that she heated on the stove. After a hot meal, Marcus retrieved his new, rolled up, store bought clothes and entered the bath, switched Bonnie's letter and his money to his new garments and poked his old colorful suit out the door for Mrs. Dunigan to wash for him. As Marcus lay in the hot water, he thought about how God had blessed him and led him through the valley of death even though he had lied to save his life. Marcus felt guilty about his sin. He reflected back to the lowest point in his life, lying in the cornfield covered in blood and feces. As he rubbed the warm soapy washrag over his arms, he said a silent prayer, thanking God for guiding his path through all the dangers he had encountered.

This was Marcus's first hot bath since staying with Genia. He was aware he smelled awful. He soaped up his head and washed and scrubbed his hair. When he finished his cleansing and emerged from the bath he looked like a new man. The lady had already washed his suit and had it hung up near the stove. "These things will be dry by morning, I expect."

"Mrs. Dunigan, you didn't have to do all this. It's getting late. I could have washed them tomorrow."

"Yes I did, if you're going to stay in my house. You were a little rank before you bathed," she smiled, being very frank with Marcus. "Now that you're clean, follow me upstairs and bring your things."

She escorted him to a guest room upstairs and opened a closet door where Marcus could store his meager belongings and leave his guns. Mr. Dunigan told Marcus he could stay at his house while they reconditioned the old boat.

The next day, workers pitched in and took the ideas the old man had drawn and applied them to the old boat, using tools and techniques Marcus had never seen. He tried to run errands and make himself useful, but for the most part, stayed out of the way, letting the craftsmen do their work. By late afternoon of the third day, a coat of red paint was applied and an old iron wash pot was secured near the stern.

Two round heavy dowels, slightly larger than a broom handle could be inserted vertically in metal brackets to form masts near the front and back of the boat. A rope could be tied at the front, laced through metal eyelets at the top of each mast and then tied tightly at the rear, creating a rope spine down the entire length. A canvas could then be thrown over the rope and secured along each side forming a tent, with flaps overlapping the sides, preventing rain from entering the boat except at the ends. A canvas flap was sewn in at each end of the tent that could be rolled up and tied when it was fair and sunny or lowered and secured when it was cold and rainy.

After renovation, the middle seat was closer to the stern, leaving more room for a bed in the front by unfolding the flat seats, like opening a book, to fill in and level the space between the front and middle seats. When the tent was up, it covered the bed and was closer to the front leaving more room to move around in the stern.

The boat genius had designed a rudder that Marcus could steer with his feet by pushing a right or left pedal attached to the rudder with small cables from a position at the rear of the tent. The boat was finished and ready to be launched, but the man insisted Marcus wait several more days until he could apply several coats of red paint; so Marcus stayed with the boat builder and his wife for another week, ate well, and gained his strength for the adventure ahead. On the morning of his departure, Marcus noticed that during the night, Mr. Dunigan had one of his skilled workers paint the word Bonnie on each side of the boat near the front and along the back, letting the rudder split her name.

Marcus realized his new "old friend" had put much effort and money into this boat and insisted that he pay him in some way. Mr. Dunigan told Marcus he was loaning him the boat so he could float to Louisville, and there, leave the unique vessel with a boat dealer named McKenzie who he did business with in Louisville. Then a steamer could tow it back to Pittsburgh when it came upstream.

23

After seven days both coats of bright red paint were dry. Marcus secured his gear in the special storage compartments under the seat. Over the past week he had been introduced to friends of the boat workers and they brought him extra food, blankets, more fishing hooks and lines, and other small items he might need on his journey. A bracket was made on the back corner of the boat that would hold a long cane pole in a vertical position, making his fishing line available on a moment's notice. Another neighbor brought him a tin container filled with large worms. One lady had even baked him a cake to take along and wood was stacked in the wash pot. One of the metal craftsmen had made a spit and grill that could sit on top of the wash pot providing Marcus with a convenient grill. Marcus had also purchased some tools including an axe and three metal buckets that fit inside each other. He could use the buckets to bail water in case his boat got flooded in a heavy rain.

During construction, Marcus had mentioned Deputy Allen's warning to be alert for river pirates. As a result of the conversation, the ship designer installed a thick wooden board on hinges on each side of the boat that could be raised to provide more protection from small arms fire. This boat was truly a work of nautical art that had not been seen on the river before. Mr. Dunigan added, "If you choose to, with this rig you could run past the guns down at Vicksburg," he thought a minute, and added, "If I was thirty years, younger, I'd just jump in there and go with you!"

Everyone laughed. They were so pleased to see their old grumpy boss enjoying himself. Since Marcus had arrived, the old man had taken on a new demeanor, focusing on the construction of this new boat and helping this young man get home. They all knew down deep he was a kind man with a tough façade, who lost his snort and horns and turned into a gentle lamb under the right state of affairs.

The men rolled the boat down to the river. The tent was packed up under one of the seats. Marcus tried to pay him for his kindness again, but like the owner of the eatery, the boat builder refused to accept any compensation from a soldier going home. Marcus gave each and every one a big hug, got in his new home, and waved to all who had helped him and told them he would write them when he got home, and he would leave the boat in Louisville.

With that goodbye, one of the workers untied his boat; Marcus took an oar and pushed against the pier that launched him into the current of the Allegheny River that within two miles joined the Monongahela to form the mighty Ohio River. Although his new ship was heavier than the other, and two feet longer, it steered well. He tested his new rudder, but it seemed slow to respond since he was floating the same speed as the river. He would drag a paddle in the water to turn the boat left or right. He waved to all his new friends who had been so kind. All were waving, wishing him the best, but as he got farther away, they became sad knowing they would never see the handsome young man again. They would miss his pleasant company.

It was a nice, cool, fall day; it had rained during the previous week, and Marcus looked forward to his new adventure with much excitement. He would soon be home. He had all of the weapons loaded and was prepared for whatever came his way. For the first time in many months, he felt totally free setting forth on a new adventure.

Marcus sat near the center of the boat facing forward so he could manage the oars and see what lay ahead in the river. He adjusted to the handling of the boat and let the river do its work, pushing him closer to home at about three miles an hour, only dragging the water with a paddle to straighten his craft. "This is better than a horse or steam engine," he thought. "I don't have to feed it oats, coal or water. This is going to be a good trip."

He watched the smokestacks and houses of the city grow smaller and less human activity on shore as he floated out of town, only seeing a lone farm building or a fisherman running his trotlines, but he was astounded by the amount of traffic on the river. Every few miles he noticed large stacks of firewood on small rafts tied to the shore and reckoned it was cut for the people in the larger cities. He soon observed, however, the wood was sold to steamboats that would pick up a load of wood and leave an empty barge to be filled later.

One of his new friends had given him a compass to help him navigate, but it did not matter; he had to go with the flow of the river. He watched the needle that indicated he was moving northwest for a while and then north. Later in the day he saw that he had turned and was going southwest. It was a cool day, but he was comfortable doing little work to keep the boat in the center of the river and avoid the heavy river traffic. After he turned back south he estimated he had three hours of daylight and decided to catch a fish to fry that night. He had all the ingredients to cook it up right. He had grown tired of the sweets he had nibbled on all day.

He took down the long pole rising eight feet above his head and removed the small red flag someone had attached, baited the hook and hung it over the side while steering the boat closer to the bank, expecting the fish to be in shallow water. Within a few minutes he hooked a nice two pound fish using the worms for bait. He pulled it in and dropped it on the floor where it flopped a few minutes before it died. It wasn't long until he had another, then another. He had enough fish and not wanting to waste his worms, he decided to land and come ashore in a remote place away from people to camp.

He feared traveling at night; he wanted more time to adjust to his new environment and learn the ways of the river. He did not fear the pirates yet; they were more apt to be in the remote areas of the river far from the big cities.

The river banks were high and close to the water on the northwestern side, but low and spread out on the southeastern making it possible for people to establish farms in the flat river bottoms. He noticed a small cove against a steep cliff that would be almost unapproachable by land. There was a small rocky beach to land his boat. It looked like a perfect site to camp.

He steered the boat into the bank and looked for a flat space where the boat could run up on the bank without hitting a rock. He saw a flat sandy place and paddled hard to run the heavy boat ashore. Because he and the wash pot were at the back, the nose was slightly out of the water and went ashore as planned, but not far enough to anchor it, so the stern, still in the current, was pushed around and was about to suck the boat off shore, but Marcus jumped out holding the front tie line and pulled it up the rest of the way, just enough to keep it from floating away.

The beach, if you could call it that, was not very wide and became very steep as one moved away from the river. But Marcus did not need much space to clean three fish. There was really no reason for him to land except to get off the river at night. He had everything he needed in the boat. His wash pot stove was there stoked with wood and ready to light. His new spit and grill were stored under the seat next to extra firewood, and he was going to set up his new tent and sleep inside his new house boat that night.

Rather than use the specially cut firewood stored in his boat, he took the wood out of the pot and stored it for later use. He got out on the rocky shore and gathered a few pieces of driftwood and small limbs that had fallen down the cliff. He noticed a spot between two rocks that was sooty and the obvious place that had been used by many river travelers over the years. He retrieved some leaves and twigs for kindling and started a fire in his wash pot stove.

He discovered, as he tried to move around on the boat, that space between the seats had been sacrificed to storage bins along the sides, and what space he had was filled with tools and gear like his spit and grill. He set the grill over the fire and cleaned the fish on shore as the flames turned into hot coals, just perfect for grilling his fish. He hung a pot of water to boil on the spit.

As the fish roasted, Marcus inserted the slats in the front of the boat, unrolled a thin cotton mattress, just long enough to support his body, and lay down and looked up at the darkening blue sky above him. "This sure beats lying in a trench full of blood with somebody shooting at you." He said a prayer thanking his Lord for the blessings He had bestowed on him since leaving the Antietam battlefield. After his prayer he slipped the picture of Bonnie out and longed for the time he would see her again in person. Each day that passed, however, was shortening the time until he was with her.

It didn't take long for his fish to grill, and with a cup of sweetened coffee and a torn chunk of bread that Mrs. Dunigan had sent with him, he was soon dining on a delicious fish. He didn't know what kind of fish it was, but he figured it was some kind of bass. After his tasty meal, he found a bag of cookies that a kind lady had given him. He intended to make them last and eat only one, but instead, they were so good he ate three. "Yes sir, this is the life he thought."

After supper, just as daylight faded away, he set up his tent. He took his two masts and inserted them in the holes provided and ran the rope through the metal eyes at the top of each mast to create the spine of the tent. After making sure it was tied securely he unfolded the canvas top and centered it over the rope and hooked the sides over little hooks provided on the outside of the boat as instructed by the boat builders. When both sides were hooked the top was pulled taught. He found one of his two new lanterns and lit it. Using the ample light, he washed his cup and plate in the river. Not wanting to bring attention to his camp, he blew out the lantern, closed the front flap of the tent, and then sat at the back with his hands over the hot embers, absorbing the heat from his dying fire as the night chill consumed the river. When the fire was nearly gone, he climbed inside and closed the back flap. He lay back on his comfortable bed with his loaded firearms beside him. It was his first night on the good ship "Bonnie."

24

Early the next morning, shortly before daybreak, he was awakened by the whirr of a strong cold wind singing a new song along the flaps of his tent. The boat was far enough on shore to be secure, but the strong wind fluttered the edges of the flaps that hung over the side past the hooks. Marcus raised the stern tent flap to peek out in the dim light to see boiling gray clouds above him as if Noah's flood was soon to be let loose on him. He feared this could be a day that would test his new boat.

He expected rain at any moment. The only thing not under the tent was his wash pot stove and the wood left beside it. He quickly got up and placed a top on the iron pot, got out of the boat, and retrieved some more kindling to stash away under the tent. He wished for a fire so he could make coffee and fry some eggs and bacon, but he drank water instead and ate a piece of cured ham with a piece of bread. "Pretty good," he thought, "considering the conditions."

Marcus studied the situation. He had noticed yesterday, there were round windows on the side of the tent, covered with flaps enabling him to poke a paddle out and row and stay dry during a rain. Suddenly a clap of thunder echoed down the river valley. Marcus's father had five cows killed by lightning when Marcus was a young child, and from that day on, he had been deathly afraid of lightning and its potent power to kill. He felt sheltered next to the steep slope, so he lay back down and took advantage of this free time to try and doze off again.

The bottom fell out of the cloud, and he heard the huge drops of rain patter distinctly on the tent, falling slowly at first, and then increasing to a roar. He lowered the open flap to seal the cozy interior of the tent. As he relaxed and heard the rain he saw water creeping in under the tent from the front and back of the boat. He looked in the bins under the seat and found a hand towel that one of the worker's wives had included for him to use when washing his hands. He took it and soaked up the rain now accumulating at the back of the boat. The new paint beaded the water and made it easy to soak up with the cloth. He wiped the floor and then squeezed the water out using the oar holes. He was busy for a half hour, but the rain finally eased up and only drizzled, making his job much easier.

The temperature had dropped about twenty degrees in an hour and now felt slightly above freezing. He had heard the thunder pass over to the southeast, so he decided it was safe enough for him to float on down the river. While it rained, he had watched the shoreline to see if the river was rising, but the river was so large he noticed no change.

He got out of the boat in the mist now and pushed hard to get the vessel back in the river, and as it floated out into the current, he jumped on the wide bow, and he was underway again. He stuck the oars out the side of the boat and raised the front and back flaps so he could see where he was headed. The compass indicated he was going west. He was impressed with the success of his tent. The wind was blowing strongly from the northwest slowing his progress and pushing his boat to his left, the tent acting like a sail. He kept the right paddle dragging the water to keep the boat aligned in the river

After a while, the wind died and the choppy waves on the water leveled out; the river turned northwest directly into the wind, but soon turned back to the southwest, then south, and then he was traveling slightly southeast. He started seeing patches of blue above and concluded the rain was over for now. He took down his tent so the tent wouldn't catch the wind. The current seemed to be increasing, possibly due to the rain, but there was no way to know for sure being out in the middle of the large waterway.

It was afternoon and Marcus had only passed a few small steamers going upstream. The men waved at Marcus and he responded; he assumed they could be pirates and kept alert. One man yelled across, "Ahoy Bonnie, have a good trip." He couldn't wait to tell Bonnie about her name on his boat.

He dug out the cake the lady had given him and cut a big chunk to eat and nibble on. People in Pittsburg told him not to drink the river water due to the many towns spewing their filth into the river. His canteen was getting low and Marcus hoped he would soon come to a town with a community well, or find a clean stream flowing into the river.

Late in the afternoon he started fishing again, and like the day before he quickly pulled in a fish, then another, and soon he had a dozen fish. He put the fish on a long stringer, so they could stay alive. Having come ashore the night before and feeling confident with his boat skills, he rode the river until almost dark, knowing he had everything he needed in the boat, and if need be, he could light his lantern to see the river.

All of a sudden, in the fading light, he saw an island emerging in front of him splitting the river. It seemed the channel to the left of the island was larger and probably the river, but he was headed toward the smaller channel. Not familiar with the river, he hoped it would come together again beyond the island and not send him down an unknown waterway. He paddled backward with the left oar, turning the prow of his boat toward the larger channel, and then rowed as hard as he could. He could see the island was not much higher than the river, and he barely cleared the end of the island to float on down the wider side of the river.

It was almost dark now, and time to get off the river and get his fish cooked. He remembered the eggs he had missed at breakfast and thought that would be good with his fish. He spotted a flat place on the island and turned the nose in and paddled hard to land his boat. Like an old river man, he jumped out and pulled the boat ashore and set about his nightly routine. It felt good to stand up and stretch. He soon had a fire going and his supper prepared in his wash pot stove. That night, he ate two fish and boiled two eggs and with the bread, cake, and coffee, that was enough. Marcus was beginning to enjoy this river life, virtually no work, plenty of food, and all surrounded by beautiful fall scenery.

The moon was above him, not full, but with the aid of the stars, scattered enough light to reveal the river and woods around him. He could see the edge of the large bluffs above the water, now far away considering he was in the middle of the huge river. While he was eating he saw a barge float by and a steamer going up stream, both with lanterns hanging from their prows. Marcus knew no rules of the river, but deducted from what he saw, that if he traveled at night he should hang his lantern from the front tent mast. Not expecting rain that night, he assembled his bed and blankets and instead of erecting his tent, just spread out the canvas over the boat to keep dew or frost out. He took off his shoes, slid in between the blankets, pulled the canvas over his head, and slipped off to sleep.

Going to bed early made it easy to get up at dawn. When he threw the canvas back, he saw a coat of frost on the top of the canvas and on the ends of the boat. What a good morning for coffee, eggs, and ham he imagined. His wood was dry, and he kindled a new fire in his iron pot. He wiped the ice off the canvas and laid it across a large rock to dry. He didn't want to fold it up wet and have it mildew.

As he was washing his plate and cup, he noticed two men in buckskins with heavy beards and large leather hats appear out of the woods about a hundred yards away. One of the men pointed at him. The two men removed their rifles from the animal skin cases as if they intended to use them. Marcus hoped they had seen a varmint to shoot, but he feared the varmint they wanted to shoot was him. He stepped in the boat, picked up his loaded pistol and stuck it in his belt, grabbed his loaded rifle, and then turned and faced them.

"Pirates," Marcus thought, and like he had been told, when they saw his arms, they lowered their rifles and raised their hands, similar to an Indian, meaning they had come in peace. When they got closer Marcus told them to stop and state their business.

The two looked like the stories that had been told about Daniel Boone and Davy Crockett, but for some reason, they did not emit an aura of valor and bravery. The two gnarly characters turned to each other and whispered something, making Marcus more suspicious of their intentions. After several moments of discussion, one of the men, yelled out, "Mister, whoever you are. You are trespassing on our island. You owe us some money. It looks like you spent the night here."

Marcus had been taught growing up that property along the river was public, and a person had the right to pull a boat up and camp anywhere on a public river. He knew now they were trying to rob him or swindle him out of some money. Marcus yelled back, "There is no sign here that says 'no trespassing' or 'keep out,' or that anyone even owns this island."

"Now boy, don't give us no trouble. We didn't come down here for trouble. We just want what's coming to us for being owners of this here island." The men started forward again.

"Stop or I will kill you without thinking about it. I am going home from the war, and I have killed over a hundred blue coats. I don't imagine the Lord would hold it against me if I killed two more thieves."

"But boy, there's two of us and only one of you."

"You got that wrong. There's thirteen of me and two of you. I have two pistols and my rifle and I don't miss when I shoot my rifle." Marcus had faced intense rifle fire in the war, and two men fifty yards away seemed trivial to what he had seen. Marcus was no longer a young boy inside, but now a veteran soldier hardened by what he had endured. "When you two shoot at me, you have to reload and I don't. I'll run and kill you before you can do that."

The two men mumbled something to each other; then one of them yelled, "Look boy, all it cost is two bits. We aren't asking for much."

Marcus thought a minute, "I'll tell you what I'll do; since I don't have two bits and couldn't pay you anyway, I'll leave you two fish I caught last night. I think that would be fair, don't you?"

Realizing Marcus had all the cards and appeared to have all the aces, the two would-be thieves agreed. Marcus yelled back, "You men back up while I get ready to leave." The men did not move. "I said back up, fifty yards!" With that reply Marcus fired his pistol and hit a tree next to one of the gentlemen, showing them he meant business and could hit what he shot at. Marcus was thankful the gun fired after sitting around for a few days next to all the moisture.

That convinced the hoodlums to back up; this kid could shoot. It wouldn't be worth it to risk their lives for two fish since he apparently had no money. The two men eased backward, but kept facing Marcus. Marcus grabbed his canvas, rapidly folded it up, and stuffed it in the bottom of the boat, always holding the pistol and never taking his eyes off of them. He got in the boat and raised the heavy planks and locked them in place, just in case they decided to fire at him when he got in the river. Marcus pushed the boat off of the shore, still watching them closely. After he got offshore a ways one of the men yelled, "Where's our fish?"

"Oh, I forgot to tell you. There's a fee for watching me shoot. Each one of you owes me a fish. I guess that means we're now even. Next time I come by, could you have a 'welcome neighbor' sign so I will be sure and stay?" The two bandits watched as Marcus floated by protected by his raised wooden armor along the side of his boat.

Marcus steered away from the island to put as much distance between him and the two men as possible. He wondered how many helpless people they preyed on or killed who might have stopped there to camp. Marcus became angry with himself for not killing the worthless vermin and possibly saving other people's lives.

Soon, he had calmed down and said a short prayer thanking God that he had survived the encounter with the thieves. The day was cool but clear and he was making progress. His compass indicated he was traveling south as he paralleled the island and all was going well again.

Realizing he told the hooligans he had no money, but he would give them fish, it dawned on him he could make money by fishing for a living. Thus far, wherever he put the hook in the river he had caught fish. He removed his long fishing pole from its mount and started to fish again, guiding the boat closer to shore where the fish most likely fed. After passing the long island, the river turned to the right going southwest and then curved to the southeast again. In the next six miles he caught fourteen fish. The river turned south again, and to his surprise he noticed a large village on the right, below the high bluffs of the river. Marcus had passed small towns and settlements, but this seemed to be larger than the others. He saw several boats tied to a pier and expected the center of town would be nearby and a site for selling fish.

As he neared the dock, a man saw him coming and indicated to Marcus to throw him his bow line, and he would help him dock. Marcus paddled backward to stop the boat and very slowly drifted up to the side of a pier and docked in an open spot between several boats. The pier did not jut out into the river, but ran parallel to the shore. Marcus stood up and thanked the man for his help.

The man looked at Marcus's craft and admired the innovations. "That's quite a ship you have there. Did you build it?"

"No sir, a man up at Pittsburgh put this together for me." Marcus pointed out the features that made the boat unique. He showed him how the tent could be erected, his wash-pot stove, his storage bins, the creative rudder, and his side armor, at which time he mentioned to the man about his encounter with the pirates.

"You mean that island back up the river about five or six miles?"

"Yes sir, I think that would be about right."

"Oh," he laughed, "Those old guys aren't bandits. They own that island. Their ancestors has lived there for years. They pick up a little money charging people who stop on their property."

"Well, I almost killed them this morning. I thought they were hooligans trying to rob me."

"No, they wouldn't hurt you, but I understand how you could think that. By the way, where you going?"

"Louisville."

"You've still got a long way to go, more than five-hundred miles, I reckon."

"I 'spect so. I want to get off the river 'fore the first of December and the weather gets real cold." Marcus then turned the conversation to the reason he stopped, "I have been catching lots of fish coming down the river. Would anybody buy them? I probably got thirty pounds of fish tied behind the boat on my stringer."

The middle-aged man thought a minute, "Mr. Flanagan runs an eatery over there and fries lots of fish. You might try him."

"What's the price of fish anyway?" Marcus asked.

"I'd guess a penny a pound. Fish is pretty cheap around this river. I saw a man sell a hunerd pounds of fish the other day. I thank he got a dollar."

"Who'd he sell it to?"

"There's a man that comes down the river 'bout three or four times a year who buys fish. He has a steamer and a crew. They take the fish and pack them in salt to preserve them. I know he would buy your fish, but I haven't seen him in a while."

Marcus thought a minute, "Would you do me a favor?"

"If it's not too much trouble."

"You see, I have a lot of investment in this boat, and I can't just leave it here while I go over there to see if he wants to buy the fish."

"I'll watch the boat for you," he replied with a grin, giving Marcus the impression, "He would be happy to steal his boat."

"No, I don't know who you are, and I am suspicious of anyone after meeting those island pirates this morning, I mean those island guys I assumed were pirates. I thought I might ask you to run over there and ask that cook if he might look at the fish I have. I'll give you two cents whether he buys them or not."

"Wait here, I'll go see." Soon the dock worker returned with the cook, and he offered Marcus thirty cents for all of them. Marcus accepted and paid the dock worker two cents. Marcus considered he had made a good deal. To him, catching fish was fun, and he just got paid for it.

Marcus wanted to take his new money and swap it back for a bowl of stew. On this chilly day a bowl of hot vegetables would warm him up. Before the cook walked away Marcus inquired if he had, by any chance, a stew or soup for dinner. The cook said he did and a bowl of stew was ten cents. Marcus had noticed a shy young boy standing by the docks. He seemed intrigued by Marcus's boat, but was too shy to come forward.

Marcus called out, "Young man, you there," he said pointing at the boy. The young boy straightened up and pointed at himself indicating, "You mean me?"

"Yes, come here." The young boy didn't know whether to run or come forward, but overcame his fear, and approached Marcus. "You look hungry. Are you hungry?" The small boy nodded his head. Marcus then looked at the cook, "I don't want to leave my boat, but I sure would like a bowl of stew. If I give you twenty cents back, will you dish up two bowls of stew and let the boy come back over here and eat with me? When we finish, will you trust this boy to bring the bowls back to you?"

"Yes, I know Micah quite well. He runs errands for me all the time."

Marcus looked at Micah, "Will you do that for me?"

"Yes sir, I would be proud to."

"If you will do that then, you can have the dime that's left over. How about that deal?"

Micah changed from a bashful little boy to a happy smiling child in an instant after Marcus offered him the dime. The deal was made, hands were shook, and soon the boy returned with the bowls of stew, covered with cloth napkins to try and keep them warm. When Marcus lifted the cloth, there was a big square of cornbread floating on top of the stew. The cook had also sent spoons, and Micah had not spilled a drop. Marcus took the soup and invited Micah to step down in the boat so they could eat. Marcus secured two cups out of a bin and filled the cups with the last of his water, the last drops dripping into Marcus's cup. "I need some more water. Do you know where I can fill my canteen?"

"Yes sir, there's a public pump over there by those stores. People in boats get water there all the time."

"When we finish would you go fetch me some water?"

The young boy agreed, and they sat down and feasted on the still warm stew and cornbread. When they finished, Marcus unwrapped his cake and cut two large slabs and passed one to Micah. They talked a few more minutes, and Marcus told Micah it was time for him to get on down the river. The boy took the canteen and disappeared around a corner and soon returned with the canteen strap over his shoulder. "Here's your water. Thank you for the bowl of stew and the ten cents. Nobody has ever paid me that much for helping them."

"You're welcome, and I thank you for helping me." As he said his last good bye and untied the boat, Marcus noticed two men on horses riding into town and knew immediately there might be trouble. He told Micah, "Run, go hide, and protect yourself. Get away from the river! Now!" Not understanding why Marcus had suddenly changed, Micah started backing up, fearing for some reason he had made Marcus mad.

The young boy stopped with his feelings hurt, "What did I do to make you so mad?"

Marcus grabbed his oars, "I am not mad at you, but those two men over there on the horses are mad at me. and if they see me there might be some shooting. Now run, go, run fast, before you get hurt." Understanding now, Micah ran away from the river as Marcus ducked down behind the pier and using an oar, pushed "Bonnie" into the flow, steering close to the bank so the two men he had confronted earlier couldn't see him. He hoped the young boy would understand why he had to depart so fast, but he saw the town fade away as he faced backward and rowed hard. Marcus was lucky the two men had not seen the bright red boat they had encountered earlier.

Marcus indeed felt lucky not having to face the two men up close. Marcus laughed to himself, "I couldn't have paid them anyway; I had sold the fish." He was proud of his fish deal and decided to fish again. He was now in mid-stream just floating along with no boats in sight. He knew he was getting low on worms, but when he scratched through the metal can he could only find one left. He baited the line and hung the pole over the side. It was time to stop and restock his bait. He steered the boat near the land and looked for a woody spot that had lots of rotten leaves on the ground.

His compass indicted he was travelling south most of the time. He was amazed how many small villages and farms had settled along banks and valleys of the river. Wherever he saw a good spot to dig worms there seemed to be a house or village nearby. He was still in Union territory and didn't want to have another dispute concerning trespassing.

As luck would have it, Marcus noticed three boys fishing in the river ahead of him. If they were fishing, they had bait. He paddled backward to slow his momentum and yelled to the boys to grab his rope when he came up. The boys appeared to be ten years old and were excited that someone was stopping. He tossed them his bow line and it took all the boys several seconds to stop the boat, even pulling them down the edge of the river a short ways.

"Thank you boys, I appreciate the help. Catching anything?"

"Yes sir, we didn't figure the fishing would be good today because it was so cold, but we've caught a good mess. Let me show you." He ran back up the river where they had been fishing and lifted a stringer out of the water that would make any fisherman proud.

"Hey! That's a great stringer of fish. I was fishing, but I've run out of worms. Do you have any worms you could spare?

"Yes sir, his papa raises worms," one of the boys answered. How many do you need?"

"Are they good and fat," Marcus added, pretending to imply he was buying an animal as important as a hog. Marcus reached in his pocket and pulled out three cents. "How many will this buy?"

"Two dozen and they are big, too," the son of the worm farmer said, taking charge of this big transaction, "And I'll throw in a few extra, too."

"You got a deal!" The boy ran to the can of worms and stirred the dirt to see how many he had. They had a lot of fish and had used most of their bait.

"Stay here. I only live over yonder. I'll be right back." The boy grabbed his own worm can and ran across a field that had been farmed that summer. While he was gone, the other two boys admired the boat. "I've never seen a boat quite like that."

Marcus showed them the unusual features in the small boat. "All the gear on board makes it crowded, and I have to crawl around more than I walk, but it is comfortable and if it's raining I can cover it with a canvas. Look at this, "he said as he lifted the heavy planks on the side, "These boards might save my life someday," as he lay down behind them and stuck his rifle through the paddle hole."

The boys were impressed. One of them asked if he could go get his father so he could see it, but Marcus said he was in a hurry and needed to leave as soon as the boy brought the worms back.

In a few minutes the boy returned with his bait can full of worms, but hidden in rich compost. "Give me your can, and I'll give you three dozen," and showing his generosity, "And six more." Marcus listened to him count to twelve as he pulled the worms from the dirt. Instead of continuing his count to thirteen, he stopped and started over again, indicating to Marcus he could not count much higher than thirteen. When he finished, he counted out another six and stuck the can out for Marcus to take. "There you are, three dozen and a half a dozen." Marcus dropped three cents in his pocket, baited his hook with a new worm, took his paddle and pushed off biding the three lads goodbye. As he left, Marcus heard the boys talking about his boat, all excited to tell other boys what they had seen.

Marcus had eaten an early dinner, and it was midafternoon. He finished off the sack of cookies the lady had given him. That should take him to supper. He noticed the sky clouding up again. It had been cold all day. He began to see droplets of rain disturbing the surface of the smooth river. It was time to set up the tent in case it started raining hard. He also wanted to keep his firewood dry.

The change in the weather started the fish to biting. As soon as he baited the hook and threw it out, before he could work on the tent, he noticed the pole bending and he stopped and pulled in the fish and strung it up. After three consecutive fish, with the rain falling harder, he placed the pole in its mount and set about weather-proofing his ship. It didn't take long, and he had everything protected, in particular, his wood for the evening meal. He crawled inside, lowered the back flap, and sat facing forward so he could watch the river through the front opening. He had enough fish for supper, but not enough to sell if he came to a small town.

As the sun was going down, Marcus saw a small village ahead and as he neared the pier Marcus yelled, "What town is this?"

"Martin's Ferry!" a man replied. Marcus had no reason to stop. He had secured the worms, the only thing he needed, so he surged on by, the boat absolutely quiet, the stillness only disturbed by the patter of the rain on the water.

Marcus felt so secure in his new home on the water. He never felt alone, for he sensed God's presence wherever he was. During his entire life, like this adventure, God, always invisible, was directing his path. He knew now he would find Bonnie. Surviving the many dangers that had come his way, and the blessings that had been given him, reinforced his faith that his Creator was real. Marcus had been taught that prayer was not only kneeling beside your bed, or bowing your head at the table, but it also meant talking to God as if He were a friend always around you, protecting you, comforting you, and directing your path. Marcus thought about how he had been tempted by the beautiful girl he had met, but rather than stain his life, God had directed him down a path that he would not have to be ashamed of the rest of his life.

As he drifted down the river, he wondered what Bonnie was doing that night in Texas. Was she well? He hoped she missed him as much as he missed her. The thought of seeing her again lifted his spirit to get out of this war, go home, and then go find her.

25

Traffic on the river had thinned out since leaving Pittsburgh, but since it was a main transportation artery to the West and the sea via New Orleans, Marcus often passed and was being passed by a variety of boats from large steamers to canoes. With night almost upon him, Marcus took his lantern and tied it to his front mast inside the doorway of his tent to keep it dry, but low enough to prevent it from catching the rolled-up flap of the tent on fire. Just as he sat back down he suddenly saw a small island with a rocky shore that seemed to be rapidly approaching in the fading light, splitting the river again; the channel on the right was small, obviously not the main current of the river. He jumped to the oars facing backward and put all his might into rowing his craft, moving her toward the main channel away from the rocks, often turning to look over his shoulder to see how he was doing. He rowed faster, but it appeared no matter how hard he rowed, he was being pulled toward the rocks. He put every ounce of strength he could muster on the handle of the oars, the pain spreading from his arms through his back, but it looked as if his beloved "Bonnie" was going to hit the rocks. Nearer the rocks came as he constantly watched over his shoulder to see if he would miss the jagged boulders. Marcus put his last bit of strength into his effort, closing his eyes, expecting to feel the powerful jolt that would damage or sink his beloved "Bonnie," but the current caught the bow and turned it away from the largest boulder, the light from his lantern revealing how close he had come to damaging the boat. Almost immediately he was moving away from the island's shore and was in the large calm current again. This near encounter with disaster taught him a lesson to be alert at all times to rocks and other boats. Marcus pulled in his oars and sighed and thanked God that by some miracle he had missed a disaster. He was exhausted now and sat inside his shelter and rested.

There were parts of the river that were very dark, the darkness only broken by a candle in the window of a lone farm house or an approaching boat. Marcus was amazed how much of the river the lantern lit in front of him. The darker the night, the better it worked. Leery now to dangers on the river, of hitting or being hit, he would step outside and look behind him to see if any large fast steamer was coming down on him. After three hours in the dark he found a little cove around a curve in the river, out of the way of river traffic, and paddled over to stop for the evening.

Remembering his encounter with the island owners, instead of pulling ashore, Marcus decided to drop his anchor and sleep on the river away from any trouble he might confront on shore. He threw an anchor overboard thirty feet from shore, climbed inside his tent, placed the lantern on the seat beside him and battened up for the night. Since it was raining harder now, it would be impossible to have a fire. His meat supplies were gone except for the fish so he dined on bread, water, and dried-out cake, drank more water, blew out his lantern, then settled down to sleep for the night.

During the night, the wind blew harder, and the clouds opened up pouring water into his boat. Marcus was awakened by the tempest beating on the sides of his canvas. When he sat up and put his feet on the floor, he heard water splash. He quickly relit his lantern. Water had come in from the ends of the boat again and was filling the back of the boat with an inch of water. He grabbed his towel and started soaking up the water and squeezing it in a bucket. When the bucket was filled, he raised the flap and poured it in the river. He determined that he was losing the battle in the heavy downpour and the boat was gradually filling with water.

At that point, he decided to head for shore and anchor the nose of the boat on solid ground rather than take a chance on losing his "Bonnie" at the bottom of the river. That would also force the water to the back of the boat where he could use one of the pails and dip it out quickly. He pulled his anchor and paddled to the nearby shore, jumped out, and took the bow line and pulled his "mighty ship" up on solid ground. Back inside, he secured his valuables on top of the seats where they would stay dry.

The wind blew so hard the tent acted like an accordion; one second the tent sides pushed out, almost to the point Marcus feared they might split, and in the next second collapsing, making a loud flapping sound similar to a large flag fluttering in a strong gale. Marcus worked to tighten the flaps closer to the bottom trying to make the tent airtight, forgetting now about the rain filling the boat. This was the second real disaster he had faced that night, but being grounded he knew his boat couldn't sink.

Marcus sat at the back and used his cup to dip the water from the boat and into the bucket. This worked better than the towel, and he noticed he was winning the battle now. About midnight, Marcus heard the clatter of oars on the side of a boat, and he peeked out to see who or what was coming up beside him. The glow from another lantern reflecting through the canvas revealed another boat beaching next to his. Apparently the man saw his light and was also seeking security on shore. Marcus scooted deep in his tent and slipped his pistol inside his belt, taking no chances this intruder might have mal- intentions. Then he heard a voice with a strong Southern accent he was familiar with, "Ahoy there! Do you mind if I stop beside you and get out of this storm. I saw your light when I passed and prayed it would be safe to pull in here."

Marcus yelled back, "You're most welcome to stay here traveler, if you come with good intentions."

"No harm intended. I wanted to travel farther tonight before I put in, but the weather made me change my mind," he said as he, too, pulled his boat on shore. Marcus opened the end of his tent so he could hold up the lantern to give the man more light to secure his boat. He noticed he was wearing a black seafaring slicker with an attached hood with a large brim, smaller in front, but hanging over his collar in back. His rubber pants secured his legs which kept him dry in the severest rainstorm. He had no tent.

Marcus noticed he was an elderly man with a deep southern drawl, a full white beard and long white hair hanging over his ears and collar. As Marcus watched, the old man went back to his open boat and pulled out a much larger canvas than Marcus had and several coils of rope. Marcus continued to give him light. The man took the largest rope and tied it to a tree as far up the trunk as he could reach and then secured the other end to another tree nearby, approximately fifteen feet across, which made a spine on which to throw his canvas. Marcus saw that he was setting up a shelter to get under. Marcus donned his slicker and came out to help the old man raise his tent. In a few minutes, with Marcus's help, the large A-frame canopy was up, the sides staked to the ground, and ends buttoned to flaps closing the ends of the tent.

Marcus brought his lantern inside and felt he was inside a huge room compared to the small tent to which he was accustomed. The aged man thanked Marcus for his help as he went back and forth to his boat retrieving gear packed in large canvas bags. After he attained all the gear he needed, he unfolded two small wooden camp stools and invited Marcus to sit down as he removed his slicker and slung it over one of the canvas bags thrown on the ground. Then he turned toward Marcus with an extended hand, "Young man, I hope I didn't disturb your peace, but it was getting wicked out there on the water. My name is Professor Jethro Jennings."

Marcus leaned forward off of the stool and shook his hand, "Glad to meet you sir, my name is Marcus Mills."

"I enjoy traveling at night," the old man added, "Matter of fact; I take pleasure in navigating the river at night, but this storm was more than I planned for. My lantern had blown out twice, and at times, I couldn't see a mortal thing. I ran ashore three times, but I don't suspect I damaged my craft."

He paused a moment and reached in his pocket to secure a long stem pipe and a pouch of tobacco. As he prepared his pipe he continued, "I supposed most of the river traffic had stopped as I hadn't seen a sign of a boat in over three hours. I saw the glow from your tent as I came around the turn. At first, in the rain, I wasn't sure what I was seeing; indeed it looked eerie as I approached until I could make out the tent shape as I got closer. Thank you for your help tonight, not only in securing my safety from the throes of the river, but for helping me secure my shelter."

"You're most welcome, sir. I was going to try a little night navigating myself, but decided I would anchor in this little cove, since I was taking in so much rainwater I feared the boat would sink."

The old man puffed his pipe, "I imagine I got three or four inches of water in my boat back where I sit. I fear some of the contents of these bags may be damaged. They told me these bags were waterproof; I assumed they meant whatever was inside would stay dry, but I presume now it means they wouldn't dissolve when they got wet," he laughed.

"Yeah, I got all my important items and put them on top of the seats. The way they built my boat, my bed can expand and become a higher floor if the bottom fills with water."

"That's interesting. You're tent-top looked unique when I came up," Jethro added.

"A hot drink would taste good on this chilly night, and I have just the thing to make that happen," Marcus suggested. "I have some dry wood in my boat. Just a minute." Marcus, still with his slicker on, exited the tent and came back with several sticks of wood and some kindling to start a fire. "We can't make a big flame, but I think we can get by with boiling some water without burning a hole in the top of your tent."

The old teacher pitched in and volunteered some coffee and a coffee pot, while Marcus kicked back the wet leaves and pine needles to reveal the bare earth, a suitable place to light a fire. Soon they were sitting around the small blaze sipping warm coffee, talking, often moving their stools to avoid the smoke, and listening to the rain and howling wind that buffeted their stronghold. All was secure, except for an occasional gust of cold damp air that blew through a hole they had provided at the end of the tent to vent the smoke.

The old man pulled his watch out and turned it back and forth in the dim light to see the time. He looked up at Marcus with a surprised look, "My boy, its two fifteen in the morning! Like I mentioned, I enjoy drifting in the dark and traveling at night, but what brings you out on the river on a night like this?"

Marcus sensed the old man presented no threat or danger. He was comforted by the old man's familiar Southern drawl, however, but to be safe, Marcus did not reveal much, protecting his true identity until he learned more about this old stranger. "I'm on my way home from the army on winter furlough. My family needs me there this winter."

"I see; are you from the Army of Northern Virginia, Lee's army?"

"Why would you think I was a Southerner?"

"Sir, your drawl, I studied phonetics and language along with math and philosophy. From your speech, I would guess you are from Georgia, matter of fact, you most likely grew up in central Georgia."

Marcus was amazed, "You hit it right on the nose. I'm from Buckhead, Georgia, just east…"

"East of Madisonville, Georgia," the old professor finished. "Well, well, we're almost neighbors. I was reared in Charleston. To finish my question, I assume then, you are a Confederate comrade."

When he said "Confederate comrade," Marcus knew he was with a friend, and felt confident when he answered, "Yes sir. I am a member of a Georgia brigade in General Hood's Texas Division," he hesitated and lowered his head, then looked sadly in the old man's eyes, "If any of them are left."

"What do you mean?"

"I was at Sharpsburg, and we were slaughtered. From what I witnessed, I might be the only survivor."

"Yes, I read in the Northern papers the Yanks gave us a pretty good whipping up there." At that point Marcus told his entire story, including the events in the 'cornfield,' the destruction of the Union artillery wagons, his capture and escape, Genia, and his boat acquisition, which brought him to his present situation.

The old man lit his pipe again and thought a minute, "That is quite a story, Marcus. You have been on quite a journey. I pondered why a young lad would be out on a river, and now I know. Can I trust you, Marcus?" the old man asked.

"Why yes, of course. I hope you are who you say you are."

The old man had no reason not to believe Marcus's story and knew what he had told him was the truth; and possibly, Marcus was a man who could help him pursue his mission for being on the river, traveling only at night. The old man reached over and placed another small log on the dying fire, took a puff on his pipe and leaned forward, as if he were going to tell Marcus the secrets of the universe, and whispered as if someone might be outside listening. "Have you wondered yet why I am on this river, traveling only at night?"

"Yes, that seemed a little odd to me."

"It's because I am on a special assignment for my country and my President Jefferson Davis."

"What kind of mission?"

"See that package over there," he said as he took his pipe out and pointed its stem at one of the bags. "It contains 160 devices built in England that enables torpedoes to explode when they are rammed into a ship."

"What's a torpedo," Marcus asked.

"It's a mine, boy! It's a mine."

"I still don't understand. A mine is a place where you dig gold and silver. Are they used to blast the rock out of the mine?"

The old man leaned back, shook his head and laughed, understanding Marcus was not educated that well. "Can you read boy?"

"Somewhat sir; I can get by," Marcus answered, embarrassed that he obviously knew nothing about what the man spoke of.

"The Latin word torpedoes, or what we also call mines, are names for weapons that float in the water and explode when they are hit by an enemy ship. These weapons are like floating cannonballs that have spikes extending out from their sides. In the tip of each spike is a detonator that will explode when hit, thus igniting the powder inside. Boom! The ship is gone, do you understand now?" using his hands to indicate a big explosion.

"Yes, I see now. Those torpedoes could stop a ship from coming up a river…."

"Or attacking our port. You see how important they are?"

"Yes, but why are you up here on the Ohio River in the middle of the night?"

"As you know, the Yankees have blocked entrance to all of our ports from Texas to Virginia. The only way we can get things into the South is smuggling them in through Mexico or Canada, or in fast ships called 'blockade runners.' The last two times we tried to bring them into Charleston, the ships met misfortune and were captured."

The old man stopped and tapped his pipe on the sole of his shoe, knocking its contents by the crackling fire, and secured his pipe back in his coat. "So this time the Confederacy made arrangements for these detonators to be sent to Canada and smuggled overland through Toronto, Erie, and finally by wagon to Pittsburgh, where I picked them up."

"Who brought them to Pittsburgh? It looks like coming overland right through the middle of the North would be the most dangerous."

"Yes, it would seem that way, but we camouflage our activity quite well. And yes again, even more dangerous now since Nashville has been captured. All of the Ohio River is under Union control since Kentucky is now a northern state, but we have made a hole we can slip through and get down to Atlanta via Nashville and Chattanooga. However, my task is to only get them to Nashville."

The detonators are packed inside crates sealed and covered with wax to make them impervious to water, or for that matter, nearly any substance on earth, but not a rifle shot. The boxes are small. For example, see those two packs there on the ground," he said pointing at two canvas sacks, "They each contain twenty boxes, each box holding four detonators."

At Nova Scotia they are taken off an English transport vessel and put on a Canadian fishing trawler that unloads fish in Toronto. From there the detonators are put on a canal boat used to haul cattle and hogs." He laughed, "For some reason those barges are never searched for contraband, I wonder why? Thus they make their way across Lake Ontario through the Welland Canal to Erie, Pennsylvania." He smiled again, "This is the best part yet; from there they are picked up by Confederates disguised as Amish farmers arriving to pick up seeds after selling their wares. The last leg of their journey is to bring them to me waiting in Pittsburgh, and I take them to Nashville. I meet an ally there who takes them to Charleston or Mobile where they are installed in the torpedoes."

"That's a lot of work and trouble to get them to the South. Why can't we make them in the South?" Marcus loudly replied to overcome the fury of the rain hitting the tent.

"We can, but our detonators corrode very quickly in the salt water. These instead are made in England out of a metal we don't have or can secure. As you said, it is a lot of work, but the Navy thinks if we can produce enough mines, we can eventually put them in Northern waterways and create much havoc there. That's why my mission is so important."

"Why are you telling me all this?"

"After I heard your story, I am ninety-nine percent sure you are who you say you are and a man I can trust. We are fighting for the same cause, only in different ways. Since we are going the same direction, you could help me in my quest to deliver the detonators downriver, and I can help you get home to Georgia. You might say we can cover each other's back."

"Yes, I could do that as long as your mission agrees with my path home."

"However, I must add this bit of information to my story. It seems the plan went awry this time at Erie. When I rendezvoused with the men in Pittsburg, I was surprised to see they had changed their disguise. I expected to meet the Amish as planned, but instead they were dressed as priests, you know with their funny hats, black coats and stiff collars. They told me shortly after they left Erie, the man who owned the hog boat got drunk later that night and announced to the world that he knew the South was going to sink the Union Navy with secret guns. There happened to be a naval officer in the bar and immediately arrested him. One of our agents, pretending to be a hired-hand on the hog barge, went down to the police station the next day and asked when his boss would be let go. They told him he was being interrogated and would probably be shot for treason. He asked if he could talk to him about what to do with the hogs. Our agent looked like an ignorant smelly wharf rat rather than a Confederate agent, so they didn't arrest him, but they refused to let him talk to their prisoner."

The professor stopped talking and took another sip of cooling coffee, then continued. "Our agent, who had been on the hog boat, left immediately to catch up with the men carrying the detonators. He knew their route, but it took him two days to find them. He warned our Amish-looking agents to change their disguises immediately in case their captured comrade told the Union authorities what was going on under their noses. If he had, the authorities were probably looking for two Amish men going to Pittsburgh. To be safe, they changed into parsons; you know, with the black coats and round collars. They filled the back of the wagon with vegetables as if they were local preachers taking food to their needy."

The old man coughed and continued, "The next day they were stopped and searched three times along the road. Our agents, the 'priests', asked why they were being searched, and the authorities told them they were looking for two Amish men smuggling guns to the South; but they were taking no chances; they were searching everyone. Fortunately for the 'priests', due to a foul up in the Union communications, the detonator boxes had been misinterpreted to mean crates of rifles. In the next six days they were stopped and searched six times, but none of the authorities ever asked to see inside the small waxed boxes marked seeds. Instead, they were looking for crates filled with guns."

"When they finally reached me in Pittsburgh, they told me the Union authorities were hunting two Amish men smuggling armaments to the South and a professor who would meet them on the river and take the weapons. We then knew for sure, the drunk had told the Union agents all he knew; but our drunk friend did not know though, how the armaments left Pittsburgh. He had never been told that information." The professor coughed and cleared his throat again, "But I was now aware they were looking for me. However, they did not know whether I traveled by land or river. At that point I loaded the detonators on my boat, bid my friends goodbye, and left Pittsburg immediately for the broad Ohio River. You can see why I am traveling at night. Thus far, I haven't seen anyone searching people on the river, but common sense dictates the easiest way to go down South would be on the river. I am definitely a hunted man. That's why you can help me now, Marcus."

"If our enemy suspects the informer's story is true, and they do, they might send out the Army and stop all suspicious boats going downriver out of Pittsburgh. I am an authentic professor, as I mentioned earlier, but since they are looking for a professor, I considered being…. maybe a gambler who got thrown off one of the riverboats for cheating and just trying to get back home to Louisville. Since Pittsburg, I have disguised myself as a 'tater and turnip' trader on the river." The professor immediately changed his elegant Southern accent to the rough ignorant language spoken on the river, "You young scalawag, grab that thar sack of 'taters and put 'um in my boat!" Then he assumed his real role again, the gentleman professor and announced his true profession, "I am also Colonel Jethro Jennings of the Confederate Army." He reached out and shook Marcus's hand again.

"No, I will no longer be a professor but a 'tater peddler. I've tried to think of other river jobs to disguise my presence, but I have settled on being a 'vegetable vender' selling vegetables along the river. I have the vegetables the priests used to disguise themselves while traveling overland from Erie, and I have torn and dirtied my clothes to match my new character. Would you believe that story?"

"Yes, I would believe you after I heard you speak like a river rat."

"Good, it is very important that we get these detonators to Mobile or Charleston. Since I know they are looking for an older man, I think it might be safer for me to give this shipment to you. They will not be looking for a young lad like you. We will continue on down the river together watching each other's back. Would you agree to do that?"

"Yes, I don't see any reason not to."

"You must know, Marcus, if you are caught with these devices, you will be shot as a spy."

"I've been in more dangerous places than this, sir. But before I get any deeper into this undertaking, I must again tell you I am on my way home and must get off the river at Louisville. I am expected to leave my boat there to be towed back to its owner."

"These little eggs I'm carrying are to be delivered to Nashville where a man will take them from me for the rest of the journey."

"How will you find this man?"

"Now listen carefully to what I tell you. I am to meet this comrade at exactly seven o'clock after dark at 'The River Roost', a bar located next to the Cumberland River downtown."

"But how will you know him?"

"Hush, that's what I am trying to tell you. I am to meet him at the most crowded time of the day when there's lots of people hanging around drinking after a day's work. We could not set a specific day or even a definite week to meet for obvious reasons. However, you'll find some pews out front, under the porch. Take a seat shortly before seven and watch the left corner of porch next to the front supporting the roof. Our man will be wearing a stovepipe hat with a red band. There will be a white chicken feather with a red tip stuck inside the hatband."

"How did you find a chicken with a red-tipped feather? I never saw one of those."

"Boy, don't you have any sense? They dipped the feather in red paint. That hat will insure that you are going to find the right man.

There will be no other creature in the entire world with such a hat like that. He will appear there every night until we contact him, but he will only be there for a minute, and then he will leave. This will also guarantee he is the man we are looking for."

"But I can't leave my boat. People will steal my belongings and maybe even the detonators while I'm gone."

"No, the bar is on 1st Street right next to the river, like I said. You could almost spit in your boat from the front porch. There's lots of river traffic there. You may have to pull up and wait until you can find a place to tie the boat to the pier. Then stay on your boat until it is time to watch for him. As a matter of fact, you could wait across the street and sit down until you see him. He is expecting me to find him, but if I die or get killed, you approach him and ask if his name is 'X'? He will answer, "Why yes it is along with Y and Z." Then ask him to follow you to the boat where you can help him remove the boxes to a wagon, mule, or boat and your mission is done. I don't know where the detonators go from there."

"That's all there is to it?"

"Yes, you are on your own after that. Most likely, I will be there too, but just in case I am not, you will now know what to do."

The old man swished his hands together as if he had finished a tough job. "Good, it will be daylight in two hours or so. Let's try to get some sleep and we'll transfer the bags to your boat and maybe cook a good breakfast. If this storm continues we might stay here until it passes over." Marcus nodded and returned to his quarters to sleep until morning, but as he left, the professor reached in a bag and pulled out an alarm clock and wound it up. "Wouldn't want to sleep late in the morning."

26

It continued to rain all night. Marcus woke up still tired from his lack of sleep. He yelled out to the professor to see if he was awake. "Yes, I'm up and cooking breakfast. I have some hot coffee; come and eat." Marcus entered under the large tent and found the professor had two camp chairs pulled up and two plates set on a small collapsible table.

Marcus saw the clock and scratched his head, "I must have been really tired. I didn't hear that thing go off this morning."

"It doesn't have to ring long, before I shut it off."

"Why, you've been busy since I last saw you. Where did you get all this gear?"

"It was in my boat."

Marcus lifted and pushed back the flap to see how the two boats compared in size. "I see. That few extra feet of length pays off in cargo space."

"Yes, and I am getting on up in years. I try to make my habitat as comfortable as possible. Here let's eat," the professor said as he offered Marcus a seat.

The two men decided to stay comfortable and dry and wait out the rain that was continuing to pepper the tent while they worked out a plan to travel the river. The professor would lead the convoy and Marcus, now with the detonators, would follow a quarter mile behind, just barely keeping the old man in sight. This would enable Marcus to come to his aid or possibly destroy or sink the detonators if the professor encountered a problem.

The old man continued to talk. "I am concerned about what I heard back in Pittsburgh about the Federal authorities being aware of our operation, but I wonder how much credence the Union Army would give to a drunken sailor. However, we must keep alert to the fact that the authorities may be chasing us at this very moment. This is the second time I have run the river with a load of detonators, and I have had no trouble thus far. We are on a northern river that seems secure to the Federals, thus they have no suspicion to search anyone, but like I said, I am worried now after our breach in security." In the daylight the professor had noticed Marcus's red boat and laughed, "There's one thing for sure, that red boat of yours stands out like a peacock in a chicken yard; I doubt they would ever suspect a smuggler would own an outlandish boat like that."

But just in case, and to Marcus's surprise, the old man told him he carried three buckets of paint, all containing different colors, and if necessary, he could pull up on shore and stay long enough to change the color of his boat and appear to be a different river runner the next day. "I have tried to give myself every advantage that I can; I want you to take one of those cans and two brushes also. If for some reason the authorities are hunting a white boat, then I can be black one. That's the only way we have a chance of getting away, since they most likely conclude we will use the river to travel south if that drunk told them everything he knew," the old man added.

"Ohhh, you've thought of everything, you old fox."

"When your life's on the line, you better!"

"Yes indeed, over the past month or so I've had to do some fancy thinking myself," Marcus grinned recalling the pox, coons and his train ride.

As the rainy day passed, the two men took advantage of breaks in the rain to transfer the deadly cargo and a can of paint to Marcus's vessel. They spent the day talking and reminiscing about the war.

Marcus told him about his escapes and close calls with the lawmen. "I hate to tell a lie, and I know God will mark an 'X' beside my name in his heavenly book as a sin, but I hope He'll draw a circle around it to remind Him I had to lie in wartime to save my life."

"Yes Marcus, it is wrong, but sometimes you just have to twist the truth. You know, when an ugly woman asks you if she looks nice, and she's as ugly as a possum with pigtails, you can't tell her the truth; you have to say she's pretty."

Marcus told him about making a few cents selling fish he had caught on the river and his encounter with the two brothers. The rain continued to pour, so the two continued to visit and get to know each other more and more, building their trust, knowing what they heard was the truth. They decided to stay put on the riverbank until dark and hoped the rain would abate by then. The river had risen slightly and maybe the current had increased also, but since it was such a large river, even a heavy rain did not affect it much.

Dark came, and it still drizzled. They ate two fish Marcus had caught that afternoon for supper. Marcus sat back in his chair; the Colonel lay on his cot, and they chatted more about the war, their past lives, and their future plans ahead. About two hours after dark during a moment of silence, the Colonel suddenly rose up from his cot and yelled out, "Great goose feathers, man, what are we doing?"

Marcus looked over at him surprised, "What's the matter?"

"Nothing, but get packed; let's get out of here as quickly as we can. I got one of those 'goose-feather feelings' on the back of my neck," he said as he jumped up and started stacking things together.

"What is a 'goose-feather feeling', Colonel?"

"It means I feel danger present. While I was lying there I got that 'feeling' that the Federals are about to find us and are coming down the river as I speak. Hurry, let's get on our way! Remember, if they catch you, you can always say you know nothing about detonators and you thought you were carrying a load of seed an old man gave you… and be sure and say, I think he was a professor. Yes, that's a better plan."

"What if they don't believe me?"

"Then they'll shoot you!" the old man laughed.

"It's not that funny, but what about your 'feelings'? Have you had that sensation before?"

"Yes! You have eyes, ears, and a nose, but I also have hairs on the back of my neck that quivers when I am in danger. I've had this ability ever since I was a boy. I was camping when I was a kid down there in Tennessee," he continued while he packed and stowed gear. "One night I got that 'feeling' and I sat up. The air was filled with danger and caused by neck hairs to wiggle. I slid out of camp and hid nearby, so I could watch my camp from the light of the fire. Soon, two men charged out of the dark with their axes raised and were surprised I wasn't there. They immediately looked about for me, but I was hidden behind a tree. One of them came directly toward me; I waited, and when he came beside me, I clubbed him in the head with my ax and shot the other before he knew what hit him. They were wiggling on the ground groaning and hurtin' so I did the humane thing and finished them off with my skinning knife. It wouldn't have been hospitable to leave them out in those dark woods in their condition."

Marcus was grabbing his gear and getting it ready to put in his boat, but curious about his friend's talent, "Did you ever get that 'feeling' again?"

"Oh yes, boy! One night, when we first settled over in Kentucky, I woke up with the 'goose-feather feeling.' Everyone was asleep so I eased to the front window of our cabin and saw figures approaching the cabin in the moonlight. I woke up my father and three brothers, and we all took a window and watched. It ended up to be a band of thieves that came in to steal our horses and burn our cabin. When we saw them approach with torches, we threw some lead at them and killed three out in the front yard and one in the chicken yard. They definitely weren't coming to welcome us to Kentucky. I had that same 'feeling' two times during the Mexican War. All I know is, when I get that 'goose-feather feeling,' get out of the way, 'cause something's coming to do me in; so let's get out of here."

"You've proved your point. I'm ready; let's go!"

The two men put on their rain slickers and carried gear to their boats, their paths lit by a lantern near a tree. They hurriedly bailed out their boats as they had done off and on all day. Marcus helped the Colonel break down his tent and fold it up. Before he left, the elderly man checked his watch; it was ten-thirty. He then hung the lantern on the front of his boat, and Marcus pushed him away from the bank. "Marcus, don't put a lantern on your boat, but stay behind me following my light. I am not sure what's going to happen, but I still have that 'goose-feather feeling.'"

"Aye, Aye, captain, I will be right behind you with all my guns loaded." Marcus giggled to himself about whether what the old man had just told him was true, or was he just tired of sitting around and wanted to get on down the river.

As they left the bank the old man added, "Oh, by the way, I have another surprise for you down stream."

Marcus wondered what that could be as he pushed his boat into the river and jumped in with the rain still falling. The old man was exposed to the rain, only protected by his warm coats, wool hat, and the rain slicker. Marcus's boat was the same as when he landed. He had prepared his boat so he could stay dry and still guide his boat. As instructed, he lined up a few hundred yards behind and followed the path of the Colonel's lantern, the glow clearly seen on such a dark night.

27

Back in Erie, the drunken Confederate agent had been arrested and jailed by the Union Army until he came out of his stupor and talked sane again. The next day upon waking up in jail and being his old self again, he yelled for someone to come and tell him why he was in jail.

A Union Captain had been summoned to help with the determination-whether this guy was a local wharf rat or a real threat-and whether what he had uttered the night before was true. The guards escorted him to a small room and told him to take a seat. "What's your name?"

"Why do you have me in jail?" he asked in a pleading voice. The man was about thirty-five years old, and his dark leathery skin revealed he had spent many years in the hot sun and cold winds as a seaman.

"First, tell me, what is your name?"

"Hawthorn Biggs," he said as he hung his head in shame, then looking up, "Did I kill somebody last night?"

"No sir, it seems in your drunken stupor you screamed out for all to hear the Union Navy blockading Southern ports would soon be blown to bits, and there was nothing we could do to prevent it."

"I was drunk! I can't imagine why I would say something like that. I just transport cattle and swine on the St. Lawrence River. That's all."

"Are you a Southerner?"

"Not really; I live on my barge and spend most of my time between Toronto and Erie."

"Did you ever live in the South?" the Union officer questioned trying to connect the suspect to a Southern plot to destroy the Union Navy.

Mr. Biggs was silent after the question, as if he could feel a noose tightening around his neck, and therefore chose his words carefully to sever his involvement with the smuggling operation and any connection to the South whatsoever. "No sir."

"Why did you say 'not really'?"

"Years ago my travels took me to Southern ports and I was alive when I was there, but no, I never had a residence on shore there."

"Again, why did you say what you did when you were drunk? Sometimes alcohol lets you spill out things you would not otherwise reveal."

There was a knock on the door and another uniformed soldier came in and gave the officer in charge of the interrogation something and whispered in his ear. Then the officer approached Biggs again. "My colleague just told me that one of our policemen found this newspaper inside your coat last night along with a note that says to meet two men named Heywood and Shaw at The Red Owl Inn on Percy Street a week before or after September 20th. May I ask what business you might have with these men?"

"They buy my hogs. I transport and sell hogs. That's my business."

"Do you know their last names?"

"No sir."

"How did these men find you, and can you tell us where we can find them to verify your story?"

"They sent me a letter in Toronto. That note told me where to meet them in Erie, and I don't know where they live. We've done this before."

"What's your address in Toronto?"

Mr. Biggs was digging a hole that is often dug by liars, too deep to get out of and difficult to wiggle in. "Well, I don't have one. I live on my boat, and people just know me as Hawthorn Biggs."

"You mean to tell me that I can be in San Francisco and write Hawthorn Biggs, Toronto, Canada, on an envelope and someone will deliver it to you?"

Mr. Biggs smiled back with pride, "Yes sir, that be's the case."

"But what if you are in Erie?"

"Then they just put Erie, Pennsylvania."

"Do you have a mailbox in Erie or Toronto?"

"Yes sir, the post office holds my mail, and I just go and gits it."

"I see," the officer said as he turned to one of his men, "Go down to the post office and see if they have a mailbox or have ever heard of Hawthorn Biggs." The officer turned back toward Hawthorn, "Then what about this newspaper, The Charleston Gazette?" he asked as he unfolded the newspaper to show Hawthorn the headlines. When he did, a brown envelope fell out from between the pages. When it hit the floor the envelope popped open and the edges of U.S. paper money could be seen. Apparently the authority who had discovered the newspaper had not examined it closely, only seeing the importance of the paper's origin and only reading the source of the paper and the note inside. The officer looked at the dollar bills sticking out of the envelope, bent down and picked them up, and started thumbing through them. At the very back of the stack were two Confederate fifty dollar bills. The Captain realized the plot had just thickened. He looked up at Hawthorn, "Mr. Biggs I don't think you are telling me everything I want to know. I am indeed fearful now what you revealed last night may be true, and now, I fear for our sailor's lives."

Hawthorn started pleading, realizing the noose had just tightened again on his lying neck. In a panic to explain where he got the bills he said, "I got those dollars before the war when I had visited there. I just kept them to take home to show my friends."

"That's real interesting, Mr. Biggs. How could you get Confederate money before the war started?" he yelled. The Union officer knew now for sure that his man was a Confederate spy at the least and might indeed be involved in a plot to sink Federal ships. He eased closer to Biggs and grabbed him by the collar and shook him violently, demanding, "Now, tell me why you're in Erie, Pennsylvania? Tell me!"

In a whimpering voice, trying to gain sympathy from an unsympathetic man, "What I told you is true. I am just a swine merchant and nothing else. Do I look like a spy?"

Indeed, this dingy pork salesman did not look like a spy. From the way he spoke, he exuded a façade of stupidity, not having enough intelligence to be part of a complicated smuggling ring, just the type of man to be in such a plot, a hog-mover no one would ever suspect. However, knowing he was lying, the officer painfully struck him across the face with his open hand. Hawthorn, still untied, suddenly leaped for the door, pushed the startled guard aside and ran down the hall. The interrogator reached for Biggs as he went by but missed him. Realizing he could not let this man escape or be shot he yelled, "Stop him, stop him, but don't shoot him," as he also took up the chase. The yelling immediately brought attention to Hawthorn's flight and after several minutes of elusive maneuvers several policemen blocked his getaway and cornered him; all the time the officer in charge was yelling, "He knows too much, don't shoot him." The men wrestled him to the ground, bound his hands, and placed him in a secure cell to await more interrogation.

The army officials and police gave Biggs time to think about his predicament, until they heard the truth about the mailbox. Within the hour they learned there was no such man as Hawthorn Biggs registered with the postal service to receive mail. With that news they returned to Biggs suspecting they had stumbled on to a possible toxic spy ring around Erie.

The Union officer had been a police captain in the New York police department before the war. He was convinced from what he heard that Hawthorn Biggs was a Confederate agent of some sort. However, due to his poor use of the English language, and apparent ignorance and lack of thought by telling them he had gotten the Confederate money before the war started, instead, made Hawthorn look like a patsy. His past experience as an interrogator would serve him well now to find out the truth about the swine man, Hawthorn Biggs.

With the cooperation of the local police the Captain decided to pull a ruse on Hawthorn and scare the information out of him without torturing or hurting him. If the deception did not work, torture and pain would come later. The sacrifice of hundreds of seamen for the comfort of one of the enemy was not justified. He was going to get the information by whatever means it took.

The Captain called his group together in a small room in the basement of the building to explain his plan. "I want to scare the information out of Mr. Biggs rather than beat it out of him. This ruse worked several times when I was a policeman back in New York, and I sense it will work here. We are going to prepare a stage for our actor, Hawthorne, to enter right here in this room. I want some of you to play the part of other prisoners and some of you to be the disciples of pain. To put it simply, "I want to scare the hell out of this man. I want him to listen to the groans of horror taking place down here in this room performed by you men. Be good actors and use the whips and other items to make this a room in hell. Kick the walls if you have to; make a place of bedlam. I think this man is ignorant though, is not a hardened spy, only getting involved for the money, and because he had a hog boat. He will tell us what he knows to avoid the pain he thinks he is about to get."

Under the Captain's direction a small storeroom in the basement was converted into an alleged torture chamber. They even adorned the floor and walls with splatters of blood obtained from a nearby slaughter house along with borrowed meat hooks they screwed into the ceiling. They hung whips, clubs, and chains on the walls to add a background of horror for their stage. Inside they placed an old table smeared with blood. One enterprising young policeman put a sign over the door that read "Torture Room" not knowing whether Hawthorne could read it or not. The men would have to work hard to prepare and carry out their ruse, but the information was important and worth their effort.

When the stage was ready for Act I, Hawthorn Biggs was led out of his jail cell back into the interrogation room with his hands bound and his feet shackled and pushed down in a chair. Fearing another escape and not knowing the importance of their prisoner yet, guards were placed inside and outside the room, and the entire police building had been put on alert for a possible attack by unknown outside accomplices, not only to free him, but perhaps to kill him to keep him from revealing the Confederate secret.

After all was secure, the Union Captain entered to resume his questioning and begin their ruse. "Mr. Biggs, as you know, we could not find a mailbox or anyone who ever heard of Hawthorn Biggs. The postal clerk went through piles of undeliverable mail trying to find any trace of your name."

"Have him look again. It has to be there," Hawthorn pleaded.

"Don't waste my time! Your slip of the tongue the other night will be a painful mistake if you don't tell me the truth. Why not make it easy on yourself and tell me what I want to know."

"I swear I don't know why they don't know me at the mailbox, and I found that old newspaper out on a bench. When I saw it was from another town, I just picked it up and put it in my coat pocket. I didn't know it had any Confederate money inside. You've got to believe me."

The Captain nodded his head to a policeman that indicated for him to tell them downstairs to raise the curtain for Act I of the play that was to follow for an audience of one. The Captain turned back to Hawthorn, "I am going to take you downstairs and use some therapeutic methods for getting information out of stubborn acorns, if you know what I mean. We had some people before you they are working on now, but they should be finishing up soon. Let's go."

The guards shuffled Biggs out the door. Biggs, only able to take small steps, was led to the stairs that descended to the torture room. As they got to the stairs a policeman came up the steps and told them to wait a few moments; another prisoner was coming up. Behind him came a bound man, his head covered in blood, followed by two more policemen. When he got to the top of the stairs he looked at Biggs, "Mister, tell them what they want to know," and he bowed his head as if he took all the punishment he could stand. As he was shuffled away, he yelled back, "You must tell them, or they will kill you."

The Captain was amazed at the effort and realism the policemen added to his plan. From below, the sounds of another torture started with the lash of a whip and the whimper of a man responding to the pain. The whimper turned to cries, then groans as the supposed whipping continued. Finally, Hawthorn heard the sufferer cry out, "Stop, stop, I will tell you what you want to know." After about ten minutes the torture room door opened, and a bloody body staggered out of the cell, almost being dragged by the guards. The Captain thought again what good actors these policemen were. It was going better than he planned as he watched the perspiration appear on Hawthorn's face, and his eyes flashed with fear as he watched the next prisoner enter the cell.

The next detainee pretended to be tough and wasn't going to confess to anything. He started fighting the guards trying to escape, causing a raucous Hawthorne couldn't see but imagine. From the sounds, the guards had forced him to the ground, all the time the prisoner yelling, "I ain't telling you guys nothing. You can kill me but I ain't squawking." Then the sound of the whip was heard, and then they starting kicking the walls as if the prisoner was getting a terrible clubbing, him still screaming, "I will never tell!" The sounds of lashes and clubbing went on for another minute or so. A guard was then heard to say, "Is the red-hot poker ready now? This guy is a hard nut to crack all right, but this will make him talk." Then another horrible continuous scream echoed out of the room as if the man had been thrown into Satan's lake of fire. Then the screaming stopped. No one outside said a word, pretending to ponder what had happened. Hawthorne now had a grimace on his face, beads of sweat covered his brow, and the same look one might have if he had been sentenced to hell by God.

The actors inside played their part to perfection. They used time to give Hawthorne an opportunity to think about his fate. After ten minutes, the door opened and one of the policemen came out and went upstairs. After a few moments, he returned with four men with a stretcher. They went inside and closed the door. There was no more sounds of torture. After what seemed an eternity, the door knob rattled and the door creaked open slowly as if the sounds had been scripted into the play. Hawthorn saw the policemen come out of the blood splattered room bearing the body of a prisoner. Another guard appeared at the door wiping his hands with a towel. "I'm sorry guys; he wouldn't talk. He was a hard nut we couldn't crack. Whatever he knew, he took it to his grave. I guess we beat him too hard with the clubs before we made him grab that red hot iron." Then he looked at Hawthorne. "Bring him in. Let's see if we can do better with this guy."

Biggs had seen enough. The Captain's plan worked. He looked at the officer, "Don't beat me. I'll tell you everything I know. I am just a small cog on a bigger wheel, but I'll talk."

The Captain stared into the man's eyes and saw sincerity of truth reinforced by fright he had not seen before in Hawthorne's eyes, but added, "That sounds good, but let's go in and just take one lash on the back to remind you what's going to happen if I find you lying again."

"No, please, please," Biggs begged, falling to his knees lifting his tied hands into a praying position, "You don't have to beat me. What I say will be the truth."

"Alright, let's go back upstairs and see if you really mean it." As they turned toward the stairs the guards were leading another prisoner down to evidently take a beating. After Biggs had gone upstairs, the Captain turned to the guards, "Men, you guys need to put that play on stage in New York. By the way, for a little place, we sure have lots of torture and prisoners. I figured he was so scared he did not think about that idea. Also, be sure and clean all that blood up before it starts stinking and runs us out of this place."

"Will do, Captain. That scheme of yours worked well."

Back in the interrogation room, Hawthorne knew what he was going to tell the Captain would most likely sentence him to the firing squad. Before he talked, he pleaded with him to spare his life. He said he had always been poor and had a wife and three children back in Toronto. He assured him he was only a transporter of livestock and had no sympathy for the South whatsoever, but one day when he was loading swine to take to Detroit a well-dressed man approached him and asked if he could deliver two boxes across the lake. "He told me he would pay me fifty dollars if I would take the boxes to Erie and find two men named Heywood and Shaw, you know, the names on the note you found. The man told me to keep my mouth shut and not tell nobody. When the two men got the boxes, they would give me another fifty dollars."

"I figured they were smuggling whiskey when he showed me the boxes, but being curious I insisted he tell me what I was carrying to Erie. He wouldn't tell me at first, but I finally got him to say that the two boxes contained hardware for the Confederate Navy that would sink Union ships, and the easiest way to get them down South was to come through Canada. He told me he had more business for me later and would pay me even more if I kept my mouth shut and did a good job. That's all I know about what's inside. He did say to handle them with care and not open them or drop them. He also mentioned the boxes should never get wet."

"What did the two men in Erie look like?

"Amish, they were dressed like the Amish. At the time, I thought it peculiar to find Amish going in a tavern; they are such good people and all. Ever since the man in Canada told me I had to keep quiet, I figured there was something illegal going on, but I could look the other way for a hundred dollars."

"What did these boxes look like?"

"I really didn't see the boxes, they were in large burlap bags, but I could tell by their sound and feel when I loaded them they were wooden boxes, two of them about six inches high and a foot wide and about two feet long."

"Did they have any distinguishing marks or labels?"

"No, like I said, I never saw them. I can't read, but I know writing when I see it. There was no writing on the bags.

"I see. How many times have you done this?"

"This was the first time."

"Where did you get the money and the newspaper? Tell me the truth this time."

Very humbled now, he feared he was doomed. Biggs was going to cooperate and tell everything he knew in hopes of saving his life. "The man that picked up the boxes had the newspaper in his pocket. When he left, he handed it to me and said for me to learn something about the South. I didn't tell him I couldn't read, so I just put in my pocket and thanked him; that's all."

"Then why did you say what you did that night in the tavern about hoping the Union navy would be blown up."

"The Lord knows I didn't mean that. When I got to Erie I went to the Red Owl and soon found the two men I was 'spose to meet. They followed me back to the boat, and I gave them the boxes. One of the men reached in his pocket and gave me the envelope filled with the other fifty dollars in U. S. money. Captain Sir, I now had a 'hunerd dollars. Sir, I had never seen that much money before. That's higher than I can count and more money than in the whole world. He said at the back were two Confederate fifty dollar bills for doing a good job. When I saw the Confederate bills I got scared a little that I might be gettin' myself in deep trouble, and shore enough I have. I started to give him his money back, but a 'hunerd dollars…. Sir; you would have taken it, too."

"Yes, I probably would have," the Captain sympathetically agreed. "What happened next?"

"Then the man said, if I keep my mouth shut, there would be more business for me later. He said, like the other guy, with my help the South could sink the Union Navy, and the two walked away. After he said that, I felt pretty important you know. I took my 'hunerd dollars; I didn't want to lose it or get it stolen, so I put it inside the newspaper and folded it up several times until it was small enough to fit tightly inside my coat pocket for safe keeping and went to the bar to celebrate my good fortune. Soon, another fellow that I didn't know joined me. From what he said, I think he was one of them Southern fellers, too. He talked to me about how great the South was and how they would win the war. Anyway, I kept drinking and listening to this fella', and 'fore I knew it, the Devil's brew had me under its control, and I must have become confused and spouted out what I heard them say about sinking the Union Navy. About then I must have passed out; I don't remember anything until I woke up in your jail."

"You know what you just told me will cause you to go on trial for treason, and if found guilty you will be shot."

"Oh, don't do that. I'm telling you the truth. That's all I know."

"Could you recognize the men you had dealings with if you saw them again?

"Yes'er, I remember people good. I'd know them anywhere."

"Good, then maybe there is a way I can save your life if you will help us catch the big fish in this operation. I am going to let you keep twenty dollars of your money, and I want you to go about your business as usual as if nothing happened. However, these folks may try to kill you to shut you up. That fellow you were drinking with in the pub may indeed be another Confederate agent sent to keep an eye on you. He may know you were arrested that night for what you yelled out in the bar. To insure your safety, I am going to send one of my men dressed as a civilian to go with you and watch your back. He will pretend to be a worker on your boat. I pray you will be safe. If the Rebel smugglers see you have been released, they will assume we thought you no more than a loud drunk in a bar, and that we have heard no information we could use. I am sure this is a group of Confederate smugglers, and you will hear from them again, either to find out what you told us, or to use your boat again. Stay around until I can arrange for one of my men to go with you," he added as he removed Biggs' shackles.

Hawthorn stood up and rubbed his wrists, then added, "I don't know if this is important or not, but to prove I am sincere in what I told you and I'm now on your side, I heard one of them Amish guys say they were going to Pittsburgh to meet a professor."

"What else did you hear?"

"That's all. I don't think they knew I heard that. They were going out the door."

The officer knew now that Hawthorn was only guilty of a little greed and not treason. "Now, go back to your hogs and continue your life as if nothing happened and if you are a free man." He dismissed Hawthorn and told him to return to his boat and keep alert.

With the information gained from Hawthorne, a network was set up to catch two Amish men now crossing Pennsylvania traveling south carrying some sort of naval devices. Since the cargo couldn't get wet or dropped the Union forces concluded that it was probably explosive devices that were to be used in the manufacture of torpedoes. Union spies knew the Confederates were developing such devices in hopes they could sink Union warships. It was imperative they capture the cargo before it could get to the Confederate Navy.

The Captain told one his men to telegraph the cities and towns between Erie and Pittsburg and locate and arrest two Amish men apparently in a wagon carrying two boxes of naval armaments for the South. He also wired Pittsburgh and told the authorities to watch for a professor who was to pick up the weaponry. Fortunately for the professor, the Union forces did not know how the professor was traveling. The authorities watched the roads, stages, railroads, and larger steamboats, not expecting the professor to be traveling in a small flat boat. Union agents ignored the small piers and docks around Pittsburgh.

The Confederate spy, who witnessed the arrest of Hawthorne Biggs, assumed Biggs would tell the Union authorities all he knew. Aware now of a possible leak in the spy ring, the spy had raced after the Amish pretenders and before they had gone far, caught them. He warned them their disguise as Amish may have been exposed. That's when the two Amish men turned into priests. They figured wooden crates would look suspicious and would be opened by the authorities to see what they were carrying, but if they were hidden with produce, like potatoes, they had a better chance of getting to Pittsburgh. When they opened the crates, to their surprise, they found the detonators were sealed in waxed waterproof boxes. To blend in with the potatoes they carefully printed "seeds" on large white paper labels and attached them to the outside of the crates with more melted wax. It made the two smugglers look like pastors taking supplies to needy farmers in their area, a perfect pretext for the occasion.

The Union authorities searched diligently for two Amish men in a wagon traveling south, but it seemed they had disappeared. In Pittsburgh, they had watched all the modes of transportation and found several professors, but none that fit the role of a spy. The detonators had to be found, however, and after failing to find the professor or the detonators after a week of extensive searching, they focused their search to the Ohio River, the only way their prey could have escaped using a small boat or barges that would not be noticed in the river traffic. River towns were soon notified to be on the alert for a professor carrying wooden crates in a wagon or a boat.

28

Marcus followed the distant glow from the professor's boat about a quarter mile ahead of him as he navigated precisely behind him on that cold rainy night. He hoped the bright light from the professor's lamp could see any danger and keep them from running aground.

He was protected from the drizzle by his tent, but the old man steered his craft covered only by his rain slicker. In the few hours he had known the old man, Marcus had grown to appreciate his knowledge, humor, and his "goose-feather feelings." He wondered if his sixth sense was real or just something to talk about around a campfire; or was it a ruse to just get them moving on down the river in the rain.

Just before dawn, when night seems the darkest and people are the sleepiest, Marcus tried to concentrate on the speck of light ahead of him. He started nodding slightly, his eyes almost closing, but caught himself before he fell over; then seeing the beacon ahead, he came back to his senses. Staying awake when one is so sleepy is torture in a way. He fought to stay alert, but in a few minutes his chin was rested on his chest, all but out, but he recovered again when he almost fell over and looked up to see his guiding light had disappeared. Marcus was not worried; he had lost the light once before when the professor went around a curve in the river and could not be seen.

Marcus traveled another quarter mile and saw a small steamer coming up the river and at the same time heard the Colonel calling from the side of the river. "Marcus, don't light your lantern. Come over here. There's a ship coming. Come to the sound of my voice," he yelled, but not loud enough for the steamer to hear a mile ahead across the water. Marcus had learned sounds traveled far across the flat water.

A right oar was plunged into the water and the boat swung around toward the voice in the dark and paddled in that direction. The old man spoke softer and softer, "Come on in, I'm over here…come on…. come on in." The night was so black, he couldn't see anything.

"I lost you for a few minutes," Marcus informed the old man as he slowed and pulled alongside.

"Yes, I doused my light the instant I saw the steamer appear ahead of me. I hope he didn't see me. It's probably just a cargo boat plying the river, and will most likely pass and not see us over here against the dark bank, but I still have my 'goose-feather feeling.' If that's a Union ship hunting for an old professor with contraband they will only find an old river rat with a bunch of vegetables. I doubt they will see us, but to be safe, why don't you lower your tent momentarily and ease on down the river hugging the shore and let's separate as far as possible before he passes us. Use your paddle to push yourself against the bank, I am resting against it right now. If they catch you, hold up the fish you've caught and tell them you're an orphan that fishes on the river. I doubt they will even bother us; as dark as it is, they probably won't even see us," the old man whispered, "I'll catch up with you later, now get out of here before they see us together."

Marcus found the shore and used his oar to push against the bank and propel himself away and on down the river. When the steamer neared him, the light from the front of the boat about a hundred yards away dimly lit the shore line, but Marcus was hidden next to the shore lying low in the boat making no human silhouette. The horizontal rock formations behind his boat tended to camouflage the boat's silhouette which would be hard to see, even in better light.

Marcus watched the small steamer pass in the dark and suddenly felt the wake rolling his boat from side to side, pushing him momentarily against the rocky shore. The distance had grown between him and his old friend, and since the steamer seemed to be plowing ahead on the straight and narrow, he concluded he had not been seen. Marcus continued to watch closely to see if the ship was going to pass the professor farther up the river several hundred yards. When the Union boat got in the vicinity of the old man, Marcus heard a loud blast from its steam whistle. "Did that mean they saw the Professor's boat and would soon approach, or did it mean they wanted him to know they were there and for him to stay put; or did it mean something else?" He quickly learned the answer when the steamer veered to the left and headed right for his friend. Fortunately for Marcus he had eased around and stopped behind a large rock, unable to be seen by the Navy ship just as Marcus heard a voice yell, "Ahoy, the United States Navy approaching."

There was no reply at first. Then they called again. Marcus knew the old man heard him call, but he was pretending to be asleep. Then he heard the Colonel yell back in his best ignorant drawl, "What's going on out thar?" To Marcus, that didn't sound like the professor's eloquent use of the English language. Marcus wished he was closer and could hear the quiet conversation taking place now that the hollering was over. Marcus had pledged to the professor he would help him if he got in trouble. Marcus debated whether to float on down the river and get away and wait for the professor later, or tie up and go see if he could help him in case they arrested him for some reason.

Marcus quickly made up his mind. He had shot Yankees before, and it wouldn't be no difference to him if he shot a dry one or a wet one. He tied his boat, still hidden behind the large stone, and slipped ashore with pistols inside his belt. He got behind the tree line and made his way toward the light on the steamer. While the larger boat prepared to check out the professor's boat, Marcus eased closer. He used the trees and dense river growth to approach within thirty feet behind the professor. There appeared to be only four sailors on the small naval steamer, two of which had come ashore on a small dinghy to search the suspicious boat. Both craft were close to the professor's boat now, and If need be, Marcus sensed he could kill all four sailors before they were aware of any danger with his two pistols.

There were two sailors who had come on shore, one being an officer, using a small dinghy. They made the old man unload all his vegetables. He heard the professor using his worst English, pretending to be a river rat peddling vegetables on the river. "Whut are you after me fer, can't you see I'm just a hawker selling 'taters,' carrots, and beets on this here river?" His voice was raspy and hoarse, further hiding the fact of who he was.

After finding nothing of military importance the officer told the old man, "Put your potatoes and beets back in your boat and we are sorry we stopped you."

Pretending to be a little angry, the professor replied, "Why are you serchin' people like me? I ain't done nuttin and I ain't never been serch'd b'fore."

"Rumor has it there's an old professor on the river carrying munitions that can blow up our ships. We are going to find him. Have a good day."

"Well, how 'bout 'dat; but one thang more? Is I gonna be stopped every few miles and have to unload my 'taters' for you'uns to look at?"

"Maybe, but let me write you a note that, in case you get stopped again, might, just might save you from being searched." He took a small tablet from his coat pocket and scribbled a note which indicated he had been searched and approved by Captain Hamilton. "Use this if you get stopped again. Most of my men know me on the river and know my signature. The paper also has a navy insignia right at the top. This may help."

"Why, thank you, sir! 'Dat's very kind of you."

After the officer was convinced the vegetable vender was who he said he was, returned to the small steamer several yards from shore.

As he boarded the craft the officer turned to his men and grinned, "He's definitely not a professor."

As the seamen steered their steamer back into the river towing the dinghy behind them, the Professor hollered as he waved goodbye, "Ya'll be careful now, and catch that man that's caused me so much trouble!" He stood and watched the boats as they disappeared in the drizzle and dawn of the earliest morning light.

When the steamer was out of sight, Marcus came out of the woods and quietly slipped up behind the old man. "You were great!" Marcus laughed, surprising the Colonel for a second, causing him to jump around suddenly. "Don't scare me like that. I'm just getting over another fright. That was close. I am sure glad we unloaded the detonators into your boat. I could be on the way to gallows right now if we hadn't done so."

"I crept up here in the dark to see if you needed any help. I brought my two helpers here," patting his pistols in his belt. I thought about shooting all of them, but I didn't 'cause you were doing such a good job pretending to be a river rat. I just thought I'd let you go ahead and handle the matter. I must say that was a great performance. At first I thought they had stopped somebody else," Marcus laughed.

"Yes, they believed I was a river rat, and by the way, will you believe me the next time I get a 'goose-feather feeling?'"

"You bet!"

29

The next few days were clear and the two comrades floated down the river with no searches or aggravations. Things were going well; they traveled during the night, rendezvoused at dawn and hid their boats during the day up small rivers and creeks that flowed into the mighty river. They dined on the professor's vegetables and ate Marcus's fish and slept most of the day. In several weeks they arrived on the outskirts of Cincinnati.

Due to the increased river traffic, the Colonel decided to begin traveling during the day to avoid a possible collision during the night. The professor concluded, due to amount of river traffic near the large town, they could pass by Cincinnati and never be noticed. However, by happenstance, they arrived above Cincinnati shortly before dark rather than during the day. The professor slowed and motioned for Marcus to come alongside.

The professor spoke with concern in his voice, "This is a large town; matter of fact she is called the 'Queen of the West', and we are going to have to keep our eyes open. Railroads intersect here and disperse supplies to the Union Army on the Mississippi. If any town is searching for me, it will be here. Instead of passing through during the day as we planned, we will have to travel again at night. Stay a little closer now, about half the distance you were before. When we get past this town and get back in the dark, we will pull in and rest.

The two small boats reached the edge of the city shortly after nightfall. The old man calculated that they could pass by Cincinnati and be long gone before morning if they pushed on now. The professor had encouraged Marcus to fish and have a large stringer of live fish to show the authorities if he was stopped, pretending to be a commercial fisherman, and the professor would continue to be the beet and tater salesman that had gotten him through so far. They would have no contact with other until they joined up again below the town.

The night was cold, near freezing, and they noticed river activity had rapidly slowed at dusk. They saw one river steamer either entering or leaving the city; the other river craft were stopped along the many piers and docks. Except for one lonely human scurrying in the night to find protection from the cold, the docks appeared to be abandoned.

Many boats from large paddle wheelers to small steamers, were tied to the piers as the two silently floated by in the middle of the river as far from either shore as possible. Their black silhouettes barely stood out from the faint glow from the city, their presence only known by the lanterns at the front of their vessels. There seemed to be more riverboats tied up in Cincinnati than in Pittsburgh. On this cold night the town had buttoned up and the authorities would not be out looking for an old bearded man in a boat. All was going well.

The two river riders were nearly past the heart of the town when the Professor saw two large dark shapes ahead of him, one behind the other, chugging up the river, spouting steam and smoke in the frosty air. On their present course the first ship would pass right over the professor if he didn't steer to the side of the river. The old man plunged his oars in the water and paddled fast toward the south shore to avoid a collision. He hoped Marcus was watching and would follow him. The captain on the other larger ship finally saw the small craft and gave the Colonel a warning with his steam whistle.

The Colonel navigated out of the boat's path and waited for the extra wide craft to pass, awaiting the large wakes from the big boats. He looked ahead and saw the other ship, a twin of the first approaching, too. As the first ship came alongside he was amazed to see it was one of the heavily-armed Union ironclad gunboats that were used to bombard the Confederate forts on the Mississippi and Tennessee Rivers earlier in the war. As the dark slant-sided ships eased by, the old man thought what a prize it would be to the Confederate cause if he and Marcus could send them to the bottom of the river. He detested the iron monsters that had caused such havoc for the Rebel river forces, but he was in awe and admiration of their strength as they passed.

He looked behind him and saw Marcus also had seen the iron behemoths and was veering off the river channel. The professor stopped and watched the flotilla go by. He saw the stars and stripes flying on the stern of each ship. He wondered if the ships were going on up the river or would stop in Cincinnati.

A few moments after the large ship passed, the professor saw the huge wakes approaching his small craft. He quickly turned the front of his boat to take the wake head on, rather than take a chance the large wave would capsize his smaller craft. After he rode over the waves, other smaller waves followed and he held his boat straight. He looked back at Marcus to see that he had rotated also to encounter the danger. Soon the other wake from the other warship approached.

Before long, Marcus pulled up alongside, grabbing the side of the professor's boat. "Ugh, did you see the size of the wake? I wondered at first why you had turned, but then I caught a glimpse of that big wake in the dim light. From the size of that wave, if we had passed them in the darkness of the river and did not see the size of that thing, it might have turned me over. As that monster approached me, I did what you did…. by the way, why are we stopping? Did the waves hurt your boat?" We've just about sneaked by this place."

"I know, I know, boy, but did you see those big gunboats go by. Let's watch them a minute and see where they go. If they stop here in Cincinnati, it might behoove us to stop, too."

"What do you mean 'behoove' us?"

"Benefit, benefit, it would benefit us to stop also."

"Why?"

"Boy, can't you see what just passed by? Those are Union gunboats. If we could put one of our eggs we're carrying in their nest, we could help our cause a great deal. You and I would have sunk a powerful portion of the Union Navy on the Mississippi. I hope they will stop and nest here for a few days."

As the two men watched the warships approach the center of town, the ships slowed and steered quietly toward an open pier. They blew their whistles to alert dock crews to help them tie up the heavy craft. Suddenly the pier came alive with activity. It took the dock hands about half an hour for the captain to maneuver in and tie up and get everything secure. The two ironclads were docked end to end, parallel to the river. The Colonel admired the skill of the two captains as they had eased their ships against the pier.

The professor turned and looked at Marcus with a great smile on his face. "It looks like they built a nest in Cincinnati. Let's go see if we can hatch an egg under those two monsters."

Marcus was afraid and argued that they were in deep trouble as it was, and they needed to deliver the detonators to Nashville. The professor argued whether they got caught now or after they blew the ships up, it would not matter, they would both be executed anyway if caught. They couldn't pass up such a good opportunity to help the South win the war.

After all Marcus had been through and survived, he felt his luck might run out. After much persuasion and patriotic talk, Marcus finally agreed and followed the professor's boat over against the riverbank below Cincinnati just outside of town. The area was thickly populated for several miles above and below the large city, but the riverbank was steep where they rested and there didn't seem to be a house close by. They pulled their craft ashore to sketch out a plan that would accomplish their goal.

The professor spoke, "You stay here and watch our boats while I go in and reconnoiter the warships, find out how they are tied up, and see who watches them. When I get back, I'll tell you what I found out." He grabbed a sack and filled it with some turnips and started climbing the steep side of the river. "I'll try to find us something good to eat before I get back. I'm getting hungry for something sweet."

"What if you don't come back?"

"Don't worry, I'll be back, but just in case I am not back by midafternoon, take my vegetables to eat, and take our cargo on down to Nashville. Remember, the man in the tall hat and the white feather with a red tip." With that he climbed the bank and was out of sight.

Marcus got in his tent and sealed it tight and would try to sleep until he returned. Having been up all day, he quickly fell sound asleep. Several hours after sunup Marcus was awakened by the sound of small rocks bouncing against the side of his boat as the Colonel descended the bank, loosening the small rocks as he came down. Startled at first, Marcus grabbed his gun and peeked out, hoping he would see the old man.

Sure enough, there he was with his sack of turnips and a small paper bag. Marcus rubbed his eyes, "What time is it? It seems I slept longer than I wanted."

"Boy, I'm glad you're here. I was afraid you thought I got captured and left. I stayed longer than I planned. Here, have a couple of these things," the professor said. Marcus took the bag and looked inside to see several large sugar cookies.

Marcus looked up, "Some coffee would taste good with these sweets. Let's make some and fry some fish. I am starving to death."

"I'm hungry, too." The two river rats got busy and started a fire in Marcus's stove, and in less than an hour they were eating a late breakfast of fish and fried potatoes, finishing off their meal with the cookies and coffee sitting out of the wind under Marcus's tent.

The professor peeked out the end of the tent to see if anyone was nearby, always alert before he talked about ideas that would hang him if heard by the wrong party. He leaned back inside, took out his pipe, sucked air through it to make sure it was clear of debris, and started telling Marcus what he discovered, while at the same time packing his pipe with fresh tobacco he had just purchased in town. "The two ships are docked about a hundred feet apart parallel to the pier with a smaller steamer between them. I walked up next to the pier and looked at them as if I was completely awed by their presence, and I might add, indeed I was. After hearing about the arrival of the large warships, needless to say, a small crowd gathered on the pier, even on a cold night, to see the magnificent ships. There was a guard standing by the gangplank where the sailors went on board and two others on guard at each end on the ship. Both were armed with rifles and pistols. I walked up to the one on the dock and using my best ignorant vernacular said, 'I never saw any thang like 'dat 'fore and laughed as if I had seen a miracle. I told him I figured those Rebels are in trouble now, and then I gave a loud howl like I was happy they were on our side."

The guard looked at me like I was an old fool who just came into town and was completely harmless. I asked him if he would be so kind as to let me go on board, but he said that was prohibited, but I could walk over to the edge of the dock and look at her. The name of that ship is the *Chicago* and the other is the *St. Paul*. It appears the *Chicago* has a problem with her boiler and will most likely be here a week. I studied both ships carefully. Every square inch of the ship above water is covered in iron, but she has a wooden hull, and I suspect it is vulnerable to one of our little eggs. If we can figure some way to get alongside and attach a torpedo, we can sink that giant. Imagine that; David slays Goliath again."

"By the way, what took you so long to get back down here?" Marcus wondered.

"After I studied the boats, I went in an eatery to get a bite to eat. Apparently it stayed open all night to feed the dock workers. You know, this is a busy place all the time. I asked a server if I could borrow a pencil and paper to write a letter back home. He was a friendly guy and quickly accommodated my needs. I wrote the first page of a letter as a ruse and then set about making sketches of the ship and its dimensions. While I was next to the beasts I paced off their length." The Colonel laughed, "Every time I saw my server approach I covered my drawings with the fake letter. Once he asked me, 'Sure takes you a long time to write a letter.' I looked up and replied, 'I ain't very smart, but I needed to pen this here letter to my brother and tell him that I bought a barge load of sows today; the reason that I come up here fer. I hope this letter gets back down the river 'fore I do.'"

"I see. Then take all the time in the world to write your letter. We aren't very busy now and have room for you to pen your letter. Besides, it's cold outside. Stay as long as you need."

The professor grinned, "That gave me a perfect place to work. A hot cup of coffee, a table, and a nearby candle to see. That's where I spent the night, and when morning came, I wanted to check out the town to see if I could find some materials I would need and a shop to work in. Now, let me get some sleep; I haven't slept in nearly twenty-four hours. I'll see you later today." With that said, the old man returned to his boat and was soon snoring and fast asleep.

"Let him rest," Marcus thought, "He had a pretty long day."

Marcus had slept soundly deep into the morning. The professor was asleep, so while he slumbered, Marcus opted to go look at the gunboats and explore the large town for himself. He climbed the steep bank and soon found a road that led into Cincinnati. He had not walked long until a man in a wagon gave him a lift. Marcus thanked him for the ride and walked toward the nearby river. There they were, the two mighty beasts that had dealt death and destruction along the western rivers. Marcus walked up and joined the now larger crowd that had gathered on shore to see them. Marcus looked at their size and the black steel dress punctuated by large steel rivets that covered both structures.

"If the Confederate forts could not sink them, how could two river rats have a chance," he thought? "But the professor was right; she was hard on top but soft on bottom." The slanted iron plates came down to the waterline and stopped. Below the edge of the iron could be seen a wooden hull. If he could approach the boat, maybe at night and attach a torpedo, she could be blown up, maybe not to smithereens, but at least a hole that would sink her.

He knew she would be guarded night and day, and they wouldn't let some stranger just row up and plant a bomb on her. How could he get near the ship and not be suspected? Marcus left the boats with that question on his mind.

He walked down the sidewalks looking at the stores. He could see the war had a prosperous effect on Cincinnati and businesses were doing well. After a brief tour, he headed back down the road toward the Colonel. As the sun sank toward the horizon, it was getting colder. Another kind fellow offered Marcus a ride. Before reaching their anchorage he told the old man to let him off, that he lived nearby, disguising the fact he was living on the river and had further to walk.

30

That night both men reclined in Marcus's boat talking softly about their predicament and what options might be open for them. Should they leave the gunboats and fulfill their original mission or stay and see if they could damage the Union Navy?

"If we could get a torpedo under the edge of the armor I think she would sink. It wouldn't take much of a hole to sink her with all that iron plating. She is probably barely afloat as it is and top heavy, and she would most likely roll over if one side started to sink," the professor contemplated.

Marcus lay quietly, listening to the Colonel's thoughts as the wise old man continued, "If somehow we could row up to the hull and one way or another attach the torpedo and leave without them knowing it; that would be perfect." The professor rose up on his elbow and looked at Marcus in the light of the lantern, "Marcus, can you swim underwater?"

Marcus turned his head toward the old man, "I know what you're thinking and yes, I can swim underwater, but not this time of the year. Have you touched the water? It feels like ice. I would freeze to death or get frostbite or sick and die of aches and chills." Marcus rolled over away from the professor, "No, thank you, let's think of something else."

"One way or another we must get next to the ship. I would expect to be shot if you just started rowing toward them in the middle of the night. There are sharpshooters all over the top of that ship, I noticed."

Suddenly Marcus rolled over and sat up, "I know how I can get close to the boat by just being friendly."

The professor laughed, "How are you going to do that? Write them a letter and say, 'I just want to look at your ship up close while I attach a torpedo?'"

"No, I think I have a good idea. Listen to me. Coming down the river I stopped at small towns and sold people fish. Everyone was very friendly. My price was cheap, and I don't think I was ever turned down once. Those sailors have to eat. If I hold up a stringer of big fish as I paddled by, you know just showing the sailors what I have caught, grinning, bragging in a way, showing off like so many young boys do, proud of what they did, I am sure they would ask me to come closer to their boat to see what I had."

The professor sat up and put his feet on the floor at the front of the boat, "Hey, you may have something there!"

The boy stared at the side of the blank tent wall as if he watched a plan being drawn on the white wall in front of his eyes. "Yes, yes! And if they want fish, I will say those are already sold, as if I was not interested in their business." This is perfect, "Listen, to this," Marcus spoke, all elated, as he revealed his plan to the wise old man. "Then I could say, 'if I have any fish left after my regular customers tomorrow, I'll sell you what's left. The next day I will come back with more fish, good big fish, and row up close to the boat and yell that I have some fish if they want to buy them."

"This is brilliant!" the old man chirped.

"If they want the fish, I'll row right up beside the boat, pretending to be clumsy and bump the side of the ship getting around to the gangplank. I'll sell the fish cheap, hoping they will ask me to bring more the next day. There are two ships there with lots of sailors to feed, and from what you said they will be here a week." Marcus went on, "The next day I'll paddle by and ask again if they need some fish, and of course they will. Don't you see then, they are asking me to come up near their ships. They will soon take me for granted, and I can probably row anywhere I want to around those beasts. They will think I am harmless and a friend. A few days later, after I gain their trust, I will carry two torpedoes, and I will attach them or hang them on the ship someway." He thought a minute, "Can you build a torpedo that can explode after I attach it to the side of the ship?"

"Yes, with some time and tools I could do that. It would have to be heavy so it would be underwater as you approached the boat so no one could see it," the professor pondered.

"By the third day, they would be expecting me. I doubt that would pay much attention to me by then. After they get the fish I could hang the torpedo on a nail. I could drive a nail underwater into the wooden hull in preparation for the torpedo."

The professor halted his story, "Son, have you ever tried to drive a nail underwater?

"No, as a matter of fact, I haven't." After thinking a second and looking the old man in the eye and feeling a little foolish, he said, "I guess that won't work."

"No. But even if you could, when they heard someone driving a nail in their ship they would come and investigate. People inside could hear the reverberations throughout the ship. You know how sound travels under water?" The professor thought a minute. "Nevertheless, there is one way we could stab a steel spike in the side of the boat and would never draw suspicion."

"How would that be done?"

"A ram, son; just ram a spike into the side of their ship using your boat." The professor jumped up and went to his boat and brought back some sheets of writing paper and a pencil. "I have an idea. Tonight I will draw a picture, and tomorrow I will build a frame that will attach to the front of your boat. I already see how I can build it. This frame will support a sharp spike pointed outward. When you approach their ship, paddle hard and speed up and ram this nail into the side of their wooden hull. Several hundred pounds of weight moving forward against that nail should drive it deep enough into the wood to hold the torpedo."

"If they could hear a nail being driven into their hull, wouldn't they hear the spike hit their boat?"

"Yes, but when they investigate they will find a clumsy oarsman who cannot handle his boat. The old man continued thinking, "Of course this 'nose' will be underwater and not seen. Yes, this idea should work perfectly. In the morning I must find a small place with some tools where I can work. I can also build the torpedoes there. Let's get some sleep and figure it out tomorrow."

The next day, the two schemers were up early; the professor seemed sleepy to Marcus and admitted that he had stayed up most of the night designing a torpedo in his head. After a good breakfast, the professor set out to find a workshop he might rent for a few days, while Marcus guarded the boats. Late in the afternoon, the professor returned smiling, indicating that he rented a pier with a small workshop at the end. It was behind a blacksmith's shop that did a lot of work on riverboats, but the owner was working on a project and didn't need it for a few days. "I'm lucky to have found that place. Every building in Cincinnati seems to be used for something. Business must be good here."

Marcus reached down in the water and pulled up a big stringer of fish. "When you left, I started fishing, and the fish are biting. Tomorrow, I will sell some fish."

Before Marcus could finish his sentence, the professor added, "And I will start building the ram. I haven't come up with a reliable torpedo design yet." The old man pulled some folded paper out of his pocket and began sketching ideas that he had thought about the night before. It seemed now their plans were made, and the first act of a life threatening drama would begin the next day.

The next morning, a small miscalculation had been discovered in their plans. While Marcus was selling fish and the Colonel building bombs, how could they keep an eye on the professor's boat? They agreed it would be better for Marcus to sell his fish early and test the first part of their plan before the professor spent time building the torpedoes. That way the professor's craft could always be watched and protected.

Marcus had lowered his tent and had packed it up. The professor bid him well, and Marcus pushed his boat into the water and rowed upstream back into town to find the two iron ships. Marcus found it much harder to go against the flow of the river than to float with the current. This was the first time since leaving Pittsburgh that he had gone upstream against the current, but after what seemed an eternity, he saw his black iron prey resting against the pier. The craft that had been between them had left, and the two warships were docked one behind the other, the *St. Paul* ahead of the *Chicago.*

Marcus thought a minute and sensed it might look suspicious if he rowed directly up to the warships, so he pulled up next to a steamer about five vessels down from the ironclads. The first boat was a barge of some sort with a small crew quarters. Marcus rowed up beside the boat and got the attention of a man in the pilot house who approached to see what the young man needed. In a few moments Marcus had sold the man four fish. It had been so easy, Marcus wondered if he should raise the price of his fish.

No one was on the next boat, but a group of dock workers saw what he was selling, and they bought six more fish. Marcus had placed only his best fish on one of his lines, expecting to sell only to the two naval vessels, but due to his change of plans and his success as a salesman, he only had three large fish left; but he still had the stringer of smaller fish that he had kept for himself. The next two small steamers bought a dozen of his smaller fish. Apparently, working men around the docks were so busy they had no time to fish so there was a demand for his product.

While he made his last sale, he noticed the guard at the stern of the warship had been watching him closely as he came down the line of boats. Marcus spoke and laughed loudly to bring attention to the fact that he was a "fisherman" and not give any hint to the sailors he might be a "saboteur." He thanked the man and told him loudly, "I'll be back tomorrow if you need some more fish."

Finally, he was at his prize. His next sale might determine the success of the mission. Instead of rowing directly toward the big warship, Marcus swung his bow away from the steel monster and acted as if he was going to steer around the warships and go on past to sell his fish farther down the pier.

The sailor standing guard yelled out to Marcus, "Boy, don't you love your country? Us sailors like good fish, too."

Marcus acted surprised, "You want some fish too?" I was skeered to come close to your ship. My Pa said to stay away from those iron ships; they got big guns sticking out the side and will shoot you if you get too close."

The sailor laughed and the other marksmen standing guard heard Marcus's reply and laughed, too. "Boy, we shoot Rebels, not our friends. Come over here and let me see what you got."

Marcus turned his skiff around and rowed toward the black warship that bristled with cannons, their mouths much bigger than he had ever seen on a battlefield. It was easier to move big guns on water than on land.

"Come over here boy, come around by the pier. There's enough room for you to squeeze in there."

Marcus couldn't believe what he was hearing. They were asking him nearly to come and plant a torpedo on their ship. Realizing he was going to give them a good bump later, Marcus purposely bumped into the ship hard as if he had not mastered the art of "rowing" yet. His knocking on the wooden hull brought some attention from the inside of the ship. Suddenly, a man in a white apron appeared, along with several enlisted men and an officer. "What's going on out here? Who's beating on the side of this ship?"

The guard stood at attention, "Sir, I asked this young man to row his boat up near the gangplank so he could sell us some fish."

"Oh, I see. That would be tasty. I'm getting tired of that canned stuff we've been eating." The guard looked at the man in the white apron holding a knife. "Cook Major, how about cooking us some fresh fish tonight?" When the ship was in port the cook often purchased fresh meat for his crew.

"Yes, I can do that if the boy has enough fish. How many pounds do you have to sell? This is a hungry bunch, and we eat a lot. Have him row on around to the gangplank, and I'll meet him there, and I'll see if he has anything I want. I ain't gonna buy no trash fish!"

Marcus rowed as close to the steel sides as possible, trying to learn everything he could about what the ship looked like underwater, and aware of the ends of the cannons staring out above him as he passed. He couldn't believe how large the ships were when he got up close. He figured they had to be over 150 feet long and 50 feet wide. He eased on down the side of the *Chicago* and rowed on around to the wide front of the ship; now in front of the *Chicago* and at the stern of the *St. Paul,* Marcus was in the center of the enemy's nest. At that point, while the guards and the cook watched, Marcus saw an opportunity to hide the move he would later use to plant a spike in the side of warship. Pretending to be a little inept as he rowed and steered around the front of the *Chicago,* he turned too sharp and gave the ironclad another good bump with the nose of his boat. The guards looked down and laughed at the awkward kid. Marcus acknowledged the laughter by hollering back, "I ain't use to rowing between two big warships. I'm a little scared they might blow up."

"Boy," the cook answered in a friendly manner, "Don't be afraid. We're not going to shoot you, nor or these ships going to blow up. Let me see what you got."

Marcus reached over the side and pulled up three large fish, each weighing about eight pounds and adding, "Sales have been good this morning. It seems everybody wanted fish today."

"Young man, I have a crew of 250 sailors. I need more than three fish. However, most of the crew was given a three-day shore leave while we are getting the boiler fixed, but I still need to feed the skeleton crew of about twenty men."

Marcus lowered the three fish and pulled up his other long stringer of fifteen, each fish weighing up to five pounds. "These are smaller, but they are still pretty good size. I'll sell you all I got."

The cook thought a second or two, "All right, I'll take them. Wish you had some more though. Can you bring me some more tomorrow?

Again Marcus couldn't believe what he just heard. He had been invited back tomorrow, his plan was working perfectly. Marcus traded his fish for a few dollars, the money not really mattering to Marcus now. Just the fact he knew how easy it would be for him to plant his deadly eggs was what was important. He bid the guards and cook goodbye and said he would be back tomorrow.

Marcus eased his boat back, bumping the side of the warship again, still pretending to be ungainly, and caught the current to carry him back to the Colonel with his great news. Then Marcus realized he had spent three days catching that many fish. He would have to fish for the rest of the day and all night and hope the fish were biting to secure that many fish. In addition, he had to stop fishing that day because he was out of bait.

About a half mile down the river, Marcus saw a rundown looking shop with a rickety pier that sold fishing gear, nets, and live bait. He had plenty of money now and could buy plenty of worms and minnows. He docked the boat next to the ladder and climbed up on the pier.

As he walked in the shop, Marcus remembered a technique his family used to catch fish when they wanted to have a "fish fry," a social event back home where people got together to party and eat fish. He felt stupid for not thinking about a "trotline" earlier.

Marcus grew up using a trotline, a heavy string stretched across a river or creek with many hooks attached. The river at Cincinnati was a quarter mile wide where he stood, much too far to stretch a trot line, but Marcus would use another trotline technique by tying one end of the line at the edge of the river and the other end to a floating bottle out in the river, the bottle held in place by an anchor, keeping the bottle in the river rather than pushing it around against the bank.

Marcus purchased enough line, hooks, bait, and small lead weights to make three trotlines about 60 feet long. He hurried back to his boat, anxious and excited to tell the Colonel about his small adventure. As he arrived, he saw the old man sitting on the riverbank, wrapped in a blanket, smoking a pipe and sketching the final details of his torpedo design.

Marcus hailed to the old man when he was near. The old Colonel stood up and immediately saw Marcus was excited, at first not knowing whether it was good or bad excitement, but when Marcus stood up and emitted a broad smile, he knew the news was good. "By the look on your face, you must have something good to tell me!"

Marcus jumped out of the boat and pulled it up on the bank, "Oh, you won't believe what happened." Marcus told him how he worked the other boats first, and then how easy it was to approach the warships. "I was next to the big iron beasts. You can't believe how big they are. I bet they are 200 feet long, now exaggerating their length. I rowed right under the ends of the cannons. If I had a torpedo I could have dropped it down the barrel."

"Did you sell them some fish?"

"Oh! That's the best part. At first, I pretended I was avoiding them and started to row around them, but the guard insisted I come up close and sell them some fish, too. I didn't know that fish would sell so fast."

"People have to eat, including the Navy."

"And…and when I got to the *Chicago,* I was almost out of fish. By the way, the cook told me most of the crew has left the boat."

"I can believe that."

"Anyway, there were only twenty sailors on board to tend and guard the ship. I found out the two ships will be there about a week to get a boiler fixed on the *St. Paul.* Anyway, they were real friendly and the cook told me to bring him some more fish tomorrow. He bought all I had. I didn't have any fish for the *St. Paul,* but they indicated they would buy some, too."

The old man took the blanket off his shoulders and tapped the burned tobacco out of his pipe, as if he was saying, you have done a great job, now let the master take off his cape and get to work. "You've done well, Marcus; better than I expected." He walked to the front of Marcus's boat and used his hands to roughly measure the dimensions and made notes on his sketches. After a few minutes he had what he wanted and told Marcus to hold down the fort but not to worry if he didn't come back until after dark, "I have work to do." He dug around in his boat a few minutes gathering several tools he had on board, then climbed up the river bank and disappeared. He worked at his workshop until dark.

Marcus was out of fish to cook, so he nibbled on peanuts to hold off his hunger until he could catch some supper. He set about making his trotlines, and in two hours he had three long trotlines attached with hooks every two feet. He estimated it was about two o'clock from the position of the sun. He returned to his boat and went down-stream, slightly below camp but close enough to watch the professor's boat, and tied one end of the line to a tree root exposed near the water's edge. He then rowed out into the river unwinding his line until he reached the end. Since he had no large bottles handy, he substituted a large, piece of nearly rotted wood, full of air, which floated well, and attached it to the line. He used a small rock on a string to find the depth of the river there. He then added that much more line to the trotline, tied the end to a large rock he had secured to the very end of the line for an anchor, and dropped it all in the water. He repeated that procedure three times. Now he was ready to bait the hooks. He rowed back to where the lines were tied to the shore, and slowly, using the trotline, pulled himself along, baiting each hook as he went. When he baited the last hook he dropped the entire line into the water. In a few hours, he would come back and put his fresh fish on his stringer if they were biting that night.

Done now, he paddled back up the river and came ashore next to the professor's boat. That night he returned to the first trotline tied to the root. When he lifted it up he could feel a fish moving the line. He smiled. He could feel the line had something on it, and apparently it was something big. He worked down the first line, harvesting his catch and baiting empty hooks with fresh worms. Most of the hooks were bare, but some still had a dead, shriveled up worm attached. After he ran all of his lines, he had twenty three fish. He put them on his stringer and rowed back to camp. He would check them again later that night. He was satisfied with his catch having hooked about a third of what he wanted. He figured the fish would bite better later in the night.

Even though it was late, Marcus fried fish and was about ready to pull two baked potatoes out of the coals. Earlier he had wrapped paper around the taters, then packed river clay around them and buried them under the hot coals. He had made a pot of coffee and cooked some cornbread in his iron Dutch oven. He hoped his old friend would show up soon and get to enjoy the food while it was fresh and hot.

When it was done, Marcus ate up. He had not eaten, except for the peanuts, since morning, and he was hungry. He had fried more fish than they needed, but if anything was left, they could snack on it during the night. He worried about his friend, but he had said not to expect him until maybe after dark. After he finished eating, Marcus washed his plates in the river, gathered the uneaten food, and put it in his Dutch oven to keep it warm.

It was time again to run his trotlines, but he did not want to be gone when the professor got back. He spread a blanket on the shore, wrapped up in another one and watched the lights reflected on the water from the lit homes across the river, the light sometimes broken by a passing boat. He looked up at the cold night air and looked at the heavens above him. He wondered if Bonnie was out that night watching the same stars he gazed at and was thinking of him. He could not wait to get home and tell her of the many adventures he had faced. He prayed a short prayer for her and hoped she was safe.

His moment of silence was broken by a stream of pebbles and clods of dirt falling on him as he spotted the old man standing on the edge of the bank above him. He was holding an odd-looking contraption that at first glance looked like a chair made by a fool. "I figured it out and got it made. This thing is heavy though. I pulled it down here in a small cart I borrowed from the blacksmith. Come up here and help me get this thing down this steep slope." Marcus climbed the hill to help him. The professor continued, "That guy in the blacksmith shop really knows his trade and is very likable, but a true-blooded Yankee. If he knew what he was making, he would kill me, or at the least turn me into the authorities, so I will have to be real careful working around him. I only need him to shape my metal parts. He thinks he is helping me build a harness to fit on the front of a boat that will support a net that can scoop up fish." The professor laughed, "You know when this war is over, I might patent that idea."

"I cooked you some fish and taters, cornbread too. It's in the wash pot. It should still be warm. I made the trotlines and caught about twenty fish. I'm going back and run them again right now. I'll be back in half an hour, I reckon," Marcus said as he pushed his boat into the river. In about an hour and a half he returned, and as he eased up to the bank, his face became visible in the glow from the campfire, and the old man knew the fish were biting. Marcus pulled up a stringer with ten large fish so heavy Marcus had to strain to make them visible. He eased them back in the water and pulled up another on the other side with twenty or thirty smaller fish. "If the fish keep biting, I will have more than enough fish for the gunboat and enough to sell on the side.

"Our plan is working well, better than I expected," the professor proudly claimed as he stood up and took his contraption to the front of Marcus's boat. "I need to see if I can fit this harness on your boat. Get out and help me with this." He slid the metal harness on the snout of the boat similar to putting a muzzle on a dog. It almost fit but needed to be a bit wider so he could slide it farther back and fit it against the nose. "It needs to fit snug so it will not bend or damage the front of your boat when you ram the spike into the ironclad." He took a measurement and removed the harness. He showed Marcus where the spike would be cradled in the harness. "I think this idea is going to work well," the professor added while scribbling some notes in his small journal.

"I'll run my lines one more time in the morning before I go sell them sailors their fish. I am tired and need some sleep." The old man watched Marcus climb in his tent. In a few moments he heard a slight snore.

The next day Marcus returned to the warship, selling his fish to the boats tied up in front of the ship as he had done the day before. The armed guards were expecting him and glad to see him. Again, he pretended to be clumsy, approaching the warship and gave the side of the ship a good bump, hard enough to get a sailor's attention sleeping inside, issuing a mild oath to whoever was outside banging on their ship. Marcus delivered the fish and was paid well. The cook informed him to bring him about 100 pounds two days from now. Marcus thanked him for the business and said he would see him then. He backed up his boat, banging it against the side again. He went to the other iron clad that had missed out the day before and secured new sales from that naval ship. They ordered some fish for the next day. Marcus continued on down the row of small boats and steamers selling his fish. His guise as a fisherman was secure now, and he had his prey literally eating out of his hand.

The next morning, Marcus made his rounds, sold the *Chicago* the fish they ordered, but only gave the *St. Paul* a friendly wave and smile as he went by. When he returned to camp, he found the old man had revisited the smithy and his workshop on the pier. He adjusted the metal harness so it would fit perfectly on the prow of Marcus's boat. By early afternoon, the corrections had been hammered out. He pointed out to the iron smith how his net would fit in the round holes at the front of the boat, that in reality, would hold the iron spike that would protrude out underwater and spear the side of the ironclad deep enough to support a mine that would be hung on the spike.

That evening, the two Confederates attached the iron frame to the front of Marcus's boat with brass screws. Then the professor inserted a thirty-inch iron ram into the harness. It was an inch in diameter, sharpened to an extremely sharp point with barbs along the point to hold the spear inside once it penetrated the wooden hull. The professor had hired another blacksmith to create two spears, one for each warship that would be inserted in the metal harness. He slipped one of the sharpened iron points into the frame, and the device was ready to be deployed into the side of the Union ship.

During the night they were awakened by a light rain that tapped on their tents. It was two hours before daylight. Marcus rolled over and went back to sleep, not worrying about what he couldn't control. The professor, however, had not slept well. He had one more problem to solve before the two saboteurs could complete their task of sending two Union warships to the bottom of the river. No matter how hard he thought, sketched, and figured, he could not design a timer that he could depend on to blow up at a certain time.

He sat up on his cot and lit a lantern and studied his ideas in his journal. The Union ships might leave at any time now so he had to work fast, but no solution seemed in sight. He continued to ponder his dilemma until daylight when his alarm clock went off. As he reached over to stop the alarm, he noticed the winding mechanism going around as the alarm sounded. Suddenly he stopped the clock and rewound it. He had a new idea. He hunted through his gear and found a box of safety matches protected in a small water-tight bottle. He tied a match to the winder on the back of the clock and set the alarm off, watching the match moving around in a circle. He thought, "How simple! All I need is something rough for the match head to rub against and strike as it goes around."

When the alarm went off again, Marcus yelled across to the professor with a little irritation in his voice, "How many times are you going to get up this morning?"

"Marcus, Marcus, come here. I have solved my problem." Soon the two were looking at the Colonel's idea. "I will mount this clock in a wooden box filled with black powder. On the winder of the clock I will secure a match so that when the alarm goes off the match will strike a rough surface…," he thought a few seconds, "like sandpaper, yes, like sandpaper. Any spark that's made inside that box will ignite the powder and boom; there goes the ship to the bottom of the Ohio River."

Marcus was in awe at the professor's ingenuity and then asked, "How big will the box have to be?"

The professor used his hands to show Marcus an estimated size of the mine. "I image a cubic foot of powder would blow a large hole in the side of the ship. All we need is a small hole; the water will do the rest. But here is another problem. The box must be weighted with rocks so it barely sinks so it cannot be seen, but yet, float enough that when we hang it on the spear it will be light enough as not to pull the spear out of the boat. Next, how do we make a waterproof top that can be opened and closed without leaking and ruining the black powder?"

Marcus thought also. "Why not use a large bottle rather than a wooden box? The bottle would be easy to seal by using a cork," remembering how he had wanted to use a bottle on the end of his trotline.

"That's a good idea, Marcus, but how could I put a clock down inside a bottle? Let's eat something, and then you go sell your fish. See if you can find out when the ships might leave. I'll think of something while you are gone."

When Marcus left, the professor studied, sketched, and finally came up with a solution to his problem. He would create a metal cylinder made out of thin metal about eighteen inches long with one end sealed and soldered together. A top could be attached with screws and sealed with hot wax along the seam. Rocks could be placed in the bottom that would make it barely buoyant. "This is going to work," he assured himself.

Shortly before noon, Marcus came back and reported the ships would leave in two days. The professor left immediately to work on building the two torpedoes. He found two coal-oil cans and had the blacksmith add a flange at the top so he could attach a top with brass screws. The professor explained to the smithy he wanted these cylinders for live boxes to hold the many fish he planned to catch with the net on the front of his boat, however, the blacksmith suspected he was building some type of steam engine. After he got the cylinders he bought some copper sheets that he cut circles from that would make a top that would seal the open ends with screws and wax. Later that day, he purchased two small alarm clocks, two pounds of wax, two sheets of sandpaper, and some fine wire to secure the matches to the winding mechanisms. He had everything but the gunpowder. It was now time to test his idea.

The professor worked in his rented shop to assemble his design. He filled the bottom third of the canister with rocks he had carefully selected along the river and stuck them together with an industrial wax. The old man wound the clock and attached two matches securely to the winder using the fine wire he purchased, each match sticking out like blades on a propeller. Next, he glued a piece of sandpaper on the side wall of the cylinder and secured the clock on top of the rocks with the strong wax that quickly cooled and held the clock firmly in place. Before the wax set up, he adjusted the distance from the sandpaper so the matches would precisely strike the sandpaper and ignite when the alarm went off and spun the matches around. He tested it time and time again. He found if one match didn't ignite, it at least made a spark, all that was needed to ignite the powder. He was positive it would work.

The next morning the professor purchased two kegs of gunpowder from two different hardware stores, hoping to remove any questions why he needed so much powder. He used the blacksmith's wagon to pull them back to his workshop at the end of the pier to finish his task. The professor opened a keg and carefully dipped out the powder with a wooden spoon until one of the torpedoes was nearly full, filling the spaces between the rocks.

As he filled the first can, he saw a flaw in his plan. When the cylinder was full of powder, the match could not spin around to scratch the sandpaper. He continued to fill the cans until the powder reached the bottom of the clocks. That fixed the problem. A little less gunpowder would not matter. Now there was a space for the winder to spin and ignite the powder. He filled the other torpedo with powder and screwed the tops on, but did not seal them.

Early the next morning, Marcus inserted the spear into the harness attached to his prow. He rowed back away from shore several feet. Then with all his might he rowed *Bonnie* forward and rammed a piece of timber they had stood up near the shore backed by a large rock to test the penetration of the spear. The first attempts failed to pierce the heavy timber, instead sliding off and rapidly turning Marcus's boat. After several more attempts they discovered the spear would have to hit perpendicular to the side of the boat with lots of speed to stab the boat successfully, otherwise, it would slide off. Marcus practiced it several times until he got the feel and the speed needed to plant his spear.

All the preparations were made and today would be the day they would sink two Union gunboats. Marcus readied his boat and got his supply of fish ready. The cooks on board the ships would expect him soon.

The professor set both clocks to go off at nine o'clock that night, giving the saboteurs eight or nine hours to get their work done and get out of town. He sealed the top with hot wax and secured it with the brass screws. They could hear the ticking of the clock inside as the professor lifted it up by the metal ring he had brazed to the copper top that would be used to hang on the spear. One last test had to be made. The Colonel lifted the torpedo up and placed it in the water by the boat and it slowly sunk, exactly according to his calculations on weight and displacement in a cylinder. He slid the torpedo over the end of the spear and pushed it back toward the boat, then lifted it up over a shallow steel finger that prevented the torpedo from sliding off the spear in case the spear slanted down in the water after attaching itself to the hull. If the spear stayed in the side of the ship, the torpedo would stay on the spear.

He looked up at Marcus, "Go! Do what you need to do. Come back immediately and I will have the other torpedo sealed and ready to plant on the *St. Paul*.

Marcus pushed away from the shore. "Wish me luck," and with that statement, he gave the professor a serious look, grabbed his oars and headed upstream.

Marcus rowed upstream; he was excited about what was about to happen. If he was discovered, he would be shot as a saboteur, but if he was successful, the Mississippi River would be safer for the Confederate boats trying to defend the river. As he neared the row of boats he saw the *St. Paul* was gone, but the *Chicago* was still tied up. If he couldn't sink both vessels, he could still send one to the bottom of the river.

He proceeded alongside of the row of boats, trying to appear as normal as possible. When he got to the *Chicago* several sailors were sitting in chairs sunning themselves on top of the ship, seeking warmth in the chilly morning air. Familiar with him now, they waved him to come forward. He passed by the large iron monster staying some distance away until he arrived near the front of the beast. The moment had finally arrived. Still appearing to be awkward, Marcus determined his position and adjusted the front of his boat to be perpendicular to the side of the large ship. Now with all his might he grabbed the oars and rowed rapidly toward the iron monster and rammed the spear into the side of the wooden hull. Marcus backed off and the harpoon stayed in the side of the *Chicago*. The torpedo was underwater and apparently buoyant enough not to pull the spear out, but yet heavy enough to stay hidden beneath the waves. Marcus thought, "The chicken has laid the egg."

Marcus got control of the boat and ineptly rowed the boat around the prow of the warship like he always had done and pulled up alongside of the pier. Suddenly an officer came out of the ship, hollering, "Who hit the side of our ship?"

Pretending to be embarrassed, Marcus volunteered, "Sir, I bumped the side of your ship with the nose of my boat, but it didn't hurt my boat."

"Your boat? What damage did you do to my ship," he yelled. I was inside there and it was a loud thump. One of you sailors go down there and see if he damaged our ship."

"Aw, no," Marcus thought, "I am going to be discovered after everything had gone so well."

The sailors on top of the ship started laughing which, caught the officer's attention. "What are you men laughing at?"

They immediately stopped laughing and stood up at attention, "Sir, this gangly kid comes by here every day to sell us fish. He seems to be at the age when his arms and legs are not connected securely to his body or his brain. Sir, he has bumped our ship almost every day trying to get around to the pier. I am sure if the bump didn't hurt his boat, it didn't hurt ours."

"Very well then, at ease. Go on about your business." Then the officer noticed the iron prow on the front of Marcus's boat. "What is that device on the front of your boat, son?"

Marcus thought quickly and remembered the professor's idea. "Sir, how do you think I bring you so many fish everyday? I have an invention my father made before he died that lets me catch lots of fish."

"How does it work?"

"It's easy. I have a square metal frame, about ten feet wide and three feet deep that holds a net and sticks in this hole right here," as he leaned over the front of the boat and showed the captain where the spear had ridden. "All I have to do is row up and down the river all night and take the fish out of the net. Some nights I catch so many fish I can't keep them all."

The officer and the sailors were amazed at what he told them, but the officer was still skeptical. "You mean all you do is row down the river and fish get in your net?"

"Yes sir, but I didn't tell you my secret."

"What's your secret?

"I can't tell you what my secret is or it wouldn't be a secret."

Marcus knew they had forgotten about the bump to the side of their ship and were interested in the lie he was telling, all of his listeners seeing an easy way to get rich if they could discover his secret. "I can tell you part of my secret, but my daddy said never, never to tell anyone all of the secret until I was about to die."

"Go on boy, tell us what you can. What is part of the secret then?"

Marcus hesitated and put his hand to shield the sun out of his eyes. "You sure you won't tell nobody."

"No son, we won't tell anyone," they answered as if they were talking to five-year-old, not realizing they were conversing with an enemy agent about to send their mighty warship to the bottom of the river.

Finally after a long wait, Marcus said, "'Stink'um'…., 'stink'um', that's the secret.

"What in the world is 'stink'um,' boy? I have never heard of such a thing."

"I know, that's what I can't tell you until I die." Marcus was enjoying the dialogue with the naval officer as he led him along.

"But I can tell you this. Before I go out in the river with my net, I go up the river and spread 'stink'um' on the water. That's what brings up the fish so I can catch them."

"What's it made out of?"

"That sir is the part of the secret that I can't tell you." With that answer Marcus picked up a stringer of fish and handed them up to the cook who had come out and had been listening to the conversation. He and another sailor removed the fish and placed them in a tub. After they emptied that stringer, Marcus gave them two more stringers full of fish to fill the order that he had been given two days earlier.

As the fish were exchanged and Marcus got paid, Marcus asked where the *St. Paul* was. He acted disappointed since he had an order of fish for them. The cook told him, not to worry, but come back later in the day. They were testing the repair they had made on the ship. That was perfect. This would gave Marcus time to go back and get the other torpedo without drawing any suspicions as to why he would arrive again later to plant another torpedo. Marcus couldn't believe how well the plan was working.

When Marcus arrived back at their camp, the Colonel was holding the second torpedo in the cool water to help harden the wax and test its buoyancy. "How did it go up there?"

"Our plan is working perfectly. I had a scare though. One of the ships was gone when I got there, and I thought they were going to find the torpedo after I planted it."

"What do you mean it's gone?" the professor asked with a frown on his face displaying his disappointment.

"It went up the river to test the repairs on her boiler, but for us, it couldn't have worked out better. I told them I had some fish for the *St. Paul*, and they said it should return around four o'clock."

"Our prey is making this job easy," the professor smiled as he took the other spear and inserted it in the front of Marcus's boat, preparing it for another attack. He lifted the second torpedo out of the water and hung it on the lance. "This one is set and ready to go at nine o'clock, too. I am going to return the blacksmith's cart while

you plant the second mine. I am also going to stay up there near the ships and watch the master work his magic," he said referring to Marcus stabbing the ship and planting the bomb. "I'll meet you back here when you finish." He paused and thought a few seconds with his hand on his chin, "You know we should leave immediately and hope our work succeeds, but I must stay and see those monsters sink in the river after the explosions."

"You can stay since they aren't suspecting you," Marcus surmised, "But I am getting out of here. I don't think it will take them long to put two and two together to realize I was the only person who could have planted those bombs. I am getting out of here and going on downstream. I will pull in and find a place to hide before daylight. You know everybody on the river is going to be looking for a red boat named *Bonnie*. I will watch for you, and we will rendezvous then."

"That's a good idea. But to insure your safety, take that paint I gave you and paint your boat another color and paint another name on her. Put up your tent. Those naval guys haven't seen you with the tent up. It will make your boat look larger. All those changes should throw the authorities off your trail if they are looking for a red boat named 'Bonnie.' Also, a coat of black paint will make it hard to see at night." He laughed, "Why don't you paint the word 'Midnight' on the back of your boat." Marcus hated to paint over Bonnie's name, but agreed it was a good idea.

Shortly before noon, they boiled a dozen eggs, ate together for the last time in Cincinnati, cleaned up their camp and Marcus bid him goodbye and the professor said "good luck," and the two departed. For the first time, the old man's boat would be left unguarded, but they had seen little traffic during their stay so they felt it would be safe while the professor was gone to watch Marcus play his part in the war.

31

Marcus rowed down the river and ran his trotlines one more time. After he retrieved the fish, he wound the lines and hooks around the piece of soft wood that held up the end of the line. The lines had been so successful, he wanted to use them again when and if the chance permitted, or until he could make the lie come true about the fishing net and "stink'um" he had told the sailors that day. He laughed to himself as he stuffed the last trotline in one of the side compartments in his boat.

He took a deep breath and put his back, shoulders, and arms into the oars to push the boat upstream. Again, like Edward, he had become friends with the sailors he was about to send to heaven or wherever, and he didn't like that feeling. He liked the friendly cook and wished he could save his life, but like he had told Edward and Edward had told him back, "You have to do what you have to do." He wished he could destroy the boat but save their lives.

When he came in sight of the *Chicago*, he saw the *St. Paul* tied against the pier, but facing downstream. "This should be no problem," Marcus imagined," as he rowed upstream, coming up along the warship as if he were going by and not stopping. The guards yelled, "Don't you have us some fish today?"

Trying to remain indifferent, he yelled back, "I came up earlier today and you had left. I didn't think you were coming back, so I sold your fish."

"You sold our fish? Do you have any now?"

"Yes, I have a stringer or two but I had an order upstream and going there now."

"Boy, turn that boat around and bring us the fish. You can do that other order later. We're the Navy defending you against all those Rebels down there," he added pointing south of the river.

"Alright, if you insist. I'll sell you some fish, but it sure makes my work harder. I got to go back down the river and run my trotlines." Marcus instantly wanted to take back what he said when he had yelled "trotlines." He was aware the sailors on the *St. Paul* were convinced he used the rake on the front of his boat and "stink'um" to catch his fish, not a trotline. Apparently no sailors on the *St. Paul* had heard his remark and no harm was done. Marcus awkwardly spun the boat around, making the sailors aware again of his poor performance in steering a boat. Finally Marcus got the boat lined up and rowed hard toward the side of the *St. Paul* with his lance aimed perpendicular to the side. He pretended not to realize how fast he was approaching the side of the ship.

The sailors saw his rapid approach and started yelling, "Slow down, kid, you are going to ram our ship!"

Marcus looked around as if he was surprised he was so near the large vessel. Instead of putting his oars down in the river to slow his momentum, he raised the oars and braced himself with his hands and feet for the sudden stop. Marcus could feel the javelin and hear a muffled "clunk" as it penetrated the hard wooden hull. The boat bounced back leaving its deadly weapon hung on the side of the ship.

The sailors all laughed at the clumsy boat, not knowing his little small craft was soon to sink their mighty fortress. Suddenly a sailor on board the *Chicago* yelled, "Hey boy, I think you need to stay with riding horses maybe; your seamanship stinks. I've watched you all week; you just can't handle a boat."

Marcus suddenly thought of an excuse that would explain his difficulties in the water and gain sympathy at the same time. "I can't help it. When I was a young'un I got throw'd from a horse and he trampled me. He tore my shoulders up, I guess. When I healed, I could move my arms, but not in the direction I want them to go. I also have spasms in them, too. I am sorry if I bumped your boat, but fishing is the only means I have to provide food for my grandmother. She's my only living kin. You know she can't walk," Marcus went on weaving the saddest story he could imagine. When he finished, the sailors stood, their mute mouths unable to utter a word, and felt guilty for laughing at the young man.

Two men who had been resting inside near the spot where Marcus hit their boat came out of the innards of the black beast to investigate what made the tremendous clunk on the side of their ship. They came out as Marcus was beginning his story. When Marcus finished he looked up at the sailors on board, "Do you still want your fish?"

The boats chef, feeling sorry for Marcus, bought the rest of Marcus's catch. As the cook paid him, other sailors came up and apologized for teasing him and gave him a few coins they could spare. Now the sailors knew the reason why he was so clumsy in the water. Marcus couldn't believe their kindness as he backed away with several dollars. He looked at the magnificent ship and the brave men on board who were going to be blown into eternity in a few hours. He wished he could warn them, but with their demise, the Union Navy would have to train more men to operate new ships. Marcus hoped this would buy the South more time to get stronger. Marcus backed away and waved goodbye, the sailors unaware they were waving at their executioner rather than a gentle young lad.

The professor had taken a seat on a coil of rope near the pier and watched Marcus's outstanding performance, how he camouflaged the hard bump and explained his incompetence with his boat, and how he had the sailors literally eating out of his hand.

Shortly after Marcus had sold his fish, a commotion was stirring down the street. The professor turned and saw the blacksmith walking toward him with two Cincinnati policemen walking with him.

Unexpectedly the blacksmith stopped and pointed at the professor, "There he is, he's the one I was telling you about, and see, he still has my wagon. I tell you, he's up to no good!"

The Colonel looked around to see if the blacksmith could be pointing at someone else, but it was obvious he was the man they were seeking. Although an older man, but still in good physical condition, the professor jumped up and started running away, a good thing to do if he could escape, but a bad reaction if he was apprehended.

Marcus, the sailors, and the cooks watched as the policemen ran by chasing after the old man. "Stop that man," they yelled. Several of the young sailors joined the pursuit and within two city blocks they caught the Colonel, tied his hands, and marched him past the two warships as Marcus watched, wondering what had gone wrong in their plan. He hoped it wasn't some error he may have made in carrying out their covert attack, but neither the police nor anyone else paid any attention to Marcus. The cooks had paid him, and according to their plan, he should be high-tailing it down the river. However, from what Marcus witnessed, he could not leave now, knowing his friend was in trouble. He watched as the professor was marched away. Marcus rowed on down the river until he was out of sight of the ironclads. He saw a lad fishing off of a pier and rowed up to him and pitched him a line, indicating he wanted the young lad to pull him on up and tie the boat, which he did.

"Young fellow, I need to go buy some things before I go on down the river. I am also going to try and find my mother's sister who lives back up against the hills. If you will watch my boat for me I'll give you a silver dollar when I get back. Can you do that for me?"

The poor little boy had probably never seen a silver dollar before. He looked as if he came from a very needy family and would be proud to bring a silver dollar home to the family with a grin on his face that said, "Look what I got."

"Why don't you jump down here and rest on my boat. I have some more worms if you need them." The boy was excited to get to come on board the beautiful red boat. "If anyone comes looking for me, tell them I went to look for my kinfolks and should be back soon."

Marcus pulled out a shiny silver dollar to reinforce the young lad's dedication to the job at hand.

Marcus walked rapidly back to where he had last seen the professor. He found some workers who had witnessed the arrest. He soon learned the professor had been taken to the police headquarters back toward town, away from the river. Marcus soon found the building and made his way inside. After several inquiries he found the professor sitting in a cell, guarded by several policemen standing around the room. He was waiting for an authority that was soon to appear and determine the charges and determine whether to jail or release him

Marcus asked a policeman why his uncle had been arrested and could he go talk to him. The guard raised his shoulders up and tilted his head that indicated he did not know the answer to the first question, but told him he could visit his kinfolk while he waited. Marcus walked down an aisle and turned in and scooted up next to the professor seated at the end of one of the long smooth benches. The professor smiled and raised his tied hands to shake hands with Marcus. Yelling loud so the guards standing around the room could hear him, "Uncle Josh, what are you doing in here? You're supposed to help me fish this afternoon." His loud question tipped the professor off that Marcus had something up his sleeve to get him out.

The professor answered in an ignorant accent, also loud enough for those in the room to hear, "I don't know. I was waitin' on you to pick me up down on the dock next to those big black ships when I saw a man and some policemen hurrying toward me and pointin' at me. I looked 'round to see who they was a pointin' at, and when I see'd they were coming after me I took off. I didn't want to be arrested 'cause me ain't done nothin' to be put in jail fer."

"You shouldn't have run, Uncle Josh. That made you look guilty of doing som'en."

"I know'd that now," but before they could continue their talk the door opened and a police sergeant, followed by the two policemen who arrested the old Colonel came into the room. The sergeant apparently was in charge of the proceedings and took a seat behind a large tall desk, giving him a superior look and position in the room.

"Mr. George Kimball, will you come up here."

"George Kimball?" Marcus thought. He wondered where he got that name.

The professor got up and exited the pew and came forward to face the charges. The professor knew the law well, but still wanted to wear the guise of an ignorant river rat. The policeman noticed Marcus and asked the professor in a sarcastic remark if that boy was his lawyer. Pretending he had not comprehended the snide remark, the Colonel replied, "No sir, he's my nephew," remembering Marcus had called him uncle, "Unlike me, he ain't had no skool'in at all." After these few sentences, the judge understood he was talking to a dim-witted individual.

"Mr. George Kimball, it seems that….," before he could continue the policeman standing guard by the door approached the tall desk.

"Sergeant, when that boy came in he called him Uncle Josh. George Kimball may not be his right name."

The sergeant asked the professor, "Why did he call you Uncle Josh if your real name is George."

The professor laughed, "That's easy mister policeman. My middle name is Joseph and all my friends have called me Josh since I was a small boy. I would have told you Josh but I thought you wanted my important name."

"I see, let's get on with this. It seems a man has accused you of making bombs. He found gunpowder in the workshop where you were working and suspected the powder had gone into two large canisters he had helped you construct. Is that correct?"

"What does construct mean?" the professor wondered, adding to his role as a fool.

"Build, make, or create! Did you make a bomb?"

"Why, yes sir, I made two bombs, but they were just small ones."

"What were you going to blow up with those bombs?"

"Fish," the professor answered acting if he was slightly embarrassed that he was going to blow up fish.

"Fish? Fish? Why do you need a bomb to blow up a fish?"

Pointing over his shoulder at Marcus, "He and me fish to make some money. I was down thar' on the river one morning cleaning fish, and this guy rowed up with a tub full of fish trying to sell me his fish. I asked how he got all them fish, and he said he killed them. I wondered how he killed a fish. You and I know'd that a fish will die off when you take him out of the water so I asked him how he shot them. He laughed back at me and said he didn't shoot them, but bombed them."

"Yes, I have heard of people doing that," the sergeant added.

"Well, sir, that was all I was trying to do. He just told me to find a metal can and put some gunpowder in it and put a rock on it so it would sink. Then light a fuse and throw it in the river where I thought the fish might be…you know, a deep hole where the fishes stay." The professor scratched the side of his head, "You know I thank that guy was hurrahing me. Me and Marcus rowed them bombs down the river to a deep hole where we have hooked lots of fish, and we lit the bombs and pushed them off the boat. They sunk, but the bombs never went off. I got to thankin' about it and I figure the water put the fuses out when we dumped them in the water."

Marcus jumped up, "That's right; nary a one of them there bombs went off. Uncle Josh wasted all that time building them thangs and they didn't even work."

The sergeant realized he was dealing with two simpletons who did not have the ability to have any clandestine plot to do any harm to anyone or anything. "I don't see you have committed any crime. You are released Mr. Kimball. Get on about your business."

Marcus thought, "If he only knew what business the professor was about to do, he might reorder that remark." With that statement, Marcus and the professor left the building and hurried back toward Marcus's boat. Marcus paid the boy a dollar, thanked him and rowed away leaving the two warships ready to explode at nine o'clock.

It was nearing four o'clock when they arrived back at camp. The professor jumped out and pulled the "Bonnie" up onshore. When Marcus stepped onshore the professor told him to help him pull the boat entirely out of the water so they could paint the craft as planned. "After nine o'clock everyone on the river will be looking for a red boat with Bonnie on the sides and stern. Let's hurry."

"Let's eat. I am starving to death." Marcus complained.

"We can eat later; we must hurry!" There are eight boiled eggs left. Take four of them for your boat. That will give us something to eat until we rendezvous again." The professor grabbed another paint brush and helped Marcus apply the paint down below the waterline. He told Marcus to remove the iron frame and throw it in the deepest part of the river after he got underway. Marcus unscrewed the brass screws that held on the harness and set it in the middle of his boat. Like magic, the old man handed him some putty to fill the screw holes and hide any trace of a metal frame being attached. Marcus was amazed at what the old man had on his boat.

Marcus filled the holes and painted over the soft putty. When Marcus came to the name *Bonnie* he stopped painting and paused. "Goodbye Bonnie, but every day I am getting closer to you." He bent down and kissed the name and then, almost crying, took the brush and covered her name forever. The old man saw what Marcus did, but said nothing, but knowing what emotion Marcus was feeling.

Marcus had not raised his tent while he was around the warships so it did not matter whether it was painted black or not. They left the inside of the boat red so Marcus wouldn't get wet black paint all over him. It would take the coat of paint nearly two days to dry and the paint near the bottom would probably wash off, but at a distance the Bonnie would look black. They would find a hidden inlet off the river later and put another coat of paint and cover the rest of the red. The professor took a smaller brush and very carefully lettered *The Crow*" on the back. "I like this name better than *Midnight*."

With that done, he threw the brushes in the water, not taking the time to clean them, sealed and stored the paint cans, and helped Marcus push *The Crow* into the stream. "Go on downstream like we planned. I am going to row over on the Covington side of the river and watch tonight to see if our torpedoes do their job. It will be dark in an hour, so drift until this time tomorrow, that's twenty-four hours. After I see what happens, I will set off and drift until tomorrow night. Watch for me; I will have one lantern on the front of my boat and another at the back. When you see me go by, row out and catch me, and we will pull in and eat and sleep."

With that Marcus pushed away from the bank and caught the river's current and told the professor, "Be careful now, I don't want to have to row back up here and get you out of jail again."

"Don't worry; I am going to change my looks right now before I go across the river. I suggest you do the same. When you see me again, I will be totally bald and rid of any facial hair. So remember, when you catch me tomorrow night, look for a hairless head."

Marcus sat down facing backwards in the boat to row forward and watched the professor give him a last wave and then slowly fade to haze as he floated away. When he was in the middle of the river he pitched the iron frame overboard.

The professor immediately grabbed his razor and soaped up his face and head and shaved his head and face. After he cleaned himself up, he scrambled around in a wooden box until he found a small glass bottle. He opened the bottle and rubbed the dark black juice on his head and face, neck, and hands. It was a stain made from green walnuts and could immediately darken a person's skin. If he was captured now and had to appear before the police sergeant again, the sergeant would never know this was the man he interviewed earlier in the day. He would talk with a British accent, as if he were from Nassau.

The Colonel changed shirts and went back to selling vegetables on the river. His boat had not been seen in Cincinnati since they had passed through that first night, so it did not need a new coat of paint. He gave his boat a final check for the trip downriver, then rowed across the river and navigated upstream and tied to a pier at Covington, Kentucky, with the ironclads in view across the river.

He observed eight rowboats surrounding the two ships which seemed to be on alert for an attack. The old man figured they guarded the boat every night and didn't think much about it. Just to be safe though, he eased back into the current and floated farther down the river to be less noticeable from the ironclads and anchored near shore. Now, all he had to do was wait. He pulled out two blankets and curled up in the bottom of his boat to sleep. He knew he would be awake for over twenty-four hours after he came to.

Just before dark and shortly before the police sergeant left headquarters, the blacksmith came in to find out what had happened to the old man he thought was building bombs in his workshop. The sergeant told him he had been released; there was no way that ignorant old man and his nephew could blow up anything.

The blacksmith became outraged, "What are you telling me? That man is a genius. I worked with him for three days, and he is a master of many skills. Are you sure you had the man I had arrested?"

"Yes," answered the sergeant as he put his coat on to go outside, "His name was," he thought a second; "George Kimball, and he hardly could use the English language. He didn't even know what the word 'construct' meant," the sergeant laughed as he approached the door.

"You idiot, that's not the name he gave me, and like I said, he is some sort of scholar, and he spoke and wrote the English language perfectly. He was also an artist or architect who drew precise plans for what he wanted made. Before the bombs, I built a metal frame that could be put on the front of a boat. He said it was used to hold a net that could gather fish as he rowed down the river. He showed me his notes on how he wanted me to make the frame. He had numbers calculated that I did not understand, explaining angles and so forth. There is something fishy here, and it isn't the kind that swims in the river. When I found the grains of black powder, I put two and two together. Think about it. When I found him today, he was sitting watching the gunboats. It all adds up, and there can only be one answer, he is a Confederate saboteur!"

"He admitted he was making small bombs alright, but to kill fish."

"Small bombs to kill fish," the blacksmith said. "Are you kidding me? They were big enough to kill a fish as big as one of those ironclads that are docked along the river."

All of a sudden both men stopped talking and looked at each other. Both ran for the door, the sergeant calling for other policemen to follow him. They ran toward the river. The sun had disappeared over the horizon, and there was only an orange glow in the western sky.

The sergeant had outrun the blacksmith, but some of the policemen had caught up with their sergeant and in all, five policemen ran up to the *Chicago*. Sailors on watch turned to see what was happening. The sergeant asked a sailor to go get his captain. He had something important to tell him. Soon the captain came out, while slipping on a warm coat, and came ashore down the walkway. "Yes, officer, what seems to be the matter here? What's going on?"

"Sir," the sergeant saluted not knowing why, "Sir, we think we have discovered a plot to sink your ships."

"What are you talking about? Our ships are safe. Look around, they are guarded twenty-four hours a day."

"We do not think so. Mr. Garrett here, a local blacksmith, informs me that he may have been helping a Confederate agent build two torpedoes that could be used to sink your ships. Matter of fact, we arrested the culprit today while he was watching your vessels."

"Yes, an officer told me about that incident."

"We think you need to check your ships immediately, he could have planted one of those torpedoes on your ship."

"There's no way he could have come on board our ships. There are two men on the gangplank at all times, with sharpshooters standing up there," pointing to the top of the ship next to the smokestack."

"Captain, don't take any chances. Search your ship for boxes or large metal cans, crates, anything that might hold a torpedo.

The captain immediately called all the guards that had been on duty that day to come out and line up in front of him. After they assembled, he asked them to volunteer any suspicious information they might have seen today. By now the captain of the *St. Paul* had come over and listened about the possible attack on their ships. The guards had seen nothing suspicious that day, nothing out of the ordinary. The only place on the ship that a torpedo could be attached would be around the paddle wheel and rudder area. The captains immediately sent their seamen to climb down and row out and check the sterns of both ships. They even had the interior of the ship searched, but nothing was found after a thorough examination.

The sailors never reasoned that anyone could have stuck a metal can to the side of a wooden hull without using nails. Waterproof glues did not exist at that time. They had rowed around the boats several times looking for a string or any suspicious fabrication that would reveal a mine, but the black torpedoes hung on the steel spikes three feet below the waterline and could not be seen, invisibly deep in the murky water. One of the sailors almost hit one of the torpedoes with an oar as he maneuvered his boat close to the *St. Paul* looking for the possible threat to their ship.

One of the guards mentioned to the captain that a young boy came by selling fish, but he was obviously innocent since he sold to everyone on the river and came by with lots of fish everyday. "No," the captain said, "That kid sells fish, besides he's just a kid, too young to be in a war."

The sergeant spoke up. "When I questioned the suspect this afternoon, he had a young boy, I expect about eighteen, with him."

"No," the captain said, "This kid is younger than that."

The captain thanked the policeman and the blacksmith for warning them and said they would place extra guards out until they left Cincinnati the next day. The captain stationed sixteen sailors in four rowboats to surround the ships and watch for whatever might come from the river. Everything seemed secure. The captain retired to his quarters to get a good night's sleep.

Shortly before nine, three officers came on board after having a good time in a local tavern, celebrating their last night's freedom before entering the sanctuary that permitted no alcoholic beverages. As they walked up the gangway they immediately noticed the extra guards stationed around the ship and asked what was going on.

After hearing what happened, one of the officers became excited. "Where is the captain? I need to speak to him immediately." This was the officer who had heard the bump on the side of the ship that had brought him outside to question the boy as to why he had an iron frame on the front of his boat. "Stink'um," he yelled, "Yes, there is something that smells, alright."

He went to the captain's quarters and knocked on the door. In a few precious moments, the captain appeared clad in a robe. "Captain, I need to speak to you immediately. I have some news about the possible torpedo."

The officer's report turned the Captain's face white. He looked at his watch. It was five minutes before nine, a perfect time to set a possible timing device on a torpedo, or maybe it was ten, or eleven, any hourly time might be the chosen time for a blast. "Where did the boy bump the ship?

"Apparently he rammed our ship on the starboard side, just behind the anchor chains where the ship flattens out."

"I don't know how a kid could plant a torpedo on this large ship without one of us seeing it, but to be safe, evacuate the ship in case it is to go off at nine o'clock. If we don't hear an explosion at nine, we'll send swimmers into the water and check our hulls. I would do it now, but we could lose many sailors if what I said was true." He ordered the *Chicago* to be evacuated immediately and sent word for everyone to abandon the *St. Paul* as well.

It was one minute past nine when all the sailors had spilled out of their gunboats and assembled on shore facing their captain several yards from the ship. The captain spoke, "We think there is a torpedo attached to our ship. I need someone to volunteer," he hesitated, "To possibly volunteer his life to see if there is a mine attached on the starboard side of the ship behind the anchor chains."

Immediately, forty sailors raised their hands and said they would go. "Come forward then and strip off your clothes. Only one of you needs to risk his life. One young volunteer came forward, "Let us all go and check our ship."

The captain agreed after seeing such valor. The sailors pulled off their shoes and jackets and were pulling down their pants to jump in the water when a loud but muffled boom was heard behind the *St. Paul* and the large ship quivered and sent out small waves from its waterline. Then drops of water fell on the sailors as they had instinctively fell to the ground at the sound of the explosion. It was too dangerous now for the men to get in the water, and the captain ordered everyone back from their ships and to find shelter, all hoping there was only one deadly egg that had been laid in their nest, hoping the explosion would not set off the huge amount of ammunition inside.

The explosion had not been extremely loud, and although it spewed water in the air, the *St. Paul* was still afloat. When no other explosions went off after a few minutes, the captain ordered four officers to go on board and report any damage. While they were on board, the second alarm clock went off and there was another loud boom similar to the first. They ran back, hoping again the munitions on board were not ignited starting a fireworks display that might catch the stores along the river front on fire. After the Captain assumed it safe, another group of sailors entered the *Chicago* to determine if it would sink. Both ships had been damaged, but would they sink? The captains anxiously waited to hear the news.

32

Suddenly, the old man was awakened by a deep boom from across the river. He rose up to see crowds of sailors getting up off the ground next to the *St. Paul* and others sailors, near the *Chicago* retreating backward, bent over, holding their hands above their heads, trying to protect themselves from expected falling debris. The professor watched intently, proud all his work had not gone to naught, and that at least one of his deadly eggs had worked. He watched the seamen scurrying forward one moment, then retreating again, trying to obey the orders from their superiors. But to the professor's surprise, the *St. Paul* did not sink. Why was it still afloat? Had he not used enough powder to puncture the heavy wooden hull? Why had not the other ship exploded? Both clocks were set the same.

When the ship didn't sink and the expected explosions inside the ship didn't occur, he saw sailors going back on board the crippled ship to investigate. In four minutes, what seemed like an hour to the old man, the next torpedo revealed itself. He saw a high column of water spew into the sky near the front of the *Chicago*. Again he saw the sailors running away, and then returning. But why were the ships not sinking? He continued to watch, and in the next half hour, he observed the stern of the "St. Paul" was lower in the water and the hull was listing to its right. The *Chicago's* bow was slowly sinking, obvious now; both ships were slowly descending into their watery graves. The holes must not have been large, but in the end lethal, and just large enough to send the iron beasts to the bottom of the river by morning.

The professor had seen enough to honestly know, they had destroyed two Union ironclads. He could hardly wait to tell Marcus and his superior officers what they had accomplished. The bald-headed man lifted his anchor, grabbed one of his oars, and paddled into the stronger current, but stayed close to the dark shore until he could no longer see the warships. He found the fastest flow in the river and floated away from Cincinnati knowing he had accomplished his mission.

Cincinnati was one of the largest cities on the Ohio River and was heavily populated above and below the river for many miles. Dim light from candles and coal oil lamps trickled out of houses; light from lanterns on small craft traversing the river, and the moon that appeared briefly between the clouds gave the professor enough light to see where he was going without having to use his own lantern. It was cold, but not freezing, and he stayed wrapped in his blankets. He was hungry, but he was elated over his success back in the city, and could endure hunger until he was safe with Marcus again. He drank lots of water and ate a boiled egg and nibbled on a biscuit he remembered he had stowed away at the front of the boat two days ago.

Back in Cincinnati, the captains got the report that the two great ships were going down. The explosions had awakened many people and word spread quickly through the town that the ships had been wounded and would most likely sink before morning. People hearing of the incident woke their neighbors, and within an hour a huge crowd had gathered to watch the pride of the Union Navy go to the river bottom. Both ships seemed to fight their demise. The *St. Paul's* stern went down and rested on the river bottom, but air in the bow kept it afloat until finally it sunk at daylight. The *Chicago's* stern stayed afloat and the boat's paddle wheels were visible for a long time, but shortly after sunrise, it joined its sister at the bottom of the river.

The ships rested on the bottom of the river, but the top of the armor plate above the gun ports and the two smokestacks near the front of the ship could still be seen; the river not deep enough to entomb them entirely. Eventually, they would be raised and floated again.

The Navy and the police knew now the blacksmith's story was true, and the two saboteurs had found success. They knew who they were hunting, an old man with a full white beard and long hair down to his collar, brilliant, but would probably appear to be ignorant, and a young boy in a bright red boat with an iron frame attached to the front. The name Bonnie, written in white letters, could be seen on each side of the prow and across the back.

Telegraphs wires were busy spreading the word about the incident and who the culprits were. Most likely they were on the river, but they could have abandoned the river and be traveling overland. By the end of the day, everyone on the river friendly to the Union cause would be looking for a young lad accompanied by an old man. The authorities were not aware their saboteurs had two boats.

Marcus, now disguised in his black boat, pondered what the professor said about changing his looks. Marcus thought about what role he could play on the mighty river as he sat at the front of the boat and drifted, using the pedals that Mr. Dunigan, the boat builder, had made for him to steer the boat.

He knew if the torpedoes had done their job, the Union Navy would know it had to be him who planted the bombs. He sure didn't want to look like a fisherman now. Thinking about that he took one of his poles and baited it and hung it over the side, then took two of his trotlines and threw them overboard, ridding him of any evidence that might prove he was a commercial fisherman, however, a couple of poles and a trotline were common around a river and wouldn't look suspicious. Those items were essential, if you lived near the water.

But he had the detonators, and if he was searched, he assumed the authorities would see what was packed inside those waxed boxes labeled "seeds". The Union authorities would be searching all the boats on the river closely now since their mighty ships went down.

Marcus was anxious to hear from the professor if the bombs had done their work.

Before morning, the wind increased. Marcus assembled his tent and got inside to keep warm. His tent slowed his speed as it caught the wind, almost forcing him backward, so he manned the oars and pushed the boat against the wind. He passed three large riverboats during the night, but due to their size and lights, he saw them coming, and pulled over next to the shore to wait, unseen, and let them pass. During the night, he passed smaller steamers, and on one occasion before sunrise, he saw a larger vessel coming up fast from his stern. Marcus had no lantern, still using the night sky to show him the way. As the craft rapidly closed the distance, Marcus turned to starboard and out of the strong current to let the steamer pass. As she approached, she suddenly veered in his direction and pulled up alongside. Marcus was afraid this was going to be the feared search he dreaded, but as the boat neared, he saw only two men and one yelled, "Ahoy sir, did you hear what happened in Cincinnati?"

Marcus emerged from his shelter, stretched, and rubbed his eyes as if he had been sleeping. "No captain, what happened?"

"Saboteurs sunk the *St. Paul* and Chicago while they were tied up next to the pier."

Marcus appeared to be aghast at the news, "Oh how awful. How did they sink them? Was it Confederate gunboats?"

"No, they say that torpedoes did them in. We are looking for an old man and a young boy in a red boat named *Bonnie*. If you see them, stop at the next town and tell the authorities."

"Thanks for the information. I'll keep my eyes open." With that the officer saluted good-bye as the faster steamer pulled away. Marcus got his answer. They had sunk the ironclads! He thought about the sailors that he may have killed, and imagined in his mind the cook and the other friendly salts he had visited when they had bought his fish. In a way, he regretted what he had done and wondered if God would hold him accountable for lying and killing during the war, appearing to be someone he wasn't. He remembered his Sunday school teacher, Miss Ellie, teaching him liars and thieves would never go to heaven. Again he thought of what he told Edward, "You had to do what you had to do; this was war."

As the naval boat disappeared in the dark Marcus realized he had passed his first test. The new black cloak and boat name had saved his life. He felt safe now to travel the river.

Soon, the glow in the eastern sky began to light his way, and he could see the river now. He remembered the boiled eggs and ate all of them to stave off the hunger pangs the morning light had brought. At dawn, traffic on the river increased with the brightness of the day, river men leaving their ports early to take advantage of the daylight. He thought about pulling ashore and getting off the river. He knew the Union Navy would cut no corners in order to catch the culprits that killed their dragons, and Marcus expected to see authorities setting up stops in the river to look for suspects; but the day passed without encountering new dangers.

His boat was still visibly red inside. He was lucky the steamer that stopped him did not see the red interior. Even risking getting in wet paint, while he drifted, he took the black paint and covered what an outsider would see from another boat. He shuffled boxes and spread out bedding to cover the inside under his tent. The soles of his shoes might be black, but that wouldn't matter, and he would be careful to avoid the black oily stuff until it dried.

During the day he caught several fish and stringed them up. Later he scaled and gutted the fish and took his last dry wood and grilled them over a fire in his black wash pot. He calculated that if he made only one or two miles an hour pushing against the wind. He guessed he was fifty or sixty miles from Cincinnati. He had passed many small villages and towns not knowing where he was, but to stay safe, he did not want to stop and ask either.

Dark was coming on, and he wanted to find an isolated place to land his boat and wait for the Colonel. Due to his first encounter with the Navy he did not wait for his friend. He felt it was important to put more miles between himself and Cincinnati. There was no place to hide against the shore since the rise and drop of the river kept the edge clean of foliage. Just before total darkness, Marcus saw an isolated section of the river that was below a steep bluff which made it difficult for anyone to descend down to the river's edge, similar to where they stayed in Cincinnati, but it was even steeper here. He turned toward shore preparing to land when he saw a fast steamer come around a bend in the river and head straight for him as soon as the craft spotted him.

Before the steamer got to him, a man yelled for him to stop for an inspection. There was a United States flag mounted at the rear. Marcus feared this was the end of his adventure when they found the detonators on board.

The small fast boat came up and stopped several feet from his bow. Marcus heard one of the sailors say to another, "That's not one of them. The boat's black." Then one of men spoke out, "Young man, we are searching for two saboteurs who blew up two warships in Cincinnati yesterday. Is there anyone inside your tent traveling with you?"

"No sir, it's just me. You can look if you like. I just live up the river thar, a ways."

"Have you seen two men in a red boat, similar to yours pass by, maybe acting suspiciously?"

Marcus thought, what a stupid question and responded, "Captain, I have been on the river since noon and have seen many craft go by, some red, some yeller that would fit that description, but I don't know what acting suspicious would mean."

The two boats had drifted closer, but it was too dark for the men to notice the thin red line at Marcus's waterline. Another sailor reached out and grabbed the front of Marcus's boat, the previously painted nose, now dry. "Naw, there's no metal frame on this boat either, it ain't him." The darkness, the paint, the putty hiding the holes, all did their job to conceal where the harness had been. Marcus feared black paint, not thoroughly dry, would reveal his disguise, but the man did not seem to feel anything wet and leaned back in his boat and bid him good night. As Marcus watched the boat disappear in the dark, he said a short prayer thanking the Lord for the strong winds that had dried the paint so quickly.

He neared the edge of the river and instead of going ashore, threw his anchor in the river so he could stay in the tent and keep warm wrapped up in his blanket, yet look out the end of his tent and watch for the Professor to pass. Marcus reckoned it was four hours past sunset, and he had seen several boats pass by in the dark, including the largest of the paddle wheelers.

After another hour passed, Marcus started worrying about his ally and friend. Had he been captured? There was nothing he could do now, and there was no way of knowing. Marcus had just been stopped and checked out, and maybe they had stopped the old man too, but maybe the professor hadn't been so fortunate.

While he waited, Marcus had a strange feeling come over him, and in a memory from the past, he saw his mother squatted down in front of him wiping his forehead with a damp cloth. They had just heard his father had fallen from a horse and had been taken to the doctor in the back of a wagon. The messenger, who had a reputation for spreading the worst situation concerning a story, said that most likely, his father had died. As his mother wiped the tears flowing out of his eyes, she told him something he had almost forgotten. "Have Faith, Marcus. It is a sin to worry. If you worry, it shows God that you don't think that He will keep you safe. Believe in God and have Faith everything will end up well." In a few moments they heard another rider galloping toward the house. The family ran out in the yard expecting to hear the worse, but the rider said, "He's alright. He was just knocked unconscious, and he will be fine now." His mother grabbed her little boy and pulled him close, "Have Faith, Marcus, always have Faith and everything will be all right."

It was ironic that he thought about his mother's lesson now after what he had been through in the last few months. He had always expected to survive, though at times he wasn't sure, but now the voice had told him to believe, so Marcus continued to wait and search the dark water with his eyes even though he had gone farther than the Colonel expected. His worry had left him, and he was encouraged he would soon see the prearranged signal.

Later that night the Lord answered his prayer. Marcus saw what he had sought to see, a small boat come around the bend with a lantern on each end of the boat. Marcus lifted his eyes toward Heaven and said, "I have Faith, thank you precious Lord." He knew it had to be the Colonel, and he couldn't wait to talk to him. He pulled up his anchor and rowed hard to catch the two lights a few hundred yards ahead of him. He was now in got in the stronger current. The Professor looked behind him and saw Marcus approaching, the white tent emerging into his dim lantern light.

While Marcus approached, the old man turned down the wick in the back lantern to save coal oil and soon the two boats were side by side. Marcus yelled, all excited in a high voice, "I heard we did it!"

The Colonel 'shushed' him and said, "Not so loud; sound travels far on the water. Somebody might want to know what we did if they heard us. Yes, we did; they didn't go down quickly. I guess the blasts did not blow large holes, but they did blow a hole big enough that eventually put them under. I watched until I was sure they were goners. You know, I don't think any of the sailors were killed. Somehow, they got warned about the blast and were standing on the pier when they exploded."

Before the Professor continued, Marcus grinned, "You did shave your beard and if you hadn't said anything before I saw you, I would not have known for sure it was you except for the two lanterns on your boat."

The professor could see Marcus's teeth in the lantern light that indicated he was satisfied their mission had been accomplished and the two friends had been reunited. The old man jerked his hat off, "And look at this! I told you I would be bald."

Marcus laughed, "They'll never find you now. I feel you are safe."

The professor continued his disguise, "Would ye like to buy some taters, turnips, carrots, or beets?" using an Irish accent."

Marcus was awed by his friend's talents, but curious about the torpedoes, "Did they go off at the same time?"

"No, there were several minutes between the blasts. At first the ships didn't seem to be hurt, but in ten minutes I saw the bows were lower and the *Chicago* was listing in the water. I guess I waited about an hour, and when I saw them both creeping into the water, I headed out; but we have stirred up a hornet's nest. The next day I got stopped three times and searched, but my new masquerade completely fooled them," as he pulled his hat off again to show his bald head.

"Did you do something to your skin? You look darker?"

"Yes, I rubbed some walnut juice on my head and hands; it makes me look darker. If I get stopped again, I may use a Caribbean accent as if I might be from Nassau or Jamaica instead of Irish."

Marcus added, "I thought I might need a better disguise, but I got stopped before dark and from what I overheard, they were looking for a red boat with an iron frame attached to the front and they let me go. But if they ever search my boat they could find the torpedoes."

The old man thought a second, "You know, let's put them back in my boat now. The bags are labeled seeds. I feel my deception is safe as a Caribbean turnip seller, and a feller who sells taters just might have a bag of seeds. I'll lay them in plain sight next to the other vegetables, showing the world I have nothing to hide. Let's switch them over here on the river; there's no boat in sight." The two comrades quickly transferred their cargo again and then separated with the professor following Marcus, this time. The Professor stayed far back barely keeping Marcus insight to convince anyone concerned they were not traveling together. They were both hungry now and wanted to eat something solid. With their disguises working and proven safe, they decided to stop at the first opportunity after daylight and purchase some meat other than fish.

Right at dawn Marcus noticed a farmer and his young son near the river beginning their daily chores, taking advantage of the early morning light. Marcus turned toward the shore and hailed the man. "Sir, by any chance, would you have some fresh meat to sell?"

The farmer ambled toward his fence, motioning for his son to move back; his walk indicated he was not sure what this man on the river wanted, always suspicious of strangers coming down the river. "What did you say you needed?"

"Meat sir, beef, pork, or chicken."

"I can sell you a chicken or two, but wouldn't want to spare any more than that with winter coming on and the war and all, and they're not gonna be cheap, either," he said shaking his head indicating he hoped the man would go on down the river and leave him alone.

"How much do you want for a chicken? I need two of them."

"I'll take fifty-cents for both chickens."

"You drive a hard bargain, but that's a deal," Marcus agreed as he rowed up onshore below the bank of the river, not being able to see the man inside his fence. Marcus got out and pulled his boat ashore and looked back to see the Colonel approaching, not turning toward Marcus, but continuing down the river. From what they had spoken about earlier, the professor knew he was most likely seeking something to eat from a farmer. Marcus showed no interest in the small boat passing by.

When Marcus got to the top of the river bank, he saw the boy was running back toward a large house built on the side of a hill above the flood level of the river. Blue smoke from the chimney twirled through the bare trees, and a large wide porch reminded Marcus of his home in Georgia. He also saw a woman beginning a fire under a wash pot that probably meant the day was Monday. As the boy approached the house, she turned toward the henhouse and soon wrung the necks of two hens and gave them to the boy. While this was happening, Marcus climbed over the man's fence and shook hands with the farmer thanking him for the chickens, although down deep Marcus felt like the man had gouged him on the price.

The boy arrived with the two hens, carrying each one by the neck, one in each hand and gave them to his father. Marcus paid the farmer his money, thanked him, and carried the chickens back to his boat. The farmer, still suspicious of evildoers, held the money in his hand and counted the coins several times with his index finger, stirring the coins in his palm.

Marcus laid the chickens on the seat and used his oar to push away from the riverbank. He saw the professor had slowed and was pointing at an isolated spot on the river. In a few minutes, they were busy plucking chickens and getting them ready to cook. Marcus took his wire grill and put it over his wash pot and pulled out a skillet given to him by the people in Pittsburg. The professor had a jar of bacon fat and after the chickens were cut up and floured, they were soon frying above a fire in the wash pot.

It took three fryings to get all the large chickens cooked, but while they fried the next batch, they dined on the first. They were out of bread, but it seemed both men just craved something fleshy and heavier than fish. As they ate and talked, Marcus noticed one of the chicken heads lying on a rock. All of a sudden, he stopped talking and his eyes opened as if had seen a ghost, or as if he was about to choke on a bone, "What's wrong, Marcus?" the professor noticed."

"The chicken head! The chicken head!" The old man quickly turned and looked, expecting the chicken head to be moving or doing something eerie. "That chicken head can make our trip safe all the way to Nashville." Marcus had remembered Genia's ruse that saved him from the cavalry north of Shepherdstown. He put his juicy piece of chicken down and picked up the chicken head and squeezed a bit of dark red blood out on his finger, then looked at the old man.

"You know what this is?"

The Professor was mystified by Marcus's strange behavior all of a sudden, but answered, "It's obviously chicken blood."

"No! You are looking at a pox."

"Pox, what are you talking about?"

Marcus then reminded him when he told the professor about Genia's ruse that had scared the Union soldiers away after they thought he had the deadly disease."

The professor threw his head back and laughed, "Yes, oh how brilliant. Why didn't I think of that? What a great idea! You are right; we have a free ticket to Nashville alright. Nobody will stop us now nor want to touch the boat, much less search it." They finished eating the chicken and drinking the coffee, all excited about their new plan.

They had traveled for nearly two days without slumber and were very tired and sleepy, but before they went to their separate quarters, they spun a tale that would get them safely to Nashville. The brown bald-headed old man had a good disguise, so they decided to give Marcus a temporary case of smallpox. The professor used a stick and dabbed the red blood, mixed with a little fine clay, on Marcus's face and hands. When it dried, it resembled scabs that poxes often left on the skin. "If I hadn't seen myself do this, I would swear you had a pox," the professor grinned, proud of his finished work of art. "If anyone comes around now poking in our business, they will retreat quickly after getting a look at your face."

The professor looked around on shore and found the other chicken head and secured a small vial from his bag of magic tricks. He washed out the small bottle and squeezed the blood from the two heads into the vial in case they needed to repaint their work of art again. After more discussion about their new masquerade, the two comrades concluded the professor would tie a long rope to Marcus's craft and tow him down the river, pretending to take the infected man with a pox to a doctor when they found one. Now, with each man sated with a whole chicken, tired and exhausted; they decided it best to separate for safety concerns. Marcus rowed a half mile down the river and anchored for the rest of the day. Marcus would wait until the professor came down river, and they would get underway again after dark.

Shortly before night, the professor awoke and pushed off the riverbank to drift down and find Marcus. He had retrieved a small fifty-foot rope he kept stored for emergencies. Following their agreed plan, he would tie on to Marcus's boat and tow him down river. If anyone asked, the professor would relate he was towing a sick man to a doctor if anyone inquired.

Upon hearing the professor's approach, Marcus came to rubbing his face, seeming to forget about his smallpox spots. They were hungry again, so they came ashore and built another fire out of driftwood and boiled some eggs to eat before they set off into the night. Using the light from the fire, the professor retrieved his vial of blood and refreshed his paint job on Marcus's face. The mighty Ohio River was their mother now, and with their new disguises, they felt sure she would keep them safe all the way to Nashville.

33

The night was cold and a strong north wind started blowing; ice was beginning to form on the boat where drops of water had splashed and froze. Both men were still tired and needed to time to revive their energy, so they decided it would be better to stay there and rest until the wind receded. Marcus again departed and went down river about a mile and came ashore. He huddled under his tent trying to stay warm, the cold creeping in around him, daring to enter any seam in his cover that wasn't pulled tight. He lay on his padded mattress with two wool blankets over him, but the cold was relentless, always attacking a weak spot. He wore nearly everything he owned, but he was losing the war as he felt his feet getting numb.

When he couldn't stand the hurt anymore, he got up and kindled a small fire in his wash pot, hoping the heat would flow through his tent and give him a little relief. He would even endure the smoke and breathe through his handkerchief, if he could only find a little warmth. This night felt colder than any he had experienced since his escape. The fire only helped when he was close to the wash pot, but like all campfires, he burned up on one side and froze on the other.

Marcus wondered how the professor was doing in the terrible cold. He didn't have a tent, but instead, wrapped himself in several blankets and snuggled up beneath his rubberized sheet. But tonight it was extra cold, and he expected the old gentleman to come alongside at any time and suggest they build a large fire on the side of the river.

In the middle of the night, Marcus didn't know when, he heard a noise outside his boat. He had dozed some, but felt like he had been awake all night. Half asleep, Marcus opened his eyes and listened. Was it the authorities checking campers on the shore of the river? Marcus eased his hand on his pistol and slipped it out of his pants ready to shoot, depending on whether the intruder came in peace or not. Was it a black bear, cougar, wolf, or some animal needing a meal on a cold night? Then he heard a whine, a similar whine he had heard back home. He rose up, "Fetch, Fetch, is that you boy?" For a moment he didn't know if what was happening was real or a dream. Marcus shook his head. He wasn't asleep; he knew that now. It was a dog. It whimpered again. Marcus sat up and noticed his fire had nearly died out in the pot, only red coals producing the heat now. Suddenly the head of a large dog appeared above the side of the boat and whined at Marcus. Marcus instantly knew the dog was seeking a friend on this miserable night and just wanted in out of the cold. The dog was a yellow lab.

"Well hello there, boy. What's your name?" The dog returned a snappy bark moving his feet up and down and rapidly wagging his tail. He had found a friend. "Jump in here," Marcus said as he motioned for the dog to come inside. Marcus had been taught from childhood to be aware of strange dogs because of the rabies danger. Upon more encouragement the dog jumped inside, Marcus keeping him from bumping into the hot wash pot. He lifted the dog up on his bed and lowered the back flap to keep what heat was left in the wash pot, now only coals and not smoking so much. He pulled the dog under his blankets to help the dog get warm. After a few minutes he realized the dog was an angel of heat as they snuggled together. The dog was well behaved and stayed still, recognizing he had found what he was seeking. Soon the two were in a deep sleep.

The next morning, Marcus was awakened by the Colonel who had gotten up at dawn and came down river, eager to start a large fire and eat some hot food. He gathered some driftwood and soon had a fire kindled. He pulled his chair close to the fire to warm his hands and feet, to watch the sunrise, and wait for Marcus to come out of his warm nest. Finally, the colonel went down and roused Marcus out of his bed, kicking the side of his boat. "Boy, we're wasting daylight, let's eat and get on down the river."

Marcus heard the racket outside, jumped up, wondering for a moment where he was. He looked around for his visitor but, apparently during the night, the dog got warm and slipped off to find his home. From his physique, he wasn't a stray. Probably just friendly and wanted to get warm and get some attention. Marcus told the colonel about his visitor while the two scrounged up something to eat. They were getting low on food except for fish and the professor's stash of vegetables. While Marcus chomped on a carrot, he pondered his furry warm visitor. He had not heard or felt the dog leave… it seemed to appear out of the cold night to keep Marcus warm. Was he imagining what happened, or was the dog an angel in the form of a dog that was sent to keep him warm? "Oh, the dog had to be real," he thought. "I don't know though, it seems I am being watched and protected," Marcus imagined, recalling all the near brushes with death he had survived since the war started.

As they talked over their coffee and carrots, Marcus learned the old man had not slept well during the night and was quite exhausted and wrung out from the cold and lack of sleep. Marcus was rested from his slumber and suggested that the Professor be the smallpox victim and be towed down the river so he could sleep during the day. The Colonel agreed. Marcus washed his face and then quickly dabbed the red disease on to the Professor's face, neck, and hands so he could sleep as they traveled toward Nashville.

The two men loaded their boats and packed their cooking gear and were on the water again, the two boats attached with the long line, the old man fast asleep in the following boat. Once in a while the professor's craft would catch a bit faster current and slowly draw closer and pass Marcus. If no other vessels were near, he paid it no attention.

"This is the life," Marcus thought as he sat under his tent wrapped up in several blankets and watched the scenery, small villages, boats, and people drift by. He passed woodcutters replenishing the steamers plying the river and most waved as he passed, seeming to be friendlier than the rest. Always alert to evildoers, Marcus kept his two pistols in his belt, ready to deter any mal intentions. The river seemed particularly serene that cloudy morning, maybe a little chilly, but protected with a good alibi now, he felt safe as the river pushed him toward home.

The overcast sky prohibited Marcus from knowing the direction he was drifting, but it did not matter since he had to go wherever the river meandered. Curious though, he secured his compass and watched the needle. On several occasions he noticed he was drifting north and east, exactly opposite from his intended general southwest direction, but he understood the twisting and turning river was making its way to the Mississippi, and he would eventually arrive in Louisville.

By midday, Marcus noticed the clouds were growing darker, and he could see murky gray clouds ahead of him. The air was getting colder again after a short warm-up after sunrise, much colder than expected for late fall or early winter. The wind was blowing harder and his vessel was being slowed by the tent. He hadn't heard from the Colonel since he put him to bed earlier that morning. Marcus went to the back of his boat and pulled the other boat close so he could see if the professor was warm and protected. As the professor's boat came near he saw one of the old man's boots sticking out from under a canvas tarp he used to keep himself warm, dry, and out of the light to make sleeping easier. Marcus saw he appeared to be warm and gently let go of the rope and did not disturb the old gentleman.

Marcus rounded a bend and saw a large steamboat tied to a wharf next to a village. Marcus concluded the village most likely had a large general store where he could purchase some vittles that would enhance their fish and vegetables and make their meals tastier. They needed bread, flour, sugar, beans, eggs, and syrup. As he neared the landing, he saw people coming and going as if the steamer was about to depart. When Marcus neared the big boat with the professor in tow, she gave out a long loud blast of her whistle that could be heard for several miles. The sudden loud noise woke up the Professor and he came out from under his tarp with a surprised, "Where am I?" look on his face, his eyes open wide and his mouth agape, with the red spots all over his face.

One of the passengers standing by the railing on the large ship saw the red spots on the old man's face and yelled, "Pox! Pox! That man has a pox," as she turned and ran away. Her yelling brought more folks to the railing, and people on shore moved closer to the river to see what the commotion was about.

After people saw the dreaded speckled face, many ran away, while others began yelling and demanded the diseased men to move on down the river and not spread the pox in their town. One man on shore threw stones at them, and soon they were dodging a hail of small rocks. Marcus was amazed how in a matter of minutes they had completely disrupted the waterfront. Not wanting to draw any more attention to their flight, he turned and paddled hard for the middle of the river to find peace and calm again. The professor had jumped back under his tarp after the woman started screaming, but they knew stopping in that town was not an option. Fortunately, neither man was injured by the incoming pebbles.

When they reached the middle of the current and downstream out of sight from town, they pulled the boats together, "I don't think we were welcome back there. They weren't very friendly."

"I agree." They both established they had learned a lesson on how to enter a village. The old man cleaned the pox off of his face, but kept the vial of chicken blood ready to renew his sickness at a moment's notice. Marcus explained why he had wanted to stop there and restock their supplies, but no harm done. They knew another small town would be around the next bend or two, and they would buy their supplies there or the next village, but no town appeared around the next bend, so they rendezvoused in the middle of the river and ate the last of their boiled eggs they had cooked earlier, but chose not to stop on shore as the weather turned colder and the dark stormy clouds got darker while the unseen sun sank over the horizon.

The weather had been cold all day and hinted snow might fall at any time. Marcus felt as if he had barely endured the cold night before and wondered what he could do to survive a colder night without the dog. While the boats drifted together, Marcus pulled out a few sticks of wood he had gathered earlier that morning, started a fire in his wash pot, and brewed some hot coffee to drink as the dark cold night came on. They were out of sugar, but the hot liquid did its purpose and warmed innards and brightened their spirits.

Traffic on the river seemed sparse as the light faded, and a storm was brewing, so many of the smaller craft had taken refuge in the towns, tying to piers or pulling their boats up on shore. The old man didn't expect to be searched or stopped on the river that night, but for security sakes, the old man painted the pox on Marcus. While he dabbed the red spots, the old man suddenly stopped and sat motionless with the brush in his hand ready to dab another pox and stared off into the dark as if he had heard something. "Ohhh no, I am getting one of those 'goose-feather' feelings. Something's creeping up on me," he said and then resumed his facial art.

Marcus looked out at the dark river, "I think you're right," he answered as he stuck his hand out to catch some falling flakes that began to flutter down from the sky. "I think they call it snow. I fear the snow is sneaking up on us tonight."

"No, weather has never given me this feeling. I sense it's something bigger than that. I will keep alert tonight. I don't know what it is yet, but I fear it is going to be severe." After finishing off the hot coffee the two separated, but remained held together by the long rope. They had gone too far to let their guard down now.

It was brutally cold that night and snow began to fall, sometimes so hard it dimmed the lantern on the professor's boat and reduced the small lantern light to an orange wispy glow in the dark. Marcus had been instructed to sleep, but he worried about the old man keeping watch ahead without the protection of a canvas top and only protected with layers of clothes and his rubberized slicker. Realizing they were alone on the river, the old man in control, Marcus soon fell asleep, the fire in his wash pot, though smoky, providing him some warmth.

Later that night, Marcus woke up suddenly to the sound of something scraping the side of his boat, and he jumped up to see what had made the awful wooden growl. He could see it was still snowing and visibility was down to zero except for the golden glow at the end of his tether line. Snow was filling both ends of his boat. Apparently the professor was still at the end of the tow line at his post, always seeming to be alert to any dangers. Although the professor had shown his skills navigating at night, it would be hard for the old man to tell where he was going in the dark snowy night. "I must have rubbed against the rocks in the river bank or scraped some rocks in a shallow place," he thought to himself. Many times on this trip he had seen shallow areas in the river and bumped into underwater rocks and logs.

Assuming everything was normal, Marcus lay back down to rest. Suddenly the image of a great river steamer appeared in his mind, almost upon him, about to cut him in half. He rose up and listened. Was that the "goose-feather" danger the professor had foreseen? But he heard no blast from a loud steam whistle, nor the splash, splash of a paddle wheel. On second thought, no large paddle-wheeler would be moving on a night like this.

He felt guilty now for being warm while the old man suffered. Since it was below freezing, Marcus thought it only fair for the professor to warm up and get a chance at a little sleep before morning, too. He stirred the coals and added some wood to his wash pot and heated some coffee to warm and perk the two men up. After Marcus downed a cup of his hot brew, he came out of his tent and grabbed the rope and pulled himself up behind the professor's dinghy. As he got closer, he saw snow on the professor's shoulders as the boat slowly rotated in the river current lit by the single lantern light. The old man sat on his seat and resembled a wise Indian chief sitting before a campfire. It looked like he had not moved in hours.

"Hey, old man, what did you let me hit a while ago?" There was no reply. Marcus knew the snow deadened noise so he yelled louder,

"Hey, old man can't you hear me? What did we hit a while ago?" but there was still no reply. Marcus figured he had gone to sleep. He used the rope to pull up beside the Colonel sitting erect and very stiff. Snow was deep on his wide brim hat and shoulders like one saw on statues in the park during a snowstorm.

"Professor! Professor! Are you alright?" Marcus hollered as he reached out to tug on the old man's slicker. When he pulled on his slicker to shake him, the old man leaned over and fell against Marcus's arm, solid as a block of ice. The Professor was dead.

Marcus knew the worst had happened. The old man's body was similar to a statue of a seated man that had just fallen over against the side of the boat, and in so doing, raised his feet off the floor of the boat. Marcus hurriedly climbed into the professor's dinghy and laid the frozen body over into the bottom of the boat. He dusted snow from the old man's face; his skin was frozen hard and felt like a piece of iron. "Old man, you can't do this to me. Why did you die?" Marcus mourned and tried to shake some life back into his body. Aware the Colonel was dead, but expecting a miracle, he continued to try to rouse the old man to awaken and be with him again, but Marcus only moved his garments, disturbing the snow. Marcus realized it was a futile undertaking; his friend was gone.

The old man's eyes were open but covered with frost. Using extreme force, Marcus was able to move his arms and legs, not yet frozen solid. Marcus covered him with a tarp to protect the corpse from the elements out of respect he had for his old friend. When he finished, Marcus knelt on one knee and said a prayer for his friend. "My Heavenly Father, for reasons I do not know, you took my friend tonight. I wish you had told me you were going to do so 'cause I had lots of things I wanted to ask him, but you probably needed him to help you do something in heaven. I wish I could have told him goodbye. From my talks with him, I gathered he was a Christian, and he is there with you. That eases my heart some, so take care of him and tell him I will take the detonators to Nashville. In Jesus' name I say these words, Amen."

Marcus looked at his dead friend and said, "Old man, I wish you could have made it to Nashville with me, but I see you have other plans now. I promise you I will finish this voyage you have sent me on. I will accomplish your mission as I promised back on the first rainy night I met you. Farewell my friend." With that vow Marcus returned to his boat with the Professor's lantern and hung it on the mast of his tent pole and then let the rope out. It was time for the Professor to get his eternal sleep now.

Drifting on the river, hearing only the sounds of small waves rapidly slapping the side of his boat, and able only to see the specks of snow falling in the lantern, Marcus was aware he was alone and very miserable with the loss of his comrade. He reckoned the extreme cold had killed his friend. Marcus wasn't for sure the Colonel's age, but he figured he was about seventy. He hadn't complained about any aches or sickness and seemed excited about taking the lead again after they had the hot coffee. Indeed, the old man's "goose feather feeling" had warned him something "severe" was going to occur that night.

The rest of the night, Marcus could not think of anything else but his friend's death, and how he would miss his genius and camaraderie. The severe weather and the death made for a lonely, cold night, but he concluded the professor most likely dozed off and froze to death due to his age. Marcus would wait until morning and go ashore and remove the detonators and search the professor's boat for valuable items that he could use on his trip to Nashville.

During the night it snowed and snowed. The open ends of Marcus's craft piled up with the fluffy stuff, but the slanted sides of his tent made it easy to remove by just tapping the sides from inside the tent. Before morning, he tugged in the old man's boat. A passerby would never know there was a body on board hidden under the tarp and deep snow. He pondered how to dispose of the Professor's body as he released the rope to let his dead friend drift behind him again.

It seemed daylight would never come, the cold now biting Marcus's face and slowly penetrating his protective garments and chilling him down to the bone. Knowing the professor wouldn't need his blankets anymore, Marcus had used them to help him survive the bitter cold night. Even with the added blankets he was losing the battle, and started trembling. Shaking with cold, Marcus tried to start another fire with the last of his wood and make some coffee. With some dry newspaper tucked under sticks of wood in the wash pot, he tried to strike a match, but he was so cold and clumsy, his shivering made the chore nearly impossible.

Fear overcame Marcus, and he got a "goose-feather feeling" that this dark night could be his last if he couldn't strike the match. He held the match with both hands to stop the shaking and scratched it on the dry seat inside the boat, but not in control of his faculties, broke the head off the match. He looked in the box and noticed he only had six matches left. He took another and tried again with no success, but on the third attempt the match lit up, and he protected the flame with his shaking hands as he stuck the match against the paper. Slowly at first, acting as if the air was too cold for paper to burn, the paper finally caught fire, flaming up and giving the interior of his tent an orange glow. Marcus added more newspaper to have a big safe flame and kept feeding the paper into the fire and adding small sticks until they lit. Soon the fire was secure, and Marcus put the last of his small logs into the pot, knowing they would be consumed too soon for him to make coffee. His only chance of survival now was to head for the riverbank and search the shore for sticks of wood hidden under the snow. He hoped the snow was so cold the wood would still be dry; with the heat of the fire even damp wood would ignite quickly.

The snow continued to descend more heavily than Marcus had ever seen back in Georgia. He finally saw the edge of the river appear in his lantern light and fortunately it wasn't a steep vertical bank, but more of a rocky sandbar. He paddled fast and ran the prow of his boat onto the shore; the professor's boat glided on by, unable to escape due to the long tether, and eventually swung around and bumped up against the shore.

Marcus jumped off the boat and pulled it on shore so the pull of the other boat would not dislodge his moorage. He grabbed the lantern and walked along the shore, kicking snow off any form that looked like wood hiding under the white camouflage. While Marcus searched, suddenly, like a gift from God, he heard a large limb break from a nearby tree and crash to the ground from the weight of the snow. On examination, the snow was so dry it had not moistened or stuck to the wood. Marcus dusted it off, got his ax and immediately went to work turning the large broken branch into kindling wood to save his life. His exertion made him feel warmer, and soon he had replenished his wood supply. He immediately started stoking his fire before it died, and he quickly had his wash pot full of fire and wood. As he finished stacking the wood under his tent, Marcus heard the first signs of dawn, the sounds of birds beginning their day as the trees emerged from the dark. Finally, this freezing, gloomy, and fatal night was ending.

34

With his wooden fuel supply replenished, Marcus brewed more coffee and warmed himself over the hot fire. Warm now, but hungry, Marcus pushed away from the bank pondering what to do with the professor's body. The snow continued to fall creating a white curtain that painted the landscape colorless against what appeared to be black tree trunks. The wind had stopped blowing, but on the water, the heavy snow muffled any noise from shore.

It wasn't long until he saw the strings of blue smoke from many chimneys appear around a bend in the river. A town, finally a town; as he neared, he saw a small paddle wheeler loading and unloading her cargo. To avoid another "pox" scare, Marcus thoroughly washed his face and hands. Now, cured from the disease, he rowed up to the pier and tied up away from any human activity. He secured the old man's craft also. The professor's body was hidden and no one would suspect there was a corpse on board.

The only human activity he could see was the movement on and off the small steamer, but when he climbed the ladder he saw a row of buildings facing the river, their glass windows emitting a warm orange glow into the dark gray day. Tracks in the snow indicated the place to be was in a large general store directly in front of him.

Marcus walked across a wide icy street into the warm interior of the red brick building, the red color exaggerated by the white landscape. A bell on the door alerted the clerk, standing watching a domino game next to a large iron stove, that he had a customer. Not only was it a mercantile store, he saw dining tables in the back.

The clerk approached Marcus, "Welcome to my store," he said realizing the man was a stranger. "Can I help you find something?"

"Yes, I'm just passing through on the river and need to get some basic vittles: sugar, flour, coffee, matches, coal oil, bacon, eggs; you know, stuff like that." Marcus stopped and thought, "And some other things I can't remember now, but maybe looking around I'll see the other things I need."

You must be off the river boat over there," pointing at the paddle wheeler.

"No, I'm in a covered rowboat pulling another. I have to deliver them to a boat yard in Louisville."

"It's pretty cold out there. Why don't you go over there and stand by the stove and warm up while I gather these supplies for you." That invitation sounded good to Marcus so he hastened over to the stove and stuck his hands out over the warm heat. The gloves he had been wearing were not very warm, and the heat on his bare hands felt good. As he stood there, the four men playing dominoes and three others watching the game nodded at Marcus symbolically, giving Marcus approval to stand there in their territory.

The men were talking about the Civil War and the local goings on around the town, then one of the sentences caught Marcus's ear. "Yeah, I'm glad they finally caught those two guys who blew up those gunboats in Cincinnati. I understand they are going to be shot as saboteurs next week sometime. Apparently they nabbed a man and his son coming down the river from Cincinnati. From what I heard, they fit the description of who they were huntin'."

"Yeah, it had to be them," another agreed.

Another man chimed in, "Good! They're going to get what they deserve. They sure didn't give those guys on board those ships any chance. I heard two hundred sailors were killed."

"Naw sir, I hear'd the truth down at the telegraph office—they told us only a few sailors were killed."

Marcus knew no sailors had been killed when the torpedoes exploded. Marcus wanted to say something, but he knew it was time to keep his mouth shut; but he wondered who the innocent souls were who were taking the punishment for what he and the professor had done. Another bystander spoke up, "A firing squad would be too easy for them. If I was in charge I would drag them to death behind a pair of horses. I would drag them slowly over rocks so the pain would last a long time. That would definitely teach others what they would get if they did such a thing again."

Marcus continued to listen to the stories and after a few minutes the clerk came over and told him his purchases were ready. Marcus's curiosity got the best of him and before he left the stove he asked, "'S'cuse me fellas. I couldn't help hearing what you were talking about. So they did catch that Rebel trash that blew up them iron boats?"

"Yeah boy! They are gonna get their due," one of the players replied as he slammed a double five domino on the table.

"Well, I was passing by there the day the ships exploded." Before he could say more the game stopped and everyone focused on what he was saying. Surprised by this sudden attention and knowing all seven men wanted him to tell them more, Marcus continued. "I heard you say hundreds were killed, but that isn't so. Somehow the local authorities discovered their evil plot and warned the ships. The captains evacuated the ships, and the sailors were standing on the pier when the blasts went off. Matter of fact, I had docked my boat and was standing close-by when the explosions went off and it wasn't that loud nor did it do much damage at first. It took them several hours to sink."

Another player added, "I'm glad, if what you say is true, no sailors were killed."

"No, like I said, they were all standing on shore when those bombs went off. By the way who did they catch, Confederate soldiers or spies?"

"The newspapers said they were huntin' a young boy and an old man. You know, they captured that old man but turned him loose. The stupid policeman thought he was a village idiot, when in fact, he was a genius."

"You don't say. So they caught those guys. What about the boy?"

"I don't know whether he's involved or not, but somebody said the lad was forced to plant the gunpowder by the old man. From what I heard, he was pretty mean to the boy."

"You're right, I heard that too," another man added. "Anyway, they found those two floating down the river trying to get away and the Navy caught them on the river. They were stopping boats all around here. Old Fred there, he even got searched."

Marcus chimed in, "Yes, I know. I bet I got stopped a dozen times since I left Cincinnati. I'm glad I didn't have an old man travelling with me. I might have been arrested too."

"Yeah, you seem to be awful young to be on the river by yourself. Where are you going?"

"I'm a soldier going home to St. Louis. I got wounded in the battle at Antietam and was sent home for a while. When I got to Pittsburgh, I lucked in on a job to deliver two boats to Louisville."

"They ain't red with the name *Bonnie* written on it?" the man laughed, slapping his knee like he had cracked a funny joke, then joined by the others to let Marcus know he was welcome to the stove, but he was still an outsider.

Marcus, unperturbed, returned, "Naw, it's just black. Whoever made it named it 'The Crow'"

"That fits I guess," one of the men laughed. Marcus was amazed that the information about his boat had spread up and down the river, but maybe since they caught someone they wouldn't be searching for the saboteurs anymore.

Marcus told the men he had to get on his way and that he had enjoyed the conversation. Marcus made a sweep through the store and picked out some canned food along with a new pair of gloves and paid for his supplies. Marcus had plenty of fishing money to pay his bill. He had purchased so much food, it took him two trips to get them to his boat. He had felt good in the warm store, but he had a cold feeling about the father and his son who were to be shot for the deed they did not do.

Marcus looked down at the deep snow gathering on the professor's boat. He needed to go down river to an isolated spot and take what would be of value out of the old man's craft and destroy the rest and decide what to do with the Confederate Colonel. Supplies secured and the fire stoked up again; Marcus pushed off from the pier and soon left civilization behind. Within the hour he saw a flat spot on the edge of the river where he could land and thoroughly search the professor's craft.

After an hour or so on the rocky shore, Marcus had swept away the snow, secured the detonators, found two more pistols with black powder and lead, $175 in Federal paper money and $627 in Confederate money, small tools, and several colors of paint. He secured the paper money in his pocket for future use. As he was finishing his search, he found a wooden carton slid under one of the seats. After opening it and scratching around inside, Marcus concluded it was the professor's "junk box". Inside were bits of nails, brads, wire, string, stale peanuts, pecan shells, nuts and bolts, and other scraps of wood and iron he hoarded thinking he might use later in one of his ingenious ways.

Marcus carefully poured the contents out on the flat boat seat. When he tipped the box upside down a false bottom fell out along with several sheets of folded paper. One of the papers identified the professor as a Confederate Colonel. Another paper were orders, apparently written by Jefferson Davis, giving him authority to pass throughout the Confederacy with privileges to ride on trains and coaches and even the authority to confiscate anything he needed to secure his mission. Marcus was amazed he had kept this incriminating evidence while traveling down the river. Marcus didn't want this evidence of espionage in his possession and started to wad them up, but then in a moment of insight, he had a brilliant idea.

Marcus held the papers and continued to think. "Yes, this is a brilliant idea, and I can save the lives of the two innocent civilians who are going to be shot." He quickly packed the papers away and finished cleaning the old man's boat. He replaced the papers under the wooden box and then carefully placed six detonators in the box. His plan would sacrifice six detonators, but to save innocent lives; Marcus felt it was worth it.

During the search, Marcus had moved the old man's stiff body to the back of the boat and covered it with a canvas tarp. Several times tears came to Marcus's eyes when he thought about the conversations and experiences he had shared with him. He stared at the professor's cold face and still couldn't believe he was dead. To fulfill his mission and to save the innocent civilians, Marcus took one of his pistols, rolled the professor over and shot him in the back of the head. "Old man, I hated to do that, but I know if you were here, and under the circumstances, you would want me to do this to save those innocent people." His frozen brain prohibited any bleeding, blood splatter or exit wound.

With that horrible task done, Marcus pushed off again in the falling snow and drifted on down the river, anticipating stopping at the next town or village and revealing his greatest lie. Traffic on the river was almost nonexistent on the cold snowy day, only a few larger steamers passing him, one going upstream and three going downstream. Toward evening he spotted a town on the starboard side of the boat, and as darkness fell, Marcus came up to a low pier and tied the two boats.

There were many small craft tied there, their owners sitting and cooking under an arbor next to a small tent village preparing for the night. Some of the old tars appeared to live in this shanty tent town the entire year. It seemed these old river rats knew each other, and some passed around strong spirits to help endure the forthcoming cold night. This crowd looked a little rough, so Marcus slid his two pistols under his coat and came ashore and asked if the town had a constable or a sheriff.

"Yes sir! It shor' does. The boss done come down here 'while ago and checked on our bi'ness. He likes to push his weight around and keep all us river bums in line."

"And he's got plenty of it too," another laughingly added.

"Where might I find this here boss man?"

"Probably eating I suspect. When he left here he walked over there," said one of the men pointing at some buildings. "Follow those tracks in the snow. They'll take you right where he is," another added as he took a swig of whiskey out of a flat glass bottle and wiped his mouth with the back of his tattered glove, then passed the bottle to another.

"Thank you gentlemen," Marcus replied, thinking he was stretching the definition for the word "gentlemen." "I'll be right back," he added hoping to imply to these "gentlemen" they would not have time to ravage his boat. To insure his boat would be safe, he added, "There's a dead man in my boat."

In a few minutes, Marcus returned with the constable shuffling along beside him, somewhat addled by the news of a dead man and disappointed to be separated from his warm stew. He was a large heavy set man one might call fat, or if one was being polite, stocky or big boned. Three of the river rats had walked over and were looking down at Marcus's boat expecting to view a corpse, but not seeing one, waited to see what would happen next.

Marcus led the constable to the professor's boat, then got him to help him carefully lift the tarp so as not to spill the snow back inside the boat. They eased back the rubberized canvas and pitched the snow aside revealing the old man's body lying on his side, one of his arms sticking out in a frozen pose.

"That man shor'nough dead," one of the watchers added.

"There's yo're sorry saboteur that blew up the gunboats in Cincinnati," Marcus said as he pointed down at the body.

"How do you know that? They've already arrested two people, a father and a son for that deed," the constable commented, looking Marcus directly in the eye, trying to pick up any suspicion of a lie.

"Well, whoever they arrested, they better let them go 'cause they're innocent," Marcus confidently stated. Let me tell you how I know. Last evening about dark, back up the river away, I had landed on shore to build a fire and rest for the night. During the night I heard wooden oars clattering against a wooden boat. I thought it might be river pirates and I got my guns ready," Marcus smiled as he lifted his coat and revealed the pistols in his belt. "But instead of pirates it was this old man. I must say he was awfully nice and friendly. I helped him put up his tarp thar, and we were soon drinking some coffee to warm us up. I could tell that he was excited about something and the more we talked the more he let me in on his doings. He finished off a small flask of whiskey after supper. Due to the liquor, he started telling me more." As Marcus finished the sentence, his emotions and memories of the professor took charge of his sentiments and his voice started breaking up into a sob. Marcus realized his ruse of killing a spy was going to end if he didn't get back in control of his feelings.

"Boy, I thought you told me you had killed a saboteur. Why are you crying? You act like he was your best friend."

Marcus turned and looked at the constable. "Sir, you don't understand, I was in the army and shot lots of people from afar, but I ain't use to murdering nobody, up close. But you see, after what he told me, I had to do what I had to do," he whimpered.

The constable put his arm around Marcus, "Boy, you're all right, now calm down and tell me the rest of the story."

With glassy wet eyes, Marcus, partly crying and partly acting, continued. "As you see by the way I talk, I sound like a Southerner. My family comes from Indiana, but my mother met a man from Georgia and married him. I was raised in the South, but when my father died we moved back to Indiana. When the war broke out I joined the Indiana volunteers." Marcus stopped and showed the constable his battle scar. "I got this on the Peninsula fighting Robert E. Lee and got captured at Antietam. I escaped and got back to my brigade and the Colonel told me to go home for six months and rest."

"Then what are you doing on this river in this cold weather?

"Going home. A man in Pittsburgh felt sorry for me and said he would pay me $25 to float 'The Crow' down to Louisville. It would help me get home and I could make a little money."

"I see, continue."

"I soon figured this old man there in the boat was not a river rat but a well-educated Professor."

"How do you know that?"

"He told me. When we were talking he said he was a 'languager' or something to do with languages and could tell what part of the country I grew up, and sure enough, he told me that I was raised in central Georgia. He asked me if I liked the South, and I said I did, meaning I liked living there, and before I could say more, he revealed he was a Confederate Colonel. He and the whiskey kept talking, and I never told him I was really a Yankee. Finally, he told me he was the one who blew up the two ships in Cincinnati. I couldn't believe what I heard! He said he was taking some detonators to the Confederate Navy and was smuggling them down the river to use and blow up all the Union Navy. He even showed them to me. Here let me show you." Marcus slipped inside the Colonel's boat and pulled out the flat wooden box. "Look at these things," Marcus proudly revealed as he unlatched the box and opened it up and poured the six detonators on the seat. As he did this, and as Marcus planned, the false bottom fell out and the Confederate documents slid onto the seat. "Oh, what's this? I haven't seen this." Marcus picked up the papers and scanned over them quickly. He raised his head and turned toward the constable as if surprised, "Yes, this is definitely proof I have killed the right man who blew up the boats."

The constable took the papers from Marcus and quietly read over them. "Yes indeed, my boy, you have saved our Navy. You are definitely a hero," said the constable already thinking how he would also get credit for saving countless lives and ships. He turned back to Marcus, "But when did you shoot him?"

"As I mentioned, I fought in the war and shot at lots of Yankees," then rapidly correcting himself, "I mean Rebels, I don't know why I said that. Anyway I never knew for sure if I killed anybody although I shot at lots of 'um, but when I heard what he had done and what he was about to do, I knew I had to kill him. Being a good soldier, I couldn't let him continue on his journey and do his evil deeds. I made up my mind to shoot him when I got a chance. I had my pistols in my belt. He smoked a pipe and once while he cleaned out the bowl I got up as if to go outside, but I just turned, pulled out my pistol and shot him in the back of his head." Marcus's voice broke again, "Have you ever shot your grandfather? He was such a nice man, that's what I felt like I was doing. I hated to kill someone like that without giving him a chance, but I had to do what I had to do. I waited until this morning, packed up all our gear, loaded his body in his boat, and pulled him down the river. I wanted to turn myself in and let the law know what I had done."

"We were told by the authorities to be on the lookout for a young lad about your age who was traveling with the old man and was the one who actually planted the explosions. I might assume you would be the boy if you were in a red boat named 'Bonnie.'" Fortunately for Marcus his boat was full of snow and it was far enough away the constable couldn't see the red paint that could still be seen around the waterline and a few missed places inside. "Did he mention anything about the boy he used to help him?"

"Why yes he did. This man must have been a real evil man. He told me after they had blown up the ships, the authorities would be looking for two people. He said to insure his safety he shot the lad and sunk his body in the river. Then shaved his head and beard. He even stained his skin to look darker and not like a professor. That was another reason I took no chances and shot him when I had the chance. I figured he'd kill me after he sobered up and thought about all the stuff he told me."

"Well, boy, you certainly did the right thing, and I know your country will be proud of you. I know two other people expecting to be shot next week who will be proud of you, too. I'll telegraph the authorities and tell them what I have," the constable said as he picked up one of the detonators and looked at it, not realizing there were more than a hundred of the deadly eggs on Marcus's boat.

"I imagine, boy.... by the way, what's your name?"

"James, sir."

"James, I expect your country will want to give you a big medal and put you in a parade with a band and show you off, maybe give you a reward. I expect you are going to be a hero."

Marcus realized he didn't want to be looked at that closely, fearing that the real story would be uncovered. Again, like a great actor on stage, he pursued another scene as a Union soldier. "Sir, please listen to me. I am proud that I killed an enemy of my country, but I am ashamed I murdered a man by shooting him in the back of his head. I know some people will say I was a coward and not a hero. You know what I am saying is true. I have told you all I know about this man, and I did what I thought was the right thing to do. I am trying to get home before it's too cold to travel. Please let me go on home and deliver this boat and see my mother. She hasn't seen me in almost two years. I don't want to be known for what I did, and I don't want to be a hero or get a medal for what I did. Just let me go on down the river. Why don't you tell people my story and say you did it?"

"Oh…. I couldn't do that," the constable replied. He stopped talking as he pondered the idea. After a few moments with his head cocked and raising his index finger, he turned to Marcus, "If you really feel that way, I'll tell you what kid; just get in your boat and head on down the river and I'll take care of everything. I'll think of something."

"Oh, thank you sir, thank you. I just want to get home and get out of this snow. Be sure though, those poor folks that are accused of sabotage are turned loose. You know they are innocent."

"Yes, I will tend to that first thing in the morning. Now go on down the river and get home," as he untied the Professor's boat from Marcus. He motioned for Marcus to hurry and get in his boat and leave. Marcus climbed in his boat and disappeared under his tent and prepared to row using the holes in the side of the tent.

"That's quite a little ship you have there son. Where'd you get a boat like that?"

"This is the boat I'm taking to Louisville. I am going to miss this girl when I have to drop her off," Marcus responded as he pushed away from the pier. As he eased away two deputies rode up on horses, dismounted and came on the pier. Marcus heard the constable tell his deputies as he had examined the corpse, "To be shot in the head, there sure wasn't much bleeding or blood splatter."

"Yeah, he was probably really cold when he got shot," one of the deputies answered.

Marcus muttered under his breath, "You're right, but you don't know how cold." Then he quietly added, "Goodbye old fellow. I will never forget you, and when the war is over I am going to tell your story, and you will be a Southern champion. Even in death, you did your duty and saved two innocent lives. Thank you, Colonel Jethro Jennings." With that said, Marcus turned away and left, never looking back at his old friend again. Marcus was safe on the river now and his next stop would be Louisville.

Marcus stared at the darkening sky as the snow continued to fall. He thought about his lost comrade wondering what the professor was doing now in heaven. Marcus wondered if those who had entered heaven were allowed to talk about the war or was that subject too horrible to mention in a place like that.

His thoughts drifted toward Bonnie as the cold night came on, and he wondered what she was doing. Marcus was melancholy that night as he stared at the dark water lit by the lantern at the front of his boat. There was nothing to see but the falling snow in the lantern light, sometimes broken by an orange glow coming from a passing boat or lonely farm house built close to the river. Two hours after dark, Marcus was totally exhausted; he had been up for over twenty-four hours. Rather than take a chance and fall asleep, he decided to pull out of the current and throw an anchor out and get some rest. The constant exposure to the outdoor air and the physical and mental strains had taken their toll.

Marcus paddled toward his right and soon the edge of the river appeared in his lantern light. In the light he saw a large buck standing on the shore seeming to wonder what Marcus was. The large stag stood his ground, but when he caught Marcus's odor wafting on the wind, he quickly disappeared in the dark. For safety reasons, Marcus didn't want to pull up on the bank, but instead anchored out of the river traffic. He found a suitable place close to the shore, pitched out his anchor, stoked the fire he had tended all day, covered the ends of his tent, folded down his seats and used all of the Professor's confiscated blankets for a mattress except three to use as cover. Though somewhat smoky, the fire warmed the space, but his tent was not so tight he would be asphyxiated. He ate some chocolate he bought back in the general store and soon dozed off sound asleep.

The next morning he woke up with first light, stirred his fire back to flames, fried three eggs with bacon and boiled a hot cup of coffee. He thought about his lost friend, but things were looking up now as he pulled his anchor and drifted for Louisville.

35

It was a cool gray day back in Buckhead, Georgia, the place where Marcus called home. His father, Calvin Mills, and his mother Sarah, were sitting on the porch enjoying the delightfully cool weather that made working more enjoyable. However, the hard work was over for the year except for cutting wood, killing chickens, an occasional hog, and other common chores found on a farm in the 1800s. Very seldom idle though, the couple used this time to accomplish a task that needed to be done. Mr. Mills shucked corn for the chickens while Sarah crumpled and shelled a bushel of dried black-eyed peas picked earlier in the summer. When finished she poured the shelled peas into a pan of water to start soaking before being cooked.

There was food aplenty that fall. War had not hit Georgia yet and there were fat hogs, chickens and lots of eggs, canned vegetables, honey, and syrup. Even after giving a fair amount to the Confederate Army, people had plenty to eat.

While the couple shucked, shelled, and talked, they spotted the postman coming in his carriage toward their house, the lone horse working harder as he came up a long grade to their mailbox hung on a tree. The last dropping leaves of fall sprinkled down on the road when a gust of wind ended their brilliant glory against the sky and fluttered to their final resting place on the ground.

The postman always seemed to be in a hurry, but today he approached slower, not urging the horse to get on up the hill to their house, but let him pull at his own pace. He reined the horse at the front of their gate, and instead of waving; he stepped down from his carriage and walked across the yard following a well-worn path to the porch. When they saw a frown on his face, both Calvin and Sarah sensed he had sad news as he never looked them in the eye, but finally giving each a quick glimpse as he came up the steps onto the wide porch.

The pair put down their work and stood up; Calvin instinctively slapped the pieces of broken shucks from his pants, and Sarah looked down and pushed her hair back and then popped her neck by turning her head as Calvin had seen her do many times when she was a bit frightened. They expected to hear that a neighbor, friend, or relative had died until he pulled out an envelope and passed it to Calvin.

"From my past experience with these letters from Richmond, I am afraid I have brought bad news," the postman responded. "I hope it is about something else, but I fear it's about Marcus." Calvin quickly passed the letter to Sarah who stared at it a few moments and then tore it open to read.

As she read she unknowingly reached in her apron and pulled out a handkerchief and held it next to her mouth. "The government is sad to report your son apparently was killed in the battle of Sharpsburg, Maryland, on September 17, 1862. He did not report for muster after the conflict and no remains of his body were ever found. The Texas Division lost huge casualties, and we fear he may have been one of the brave soldiers lost that day. Please accept our deepest sympathy and regards, sincerely, Colonel Jonathan B. Browning, War Department, Richmond, Virginia."

Calvin turned and grabbed the arm of the old chair to help ease him back where he was seated and picked up his corn and started removing the shucks and staring directly ahead as if nothing happened. Sarah lowered the letter, looked at the postman a few moments and then walked to the front of the porch and looked out at the yard as if she saw Marcus playing there when he was small. The postman reached down and handed Calvin another letter and broke the cold silence, "You got another letter. It seems it is from the Staples girl who lived next to you and moved to Texas with her family a while back.

Sarah slowly turned and came back to Calvin, stopping behind his chair, and took the letter, seeming to come out of her deep thoughts. Speaking in a somber voice, "Maybe she knows what happened to Marcus. Growing up, they were seldom out of each other's sight." She looked at the front of the envelope and saw it was from Texas and addressed to Marcus Mills, Buckhead, Georgia. "I guess I better read it for him, since he ain't in a state to do that anymore," she said in a harsh manner, as if she blamed Marcus for going off and killing himself.

She tapped the letter to one side of the envelope and then tore the other end and slid out a two-page letter. "This is dated October 5, 1862. It reads:

> *My dearest Marcus, I miss you very much and hope you are doing well in the Army. I write you every week. I pray you are getting my letters. Since I have not heard a reply, I am worried that you are hurt. Don't let yourself get shot or nothing. We finally got to Texas and found my Uncle Pete's family at Fincastle, Texas. It is a bustling little town and is a storehouse for food that will help feed you this winter. It is a hilly area with rocky clay soil on the hills but good sandy farmland between and outside the hills. Mother and John came down with a fever when we were crossing Louisiana. We stopped with a family that let us stay in a small cabin near their house. It had been used by an older relative who had recently passed on. Mother and John got well, and we came on to Texas and arrived here about a week ago. Father rides out every day and*

looks for farmland. We are living out of our wagon but need to find shelter soon as the winter is coming on and it is getting cold at night. Please, Marcus, take care of yourself and I will always be waiting for you to come and find me. If you get this letter, write to the post office in Fincastle, Texas, and write on the envelope, 'To Bonnie Staples, Fincastle Texas.' The man at the post office said he would save any letters for me. I am sending this letter to your mother and I hope she knows where you are. I can't wait to see you again and I love you very much, Bonnie."

Sarah lowered the letter, like women had done since the beginning of time, forced to accept the death of her son. Like Calvin, she turned back to continue her pea-shelling, hoping being busy would ease her pain. "I know'd he'd be killed when he ran off that day when the band played and made everyone think the war was going to be a party. He was too young to go and could have waited another year or two before anyone would have thought him a coward for not going." She paused and thought a few seconds. "I don't know how Bonnie is going to do when she gets the news. I guess I'll write to that address. I guess it is the right thing to do."

The somber discussion was interrupted as Marcus's two younger brothers came running from a far-off field. They had been cutting and clearing a field. When they saw the postman's buggy stop, something he seldom did, they raced back to the house, looking for an excuse to visit, get some water, and see what was the matter. The two boys immediately sensed something was wrong as they came loping up gasping for breath. "What's the matter Pa? Something's wrong."

"Boys, sit down here on the porch," Calvin told his boys, breaking his long silence, taking the responsibility to tell his boys the bad news. "You're not going to like what you are going to hear," he hesitated a moment, then slowly uttered, "We just learned Marcus was killed in the war."

Evelyn, who had been quilting in the back room, came on the porch and heard her Father's words. Immediately she angrily rebelled, "No! No! That can't be. I will not believe that. I asked God last night, like I do every night, to protect him and He said have Faith, he will be all right." She turned and ran back in the house with Sarah following closely trying to soothe her, "You're right Evelyn, if God told you he was not killed, then he is safe." Sarah knew Marcus was gone, but she wanted to agree with Evelyn and help calm her nerves, letting time bring reality to her.

The postman added, "On days like this, I hate my job. I am sorry you have lost your son. He was a good boy, and Bonnie was going to make him a good wife." He bid Calvin and the two boys goodbye and continued on down his route telling all the neighbors about Marcus. Soon people were coming to the house bringing food and sweet things to eat, and by dark, all the families' friends had gathered trying to comfort their grief.

There was an absence of Marcus's friends since most of the older boys were in the Confederate Army, but many of the young girls who adored Marcus arrived with their parents to pay their respect. A large feast was eaten and at times, one might have thought they were at a wedding, rather than an impromptu wake, the laughing, however, often broken by sounds of sobbing.

The next day, Sarah sharpened a large turkey quill, took out a bottle of ink, and wrote Bonnie a letter:

"November 30, 1862

Dear Bonnie, It was pleasurable to hear that your folks got to Texas and your mother and brother got over the fever. I don't know how to express myself on paper about what I am about to say, but I will try. Mr. Percy, our postman, you remember him, brought us a letter the same day your letter came. Your letter brought us good news, but the other letter brought us sorrow and grief, and I am sure it will touch your heart also. The letter said that Marcus, our dear Marcus was killed at a battle in Sharpsburg Maryland. I don't know if I can accept it or not, but I guess I will have to for the sake of the other children. Evelyn believes he is still alive and refuses to accept his death. I pray she is right. Please accept our sympathy as I know you will send us yours. Sincerely, Sarah Mills."

36

For the first time since meeting the professor, Marcus felt safe on the river. The authorities would not be hunting for a young boy or an old man who sent two of the best Union warships to the bottom of the river. The saboteur had been killed, and his aid had been murdered.

It took Marcus three days to reach Louisville. There had been no trouble or searches. It had stopped snowing, and he watched beautiful snow scenes pass by as he floated the river. He cooked on his stove and had plenty to eat. The weather warmed, and the snow started to melt during the day. His next goal would be to drop his watercraft in Louisville and buy a horse and wagon using the professor's money. Next, travel overland to Nashville and find a gentleman in a black top hat with a red feather attached, sitting on the porch of The River Roost, an eatery above the river in Nashville.

Marcus arrived in Louisville with church bells ringing. Marcus thought it was thoughtful of the people to welcome him in such a magnificent way, but he knew instead it was Sunday. For the most part, the piers were quiet which indicated the sinners were sleeping off a Saturday night drunk and the righteous people were in church. He rowed up slowly and found an empty space among the many boats that had stayed overnight. He tied his boat and mingled among the few people going about their business on a Sunday morning, from mending fishing nets and repairing boats, to resting; some playing checkers.

Marcus wanted to find Mr. McKenzie, the boat builder where Marcus had agreed to leave the boat. A passerby told him it was about a half mile further down the river. He returned to his *Bonnie,* as he remembered her, to take his final ride with his old friend that had done her job so well. He rowed slowly looking for the site that would end his adventure on the river. About where the man said it would be, he saw the name McKenzie painted in large letters directly on the side of a large wooden building. Located a ways from downtown, there were no people to be seen, and the place appeared to be locked up. Marcus tied *The Crow* next to other boats secured to a pier parallel to the river's edge and walked up the embankment and searched around the building to see if anyone might be about. There was a lone horse hitched beside the large shed. At the back Marcus looked through a window pane and saw an old man working in the morning sunlight coming through the windows.

Marcus tapped on the window to get his attention. The old man put his auger down and walked to the back door and opened it. "What can I do for you, son?" the old man asked politely, like so many old men did.

"Are you Mr. McKenzie?"

"Aye, boy, I am he, Mack McKenzie. How can I help you?" he replied with a touch of a Scottish background.

"Sir, I have a boat to leave here with you. Mr. Henry Dunigan, back in Pittsburg, loaned me this boat to help me get home and said when I got to Louisville to leave it with you."

Before he could say more, Mr. McKenzie said, "You're Marcus Mills, the soldier from Antietam," as he stuck out his hand, proud to shake hands with a hero. "Come in, come in, I have a pot of coffee over here on the stove. I was just about to stop and take a sip when I heard you knock. Come over and join me."

"Well thank you, Mr. McKenzie that would taste good." Marcus and the older man walked over and sat down in some cane bottom chairs near the stove. Mr. McKenzie retrieved a cup from a nearby shelf and tapped the wood dust out and filled it with coffee. He took his own unwashed porcelain cup and poured yesterday's coffee on the floor and renewed it with fresh coffee. Then the old man revealed a secret he knew about Marcus.

"Mr. Mills, indeed you are a hero to me, but not for being at Antietam." He grinned, "You are a one eyed-jack in this War Between the States."

Surprised at what the man said, "What do you mean, sir? I am delivering the boat as I promised Mr. Dunigan."

"Boy, you don't have to hide anything from me. I am on your side."

"What? What do you mean?"

"Unlike Mr. Dunigan, a devout Yankee, and even though I live in northern Kentucky, I am a devout Southerner fighting for state's rights. I am a Confederate agent just like you."

"Why do you figure I'm a Confederate?"

"Newspapers and a little figuring. I know now you had to be the young boy that helped one of our agents sink the *St. Paul* and the *Chicago*." He eased his chair back and reached behind him and grabbed a folded newspaper from a table. "From what this paper says, a bald-headed dark skinned old man was shot by a constable on the river four days ago after he heard the old man confess he had blown up the ships. Did you know your comrade got killed?"

"I don't know what you're talking about. I am here just to deliver a boat."

"That's the other part of the puzzle. Mr. Dunigan wired me about you. He said a young lad who had fought at Antietam wanted to get home. He felt sorry for you and built you a special boat, painted it red, and painted *Bonnie* on the back."

"That's right. I am here to give it back to Mr. Dunigan. He said you would send it back to him."

"Well son, every sheriff, soldier, sailor, and constable have been looking for that boat from Pittsburgh to Cairo, Illinois, ever since the Union warships went down. The sailors said a red boat named *Bonnie* had planted the torpedo and was associated with an old professor. When I heard the old man was a professor I knew it had to be Jethro Jennings, but Jethro was not bald nor was he dark skinned." Then the elderly man cocked his head and scratched his chin and looked Marcus in the eye, "And I am expecting a red boat named *Bonnie* coming down the river from that direction. How many red boats on the river are named *Bonnie*?

Marcus concluded the man had discovered who he was and what he had done. Obviously, Mr. McKenzie would also wonder why the red boat had turned black when he sees it. Before Marcus could answer his question Mr. McKenzie went on. "Tell me, how in the world did you get down the river in that red boat without being stopped? I am just curious."

Marcus hoped he was a Confederate agent as he indicated and was not part of a trick to capture him. Marcus stood up and asked the older man to follow him. They walked down to the river and pointed at the black boat, "That's how!" Marcus also confirmed another question, "You are right about the professor, too. He was Jethro Jennings."

"But the dead man description didn't fit Jethro?"

Marcus paused and thought about his old friend, then answered with tears beginning to moisten his eyes. "That's why the boat is black. He told me after we blew up the ships they would be looking for a young man in a red boat named *Bonnie*. He carried paint in his boat so he could change his appearance in a moment's notice. As soon as it was safe I pulled ashore and painted my boat black and named it *Crow*. Then he became another man. He knew they were looking for a gray headed man with a white beard, so he shaved his head and rubbed his arms and face with walnut juice to make him look dark. We did not travel together, just close enough to keep each other in sight. We got stopped several times, but we didn't look like the people they were hunting, so they let us go on by."

Mr. McKenzie slapped his knee, "That old dog. Our cause is going to miss him. He was sharp as razor."

Feeling better now about the boat dealer, "Mr. McKenzie, you just don't know how great that man was. When we saw the gunboats in Cincinnati, he figured out a plan and built the torpedoes to sink them. He could make himself appear to be any character you might find on the river and talk like them, too."

"What was the professor bringing into the South, detonators? That's what he had smuggled in before."

"Yes, that boat contains about a 150 of them."

"Can I see them?"

Marcus pondered his question, "No, not now. I have them packed in wooden boxes under that canvas amongst taters and beets. I'll take them out later when I unload the boat. It will be easier then.

"Very well," he said, as if a little disgusted as he looked at Marcus's boat. "This is indeed a fine craft. It's almost like a floating hotel," McKenzie commented, placing his hands on his hips, taking on the air he was the designer of the craft.

"Yes, and I am going to miss this girl. She's been very kind and good to me. I hope after the war to go back to Pittsburgh and buy it from Mr. Dunigan."

"Oh, I wouldn't do that. No, I wouldn't do that," he repeated.

"Why is that? He thinks I am a hero."

"Not anymore. When the news got to Pittsburgh about the warships' demise and the fact they were blown up by a red boat named *Bonnie* he knew immediately who did it. He wired me if you ever showed up to shoot you on sight and tie rocks to your body and throw you in the river and burn the boat. He feared they would trace *Bonnie* back to his yard, and he would be implicated in the sabotage of the gunboats. You know in times of war, authorities will blame anyone and execute them at the drop of a hat if they think they are guilty."

"Yes, I already ran into that. Those people in Cincinnati were going to shoot two innocent civilians, a boy and his father, to cover their mistakes until I came up with a plan to save them."

"Let's go back inside around the stove, and you tell me the entire story. I want to hear about this plan."

Inside, Marcus made clear how he got involved with the professor, the sinking of the war ships, the professor's frozen death, and how his story to the constable freed the two civilians. "And best of all, I convinced the constable to tell everyone he had killed the Colonel. That would make him a hero instead of me and let me get on about the business of delivering these detonators."

"Where are you taking the detonators?"

"To Nashville, sir. I promised the professor over his dead body I would finish the mission." All of a sudden the acute questioning made Marcus suspicious of his newfound friend. Marcus, since Antietam, had experienced many people and horrible situations and those occurrences had taught him to be more wary and not accept his first conclusion. He was gaining the wisdom and vision of a wise old veteran about plot and intrigue, and for the moment, he did not fully trust his new ally. Could it possibly be, McKenzie was indeed a Yankee plotting with Dunigan to capture him? But if that was the case, they would have immediately arrested him and secured the detonators. However, McKenzie knew the professor's name. That would indicate he was a Confederate agent, but could he have obtained that name from the newspapers. Obviously, what had been reported in the newspapers was true. Could it be the authorities decided not to arrest Marcus, but let him go on with his mission and follow his trail to discover other Confederate comrades and expose the entire smuggling ring?

"That is a great story, Marcus. If need be, and you enjoy the river, I'll let you take the boat on further down the Ohio River until you reach the Cumberland River, and that would take you up to Nashville, but you would be rowing upstream after you reached the mouth of the Cumberland." McKenzie hesitated a moment, then asked, "So you don't know who this man in Nashville is?" as he reached for the coffee pot to refresh his cup. Marcus sensed by the way he questioned him he was seeking information, not as a friend, but as an adversary. Then Marcus saw something that chilled him to the bone; the man's hands were soft and pink, not the hands of a wood worker who used hammers, planes, and saws. Marcus then remembered the softness in the man's hand when they shook hands a few moments before. Marcus got a "goose-feather feeling" and realized he could be in deep water. Maybe he was already caught and the building was surrounded and he would be arrested at any moment after he told McKenzie all he knew. He would reveal no more information to this man.

With his body tingling with an uneasy fear, with the roof of his life about to cave in on him, he started planning a new escape if events turned out as he suspected. Marcus decided immediately to end the meeting and see what happened. "Mr. McKenzie, it was nice to meet you, sir, but I'm getting hungry, and I hope you could recommend a place for me to eat a good dinner?"

"Why yes, go out front here and follow the road three or four streets over back toward town, and there is an eatery that feeds people moving up and down the river. It's inexpensive and the food is pretty good."

"Thank you, that sounds good. We'll talk later, but for now would you mind if I leave my boat here and will you keep an eye on it for me?"

"Yes, I'd even go with you If I didn't have this special repair job for a very important customer– that's why I'm working on Sunday, you know, I got a cow in the ditch. I normally have my workers do this tough stuff, and I keep the books." Marcus was relieved slightly to hear that statement. It was still possible that he was a Rebel agent; at least he had an excuse for soft hands.

At the moment, Marcus was not concerned about the detonators, but his life. He told McKenzie he would return after his meal and make plans with him to continue his journey. As he walked away from McKenzie's, he kept looking behind him to see if anyone was following him. He would soon know if he was being watched. If he saw something out of the ordinary, he would do like the professor, change into the wind and blow away. He hoped this "goose-feather feeling" was a false alarm and Mr. McKenzie was indeed who he said he was.

Marcus walked three city blocks and found the eatery next to the river. Marcus was surprised to find it full of people from the surrounding boats and shops. The only food they sold was stew served with a big slab of cornbread. As he stood in line holding his bowl waiting for the server, Marcus wondered how often they washed the large stew pot or did they just add more vegetables and meat to the brew everyday. His bowl was soon filled with the hearty meat and vegetables with a slab of cornbread laid on top. Marcus declined the coffee, and instead, opted for a glass of buttermilk. He saw a seat by the front window and sat down there to keep an eye on the surroundings. From his vantage point he could see the street that went to McKenzie's and could watch for any suspicious activity headed his way.

He finished his meal and thought about his predicament on whether to hit the road or finish his mission. He was still devoted to fulfilling the professor's mission, but his life might be decided with his decision. Marcus thought it was similar to a person's choice in whether to believe in Christ and have everlasting life in heaven, or make the wrong decision and spend eternity in a lake of fire. Marcus watched the road and the river folks who came into the hash house, but he saw nothing that would make him apprehensive.

After an hour of eating and thinking, Marcus made his judgement and returned to the boatyard. Mr. McKenzie commented he was becoming concerned about his whereabouts when he had not promptly returned. "Oh, that stew was really good. I had to have more than one bowl," Marcus replied making up an excuse for his long absence.

Marcus, not fully trusting his new friend, began plotting how to secure his safety and fulfill his mission to Nashville and get away from whoever this man might be. "Now, about getting to Nashville, Mr. McKenzie. I'm tired of the river and dread the thought of rowing all that way up the Cumberland to Nashville. I have some money that I got from Professor Jennings. I expect it would be enough to buy a horse and wagon."

Before he could say more, he was interrupted, "You do know, because of the war, mules and horses are in great demand and their price is higher than I have ever seen. The Army comes and purchases every healthy horse they can find," then he paused, "but I think I can secure a good horse and wagon for you. I know a man south of here who deals with horses and mules. If anyone can find you a horse, he can do it. Most businesses are closed today, but tomorrow I'll contact him. Do you have a place to spend the night?"

"I have a comfortable bed on my boat."

"No, you won't have to do that; I'll provide a place for you to stay tonight. There's a roadhouse near that eating place where you can sleep."

"No, I'd rather stay on the boat so I can keep an eye on the detonators. I have survived much colder nights than this."

"Very well, but if you change your mind, let me know." Mr. McKenzie returned to his work and Marcus's uncertainties whether he was a knowledgeable craftsman went away as he watched the old man work. They discussed the war and the more Marcus watched the master with the hammer and chisel, the more convinced he became that he was not a Union spy planted to uncover the roots of the Confederate smuggling network.

However, the "goose-feather feeling" he had about the stranger would not go away. Marcus wondered why he kept looking up and asking; "Now, who are you going to meet in Nashville? What is the agent's name? I probably know him." He seemed to be probing Marcus for information that a spy would seek rather than a comrade. Playing it safe, Marcus did not reveal who he was going to meet.

"Well, to tell you the truth, all the professor told me was he was going to meet a man in Nashville. He told me we would go to the State Capitol building and sit on the front steps everyday at noon. We didn't have to find him; he would find us." As Marcus talked he caught a glimpse of a man's face, reflected from an indoor glass window pane, appear and just as quickly disappear. Marcus hesitated a moment, and jerked his head and looked behind him to see the source of the reflection, but no one was there. Had a face been reflected, or was he nervous and only imagined it?" He continued, "He said a man would approach and ask if the moon would rise tonight. We were to answer his question by saying, no; it is going to rain tonight. At that time we would give him the detonators and our mission would be over. That's all the professor told me. The old professor had secret ways and magic I couldn't understand." He also mentioned if something happened to him, when I got to Nashville, I was to put a large chicken feather behind my ear and the man would find me on the steps. I guess the feather was a backup plan he had." Marcus was telling the boat builder a lie, but he didn't want McKenzie to know his business after he left Louisville.

37

The boat maker finished carving a delicate wooden part that was needed for a specific boat. He stood up and took off his apron and dusted his pants with a small broom. "That should do it. It's been a long time since I have worked like that, but my best carver was sick today and I had not a soul with the skill to make that part. Kind of urges me to get back to hands-on work again," he chuckled slightly, obviously pleased with what he had made. "I am going home and get some supper. Would you like to join me?"

"No sir, but thanks for the invitation; I need to stay and watch the boat." As he said that he glanced out the window at the black boat. "I'll be alright tonight and in the morning I'll look for a horse and wagon, load the detonators, and return the boat to you."

"Very well, I'll see you tomorrow morning. I will be down here at seven." With that Marcus followed him out the door and returned to his tent home for one last night. He built a fire in his wash pot and grilled a few pieces of fish that were always available on his stringer tied to the side of his boat. He would have enjoyed another bowl of stew, but he didn't want to leave the boat with his valuable cargo on board.

Suddenly the eerie "goose-feather" feeling grew stronger. He had left the boat alone for over an hour while he had gone to eat. Had Mr.

McKenzie done what he promised and watched the boat? Marcus jumped up and scrambled to the two boxes of detonators. He threw back the tarp to see the two waxed boxes. They looked identical to a casual observer, but after Marcus had previously opened one of the boxes to retrieve the six detonators to show the constable, he had thought he placed it under the unopened wax crate. Yet, the opened box was on top. Had Mr. McKenzie or one of his people been on his *Bonnie*? Marcus was very suspicious again of the boat builder, but he also wasn't sure whether he himself had stacked the boxes as he found them, or had he planned to stack them that way and then forgot about it? Had his nerves finally given way to his fears and as this mission ended was the pressure causing him to be overly suspicious?

Marcus wanted to run, but without a wagon, he would have to leave the detonators behind. But that he couldn't do after all the effort he and the professor had endured to get this far. He just wasn't sure of McKenzie, but if he was his nemesis, he reasoned they had been on his boat and they were watching him now. Who was that face he thought he almost saw? In this moment of mistrust he decided to wait it out and see what happened in the morning. He dug out his blankets and spent the night on board his *Bonnie* one last time.

Nothing happened during the night and the next morning the skies forecast sleet or snow. McKenzie returned at seven and soon several other workers entered the large wooden building. Marcus saw smoke appearing from several chimneys that indicated the fires were being lit for the day ahead. Marcus boiled four eggs, something easy to do on the boat, and then walked up to the shop. The boat builder seemed to be in a good humor and when he saw Marcus, he invited him into his office, a room that was filled with large cabinets with thin drawers which contained boat plans. An iron stove was just beginning to warm the cold room, and McKenzie was doing some figuring on a paper tablet when Marcus entered the room.

Marcus took a seat. "Have a good night?" the boat builder asked as he poured Marcus a hot cup of coffee.

"Yes, like all the others."

"So, we need to find you a wagon, horse, or a mule?" McKenzie asked as he laid down his pen and pushed back from the table clasping his hands behind his head, indicating he was ready to get down to serious business. "As I mentioned, horses and mules are hard to find, and when you do, they are expensive. Do you have any money?"

"Yes sir, like I mentioned, I have both Union and Confederate bills."

"Forget about the Rebel currency. It's not worth anything this far north, but save it for when you get to Dixie. How much cash do you have with you?"

Marcus, still suspicious about this man, thought the question sounded more like an interrogation, prying into his operation, seeking to find out more about Marcus.

"Don't know for sure, but enough I imagine to buy a horse and wagon."

Sensing Marcus resented the prying, McKenzie changed the subject. "Like I mentioned yesterday, I know a farmer on the edge of town that might be able to procure a mule." Trying to gain Marcus's confidence, "It is important that we get those detonators to Nashville safely." McKenzie, still leaning back in his chair with his hands folded behind his head, relaxed and leaned forward as if he had solved a problem. Looking beyond Marcus he yelled, "Hey, Henry, send Mathew in here."

In a moment a small man came to the door. "You need me Mister 'Kenzie?"

"Yes, borrow a horse from somebody and ride out to Mr. Clark's place on the south side of town. Tell him I sent you. Have him pick out a lightweight wagon that can be pulled with one healthy horse or mule. You know about horses and mules, Matthew. Don't let him sell us something we can't depend on. Tell him I need it today, and I will pay him later. He knows I am good for the money. Tell him I have an important need for that mule and wagon."

"Yes sir, Mister 'Kenzie!" the young man happily replied, knowing he wouldn't be working in the shop today, but instead outdoors riding a horse. As he turned and left, Marcus noticed the man was crippled.

"Got his leg nearly shot off in the war," McKenzie commented when he noticed Marcus watching the man shuffle away. "You want to go with him?" he added. "I would have sent you to get the wagon, but old Burl don't know you and I doubt he would let you have a wagon."

"I better stay with the boat. The old gal and I have come a long way, and I'd hate to lose those detonators now."

"Don't worry Marcus, I'll watch them. They'll be safe here."

Marcus, still doubtful about the man's true identity and purpose, sensed McKenzie wanted him to leave. Marcus immediately decided he would find out the truth about this man once and for all. "You know sir, it would be kind of nice to get away from this river for a while and ride a horse. I haven't been on a horse in more than two years. Yes, I'd like to go get that hoss or mule. Besides, I helped my father plow with them. Yes, I know them well; I'll help Matthew pick out a strong one."

McKenzie jumped out of his chair all excited as if he had accomplished a mission. "Good then," he added as he walked around the desk and slapped Marcus on the back. "Take your time. If you don't mind while you are gone, I'll carefully get your boat pulled up here in my shed and out of the river just in case some suspicious soul might come by prying where he shouldn't. We can then put the detonators in the wagon from your boat and nobody will see us."

McKenzie just didn't appear to be an honest man to Marcus. There was something Marcus sensed that stirred his "goose feathers." McKenzie seemed to be following a script in a play on stage and he wasn't a good actor. His fake performance revealed McKenzie wanted to get him away from the boat for some reason. He or his men must have been on the boat when he went to eat yesterday and someone had examined the detonator boxes. As he had done in the past, when times got dangerous, Marcus devised a plan to save his life and maybe the detonators. He now considered McKenzie an enemy and would treat him as such. If he wasn't, however, his mission would still be completed.

"Mr. McKenzie, are you sure they'll be safe?"

"Why yes, boy. Remember, I am on your side," as he led Marcus to follow Matthew. Those waxed seed boxes will be here when you get back, but in a safer place."

Marcus's eyes rolled up in his head as he thought, "Oh, oh, I see, I see more clearly now. You *were* on my boat yesterday. How did you know they were in waxed boxes without seeing them? I kept them hid under the tarp yesterday. You just told me what I suspected. You had no way of knowing how the detonators were packed unless you or your men had looked around."

McKenzie hollered at Matthew that Marcus would be going with him and to let him ride behind him on the horse. "I'll see you boys when you get back." With that final reply he turned and went inside closing the door behind him.

Matthew did not appear to be a Union agent, but rather a local uneducated young man, now scarred for life, destined to work in the boatyard for life, at least Marcus hoped that was the case. While Matthew bridled the horse, Marcus looked carefully at the surroundings. If what he reckoned was true, he wanted to know his surroundings well. The two young men slid up on the bareback horse and headed away from the river, skirting the town on the western side. Marcus glanced over his shoulder to see if anyone was following. About a half mile from the river Marcus told Matthew to stop. Under the guise of being sick, he told Matthew to travel on and get the wagon and pick him up later. "I'll just lay here awhile and mend myself. I haven't been on a horse in more than two years. I think the bouncing made me sick to my stomach. Besides that, you can go faster without me. Pick me up when you come back."

Matthew didn't want to leave him, but finally agreed to Marcus's desires and left to go and get the wagon. Matthew rode away and as soon as he was out of sight, Marcus retraced their path back to the boatyard. He came up from behind and hid in a patch of tall dried grass that he had determined earlier would be a good hiding place to watch the goings on. As Marcus expected, there was plenty going on.

Mr. McKenzie and three civilians were in the process of pulling Marcus's boat on shore using two mules and small logs as rollers.

They pulled the black boat with the red bottom under an open shed next to the shop, and two workmen quickly removed the waxed boxes containing the detonators. It wasn't long until they returned with the detonators and replaced them in the boat and hid them again under the canvas tarp. It was obvious now; they were replacing the detonators with fake ones. Marcus had not counted the detonators, but he suspected McKenzie had taken one device from the waxed box the day before to have duplicates made. His suspicion was confirmed when he heard McKenzie say, "It took a lot of work last night. Every machine shop and craftsman in Louisville was helping us, and these look as good as the real ones." Now with the useless explosives, they were going to let him travel on, carrying fake detonators to his comrades in Mobile. The Confederates would waste their time and resources implanting torpedoes that wouldn't work. He expected they would follow him and learn as much as they could about their smuggling operation. For sure, without a doubt, Marcus knew the truth now and would be wary.

Again, Marcus was torn between running away from an obvious enemy or stay and try to get the real detonators again. He pondered the question. Since he had uncovered the truth, his foes most likely were going to let him continue the mission. He concluded they would give him a secure path to Dixieland to help insure a safe delivery of the bad eggs. After considering the situation he opted to go through with his mission and fulfill his promise to his deceased friend.

As he watched the bomb exchange, he put together a plan to get the real detonators back. When the wagon and mule arrived he would have McKenzie's men load the fake detonators from his boat to the wagon. Then, long before dark, he would tell McKenzie he wanted to get on down the road and find a safe place to camp before dark. Marcus was confident they would secretly follow him until they were sure he had left Lexington for good. When he was safely out of town and on the way to Nashville, he would pull away from the road to water his animal and wait to see if anyone was still following. If not, he would return to the boatyard after dark and exchange the fake detonators for the real ones. From what he had observed,

McKenzie's shop was left unguarded at night and he could easily steal the detonators back just like the professor would have done. With that in his mind, Marcus slipped away and returned under the tree to wait on Matthew's return. He snuggled down in the grass to keep warm.

Shortly after high noon, Matthew rode up in a well-worn wagon, pulled by a stout looking mule with his horse tied behind. Matthew yelled as he neared Marcus and saw him rising up from under the tree, "The mule's strong and the wagon; she's been through hard times, but Mr. Burl said it still had lots of pull in her!"

Marcus dusted himself off and climbed up in the wagon seat next to Matthew. "Matthew, if you don't mind, please don't tell Mr. McKenzie I got sick today. I feel a bit embarrassed about that."

"No sir, I understand; I won't say nothin'."

The two young boys rode back to the boat lot. *The Crow* was under the shed ready to be unloaded. Mr. McKenzie came out of the shop and at first appeared disappointed at what Matthew had bought, but Mathew assured his boss Mr. Burl said the mule was fit and the old wagon would do the job.

Marcus saw his chance to begin his plan. "Well, with that said lets load them eggs from the boat into the wagon, pad them good with lots of hay and let me get on my way. I'd like to be out of here as soon as I can." To Marcus's amazement McKenzie agreed. A nearby barn provided enough hay to make a soft wagon bottom for the detonators to rest on, a wall to hide them from view, and feed for the mule. With the addition of the Professor's potatoes, Marcus looked like a local farmer going about his business.

With that done the two men returned inside to get Marcus's pistols, rifles, and gear he had stowed inside from the boat. On entering Marcus observed where the detonators might be hidden. He quickly noticed a worn path to a closed storeroom, the only place they could be. McKenzie reached up on the wall behind his desk and selected a key that opened a closet that contained Marcus's gear. "Here, Marcus, get your stuff." Marcus reached inside and retrieved his equipment and at the same time checked inside for any detonators. There was none so his first assessment on where they were must be right.

The two men returned to the wagon, shook hands, and Marcus assured him he would complete the Professor's mission. McKenzie seemed pleased that Marcus was leaving and thought his deception was working. With that said Marcus mounted up on the wagon seat and clicked his tongue for the mule to move forward. It would take him a while to learn the ways of his new friend, but in time they would get to know each other.

No sooner than Marcus was out of sight, Mathew turned to his boss and said, "Mr. 'Kenzie, he ain't gone yet. He be back tonight."

"What are you talking about boy? There he goes with the fake detonators, just like we wanted him to."

"Boss, you don't understand. Not long after leaving here to go get the wagon he told me he was sick from riding on the horse. He told me to go on and get the hoss and wagon and pick him up on the way back. I wuz 'spicious of his story so I stopped a ways down the road and came back. I followed him back here and he watched you swap the bombs and heard your talkin'." He knows his bombs won't work."

"Ohhh, I see. Great job Mathew. Yes, I expect he will be back tonight when we are gone and get the good ones. I imagine a little Jethro Jennings is working in him now. We don't have time to make fakes again so we will have to cripple all the detonators and make them useless." Mr. McKenzie hollered up all his men. "Men, we don't have much time, but we must disarm all the detonators we unloaded today. There is a spring inside the detonator that we can pull out and it will disarm the firing pin. I'll show you how and then let's get started. When we are finished we will leave them out so he can find them in the dark. I don't know when Marcus will return, but I am sure he will be back to get his detonators tonight. I'll even leave the door unlocked." After dark I want three of you guys to stay with me out there in that field so we can watch what's going on." In an hour the springs had been removed and the detonators were packed in the waxed boxes, placed in plain sight on a table ready for Marcus's arrival.

38

Shortly after dark, Marcus turned his mule and wagon back toward town. He was not in a hurry. He had all night to accomplish his task. He entered town about ten o'clock and slowly made his way back to the boatyard. He stopped to look for any possible dangers. After a quarter hour he assumed all was serene and pulled up close to the front door. He eased out of the wagon and approached the entrance. He expected the door to be a challenge, but he had secured a pry bar from the professor's gear. He placed his hand on the door, turned the knob and gave it a shove to see how secure it was. The door immediately opened.

Marcus momentarily smiled at his success, then the "feathers" entered his mind. Was he entering a trap? He momentarily froze in the dark and listened. If anyone was around they stayed hid. It was very dark inside. He needed to light a candle so he could see where he was in the unfamiliar room. He felt his way to the storeroom and opened the door and went inside. He closed the door and felt for a candle or a lantern he could light. After a few minutes of touching in the dark he discovered a candle next to a box of matches. When he lit the candle he noticed the detonators were not there where he suspected. Had they moved them on to another location?

They had to be here he insisted to himself. McKenzie's shop was up hill and not close to the road and the candle was not very bright. He had to take his chances with the dim candle in the shop and hope he could find the detonators. He crouched down close to the floor so the only dim light that could be seen from outside was a faint orange glow on the walls hardly visible from the road. He crawled forth into the large room and lifted the candle up so he could see the tops of the tables, and there they were in plain sight as if they had been left for him. Marcus quickly squatted back down and blew out the candle. He had seen the boxes and knew where they were. He felt his way up to the table and touched the eggs he was seeking. Indeed, he had found the treasure. He quickly removed the boxes and had them on the hay next to the fakes. He eased the false detonators back inside and placed them where the real ones had been. "Mission accomplished!" he thought to himself as he got in the wagon and clicked his mule forward. McKenzie and his hidden men watched Marcus as he left the boatyard with the destroyed detonators. The Confederate Navy would soon possess these useless weapons.

Since his undertaking had been so perfect Marcus could not get rid of the "goose feathers," but he reasoned maybe it was his time for all the events to go his way. He concluded the door was left open by a careless worker and the detonators had been pulled out of the storeroom since McKenzie was aware Marcus had gone. Still wary though he may have walked into a trap, he would spend most of his time looking back to see if he was being followed.

Before Marcus mounted the wagon his eye caught sight of his *Bonnie* parked under the shed. Suddenly the memories he had shared with his old friend gushed force causing his eyes to tear up. He walked over and leaned against the black boat. "Old girl I'm gonna miss you. You were a good friend and a great companion." He slapped her on the side and stood motionless recalling the peaceful sunny rides contrasted with the many rainy nights that he enjoyed. He took a final look at his cooking pot and remembered the fine meals he had cooked. Deeply saddened he touched her one last time and walked to the wagon and jumped up on the seat. "Good luck old girl." He looked away and urged the mule forward never seeing *Bonnie* again.

Marcus recognized a wagon could be followed because of the ruts it made in the road, but he was also aware a large city like Louisville would have stone or brick streets where his tracks could not be followed and his direction from town would not be known. It was about eleven p.m. and by morning, he expected to have put lots of space between him and his possible pursuers. Yet he expected the road to Nashville would be busy with cavalry if McKenzie discovered he had escaped with the good detonators.

Marcus was not sure of his directions in the dark, but reasoned the road was following the river. It was obvious now he was getting closer to town. It eventually led into Louisville, and he found a paved street and a major intersection in the middle of town. The downtown was quiet except for music coming out from one of the taverns, the clip=clop of lone riders going home on the stone streets, and the occasional rattle of a wagon passing him by. He saw a sign that indicated the road would take him to Shepherdstown, Bowling Green, and Nashville. He saw another arrow that pointed to Lexington. Marcus stopped and pondered a decision that might save his life. McKenzie knew he was going to Nashville. Should he take another route and travel the backroads instead of the main thoroughfare to avoid a possible capture when McKenzie finds out he has the real detonators. Thus far he had not been followed and there was not a soul at the shop so he decided to take the chance and go to Nashville. He clicked his tongue and the mule leaned into his harness and the wagon moved forward toward Nashville.

He passed dark houses, woods, fields, and farms, and well past midnight, he was in total darkness, the sky overcast and cold. He did not hurry his mule, but instead let him pull the small wagon at the animal's own pace, somehow seeing the road in the dark. The road was good, and he made about three miles an hour. When he came to a stream crossing the road, he let his mule stop and drink. While the animal rested, Marcus dug out a blanket to protect his body from the cold. At daylight, he would buy some corn for his animal friend, whose name he didn't know. After half an hour's rest, Marcus moved on in the dark, the mule seeming to know the way.

Light began to appear in the eastern sky off to his left indicating to Marcus he was going in the right direction. He smelled morning breakfasts being cooked in the small cabins and houses that he passed which made him hungry. He approached a small town that from the sign indicated he had arrived at Shepherdsville, Kentucky. Marcus thought it ironic he was in another Shepherdstown. Then he understood it was Shepherdsville and not Shepherdstown. Even though early in the morning, people were going about their business. He saw a man and asked him where a fellow might get a bite to eat. The man directed him to continue on a ways until he came to downtown and Shannon's Kitchen that would on the right. He proceeded on and found the eatery, tied his mule and went inside. As he entered, he saw a stagecoach tied outside while a boy was putting a pail of grain in front of each mule. Marcus approached the young lad and asked if he would feed his mule if he paid him. The boy agreed, and Marcus pointed to where his mule was tied behind the stagecoach.

Marcus walked inside a large warm room sparsely filled with various kinds of workers and strangers. There were six people eating together close to the fireplace. Marcus assumed they were the passengers on the coach. As he took in his warm surroundings, a lady with a big apron came up and asked him to take a seat. Marcus pointed to a table near the front window so he could watch his wagon.

"It's kind of cold over here by the window," the lady replied as she led him to the table and pulled the chair out for him.

"I know, but I need to keep an eye on my wagon. Well, actually it's my Uncle Bob's wagon, and he told me he would kill me if I didn't bring it back."

"I understand; since the war started a man had better keep a close watch on his animals."

Marcus ordered a hearty breakfast of eggs, ham, and biscuits. He could order coffee, but because of the war it was expensive, so he drank milk instead. There were two Union officers near the stagecoach riders. Marcus looked out the window and saw two horses with army saddles tied in front of the stagecoach. They paid him no attention and hoped word about his departure had not been telegraphed in this direction. Marcus expected it was near eight o'clock and Mr. McKenzie should be finding his detonators on the table just as he had left them. Marcus doubted they would ever discover his swap. However, Marcus had been fooled and was delivering the useless detonators to the Confederate Navy, just as McKenzie planned.

"Peace at last," Marcus thought. He finished his meal and turned up the stoneware mug and poured the last of the milk into his mouth and wiped his lips with the back of his sleeve. "That was sure good," he said to himself, "I enjoyed that." He reached in his inside pocket and slid out Bonnie's beautiful picture. He hoped she was safe in Texas. Then he heard the chairs of the Union soldiers scrape across the wooden floor, catching Marcus's attention.

The Union officers had finished their breakfast and stood up. They looked around and noticed the young boy eating alone, and then approached him, paused and looked him over. "Boy, why isn't a young healthy buck like you in the Army?

Marcus looked the officer straight in the eye. "Sir, I am in the Army. I was wounded at Antietam," Marcus remembered to name the battle by the name of the creek; a Union practice, rather than by the town, a Rebel custom. "My officer, Colonel Horn, Colonel Henry Horn told me to go home and heal, and when I felt better, to come back to the fight."

"Where were you hit Private?"

Marcus stood up to pull his shirt off when the officer stopped him. "No need to show me, I believe you. Where are you from, boy?"

Marcus thought quickly, I'm from Louisville; grew up there."

"Your folks farmers?"

"No sir, I'm Marcus McKenzie, my father owns a boatyard there by the river."

"You don't mean you are Mack McKenzie's boy. I know that man very well. Before the war I worked freight on the river and bought several boats from that man. Matter of fact, Captain Kimball and I are headed up there now. It seems your father discovered a ring of Confederate smugglers, and he wired me day before yesterday to come up and lend him a hand. I am to join up with a column of horsemen up there. You know your father watches for Rebels going up and down the Ohio River."

Marcus was not surprised, but grinned, "Yeah, oh Pa had that guy yesterday, but he said they were going to let him go so they could follow him and maybe kill or capture some more of those Southern rats."

"Why yes, that's why I am meeting your father. I'm going to pick up those gadgets he was smuggling and insure they get back to Pittsburgh."

The officer stuck his hand out, "Well, well, I will tell your father I passed you on the road here in Shepherdsville."

Marcus stood and shook the officer's hand, "Oh yes, tell him you saw me by all means."

"By the way, what are you doing way down here?"

"I am delivering a load of seeds for my father's friend. I left yesterday and will be going back today."

"What a coincidence. Why don't you ride back with us? You'll be safe with a column of cavalry. We even have two cannons."

"Naw, thanks for the offer, but I have to take the seeds down below Shepherdsville. I won't head home 'til later today or early tomorrow."

"I understand. Anyway, I'll tell you father I saw you. Won't he be surprised?"

"More than you know," Marcus laughed.

The captain turned and left. Marcus quickly paid his tab and followed them out on the porch. He saw the captain mount a beautiful white horse with an unusual black face. He gave Marcus a final wave with his index finger. Marcus watched them trot off and from a side street the captain was joined by a column of horsemen who fell in behind him. The large force headed back toward Louisville pulling their two cannons.

Now, after such a peaceful start, Marcus knew he had to make plans to change his route and disguise. He hurriedly made his way to the wagon where he paid the boy who fed his mule. He got in the wagon seat and left Shepherdsville in a hurry going south. Calculating the time it took him to get here, he figured by late afternoon a squad of soldiers would be here looking for a young man in a wagon.

McKenzie, if he had discovered his detonators fake, would now know exactly where Marcus was going. He needed to leave this turnpike and find a more secluded backdoor into Nashville. Whether McKenzie had discovered the truth or not, it would be safer to travel another path to Nashville.

His mule was refreshed, and Marcus sensed his new friend had a little more steam now than she had during the night. He led the mule to the local watering trough and let her drink until she was satisfied. Now that his presence would soon be known again, Marcus pondered a new escape route as he clicked the mule to get her started out of town.

Ten miles down the road he met a large man riding a horse. He had passed many wagons and folks that morning, but this man had what Marcus needed. The man was a procurer of horses and was leading a string of five horses and a large mule.

When the man got closer he waved for the man to stop. "Sir, might you have horses to sell or trade?"

"Yes sir, I am taking these animals to Louisville. The army will give me a good price there."

"Whatever it is, I will pay more. I see you have five horses and a mule. What would you take for them?"

The large man scratched his chin while admiring Marcus's wagon. "Can l ask you a question?"

"Yes indeed, go ahead."

"I got a family back down the road here, and I need a wagon to haul them around, go to church, you know, visiting and such. Times got a little tough awhile back, and I had to sell the one I had to make ends meet and help feed all them folks."

"Yes, I understand. Do you want to buy or swap for my wagon?"

"Yes sir that be my wants."

"Well sir, this is your lucky day, 'cause I need to get rid of this here wagon and get a horse and a pack mule or two." Marcus had no idea what mules sold for, so he proposed an offer he figured the man would have a hard time turning down. Marcus paused and scratched his chin too, pretending he was figuring numbers in his head. "I tell you what I'll do. I'll give you this wagon for a horse and mule…."

The large man interrupted, "I can easily get that in Louisville."

"Now let me finish. I wasn't through. I will give you the wagon and fifty dollars and you give me a horse and mule, and I get to keep my mule. That will give me two mules to carry my cargo and a horse to ride."

The man dismounted from his horse and looked over the wagon. "Looks kind of worn to me. Pull forward slowly and let me look at the hubs." Marcus clicked the mule to move forward. "At least the hubs don't seem too worn."

Marcus knew he almost had a deal; a deal he had to get settled quickly so he could get off the main road and travel through the fields and forest, something he could not do in a wagon. "Yes, I admit, it's a little old. How about I'll throw in another ten dollars, and look at it this way, you won't have to make that long trip up to Louisville riding a horse. Instead, you can sit up in that seat like a fine gentleman….a lot more comfortable."

The man looked up at Marcus, "This here wagon ain't stolen is it?"

"No, I'm taking some seeds to a farmer that lives over in the mountains. I understand a wagon can't get over the pass that leads to his house."

"What pass might that pass be?"

Marcus thought fast, "Widow Morgan's Pass. Seems one night Widow Morgan's husband was crossing the pass and was struck by a bolt of lightning. Some say his ghost is up there still."

"Well I'll say. I know most of them passes, but I never hear'd of that one," as he took his hat off and scratched his head.

"Naw, you wouldn't. I didn't know it either. It's way off the beaten path. That's why I figure I need to get rid of this here wagon." Marcus wanted to convince him he had a good reason for selling the wagon. "Right before I left to come down here. I got a letter from the Army that said I could pay some money or I would have to go fight. I have heard how hard this war is and I have no money, so I decided instead to go back home, tell ma and pa goodbye, take them animals and go live up in the hills where they couldn't find me, and wait thar' 'til the war's over. That's another reason I needed a horse and mule."

"Which side you gonna fight fer?"

"The Yankees sent me the letter, and that's another thing, I kind of like the Rebels. I couldn't fight against my own people."

"Yeah, I see what you mean."

"Well then, do we have a deal? If we do, I'll unhitch my mule and I'll unload my wagon."

The man looked at the wagon, then at Marcus, then at his horses and mules. Finally he said, "You got a deal."

Marcus noticed the man's saddle bags, four in all, two being large packets that could hold light cargo. "Mister, I just discovered I need a saddle and some bags to carry my gear. I'll give you another seventy-five dollars for those bags and saddle on your horse."

The man looked at his saddle bags, "I'll have to have thirty for them bags. They were my Pa's. That's the only saddle I have and better not sell that."

"Alright, if you insist. Then I owe you a hundred and forty dollars; is that right?" Marcus reached in his one of his pockets and pulled out an envelope containing the money. "I guess you want Federal money."

"Yes sir, or ten times that amount in Confederate bills."

When Marcus opened his coat, the man saw the two pistols in his belt and suddenly became visibly afraid. When Marcus noticed his sudden apprehensive look, Marcus added, "Don't worry, I ain't no outlaw or bandit. Since the war started, I carry these pistols for my own good."

When Marcus started counting the money out in his hand, the man was relieved he was going to pay him and not shoot him. The large man folded the money up and pushed it deep in his pocket, then turned toward his animals. Marcus walked around the animals and looked them over. In a few moments he picked out one of the horses. The man assured Marcus the horse was broken and the mule he chose was tame. His owner assured him he could pull a wagon or a plow and would make a good pack animal.

"What are their names?" Marcus asked.

"The horse you chose is named 'Fox' for obvious reasons, being a roan and similar color to a red fox. And the mule's given name is 'Judy.'" Both animals Marcus bought had halters, but no bits. The man insisted he had worked with these animals and they were very tame and his children had played on their backs before he left home. "I don't think they will give you any trouble. If you can walk 'em about five miles down the road," pointing in the direction he had come, "Thar's a livery stable. If you have any money left, they have whatever you will need for these critters."

"Then, I'll just lead them down there and get what I need. Thank you for that information, sir."

Marcus took out all his gear and selected what he could put in or tie on the saddle bags. He looked at the man disgustedly, "I can't take all my gear so I'll have to leave some of it with you. That makes our deal even better for you."

"Thank you, I see some pots and pans my wife can use."

"I need to keep a pan or two for cooking, but you can have the rest." Marcus unloaded the detonators wrapped in blankets and hidden in the waxed boxes. Before Marcus realized it, the man was pulling one of the boxes out of the wagon. "These are the heaviest seeds I ever saw," he said as he sat one of the boxes on the ground."

"Oh, there's some other things in there too," Marcus grinned and threw his head back lifting his arm, as if he was taking a swig of whiskey, indicating moonshine had been included with the seed. That answer seemed to satisfy the man and soon the two departed, each giving each other a final wave of the hand.

As Marcus walked beside his new horse and led his two mules, he brooded over his new dilemma and the loss of some of his gear, however, he knew the woods would be full of Union cavalry soon and he needed to get his animals fit for travel. It wasn't long until he came to the crossroads and found a general store surrounded by pens containing horses, hogs, mules, goats, sheep, chickens, ducks, geese, and guineas, along with any tools and equipment needed on a farm.

As Marcus rode up to the front of the two-story building covered with signs, he saw a black man shoeing a horse and other workers feeding the animals. An older man sat in a porch swing. When Marcus dismounted and tied his horse, the man stood up and came down from the porch with his hand out to greet Marcus, "Howdy, my name is 'Buck' Adams, but my friends call me B A, and I been waiting for your bis'ness."

"Well B A, I could sure use your business right now. I bought these mules and horse up the road," before he went any farther B A butted in, "Yeah, I know'd who you got them from. He does a lot of trading around here. Tie yore animals thar beside the fence and let's go inside." From years of experience the old gentleman did not waste time and immediately produced what Marcus needed: a saddle, a bridle and two large canvas bags that laid across the back of the mules and had more space that the smaller leather bags. "If you are going to lead those mules, those rope leads will do fine, but if you need leather I got them too."

Marcus admired the saddle, "I don't think I need one this fine."

B A removed it from the counter and in a moment returned with a worn, well-used leather saddle. "This one will suit your needs and costs much less. I wanted to show you my good stuff. I didn't want to insult you by showing you the cheap things first. As I can see, you are an educated man," continuing his sales pitch to Marcus.

"Oh no, I just made it to the third grade."

"Well, it sure don't show."

Marcus shopped around the store for odds and ends he could use. He considered his needs for traveling through the deep woods to avoid the Union patrols. He purchased a small tent, not much more than a piece of canvas to be hung over a rope stretched between two trees, similar to, but smaller than the professor's. However, it would keep him dry and protect him from the cold wind. Finally, he purchased many sacks of oats and corn and started filling the large canvas bags with the grain.

Suddenly he remembered the professor's skill at hiding things. He turned back toward B A and purchased several more pieces of canvas. Uneasy now, fearing the Union Cavalry was on their way, Marcus finished packing his animals, paid B A, saddled his horse, adjusted his new gear and supplies, thanked B A and headed east, rather than south, the direction toward Nashville.

The area he passed through was covered with small productive farms, the roads no wider than a wagon's width. The people nodded or gave him a friendly wave acknowledging he had their permission to pass down their roads. Marcus also knew he was leaving a trail of witnesses that the Union authorities could use to track him down. Marcus watched the road and stayed in the most worn paths hoping to further disguise the tracks of his horse and mules.

All day the weather had been cloudy and cold. Without seeing the sun, Marcus had to ask people for directions to keep him traveling east. Marcus passed through beautiful flat valleys surrounded by small mountains. The farther east he went, the farms became scarce and the mountains more abundant. They were not huge mammoth peaks but rather large hills which contained hiding places a hunted man could get lost in.

As night approached, Marcus took his entourage off the road several hundred yards and made a camp among a grove of thick pine trees. This was a perfect hideout. He could not be seen or his animals heard from the road. There was a nearby stream that provided water for him and his animals. He watered and fed them, and by dark he had set up a lean-to shelter and built a fire. He missed his old wash pot, but he was soon eating some bread and beans. The sky indicated it might rain that night, but for the moment, Marcus felt as comfortable and secure as he had been in his river boat *"Bonnie."*

During the night Marcus thought about the brilliant idea he had at the general store to buy the extra canvas. This was an idea the old professor would have thought of if the cavalry were chasing him down. He would disguise himself. Marcus had changed his looks once by swapping the wagon for some mules, but he sensed he needed a better mask than that. Besides they would be searching every wagon and horse for those boxes of detonators labeled "seed." The next morning at the crack of light he took the detonators out of the wax boxes and removed most of the grain from two of the saddle bags. He then buried the detonators in the grain at the bottom of the bag and covered them with a piece of canvas forming a false bottom. He filled the bags back up with the rest of the oats and corn creating a perfect hiding place. Any hand that dug into the grain would soon feel the false canvas bottom and assume there was nothing hidden inside.

To back up his story he was delivering seeds, Marcus filled the wax boxes with soil. He carefully sorted the corn, wheat, oats, and maize seeds into four piles. After he had enough seed, to spread the seeds on top of the soil to make the boxes look full. He then built a small fire and used his knife to melt the wax and resealed the boxes and placed them in two of the larger canvas bags. Now with his detonators safely hidden, the seeds properly sorted in real seed boxes, Marcus traveled east feeling secure that no matter who stopped him he could pass inspection.

After his work was done he left his hidden camp and eased on down the road not really knowing where he was going. He soon saw a man picking up his tools after making a repair on a rail fence and stopped to get directions. The man seemed a friendly sort and greeted Marcus as he hung what appeared to be his black powder horn around his neck and picked up his axe and rifle. Marcus explained he was lost and was trying to go east to deliver some seeds to a farmer.

"Where that farmer be?" the man asked. The question caught Marcus off guard. He did not have a town in mind to answer him but quickly made up a name and spurted it out not knowing whether a town existed by that name or not. "McKenzie, Tennessee," he said recalling the boat owner's name.

The man thought a moment, "You must really be lost, mister. I peddle hog meat throughout these parts, and I ain't ever heard of a town or wide spot called McKenzie. There ain't no town around here by that name."

Marcus could tell by the way the man answered he immediately distrusted Marcus and became wary of his presence. Marcus was aware his ruse had immediately been detected and tried to say something that would gain the stranger's trust again. "You're right, sir. I am not here to deliver seeds."

"No, I can readily sense you're up to no good," he replied as he moved back away from Marcus fearing he might do him harm.

"Wait, wait! Don't be afraid."

"Then are you here to rob or kill me?"

Marcus saw the situation was rapidly deteriorating and quickly thought through his book of false excuses and pulled out a slightly used one. "No, I'm not a bandit or a killer. I sell unlawful whiskey, and I am trying to get some bottles of liquor down to Nashville. The roads are crawling with Union soldiers and cavalry. It seems they are looking for a Rebel spy trying to get some weapons smuggled into the South and they are stopping and searching everyone. Fortunately, a traveler told me they were searching people on the thoroughfare, so I turned off the road headed south and proceded east staying off the main roads."

"Well man, why didn't you tell me that to start with? If you need to get unseen to Nashville, I can tell you how to go. I have smuggled a few loads of tax-free whiskey down thar myself." When the man discovered he had some illegal cargo, he immediately looked around as if someone was watching, and he turned into a different man right before Marcus's eyes. Suddenly, there was something sinister about the man that gave Marcus a "goose feather feeling," too.

"Come with me, I'll show you a place to hide," he said in a low raspy voice as he turned and started walking down the road. Marcus followed on the horse leading the mules. The man soon turned off on to a small unkempt lane that ascended up from the road. "I'll hide you up here in my barn. I can feed your mules and give you something to eat. You can sleep in the barn. There's no room in the house. When everything settles down again, you can move on. How's that?"

"No, I don't need a hiding place; I just need directions. I got to git on down the road," Marcus replied fearing now more than ever this encounter was leading to something evil. Before Marcus could see the house, the man took his powder horn, to Marcus's surprise, to his mouth and blew a loud shrill blast out through the woods alerting people in a house, now appearing through the trees, someone was coming.

Marcus rounded the corner and saw a cabin nestled up against a wooded hillside. Again, the "goose-feather feeling" burst forth when he saw three large burly men pour out of the house holding their rifles with intent to use them. Marcus feared the worst; the horn had been a warning for the men inside to get ready.

The man turned around and walked backward looking up at Marcus. "Boy, don't be afraid. These are my brothers. They may take your whiskey, but I don't reckon they'll hurt you." As he said that he stumbled on a stone and fell backward and sprawled in a puddle of water caught in a low place on the muddy road.

Fearing for his safety, Marcus jerked his horse around and tugged on the ropes to get the mules moving. While Marcus whirled around, the man grabbed his muddy rifle, stood up, aimed, and clicked the gun at Marcus. Luckily for Marcus he only heard the click, the rifle misfiring after being soaked. Marcus knew now he was in deep water and needed to get away. The three brothers fired, but still being some distance from the porch, the bullets missed. He knew they were all out of ammunition, and he would have a half a minute to get on down the road. To solve one fourth of his problem, Marcus pulled one of his pistols, turned and fired two shots at the wet figure standing in the puddle reloading the rifle. The man collapsed back into the cold water. His brothers were reloading on the porch, but when they saw their brother fall, they ran toward him cursing Marcus, who was now getting some speed into his mules. Marcus turned and fired another shot to slow the men down, but the distance by now was too far for a pistol to be accurate and most likely out of range.

Marcus galloped down the road hollering at the mules to urge them on. He came to the main road and turned east, the direction he was headed before he met the stranger. Marcus knew his tracks would be easy to follow, and he expected to see the brothers on horses approaching from the rear. Marcus's mind started calculating a plan that would get him out of this new scrape. As he raced down the road, he wondered if they would chase him at all. He reasoned since he ran into the lone brother on the road some distance from his house without a horse or mule, maybe they didn't own any horses or mules. If that was the case, if he kept going there was no way they could catch him. Now his mind was racing as fast as his horses. What if they did have horses? Then, in that situation, his only other choice would be to stop and set up an ambush and kill them at close range with his pistols before they had time to use their long rifles.

Marcus reflected back on what he had just done and what he might have to do in a few moments. Maybe he had just killed a man, but his heart was becoming harder and he, like he justified in the war, did what he had to do for his own survival and would exterminate three more vermin if they pursued him.

After running the mules longer than he wanted, he came upon a grove of thick green dense myrtle bushes growing next to the road. Rather than having to look over his shoulder for the rest of the trip, wondering if he was being pursued by three angry brothers, Marcus decided to settle the matter now. He galloped past the grove of bushes and slowed the horse and mules to a walk. He dismounted and led his animals quietly into the thick woods and tied them securely, expecting to hear the sound of galloping horses drawing near at any moment. As Marcus hurried back to the road, he frequently looked back to see how well he had hidden his animals. When he reached the road, they could not be seen.

Marcus continued to listen for the sound of his pursuers approaching, but they had not arrived as Marcus hid himself in the grove of dark green bushes. He quickly took his knife and cut off small leafy limbs and filled gaps that might reveal his presence before the men neared. After a few minutes he sat down on the dried leaves and checked his pistols. He had seven shots remaining in his two pistols. He reloaded and now had ten shots ready, and at this close range with both guns blazing, how could he miss? Everything was ready. Bring on the fight. Although he was outnumbered three to one, he had the advantage of surprise, and he would have them down before they knew what hit them.

Marcus sat and concentrated on the task before him. He checked his weapons again, wondered if he could be seen from the road, even cut more twigs and placed them in his hatband to cover his hat and face. He fretted over the twenty-foot distance from the path from where they would come, whether he was too close or too far. Marcus recalled tense memories he had earlier in the war, the same anticipation he felt waiting to go forward to face the enemy. He remembered the morning at Antietam, and questioned whether he would meet his Maker today.

Time passed; ten, fifteen, thirty minutes, and then an hour. For two hours Marcus sat alert waiting for the battle to start. His animals had remained quiet, and he only heard them bray twice. Four times he heard people approaching, but long before they came in sight he could tell the folks were not chasing anyone, and one individual came from the opposite direction singing aloud. He knew the man would be embarrassed if he was aware of an audience. Marcus was pleased they passed so close and never had an inkling he was there. As they neared, he pretended they were his prey, and he mentally went through the motions of killing them. He was comfortable now that he could kill all three with three to six shots.

While waiting in the quiet forest, Marcus pulled his picture of Bonnie out and laid back on the soft leaves. Would he ever see her again? He thought about home and his thoughts revived the image of the old professor. He was getting homesick. His rest in the woods gave his mind time to think of home, Bonnie and the professor. He thought about burying the detonators, turning the mules loose, and riding the red horse to Georgia and being done with the war. But he had spent too much of his worth to abandon the professor and not accomplish his task.

After two and a half hours, Marcus decided the brothers had no horses, but he would get a "goose-feather-feeling" when he thought about leaving his concealed shelter, so he waited another half hour. Another lone rider passed, and as the man disappeared down the road, Marcus made the decision to abandon the ambush. Marcus got up and fetched his animals and led them out of the woods, mounted and started east again.

Marcus regretted he had not settled the score with these men, and wondered if they would pursue him later. But for now, he felt safe, but he would keep a lookout over his shoulder. Soon, he came to a stream running across the road where he fed the animals some grain and let them drink their fill of water, but kept alert to the men he didn't kill.

39

Marcus reckoned it was past noon when he mounted his horse and headed east leaving the security of his ambush site. He concluded the brothers were too poor or ignorant to chase him. He kept his horse and mules at a steady walk. He was lost but figured he was headed east. It was still cloudy, and he had no way of knowing for sure of his direction. He knew on a cloudy day in deep woods you could turn yourself around in a few minutes. He had done that many times when he was out squirrel hunting in the big wooded river bottom near his farm. He hoped he could meet someone that knew where he was and could give him some directions.

An hour before dark Marcus came to a small stream crossing the road. He dismounted to let his horse and mules drink the fresh flowing water. He went upstream slightly and bent down to sip some water with his hand when he heard, "Mister, don't move a muscle or I'll blow you hai'd clean off." Marcus followed his instructions and did not move as he heard rustling in the brush in front of him. He cut his eyes up to see three men in buckskin holding rifles walking down the hill toward him. It was the brothers of the slain man, but how did they get in front of him?"

"Git up and raise yore hands." Marcus saw the men clearly now holding their rifles against their shoulders ready to shoot if he did not obey. "Well, well, well, in 'nother little while we were 'bout to give you up. We been waitin' here all day. Where you been boy?" he asked as he carefully approached Marcus and removed the pistols from his belt. "This here's one of the guns that killed our brother. Which one killed my brother?"

Marcus realized he couldn't lie his way out, but he had to buy some time to figure a way out of his new state of affairs. "I don't rightly know. I used both of them to shoot at him. I know you ain't gonna believe me, but I didn't mean to kill yore brother. He was shooting at me, remember."

"That don't matter. What were you carrying that Horace brought you up to the house fer?

"Whiskey, but I didn't have any. I just told him I did."

"Why did you tell a lie like 'hat?"

"I hoped he could show me a shortcut through the woods."

"Why are you in such a hurry passing through our woods?"

"I needed to get to Nashville without anyone knowing."

"What fer."

"Army business."

"Army bis'ness? What's that?"

"Can't tell you that."

"Yo're gonna tell us that bis'ness, or I'm gonna shoot choo."

"You already said that, so why should I tell you? I will get to die knowing something you don't."

One of the other brothers spoke out, "If he won't tell us what gun he used and what Army bis'ness is, then why don't we hang him? Thar's a good limb right thar."

The other brother added, "Yeah, let's do that. I saw a hanging once down thar in Shepherdsville."

"Yeah, I was with you. Yeah, let's hang him. He killed our brother. He deserves to get hung."

"Should we give him a tri'le?"

"Yep, I'll be the judge," the third brother threw in.

"I'll be the jury," the second brother grinned showing most of his teeth were gone.

"Then I am the executioner. Does anybody have a rope?"

"I do," Marcus admitted, trying to buy more time for him to think. "It's in my leather bag over there on my horse."

Luther went and dug out the rope and looked at it disappointedly, "Kind of small, but I imagine it will strangle him if it don't kill him"

Lester asked his brothers, "Does anyone of you know how to tie a hangman's knot?"

Both ignorant brothers answered no, but one of them chimed in, "It don't have to be a noose, Lester, any loop we can tie in the rope will, like I said, strangle him."

Listening and thinking intensely, Marcus now saw a possible chance to get away. It might be his only chance so he spoke out, "I use to work for a sheriff back home. I know how to tie a hangman's knot. If you men have decided to kill me, at least give me the respect to be hung with a proper knot in the rope. You know I didn't murder your brother on purpose. He started shooting first, you know that, and I was only defending myself."

"That sounds fair," Lester remarked.

"Yeah," Luther agreed. All three brothers had Marcus surrounded with their rifles aimed at his heart. "Move over thar and set down under that limb we're gonna hang you from."

As Marcus moved under the tree, he gained confidence in his new plan. As a youngster, he had seen a hanging, and like all kids, had been fascinated by what he saw. By chance he had learned how to tie the recognizable hangman's knot. "Give me the rope and let's get this over with. I want to hurry and visit my grandmother in Heaven." He looked up at the three poor ignorant excuses for human beings, "You know, she was so nice to me and baked the best cookies. Matter of fact, a condemned man should be given his last meal, ain't that so Luther?"

"Yeah, I guess so, but we ain't got nothing to eat."

"Well, I do, look in my saddlebags again. There's some ham in there with some canned goods. Please let's have a slice of ham 'fore I die. If I can't get the cookies, I guess ham will have to do."

Lester threw the rope over to let Marcus get started on the noose. "Keep your guns on him while I check out his stuff." Lester soon found Marcus's stash of food and started gnawing the ham without slicing off a piece for Marcus, slobbering and snorting like an old boar eating slop.

"On second thought, Lester, I think I'll die on an empty stomach," Marcus replied as he started the knot. In a few minutes he had completed the famous knot as he watched the brothers gorge themselves on his stores of food to such an extent Marcus thought about making a break and trying to hide in the woods until dark. But his new plan of escape was so perfect, he knew it would work with these three simpletons.

The three filthy, unshaven brothers watched intently as Marcus had laid the rope across the ground to make the first loop in the fancy knot. Marcus started winding the rope around the top of the loop making the familiar spiral of rope that made the collar above the loop. Marcus explained what every loop meant. "Here it is. Ain't that the purti'est knot you ever seen?" he said as he held the top of the knot and beat it against the side of his leg showing how strong it was. "Now, put the noose around my neck and throw it over the limb. I am ready to die." Marcus hesitated a moment, "Oh here, let me put it around my neck. That way I can tell my grandmother I committed suicide when she asks me how I got to Heaven."

"What's suicide?" one of the brothers asked.

"Never mind," Marcus remarked back as he slipped the noose around his neck and even threw the other end over the limb several feet above his head. Marcus realized by their conversation they had only seen one hanging in their life and knew only the coarsest fundamentals of life.

The brothers held their guns on Marcus and looked at each other, not remembering exactly how to hang the man without a platform for Marcus to stand on. Marcus, recognizing the brothers were studying what to do next instructed them, "Fetch my horse. I am supposed to straddle the horse. Two of you hold that end of the rope while Lester whips the horse on his rump. The horse runs off leaving me behind hanging here until I die or am strangled. Now, let's get on with this. My grandmother is waiting," Marcus added in a disgruntled voice.

Two of the brothers grabbed the rope and held tight. "Now, Lester, don't hit the horse 'til I'm ready. Let me adjust this noose. It's a little tight on my neck. Let me pull my jacket up around my neck so the rope won't burn my neck while I am hanging." Lester waited for further instructions from the man they were supposedly hanging. Marcus was finally ready and looked at his executioners. "You know, Heaven is going to be nice, but because you hung me, you sorry dogs are going to hell."

"He called us sorry dogs, Lester, hit the horse! Let's kill 'im!" Hearing that remark, Lester, now insulted, slapped the horse, and Fox took off and the two brothers pulling tightly on the rope suddenly fell back stumbling into the nearby creek when the tension of the rope was released. Marcus had tied a beautiful knot but never secured the end of the rope into a small loop that kept the knot tight, and when tension was applied, the hangman's noose unraveled, giving only a slight tug on Marcus's neck. Marcus's hands were untied, and he was able to hold on to the rope and insure it did not harm his neck. All three men had laid down their rifles, and by the time they could aim their weapons, Marcus could only be heard galloping away back in the direction he had come. Marcus had lost the detonators and all his belongings but he had his life and a fast horse.

Marcus raced away down the muddy road in the direction of Shepherdsville. He thanked God that He had spared his life again. Only a miracle had saved his life. He had heard his Mother speak of guardian angels, and he knew his was real and not imaginary. He had never seen him, but he had seen the results, and this escape was the best. There was no way he could have gotten out of that predicament, but he did. He just kept repeating aloud, "Thank you God, thank you God, thank you God!"

But no sooner than he had gone a mile, he saw up ahead a scattering of dark blue, almost black, pieces of color seeming to appear through the trees hanging over the road ahead. He looked behind him to see if his pursuers were coming. Maybe they had cut him off again. Then he saw what he dreaded and feared most; the Union Cavalry that he expected was coming his way and blocking the road ahead. Before he could stop and disappear in the woods, the cavalry saw him and came forward. When the lead officer saw the approaching rider at a high speed he stopped his column and raised his hand for Marcus to slow down and stop. Marcus pulled on his rein and did not completely stop until he had penetrated the Union column of horses.

The captain turned and approached Marcus. "Sir, what is your hurry? I haven't seen speed on a horse like that in years," commenting in such a way as to get chuckles from his men. "Where are you going at such a break-neck speed, boy?"

Marcus excited and out of breath answered, "Sir, thank goodness you have arrived. Some bandits or Rebels waylaid me down the road a piece, I expect a mile. They robbed me of my mules, some provisions I was taking to my sick grandmother, and then tried to hang me. You can probably see the redness in my neck," as he pulled his collar back and showed them the minor abrasion where the rope had slipped along his neck.

"How many men tried to hang you?"

"Three, sir, and they are awfully dumb. I expected them to be right behind me. You can't imagine how glad I was when I saw your horsemen coming my way."

The officer turned his horse around, "Come on then. Let's capture them before they get away." He waved his hand forward and the twenty-four blue cavalry dashed back toward the creek. Marcus hesitated. He was free. He could run and escape and go home, but he was still dedicated to fulfill the professor's mission, so he kicked his horse's side and chased in after the cavalry.

In two minutes, they rode up on the three hooligans, and they immediately surrendered when they saw the soldiers ride up and point two dozen Navy Colt revolvers at their noses. Two of the ruffians were wet after falling in the creek, and the rope was on the ground. The officer dismounted and approached the men, "I understand there was going to be a hanging today?"

The three scared men started telling their story immediately. That boy killed our brother this morning. Shot him in the road to our house. We just hunted him down and was paying him back for what he did to us."

"Is that so?" The officer turned to see if Marcus was still around. "Is the boy still with us?"

"Yes sir," one of the men replied, "He followed us here."

"Bring him forward." Marcus walked his horse through the many horses to the Captain. "These men claim you killed their brother this morning. Is that true?"

"Yes sir, that is absolutely true. I shot him in the road to his house this morning with one of my pistols."

"Well, young man, I might want to hang you, too. Why did you shoot him?"

"Sir, it's not as simple as that. I saw the man working beside the road this morning and stopped to ask him for directions."

"I thought you lived around here?"

"No, I didn't say that. I am from Louisville and came down here to deliver some seeds at 'Mulligan's Pass' somewhere up in the mountains. You can look in my bags and see the waxed cartons marked "seeds." I had a map, but I guess I lost it during the night."

"Check out his bags," the officer said pointing at the mules tied to a tree. Then he looked at Marcus again, "Why aren't you in the Army? You crippled or something?"

"In a way, sir; I am a Union soldier home to get healed. I got shot at Antietam and was sent back home to Kentucky until next spring. Let me show you my wound. You will believe my story then." Marcus started taking his coat off, but like the other officer, he said he believed him and to keep his coat on.

"That still doesn't give you the right to shoot the man."

"Let me finish, sir, please."

Luther yelled up, "He's got a bunch of whiskey he's hiding. That's why he was hunt'un a back way to Nashville."

"Is that true? You got whiskey?"

"No sir, he just thinks that. When I left Louisville day before yesterday, my father told me to take these seeds down and then over to "Mulligan Pass" in the mountains. He said to stay off the main roads and travel cross country when I could to avoid thieves. He said there were lots of bad people between the Union and Confederate lines. He said the seeds were expensive and hard to get. I think he said they came from England. I was coming down that road, if you could call it a road, and ran into the man I shot fixing his rail fence. I stopped and asked him how to get to 'Milligan Pass.' He said he had never heard of a pass with that name, so I knew I was lost. He asked me why I was traveling these back roads. I didn't want to tell him I had these expensive seeds, so I told him I was smuggling whiskey to Nashville. That's when he got real interested in getting me to his house. He said to follow him to his house, and he would show me a way through the mountains that would get me to Nashville, and he would share a hot meal with me. That sounded pretty good, but I didn't know 'bout his brothers."

The soldier returned from the mules, "I couldn't find no whiskey, just mule feed, camping supplies, and some boxes of seeds."

"Your story checks out so far, continue."

"Sir, I followed him down the road a piece, then he turned and we headed up a hill. Shortly before we came in view of the house, the man pulled out a bull's horn and blew a loud blast that echoed through this entire valley. There's the kind of horn it was, there around his neck; that's the kind of horn he blew. They all have one."

"What was that about?"

"I see now it was a warning to his brothers, there in the house, that a stranger was coming, and apparently it was a warning for them to get ready to rob me. As we neared the house they came out with their rifles pointed at me. I feared for my life. At the time, the man was walking backward telling me not to be afraid, but I decided to drink my coffee somewhere else, so I turned my horse and mules back toward the road."

Luther hollered out, "Naw! That ain't right."

"Shut up until I hear the rest of his story. Go on young man."

"Fortunately for me, he fell backward; he fell in a deep mud puddle and wet his powder. To my amazement he raised his gun and fired at me, but all I heard was a click. Then these guys you see fired their rifles from their porch; luckily all their lead missed me. It didn't take me long to figure they were out to kill me, so I figured I could take out one fourth of my enemies right then, so I pulled my pistol out and fired three times, as I remember, one of the bullets hitting him. I wasn't sho're I killed him, but I didn't stay around to find out either."

"I see, continue."

"I figured they would mount their horses and chase me. I went a spell down the road until I found a thick hiding place. I hid my mules and waited for them to come along. Matter of fact, I can show you where I waited most of the day. I finally reckoned they had no horses and weren't coming, so I gathered my animals and just remembered that as a bad experience. I continued on until I got here to let my animals get some water. That's them right over there with my saddle bags; the ones you looked in," Marcus said as he pointed at the two mules.

"I see; what happened then?" the officer inquired.

"All of a sudden I heard a man tell me to stay still. When I seen who it was I was skeered to death and realized my time was done. They knew this territory and had cut me off and was waiting here at this creek to ambush me like I was going to ambush them. They were gonna shoot me at first and then I talked them into hanging me instead. That's where I tricked them and tied a hangman's knot, but I left out that final tuck of the rope so it would undo itself when it tightened on my neck."

."You mean they let you tie the knot to hang yourself?"

"Yes, that was my intent. They didn't even tie my hands, and when they slapped the horse out from under me I just took off. That's when I ran into you soldiers. These ruffians were going to kill me."

The captain turned to the three brothers, "Is what he said was true?"

"Naw, sir, he came up our road this morning with the intent to kill all of us I guess. I never saw him 'fore in my life," Lester spoke out, with the other two brothers nodding their heads in agreement."

"All four of you brothers were on the front porch?"

"Yes sir! That was the way it was. Horace, my brother, wondered who this man were so he walked down to invite him up for some coffee we had brewing on the stove. When he got close, he pulled out his pistol and killed him. When we saw that, we fired at him to run him off. By the time we got our mules saddled, we knew we couldn't catch him, but we went over the mountain and cut through the valley and waited for him to come by here at the creek. We had just 'bout given up when here he came plod'en along. That's when we caught him."

"Sir, I don't believe a word you said except for the fact you took a shortcut over the mountain to revenge your brother's killing. I can't imagine why a young lad like this would ride up a strange road and attack four men with rifles sitting on their porch." He then ordered six of his men to arrest these three men and escort them to the county jail. With that done, Marcus claimed what weapons, property, and mules were his. The soldiers found the brother's mules were tied up the creek a short distance away.

After the brothers were arrested and taken off, Marcus thanked the captain and the soldiers for saving his life. The captain recommended Marcus travel the busier roads reminding him like the instance today; the Union had control of the roads in most places. The captain returned to Marcus, "I don't believe a word they said was true. If you did what they said you did, I must say, you are the bravest young man I ever met or the dumbest. My men will take them in to the local sheriff in this county, and they will be put on trial. It will be necessary for you to come and testify at their trial, however."

"Then let them go home. I cannot come this far again unless my father sends me on a job. I am sure if you talk to some neighbors they probably have reasons to fear they have robbed people before. It's just too much trouble for me to come back over here with the war and all, and I have to return back to my Indiana Brigade in March. Just let them go if you have to. I just want to go home."

"Alright then, if that's the way you feel about it, but before you go I heard you mention you came from Louisville?" "Yes sir, I came through Shepherdsville."

"By any chance did you see a young lad with a mule and wagon pass during the night or sometime during the day today?"

Marcus could not believe what he just heard. "Now that you mention it, while I was waiting to ambush those heathens a young lad passed in a wagon headed east."

"Why do you ask? Are you hunting for someone?"

"Yes, matter of fact we are. Someone similar to you. Like you he was hauling vegetable seeds. Fortunately for you your boxes contained seeds and not detonators."

"What's detonators?"

"Small bombs. That's why we were out here on the road when you came along. The young man is a Confederate agent smuggling those bombs into the South. We had him back in Louisville; but he gave us the slip. Speaking of slippery, he's slicker than a greased hog."

"Yes, I expect I saw him today. As I recall he came by this morning shortly after I got here, sometime before noon, I expect. He passed by less than twenty feet away, but he never saw me. He never was aware he was being watched. I saw him up close and got a good look at him. He was indeed a handsome lad. Kind'a looked like me," Marcus grinned. "By now he must have about a three hour head start on you."

"Thank you, then, I guess that about does it," the captain said as he turned away to lead the rest of his command to pursue the young man in the wagon. He wished Marcus good luck and mounted his horse. As Marcus watched, the cavalry patrol disappeared down the narrow wooded lane and was soon hidden by their dust. Marcus looked up at the sky and told his guardian angel, "You know, the Lord does work in mysterious ways doesn't He." Marcus turned his horse, and with the mules following, he headed back west to catch the road to Nashville. It would be safe, now, for him to go directly to Nashville.

When the soldiers had ridden out of sight of Marcus, the captain turned to one of his lieutenants, "That boy is doing everything he can to get himself killed. If he would just stay on this main road to Nashville, we can keep an eye on him and make sure those detonators get to where they're supposed to go."

40

That night, Marcus camped below Shepherdsville on the main road to Nashville. Finally, he hoped he was over being hung, robbed, shot at, and captured, and now he expected to complete his mission peacefully. He learned he was about a week's journey from his goal to arrive in Nashville. Nashville had fallen to the Union forces earlier in the year, and as he neared the city Marcus passed small infantry and cavalry units coming and going out of the large southern town. Marcus expected to be searched, but apparently the search for the boy in the wagon stayed farther north. Although he passed columns of marching soldiers and Union horsemen, they paid him no mind. The weather had been dry and reasonably warm during the day. He finally was just a common traveler going down the road.

After eight days, Marcus neared the city of Nashville on a Tuesday morning. He had been told to camp out of town, since places to stay were hard to find. Union soldiers seemed to be everywhere. This was now a jumping off place for the war farther south and heavily defended. He remembered he had to find downtown and find "The River Roost" somewhere near the Cumberland River on 1st Street. Marcus assumed it would be easy to find. The professor had told him it was next to the river and would be easy to find. From a hill at the edge of Nashville, he saw the imposing capital of Tennessee several miles away. When he entered the town it was crowded with soldiers, traders, and the riffraff that hung around the Army and preyed on the crumbs, immoralities, and excesses of a large army.

Marcus followed the flow of horse and wagon traffic that tended toward the downtown area. He slowly descended into the town of Edgefield, just east of Nashville. He rode his horse leading his pack animals through the maze of shops and stores. He soon came to a large bridge that led into the city. There were large turrets on each end of the bridge that guarded the bridge. He heard the whistle of a riverboat approaching the bridge. To his amazement, the bridge rotated on a pillar in the center of the river to let the large craft pass by. Then it rotated back into place.

When he came near the turrets, he noticed that people entering the city were being questioned, but a thorough search of wagons and horses seemed not a priority. He noticed the guards throw a canvas back from a wagon to see what was inside, but as he watched, he saw several folks leading pack mules waved on by with only a word or two to the riders. Marcus sensed it was safe and rode up to the bridge, waiting a few minutes as the people in front of him were queried.

As he waited, he heard the sound of many hooves approaching from behind him. Marcus turned to see a large column of Union cavalry. It was a magnificent sight to Marcus, even if they were horsemen of the enemy. They rode in pairs, and at the front of the long line of riders was an officer riding alone, filled with pride as he straddled a large white horse with a black face.

Marcus stared at the horse. Suddenly a "goose feather feeling" ran though his body. He had seen that horse before, but where? Then, as the officer approached, he remembered. It was the officer on the strange looking horse he had talked to in the eatery at Shepherdsville. He was riding straight for Marcus. How did they find him? "No, no, no," Marcus thought, "This couldn't be true. Why isn't this guy on the way to Lexington looking for a boy in the wagon? They must have talked to the man who sold him the mules. Where can I hide?" Marcus was astride his beautiful red horse, and this officer was looking around at the people as he passed, not in a searching manner, but to see how his impressive position was initiating their admiration as he passed. As he neared, Marcus knew he would pass within ten feet and would surely recognize him from their previous conversation.

However, Marcus was fortunately waiting with several other riders to cross the bridge and wouldn't be alone. Marcus then heard several soldiers begin yelling for the people waiting to pull their wagons and horses to the side of the road to let the cavalry pass. Marcus dismounted and led his horse and mules to the side of the road. When the Captain came near, Marcus dismounted and slipped between his two mules and tucked his head down and did not look up until he heard the hooves of the horses rumble on the wooden bridge, knowing for sure the captain had passed. He then looked up to watch the rest of the column pass and cross the river. Marcus had dodged another bullet, but he was uneasy, now that there was a man in Nashville that could recognize him. Nashville was a large city, and the chance of facing him again was most unlikely. The officer would stay inside comfortable quarters in the nicer part of the city; not in the grimy areas next to the river.

The throng of people moved back into the road and waited their turn to cross the river. Marcus stayed dismounted so as not to bring attention to him mounted on the beautiful red horse. He felt comfortable the detonators were safe unless the guards made him empty his bags on the bridge. Marcus slowly eased forward, and when he came to the guard, the soldier looked Marcus straight in the eye like he had met Marcus before and was trying to figure out where. Then he reached out and firmly grabbed Marcus's arm. Suddenly the "feather feeling" sped through his body; "This man is going to stop and search me," Marcus feared. "After all my pain, my near brushes with death, cold nights, hunger and fright, I am going to be stopped when I looked the least suspicious. This can't be true."

Then the guard smiled and said, "I know you. It's been years since I have seen you, but aren't you Ben Farmer's son from down there below Franklin? I forget your name, but I went to school with your older sister, Margie."

Marcus was relieved as he answered, "No, no, I'm not from around here. I grew up in…in… Louisville." Marcus had to think a moment to decide where he should be from.

"No, you got to be Ben's boy!"

"No, sir, my name is Marcus, Marcus Mills; you must be mistaken.

"Well, young man, you have a twin in this world who looks just like you. I'm sorry to have bothered you."

"No problem. No problem at all." Marcus turned away and started toward the bridge; then he remembered and turned back. "Say would you happen to know where I could find the "The River Roost?"

The guard walked forward, "Oh, that's easy. When you get to the other side of the river, turn right and you are on 1st street. Follow it on down about a quarter mile or so, and you will see it on your left." He grinned, "That's quite a rowdy place I hear."

"Thanks for telling me. I am supposed to meet my uncle there. It sounds like a place he would like," Marcus grinned back. At last Marcus would be at the spot that would end his journey. Then, there was a blast from a loud steam whistle, indicating the bridge was opening and turning to let a large steamboat pass under. Marcus wanted to hurry and cross the bridge, but the guard held him back. The bridge slowly rotated and the large steamer passed under. Marcus had not ever seen such an amazing sight of engineering. As he waited, more and more people came up to the river to cross. Marcus had not been in such a crowd since he had been at Antietam. His animals became nervous, and he patted and calmed them in a soft voice. He was beginning to get a "goose-feather itch," too, but not a scary feeling. He looked around at the crowd to see why he would be anxious. He huddled between his mules to hide him from any possible unseen dangers. All of his past encounters had made him edgy, and he wondered if he would have this uneasy feeling for the rest of his life. In a few minutes, the whistle blew, and the bridge returned to its original position and people moved over the river.

Marcus, still nervous, stayed on the ground and led his horse and mules as he meandered through the herd of people. He came to the other side and turned onto 1st street. Stores and shops were on his left, and the quite steep riverbank was on his right. He walked down the street leading, patting and talking to his animals, and there it was, in old peeling black painted letters on the side of a white building, "The River Roost." Marcus was elated inside that he had finally arrived. The place was a tavern with some rooms to rent upstairs. It had a large porch accessible by stairs that ascended up from the street. Due to the slant of the ground, the porch was quite elevated above the level of the street. As the professor had said, the worn wooden porch enclosed old church pews pushed against the wall. Due to its height, the porch had a railing preventing someone, most likely a drunk, from falling off the porch. He walked up to the front of the stairs and tied his mules to a hitching post. The time was past noon, and he was hungry. Maybe the "Roost" would have something to eat.

He ascended the stairs and looked down at his mules. The only thing of value that were visible were his two rifles. He felt the detonators were safe and if any thief looked in the canvas saddlebags all they would see was a mixture of corn and oats, or find waxed boxes. In normal times people watched out for their neighbors, and thieves were looked on as the vermin of society. No one wanted to be labeled a thief, a title that was never cleansed from a person's past. But this was war time, and the town was full of every kind of human rubbish, from thieves to killers.

When he arrived at the top of the high stairs, a policeman clad in a black uniform came on the porch. His sudden presence eased Marcus's fear that the town was out of control. Even though the weather was cool, there were several people seated in the pews talking or just waiting for someone. He opened the door and entered a large room with tables scattered throughout with a bar at the back opposite the door. He heard the crackling of a fire and turned to his left to see a large fireplace, maybe the biggest indoor fireplace he had ever seen. It was warm, and he smelled the aroma of hot food. Some folks were drinking at the bar, but most of the inhabitants were eating. Marcus saw a chalkboard that substituted for a menu next to the bar. Today, it seemed, stew was available for ten cents and coffee for a nickel. Marcus saw two men get up from a table next to a front window. From behind him, he heard a lady's voice, "Let me clean that off for you, young man." He turned and saw a plump lady pass him by with a wet soapy rag and wipe the table. She pulled another dry towel from her apron and dried it. "Have a seat. What can I get you?"

"From your sign it seems my only choice is stew."

"Oh, we got other things. Bacon, pork, beans, and cornbread; stuff like that."

"Give me the stew. I am hungry for some vegetables. I have been on the road a long time."

"Where are you coming from?"

"I have come all the way from Maryland. Went through Pittsburgh, rowed a boat down the river to Louisville, and rode a horse down to here."

"Where are you headed?"

"Georgia"

"Be careful going down through there. There's been lots of killing in the war in that direction. There's a large Union Army down there around Chattanooga. Which side are you on?"

Marcus realized he was telling more about his business than he intended. "Neither."

"Then what was you doing in Mar' land?"

Marcus was now in one of those situations when talking too much got him in trouble. Was it possible this old lady was an agent like Mr. McKenzie who kept watch for suspicious people and behavior? Maybe though, she was a Confederate; after all, this was Nashville, a Southern town captured by the Yankees. On the other hand, he had better play it safe. "I cannot tell you more. I can only tell you I am a Union spy going south. I'm on a secret mission."

"You sure don't talk like no Yankee to me. Sounds to me like you are a good old Southern boy."

"That's why they chose me. I went to school so I could talk like this." Marcus enjoyed playing her along as a Union spy.

The lady studied him for a few seconds then suddenly turned away and harshly remarked, "I'll get your stew." She turned away as if he had made her mad.

Marcus wondered what had changed her attitude so fast. Maybe she was a Rebel and resented serving Yankees. That was better that her being a Yankee spy and turning him in to the authorities. He just wanted night to come so he could meet the man in the top hat with the red-tipped white feather.

From his window seat, he could only see the back of his horse and mules. At least he could see the saddlebags and knew they were still there. The lady brought his stew and coffee but did not say anything. That was strange; Marcus wondered why she had changed her disposition so fast?

Marcus ate his stew but was still hungry. He saw his waitress wiping the table behind him. He turned to her and asked, "Excuse me, could I get another bowl of stew and some more coffee?" Without saying a word she left and retrieved his order. When she set it on the table, he also asked, "Could I get a piece of cake or pie?"

Still in a surly mood, "What do you want, pie or cake?"

"What have you got?"

"Pumpkin pie or white cake."

"I'll take the cake, and excuse me if I made you mad. Forgive me for whatever I said."

"I ain't mad."

"Then could I ask you another question?"

"Yeah, go ahead," she answered, still in her impolite frame of mind.

"By any chance have you seen a man attend this tavern late in the evening, let's say around seven o'clock, who has a black top hat, a red band with a red-tipped feather in it?"

Marcus could immediately see by her eyes and slight surprised reaction, she knew exactly who he was talking about. "Why no, I never saw anybody like that." She thought a second, "Where would anybody get a feather like that?"

"You know, I thought the same thing. Apparently it is a chicken feather dipped in red paint," Marcus grinned, recalling what the professor said back to him when he asked the same question. "However, from your surprised reaction, I suspect you have seen him. Why will you not tell me if he comes in? I am a friend of his and need to speak to him."

"No! No matter how I acted, I have not seen a man like that. It just sounded funny to me since I never heard of a red-tipped feather."

"I see. You're not going to tell me."

"No, like I said, I have not seen your friend. I'll get your cake." She immediately fetched the cake and coffee pot, poured the coffee, but did not say another word. He added a little sugar to his coffee and picked up his cake and moved over to a chair closer to the fireplace. The warmth felt good. He quickly ate the cake but swallowed the coffee slowly, savoring each sip. From his new seat, he could see through an open door into the kitchen. He noticed his waitress was talking rapidly to a well-dressed man at the backdoor and pointing back toward the dining room, not noticing Marcus was watching. He saw the man nod and quickly turn away. Marcus got a "goose-feather feeling." Something was going on here, and he was afraid it wasn't good.

He quickly returned to his window seat so she wouldn't suspect he had seen her. Marcus hoped he was just imagining things. She was most likely talking to a food supplier or a woodcutter ordering more wood. Why would she suspect him? For whatever reason, Marcus decided to keep alert and watch for any situation that looked suspicious.

He finished eating and walked out on the porch. His animals were still tied and seem adjusted to their new crowded surroundings. Marcus sat down in a pew to look around and soak up this new city. Like Cincinnati, there were boats of every size tied up, while others plied the river. He noticed the buildings and trees; the sides and trunks up to about three feet were worn from people standing against it. From what he noticed, most men stood on one leg and placed their other shoe against what they were leaning against. In his mind, Marcus called it "half-sitting."

He noticed the wooden stairs had worn spots in the wooden steps where thousands upon thousands of shoes had worn them down. The town was bustling with activity. Boats were being loaded and unloaded on wagons. Many folks filled the landscape not seeming to do anything except come and go. People of all classes climbed and descended the stairs into "The River Roost." It was obviously a popular watering hole in the town. Marcus hoped the man with the red-tipped feather would show up at seven o'clock, so he could finally go home.

41

Marcus looked down at his mules. He wanted to find a place for them to be fed and secured while he waited for his rendezvous. He descended the stairs and halted a man in a wagon pulling a load of barrels up from the river's edge. He asked where a stranger in town could leave his animals. The man told Marcus to go down the street and turn left. There was a large livery stable that would feed, water and secure his animals. He also added, they took good care of their horses and mules, but they were costly because of their convenient location.

Marcus untied his mules and mounted his horse. The livery stable was easy to find, exactly where the man said it was. It was a large barn with small stalls inside, all filled with horses and mules. A huge loft above the stalls stored hay and sacks of grain. Some of the horses were being combed and groomed, the animals of the city's rich folks. There were also many pens outside, some under a roof and others uncovered. A blacksmith was busy making horseshoes while others nailed them to the hooves. In one of the stall, a large black stallion was rearing and causing a great disturbance when a mare in heat came in and several men were trying to calm him down. Like the city, the stable was bustling with activity.

Marcus could readily see there was no room for his animals, but before he could turn away, a man in a leather apron hollered at him from a small room just inside the door. "Young man, what's your need?"

"Oh, I was looking for a place that could feed and keep my animals for a day or two, but I can see your stalls are full."

"The stalls are full, but we have open pens out there behind the barns. They may get rained on, but we'll take good care of them."

"What's your cost?"

"Dollar a day per animal; includes hay and corn, but no grooming."

"Yes, I understand that. I just need a good safe place. Will my saddlebags and saddle be safe?

"Yes, we have a secure room to store that kind of stuff. What's in the canvas bags?"

"Just corn and oats, I am supposed to meet a man, I hope tonight. If I find him, I will leave tomorrow."

"We'll store them for you and give those mules a rest."

"Good then, they've been working hard and they need some time without those heavy packs."

Marcus paid the man three dollars in advance. The stable worker led the three animals down the center of the large barn and stopped the mules in front of a door at the end of the stalls. He took a ring of keys out of his apron, selected a special key and opened the door. The open door revealed a large tack room with many shelves filled with bridles and saddles, leather bags, guns, travel trunks, and other valuables. The liveryman removed all the bridles, saddlebags, and saddle from the horse, and replaced the bridle with a rope halter that had a number. Then Marcus helped him remove the canvas bags of grain. Marcus pointed out the importance of keeping his seed boxes safe and dry. "Those seeds are why I'm in Nashville." To please Marcus, the man placed the canvas bags on a higher shelf. The animals seemed pleased to be relieved of their loads. Then his small herd was led out the back door and down a narrow shoot between the corrals to a pen on the backside of the yard.

"Your animals are in pen 78. I also have their halter numbers. I'll give you a receipt when we go back inside." With that done, Marcus bid his animals a farewell and entered the stable with a sigh of satisfaction. Now he could be at ease with his belongings and rifles safe. He received a receipt and told the man he would be back in the morning to pay for another day or leave.

It was mid-to-late afternoon, and Marcus started back to "The River Roost." As he turned the corner onto 1st street a man, looking backward while proceeding down the street accidentally bumped into Marcus. "Young man, pardon me, I didn't see you. Pardon me."

"No concern. Excuse me," Marcus politely replied to the nice man.

The man appeared to be a middle aged man, well dressed, but his clothes were slightly worn. "Probably due to the war," Marcus thought.

Before Marcus could continue on down the street the man asked, "Say son, are you busy?"

"No, not until about six o'clock."

"Would you like to make a quick two bits?"

"Why I guess so, how can I help you?"

"I'm staying here in this hotel," pointing at the building whose sidewalk they were standing on. I am a hardware salesman and will be in town a short spell and have a trunk that I need carried up to my room. It is a bit too heavy since it contains hardware, and I always need someone to help me. It will only take ten minutes. Imagine that boy, two bits for ten minutes work."

"That's good pay alright."

"Then come on, my carriage is behind the building. We can go in the back entrance. Follow me." He turned and went back around the corner to an alley that went behind the building.

When Marcus turned the corner, he did not see a carriage; just a rocky alley with the back of buildings on both sides, and he suddenly sensed a slight "goose" feeling for a moment. From his past experiences, Marcus immediately became suspicious and stopped. "Where's your buggy?"

"Oh, I forgot to mention. There was a fight or some commotion in the street; it was so crowed I couldn't get by, so I parked it down there at the end of the alley. Come on, follow me; it's right down here." He turned and stuck his hand out, "My name is John Gibbons, what's yours?"

"Marcus, Marcus Mills, from Buckhead, Georgia."

Marcus's momentary "goose feather" went away, and he convinced himself the rather small man couldn't do him any harm. Besides, he still had his pistols in his belt. They walked a few steps farther, and Marcus fell unconscious, struck on the back of the head by an unseen assailant.

Marcus woke up later in the parlor of a nice house. He had a terrible headache and his arms and legs were securely tied and his pistols gone. As the images focused around him, he noticed the nice man he had just met was sitting in a comfortable chair smoking a pipe. As he looked around from his position on the floor, he saw two other men, both well dressed. They did not look like common hoodlums, but rather successful business men. "What happened, where am I?'

"We would like to know the same thing," John asked. "What are you doing in Nashville?" Two of the men approached Marcus and lifted him into a chair.

Marcus feared he was talking to the Federal authorities and went to his standard story. "I am a Union soldier trying to get back home to Georgia."

"Georgia?" the man yelled, "A Union soldier trying to get home to Georgia? Then that makes you a spy or a traitor. Which is it boy; a spy or a traitor?" He then stood up and rapidly approached Marcus and slapped him on the side of his head with the back of his hand. "Well boy, which is it, a spy or a traitor."

Marcus squeezed his eyes shut showing the severe pain and fearing another hard smack. Before he could say anything, another man standing behind him kicked his chair, then bent down and whispered, "Boy if you want to be around when the sun goes down, you better tell us the truth. Are you a rotten Yankee spy or a traitor to your homeland?"

From what he was hearing it sounded like these men were not Federals but Confederates. But how would he know it? The only person he had talked to was the waitress in "The River Roost." Then he recalled how her mood changed after he told her he was a Yankee spy, and the conversation he had seen with the man at the backdoor. These aren't Federals, they're Confederates, and she had informed them a Federal spy was in their midst. They may have assumed he was a planted Union agent sent to capture the man in the top hat with the red-tipped feather. It seemed Marcus's luck had run out. He had to take a chance and hope he was right. "All right, I will tell you the truth. It is true, I am going home to Georgia, but I am a Confederate soldier, not a Yankee spy. I was just having fun ribbing the waitress, if that's where you got the information I am a spy."

"You lying Yankee scum," John shouted, slapping him on the side of the head again.

Grimacing in pain Marcus pleaded, "Let me finish. I am telling you the truth. I fought in all the early battles of the war. I was in the Georgia Brigade in Hood's Division. At Antietam I was captured, but I managed to escape. I was trailed by dogs, betrayed, escaped again and eventually got to Pittsburgh."

"Yeah, that figures, another Yankee town," one of the men yelled as he stepped forward to kick him again. "Then why did you tell Maggie over at 'The 'Roost' you were a Yankee looking for a man with a red-tipped feather in his hat?"

"To tell you the truth, since I left Sharpsburg, everybody I meet is a Union authority or spy. Sir, it seems everybody I've met since Antietam, except for an old man on the river, was trying to capture me, kill me, betray me, or hang me. I just figured Yankees ran this town, so I pretended to be a Yankee. I didn't want to draw attention to myself. I never figured I was speaking to a comrade."

The man standing beside him gave him another slap on the back of his head causing Marcus to bend forward in extreme pain, "You lying dog," he yelled.

"Stop, please stop, I am telling you the truth. I am on your side."
Another man approached to kick him again.

Then John stepped forward preventing another kick, "Stop! Before
we kill this traitor, let's hear him out. I am interested in hearing how
he knew about the red-tipped feather."

"Please, listen to me," Marcus gasped, "In Pittsburgh, I met a
man. He owned a boatyard, and I convinced him I was a Union
soldier trying to get home to Louisville. He believed me and felt
sorry for me. He was the kindest man I had ever met. He even let me
borrow a boat to float down to Louisville. Before I got to Cincinnati
though, on a cold rainy night I met an old man who said he was a
professor."

When Marcus said, "professor," he noticed all the eyes watching
him turn and communicate. After a moment of silence, John
interrupted him, "Who did you say you met?"

"The professor, an old gentleman," Marcus coughed, trying to
clear his throat from the hit on the neck. "We quickly became friends.
We spent the rest of that cold night talking. He was a professor
of language, and he knew by the way I talked I was from central
Georgia." Marcus winced in pain, but continued. "Then he told me
he was taking detonators down the river. I didn't know what that
meant, but he told me they would blow up Yankee ships. He was really
smart, you know."

"Do you remember that old man's name?"

"Jethro Jennings, Colonel Jethro Jennings. He showed me his
papers. He knew President Davis, you know."

All of a sudden the three men changed their demeanor
understanding they may have made a mistake. After more worried
eye movement and thought, John stepped forward. "Untie those
ropes. This man may be one of us."

"That's what I'm trying to tell you. I'm one of you if you are
fighting for the Confederacy."

They lifted him up and untied him and led him to a softer chair.
"Continue your story."

Marcus rubbed his wrists, "That night he asked me to float with him down the river and help guard the detonators. He said we could watch each other's back. When we got to Cincinnati, we saw two Union warships. The Professor said we could not pass up a prize like that. That old man figured out a way to sink those boats, and we did."

The men looked at each other in amazement. "You mean you and Colonel Jennings blew up those ships?"

"Yes sir, he built the torpedoes, and I stuck them in the sides using a spear. They thought I was a fish seller, and they let me get near the boats everyday until we sunk them."

"Well, how about that! You two sunk those boats? I'm amazed," he said as he raised his knee and slapped it. "By the way, where's the professor now?"

Marcus looked down and then slowly raised his head, "Haven't you read the newspapers? He's dead. One night he froze to death on the river. I promised him before he died though, if something happened to him I would finish his mission." Marcus rubbed the back of his neck where he had been hit so hard.

"Sorry about that boy. We sincerely apologize. After what you told Maggie, we figured you were a Yankee spy who had infiltrated our network."

"Do y'all mind if I laid down a minute on your sofa. My head is killing me."

"By all means boy, lie down. What's your name again?"

"Marcus, Marcus Mills." Before Marcus could get comfortable, he heard the door open, and he saw a tall man enter with a black top hat with a red band and a white red-tipped feather. Immediately Marcus rose up and pointed, "That's him," he stood up and yelled, "That's the man I am going to meet tonight at seven o'clock. Your name is," he hesitated, then stuttered out, "X, you're Mister X!"

"Along with Y and Z." the man replied.

"That's right! That's what the professor said you would say." Marcus knew he had found the right man, and the other men now knew for certain they had kidnapped and punished the wrong man. They looked at each other in deep guilt; they had harmed a brother in arms. John approached with his hand extended, "Again, I say I'm sorry for what we did. We suspected you were a Union agent." Marcus was relieved now; he was among friends and quickly forgave them for the beating he had received and shook his hand. "We apologize to you, Marcus. As I said we thought you were a Yankee agent sent to capture 'X,' otherwise known as Captain James."

"What's going on here?" Captain James asked.

John took the Captain's elbow to move him forward, "Captain, this is Marcus Mills. He is a Confederate hero, and this is the man you've been waiting for. He said the professor died on the trip down, but Marcus here, vowed to finish the mission."

The Captain with the red-tipped feather in his hat reached out and shook hands with Marcus. "Glad to meet you, boy, but I must ask you the ultimate question, do you have the detonators?"

"Yes sir, I do. They are stored over at the livery stable across the street from where I bumped into Mr. John. They are hidden down below the corn and oats concealed under a false bottom in my big canvas saddlebags. I didn't figure anybody would search through mule food if I was stopped on the road."

"Good thinking; that was smart." Captain James looked at the clock above the fireplace, "There's no need for me to go to 'The 'Roost' and sit on the porch tonight. Instead, let's all go there and celebrate. There's enough daylight left to go fetch those little potent eggs and be on the way south tomorrow morning."

They patched Marcus back together, and all five comrades left a nice two-story house several blocks from the river. They quickly returned to the stable, riding in a wagon pulled by two horses. Marcus told the liveryman he needed to retrieve his gear for the night and would get his animals in the morning. They drove the wagon inside and loaded all of Marcus's equipment, including the canvas bags, and departed. They all agreed it would appear suspicious if they secured only the canvas bags that contained the corn and oats. The five men went back to the two-story house. They entered a barn behind the house and shut the doors. Inside was another wagon that appeared to be completely worn out.

"This wagon appears to be on its last leg, or I should say wheel," John chuckled, "but it is made to look that way. As you can see, it is filled with straw and hay, but like your canvas bags, it has a double floor that has a storage space at the front and slopes back and tapers to join the bottom at the rear so it looks like a normal wagon with only flat boards for a floor. The enemy would have to rip the old gal apart to find the deception. We had a carriage maker here in Nashville build it for us. Our little eggs will fit In that space behind the seat all padded and secure."

"That looks like the professor made that," Marcus grinned.

"Matter of fact, he did. The last time he smuggled fuses down here, he came up with this idea and drew the plans. He hoped eventually to use this wagon to smuggle them all the way from Canada."

"Yeah, that sounds like the old man."

The Confederate agent continued, "Captain James and I will take them to Mobile to insure their safe delivery. By our dress we will appear to be farmers moving hay. With that disguise, we can fit in anywhere in the South and not be suspected of doing anything illegal. If you think this wagon looks down trodden, wait until you see our clothes," he laughed. "No one will suspect us of being agents for the Confederate States of America." He hesitated a moment, "And if the Union Army searches the hay or even confiscates the hay, they will never see the deception because the sideboards and seat hide the slope of the floor."

The comrades set about taking the detonators out of the canvas bags, dusting off the bits of grain, wrapping them in paper, then in oil cloth to waterproof them, and finally in flat wooden boxes that were built to slide into the space behind the seat. While they were stowing the cargo, the barn door opened and a house servant entered carrying four bottles of Kentucky whiskey safely packed in a wooden crate. John took the box and buried it in the hay. "These are favors for Captain Tyler down at Mobile. He requested four bottles of the best whiskey the next time I came down. Now with their work complete, John suggested they all go to "The River Roost" and celebrate their success.

It was nearly dark when the five men climbed the stairs. The porch was crowded with men waiting to get a table. Marcus sensed they would have a long wait in the pews before they would get something to eat. Following the group up the stairs, he noticed John and Captain James pushed between men and opened the front door. They entered and went in the door that Marcus had looked through to watch the waitress who informed on him. John held the door open and motioned for Marcus to follow them inside. The kitchen was hot and busy. The five men made their way to the back of the room and entered what looked like a storeroom. But instead, it turned out to be a hidden entry, hidden behind a pantry wall that led to a secluded room with high windows for privacy and ventilation. The hidden sanctuary had a table with six chairs. John and Captain James took their places at the ends of the table and invited their guests to sit down.

John spoke up, "I own this place. I keep an eye on things from here. I know who's in town, and what's about to happen. We expected the professor any day now and were becoming concerned about his whereabouts. When you showed up and told Maggie you were a Yankee, we really feared the Federals had killed or captured him and were trying to penetrate our network. Fortunately, except for your beating, things turned out well. The train is back on the tracks again, so to speak."

Marcus looked around at the unique room, "Is this hideaway one of the professor's ideas, too?"

"Yes it is. He felt we needed a place to hide and carry on business and meetings after the Yankees captured our town," John grinned, proud of his secret chamber.

Soon a lady appeared and took everyone's order. John insisted they all eat the best ham in the house with a baked potato filled with butter, and green beans. The waitress brought them all beer, but Marcus declined and asked for coffee instead. While they waited, the men wanted to hear how Marcus got involved in the smuggling network. He told his life story and his involvement early in the war. He related how he escaped the cornfield and blew up the Union powder wagons at Sharpsburg. All the men at the table cheered when they heard his heroic feats. He continued with his escape from the dogs, his encounter with Genia and Edward Brewster, and how he escaped again from the prison train. The men all laughed at his ingenuity and how he got to Pittsburgh. The Confederate agents listened with the greatest concentration, almost all leaning forward on their elbows not to miss a word.

He then told them how the boat builder befriended him and built *Bonnie* with all her special features and the ultimate rendezvous with the Professor. At that point the food was served, and the men insisted Marcus continue his story after they ate. While Marcus ate, he really sensed his dreadful journey was over, and he was almost home. He would not worry anymore about risking his life to save the detonators. He had not eaten a finer meal in his entire life. When they finished, a lady brought in an apple cobbler with sweet heavy cream poured on top. That was the best thing Marcus had ever put in his mouth. He was warm, happy, full, and relieved it was over.

When they finished their meal, the lady came in and cleaned the table. Then Marcus told them about sinking the Union gunboats, the Professor's genius, and about his death. He informed them about his Louisville escapade and his discovery of the detonator switch, his escape, and the chance meeting with the Cavalry officer at Shepherdsville, and how he saw him again at the bridge. He told about his near hanging and about the cavalry saving him. The men all laughed at that and at last he said, "Now you know why I told Maggie I was a Yankee, and you know the rest."

They all leaned back with pride in what Marcus had achieved. "Marcus, you should be recognized for your bravery and courage." Captain James spoke out. "When I get back to Richmond I am going to tell Jefferson Davis about your heroic efforts and recommend that Congress give you our highest medal and place a bronze plaque to you on the Capitol grounds. For what you accomplished, you deserve it."

"Yes, I agree," John added nodding his head. "Here's to Marcus!" he yelled raising his glass of beer. They all stood and toasted Marcus's remarkable achievements.

"Thank you sirs, but I want to go home. I have a girl who I love very much." He slipped out the photograph and showed them Bonnie's picture. I have to go find her now. I expect she is somewhere in Texas. I imagine my folks and the army think I'm dead after the bloody battle at Sharpsburg. Since then, nobody 'cept you folks have heard from me."

The men passed around the photograph of the beautiful girl. "I can see now why you want to go home, but Marcus, I hoped you might join Captain James and me and travel on to Mobile with us. You would be a tremendous asset with all your knowledge about getting around the authorities," John suggested.

"No, I thank you for considering me for the job, but I have extended my luck too long. If I keep doing this, I will eventually meet the bullet that I can't dodge or a chain I cannot escape. No, like I mentioned, I just wish for home and to go find Bonnie." Marcus looked down sadly, then looked at the men with a glazed look in his eyes and spoke softly, "Gentlemen, forgive me for saying this, but no matter what we do, we cannot win this war. At Antietam, as I just mentioned, I became a Yankee for a day. I saw what they have to throw against us. At Pittsburgh and Cincinnati there are factories and stores of food, while our soldiers walk on bare bloody feet, starve and wear rags. I saw at Antietam what we lack. I promised the professor that I would see his mission to the end, which I have done, but no more war for me. I have done my part and there are no more parts to give." With that statement Marcus lowered his head as if in defeat, raised his elbows on table and clasped his hands on the side of his head.

The men looked at each other. Then John said, "Yes boy, we all fear you may be right. You have given all you can. However, we hope that England will recognize the Confederacy soon and aid us in this war. We need a great victory this spring, or I am afraid, too, the war is over. We hope if we can get these detonators where they're needed, and we can begin sinking the blockade that is strangling the South." He hesitated and looked around at the other comrades, then at Marcus, "Again, we all want to thank you for your courage."

Marcus stood up and asked for their attention one last time. "And don't let us forget Professor Jethro. He was the real hero. Be sure he gets a statue in the park. He was the smartest man I ever met."

"Here, here!" they all shouted agreeing with Marcus. The officers who had worked with the old man stood up one by one and lauded his talents, skill, and cunning. The men continued to talk about the war and ask more questions about Marcus's adventure, trying to gain any information that could help them in the future. Many lit cigars and pipes made the room cloudy.

When all the questions had been asked, John queried one more. "What did you do with the Professor's body after he froze to death?"

"I was afraid you would ask me." Marcus appeared to be under great stress as he slowly related how he shot him and told the constable he had killed the Confederate spy to end the hunt for the detonators. "Even though he was dead, it was the hardest thing I ever had to do, but I know the Professor would have approved to insure my escape. I left his body with the constable. Please, after the war, have someone locate where he is buried and bring him back home." The men were all moved and admired Marcus even more for his courage to do what he had to do.

With the final question answered, the celebration ended and John requested Marcus to return home with him and spend the night there. The next morning, they could return to "The Roost" and eat a large breakfast. At first Marcus refused, saying he was dirty and needed a bath. John said he would arrange that, too. His house servants always kept a kettle of hot water on the stove to heat bathwater. Then Marcus remembered, he had some clean clothes in his saddle bags.

The next morning Marcus felt good after his previous night's bath and hair washing, but when he got up, he was aware of the knocks and bruises he had gotten the previous day. He had forgotten what a comfortable bed felt like. The servant loaded his bags back in the wagon, and Marcus was soon joined by John in his tattered clothing to begin his trip south. "What do you think about these rags?" he asked Marcus. "Do I look like a poor farmer?"

"Not yet sir, you need to let your whiskers grow and get a little dirty to match your clothes. Your face looks newer than your clothes."

"Good idea. I didn't think about that when I shaved this morning. I will remind Colonel James to look scruffy, too." As they got in the wagon, Marcus noticed his shabby shoes that completed his costume.

Soon, the two men were eating breakfast at "The Roost." They were joined by Colonel James wearing his old dirty rags. He had not shaved that morning and was beginning to get that unkempt look. John paid Marcus with enough money, both Federal and Confederate, to see him home. "Take this money; you haven't been paid lately. I want to thank you for what you have done for our Southern cause." Marcus refused at first, but John and the Colonel insisted. After their breakfast, full, and with his needs met, John returned Marcus and his belongings to the stable.

In order to travel faster, John suggested Marcus sell one of his mules, but Marcus declined saying he would need both mules when he got home. He was going to buy a plow, find Bonnie, and be a farmer one day, and have a house full of children.

All three men mounted their rides. Marcus thought a moment, "I've been thinking about it this morning."

"What are you thinking about?" Colonel James asked.

"If you don't mind, I'll take you up on your offer and ride with you until I turn back east. If anyone asks, we just met on the road a few minutes back, and we're just riding along together. Pretend we don't even know each other's name. How does that sound?"

"I'll buy that idea. That way we can guard each other."

"Yeah, that's what the Professor would do." With that said, the three left the stable and returned to 1st Street passing by "The Roost" one last time, heading south and for Marcus, heading home.

42

The three travelers found the road patrolled by Union Cavalry and passed Union Infantry Brigades camped in fields near the road. The soldiers seemed to pay them no mind, but late in the afternoon a dozen Union horsemen stopped the wagon. Marcus had followed behind the wagon, far enough just to keep it in sight, after they began encountering Union forces.

One of the horsemen questioned the two apparent farmers on their business in the area. John replied they lived down the road apiece and had managed to find a little hay for their livestock. "You know times are hard right now. My brother told me at church, when I got the chance, to come down and get it. The Confederate Army had taken his cow and two horses, and he wouldn't need it anymore."

Marcus rode up on his horse leading his mules at the moment he heard the horseman add, "Do you have any proof that you live in the area?"

"No, I don't have the deed to my property, but if you want to follow me a ways, I can show you where I live." At that time, Marcus passed by and yelled over, "Mr. Caldwell, come by my place tomorrow, and I'll loan you that sickle you wanted to borrow. I finally borrowed Hubert's mules to start breaking the bottom for spring planting."

John turned, "Hey Josh, I didn't know you were behind us. Thanks, I'll be by tomorrow and get it." Then he turned toward the mounted soldier, "There! That should show you I live around here."

"Very well, you may pass, but is hay all you got on the wagon? You don't have any contraband back there do you?"

"Contraband, what's that," Colonel James replied, trying to prove his ignorance.

"Rifles, whiskey; stuff like that."

"No, all I have is the hay. You can search me if you like."

"What's in the box under your seat?

"Oh, I forgot, sir. Whiskey sir, whiskey; four bottles for a rich man that needs it for his heart."

"Let me look at it. Have you paid the taxes on it, or is it illegal brew?"

"It's legal. Let me show you." He opened the crate and pulled out one of the expensive bottles. "You see," as he pulled the bottle out of the box and turned it so he could read the label, "This ain't normal whiskey. This is the good stuff, and the kind a man like me can't afford. I'm gonna get a half dollar, sir, if I can get it to him, and my family sir, could shore use that half dollar."

Realizing the poor farmer's plight, the officer let him pack it back up.

The horseman, apparently an officer, commanded one of his men to take the pitchfork riding on top of the hay and give the wagon a final search. After turning the hay over and poking it with the pitchfork, he was convinced the two men were who they said they were and let them pass. "Sorry, to bother you sir, but in times of war, you Rebels get clever smuggling war goods around."

John wanted to reply, "You just don't know how clever," he thought to himself as he clicked his tongue to move the mules forward. On down the road they caught up with Marcus. "That was an intelligent remark you made back there. You may have saved us some trouble, if they had wanted to see where I lived."

"Oh, that's just what the Professor would have said," he laughed. "Even though he died, I sometimes feel he is still with us. I will never forget that man."

It was nearing sundown and as the solar furnace set, the air was getting cold. They decided to stop, build a fire, and open a large can of beans for supper. "The Roost" had sent some cornbread, and with the beans they would have a good warm supper. That night, as the three comrades discussed the day's events, it was decided it would be safer for Marcus to follow along behind them and continue their anonymity of each other and meet only at night to share vittles.

The next six days passed with no major conflicts. The wagon was stopped twice, but allowed to pass through. Their appearance did not pose a threat to anyone, only farmers fetching some hay or vegetables for their probably starving cow and mule and families.

On the seventh day, the Colonel led them off the busy road and turned southwest down a small lane. Eventually they came to a large plantation. He informed Marcus they were on "The White Oaks" plantation that backed up to the Tennessee River. The owner was a Confederate agent and expected them. After dark, they would cross the river undetected on a flatboat tethered to a pier. This was their gateway to the South. The owner welcomed them as they rode up in front of the large home. That night he wined and dined them. After dark, they loaded the wagon on a barge and poled it across the river, then came back and ferried Marcus and his animals across. They would follow the back roads until they left the river area, then get back on the main road south.

One morning, after two days back on the road, Marcus was slow to rouse and came to breakfast late as the other two men were packing their cooking gear in the wagon. From hearing all of his adventures, they knew Marcus was tired and needed more rest. Although they had finished eating, they had saved him some bacon and the last of their bread. Marcus, not wanting to slow them down, told them to go on ahead and he would catch up. He told them if they came to a fork in the road, put a large stick in the road pointing in the direction they took.

In order to save time, the wagon went on ahead. Marcus was tired that morning and was slow to get going. He still felt the results of the kicking he endured back in Nashville. He fed his animals and took his time folding up his blanket and canvas lean-to he slept under. There was no need to hurry. He was lagging behind anyway, and he figured he would catch them before noon.

Not long after getting underway, he stopped at a stream crossing the road to let his animals drink. He dismounted and stretched his arms high above him and looked up at the partly cloudy sky, wondering if the clouds coming from the south would bring rain later that day. Except for his minor aches and pain, he felt good about the day. He was going home and had not been harassed by the Federals as they left Union controlled areas and moved into Dixie. He calculated he could be home in three to four weeks. He had learned in Nashville it was the 15th of December when he left there. He hoped to be back in Buckhead, Georgia, by January 15th. When his small flock finished drinking, he mounted Red and headed south again.

After an hour's ride, Marcus came around a curve and could see his friends ahead. They seemed to be stopped waiting for him, but as he came closer he saw the mules were gone. Marcus figured they probably had unhitched them to take them over to a pond or stream to get a drink. When he got closer he noticed many hoof prints in the road and the grass near the wagon trodden down. Most of the hay was on the ground. Then he saw a sight that sent a "goose-feather" down his spine. John and the Colonel were lying face down in the weeds a few yards from the road. Both men were next to each other shot in the back of the head, execution style, and the pitchfork was plunged into the Colonel's back.

This massacre must have just happened, and the perpetrators were not far away. Marcus had seen all he needed to see. There was nothing he could do for his comrades. He had learned from the war large bullet wounds to the head were fatal. He needed to get out of there and save his life. He clicked his tongue to hurry the mules; he turned his horse and tugged the mules to follow. When he passed the wagon, he wondered if the detonators were still inside. Due to the condition of the wagon, as planned, the marauders had abandoned it, knowing its tracks would be left in the road for any pursuer to follow.

Marcus pulled close to the wagon. The hay was scattered about, and the whiskey was gone. The side boxes that carried the cooking gear were open, but most of the pots and pans were still inside. Marcus thought about his two friends and the Professor who had given their lives to the mission now in ruin.

Marcus decided to run while he had the chance. Marcus wanted to give up and leave and abandon the valuable cargo on the side of a road there in Alabama, but his patriotism and his promise to the Professor to deliver the detonators ate at his conscience. He hesitated and looked up and prayed, "God give me your protection for a few more minutes so I can finish the Professor's task, Amen." Marcus dismounted and hastily gathered up the reins and horse collars strewn about the ground. The mules apparently had been cut out of their harnesses quickly. Marcus worked swiftly, and he soon had his mules hitched up well enough he could pull the wagon. He tied Red to the rear of the wagon, turned the wagon around, and headed back toward the direction he had come, not taking the chance to go forward and run into the killers. It seemed they killed his friends for two mules. They probably discovered the whiskey after they killed them. Marcus knew they would kill him for his mules and horse, too, so he hurried back the way he came. He wanted to put as much space as possible between he and his possible predators.

After an hour, Marcus looked for a safe place to rest his mules. He had pushed them hard. Soon, Marcus saw a long small hill in an abandoned field that had been farmed the previous summer. He turned the wagon from the road and into the field. He stopped and wiped the wagon tracks out with his foot. He pulled up some dried weeds and scratched out his footmarks, making his exit from the road nearly impossible for a passerby to detect. He drove the wagon behind the hill and found a refuge that hid his wagon from the road. Marcus knew his guardian angel was with him when he found a low place behind the embankment that contained clear rainwater. He was two hundred yards from the road and felt this was the place to camp for the night. After dark, he would build a fire that could not be seen from the road. He unhitched his team of mules and led them to water.

While he was holding the reins, he heard horses coming from the direction of the massacre. He left the mules to drink, and he hurried to the top of the hill to see four horsemen pass. It was the killers of his two friends. One of the men wore Captain James's familiar hat. Two of the men led the captured mules, and the other two were holding a bottle of whiskey. Without question Marcus knew these men were guilty and needed to be trailed and executed. No trial was needed. It would be dark soon, and he reckoned they would stop then. He went back to the mules and tethered them on a long rope that would give them a little room to roam around the wagon and maybe able to graze on the dried grass. He took some of the grain and poured it on the ground. The corn would keep them interested in staying put.

Marcus mounted Red and galloped out from behind the hill. He hurried to catch the men ahead of him. Just before dark, he unexpectedly came upon them and reined in his horse. Marcus suspected the men had heard his galloping horse approaching which killed a plan to discover them before they discovered him. They stood next to a wooded area unsaddling their horses for the night. Knowing he had been detected, and they were a dangerous adversary, Marcus spurred his horse to gallop on by at full speed. Before he got to them he veered off the road and gave them plenty of room. Already feeling the effects of their bottle's contents, they jeered and yelled at Marcus to stop and have a drink with them. When he didn't stop, they started cursing him and calling him a coward, but under no conditions was he going to stop. He would see them later. Marcus raced another mile until he was sure they had heard him fade away and would assume he was gone.

Marcus reined in Red and patted him on the neck. He dismounted and led him to the back of a field and tied him inside the edge of the woods. He waited with Red to calm him down, and shortly before it was totally dark, he ran back to the road and used the heel of his shoe to draw a line across the road. He pulled up some weeds and placed them in the road, so he could find the place he hid his horse.

He checked his pistols in his belt to make sure they were ready. There was going to be a killing tonight.

Marcus began counting his steps down the road going in the direction he had seen the murderers. After 1287 steps, he saw the glow of their campfire ahead. He stopped and drew another line in the road and stuck his pistols behind him in his belt. He knelt down and crept forward, then crawled. Marcus could see one of the killers standing up swigging the last of the whiskey down, his silhouette dark against the light of the fire. Marcus dropped down on his belly and crawled further. He then exited the road and entered the trees, still on his stomach. He knew as he got nearer the fire, he had to keep his face down so as not to reveal his presence. He continued to belly-crawl until he found a low place he could hide in, close enough to hear their conversation. A perfect place to let time and whiskey do their work.

While he waited, he slowly pulled the leaves up on him until he was camouflaged, similar to his experience before in Maryland. While he listened, he reasoned they were deserters from the Confederate Army; stealing, and when necessary, killing people. He heard the heathens talk about the murder and laugh as they recalled how John and the Captain pleaded for their lives. One of the vermin remarked, "Can you imagine? Those country ignorants tried to tell us they were gen'rals or something like 'kat," he laughed and took another swig. "I never thought I'd get to kill a gen'ral. I hated those fancy dressed guys that worked me like a dog, hollered at me from their high horse, and made me march in that hot sun."

Another laughed, "They ain't on high horses now!"

The man in John's hat hollered out, "For poor farmers," he giggled, "They sure had good whiskey," as he turned one of the bottles up and took another mouthful, raising the bottle high. It was all Marcus could do to stay still and carry out his plan rather than to jump up and run forward in a fit of rage hoping to kill them before they could kill him. But Marcus was a wise veteran now and used his experience to bide his time.

After an hour, one of the men stood up and wobbled and staggered in a ragged line in Marcus's direction. Marcus reached behind him and withdrew one of his pistols, rustling the leaves slightly, but being experienced in the woods knew the man stumbling toward him was louder and would cover any noise Marcus made removing his pistol. As he came nearer, Marcus wondered if the fool was going to walk over and step on him, but before he got nearer, he stopped and relieved himself. He then turned and returned to the fire, and Marcus continued to wait.

During the next two hours the bragging, hollering, drinking, and fire died down until all was quiet. Marcus remained still, being patient, giving the men all the time they needed to fall asleep. With only a slight glow from hot embers, Marcus finally rose up out of the leaves and using the trees for cover, approached the edge of their camp. He observed the four bottles of liquor were empty, but had done their job and he could hear all four snoring. The men's rifles were leaned against their saddles. He could see one pistol, probably either John's or the Colonel's. He also knew both of his comrades carried pistols, so there was one he could not locate.

Marcus continued to study the situation and pondered where the extra pistol might be. He could see all their belts except one, whose owner was lying on his stomach. He was the one that wore the red-feathered hat. Marcus wanted to unarm them and wake them up to tell them they were going to die, one at a time, and watch them plead for their lives. He hated to send people to hell without a chance of repentance, but he had to do what he had to do.

He took both pistols and slipped them in his belt up front again and removed his hunting knife from the holster. Marcus gathered their rifles and secured the pistol he could see from the man's belt. He kneeled down by the heathen lying on his stomach and slowly inched his hand along under his belt to locate the unseen pistol he hoped was there. At last he felt the handle of the gun. He manipulated his fingers so he could grasp and remove the pistol. When the pistol came out the man sensed the movement and stopped snoring. Marcus did not move a muscle. For a few seconds the man did not appear to be breathing; then suddenly, he made a loud gasp for air and rolled over against Marcus's feet. Marcus froze for what seemed an eternity, wondering what the man would do next. Finally, he started snoring again. Whether the man was having a nightmare or he had discovered Marcus, suddenly he grabbed Marcus's leg and yelled. With no choice now, Marcus plunged the sharp blade of his knife into the man's chest and used the weight of his body to push the knife in deep. The man started shaking, and the noise alerted the other three drunks, and they started to move, but unable to quickly comprehend what was happening. Before they could rise up, Marcus drew his pistol and rapidly shot each one in the face. One of the deserters died immediately and did not move, but two lay on their backs and tried to grab their faces. Marcus pulled his other pistol and put another bullet into the squirming men to put them out of their misery. It was over in a few seconds. He had revenged the murder of his friends. In Marcus's mind, justice had been done. They had traded and eye for an eye and a tooth for a tooth, unfortunately this instead, was a bullet in the head for a bullet in the head.

Marcus thought about his predicament now. If someone came along, he would be accused of murder at worse, and at best, he would have to stay around until the investigation was over. The four bodies were near the road, but their horses and two stolen mules had been tied back next to the woods and were not visible from the road in the dark. Marcus saw the value in the saddles, weapons, horses and mules. He had a wagon now and plenty of room for the extra gear, but for now, he needed to tend to the problem of the dead men and get them away from the road.

Marcus kicked dirt on the fire until there was not a trace of smoke. Then one by one he dragged the four bodies into the woods and then searched each one for any money or valuables. They had six dollars in Confederate bills between them and sadly, a small gold band, probably stolen from a lady. He looked at the worthless carcasses who were once small lads and the apples of their mothers' eyes and wondered aloud, "How could your souls become so wicked and cruel, yet start life so pure." He thought a minute. "You didn't think that bourbon you found would lead to your death, did you? I am truly sorry I had to kill you, but my heart has hardened over the last four months dealing with human waste like you. You reaped what you sowed and may God forgive you of your sins" He looked up at the starry night and added, "And God, forgive me for what I had to do."

The road was dark, lit only by starlight, but his eyes had adjusted so he could see a little. He found the line in the road and counted the paces back to find the other line and weeds within a few yards from where he expected them. Using the mark, he walked back in the woods and found his horse. He led Red out of the woods and mounted him, leaned up by his ear and humorously told him to find the wagon. Marcus was surprised when the horse turned in the right direction when they got back to the road.

When Marcus passed the deserters' last campsite he tried to see anything that might cause a passerby to stop. He could still smell a slight odor of ashes, but he laughed, "What am I worried about? Nobody's gonna come down this road tonight but me." He spurred Red past the bloody campsite to return to his wagon and mules he left hidden behind the hill. He had galloped farther than he imagined. Eventually he saw the hill to his left silhouetted against the stars. He found his mules standing with their heads down. Their collars were still on and he had the mended harness hooked to the wagon quickly. He tied Red to the back and headed back to the dead men's camp.

At the camp, he threw the saddles and weapons in the back, retrieved the four horses and tied them next to Red who seemed to appreciate the company. He tied one mule on each side of the wagon. He was about to get in the wagon to leave when he caught a glimpse of the white feather sticking out of the Captain's hat. He walked over and dusted the hat off and put it on his head. It fit like it was made for him. He would keep it forever to remind him of this adventure when he was old. It also brought back the memory of John and the Captain lying at the edge of the road needing to be buried. He wanted to go back and bury them so the vultures and varmints would not scatter their remains before someone found them.

Marcus did not have to worry now about the people who had killed his comrades, so he turned around and headed in his initial direction. He calculated by the time someone discovered the killer's carcasses from their odor, he would be long gone and safely away.

When he returned to his two friends, he found the cold night had preserved the two bodies. Apparently no one had seen them. It was almost light now. He pulled them farther from the road so they wouldn't be detected unless someone stumbled on them or began to smell them. He didn't feel it was safe for him to stay and dig a grave, and risk being captured or even seen. He told them he wished he could do more, but he knew they would want him to finish the mission instead. He said a short prayer, clicked his mules forward, and proceeded south, leading his entourage of animals.

43

At the next small crossroads several miles away, Marcus came to a cluster of buildings beginning to resemble a small village. He noticed a post office sign on the side of a general store and stopped. The town was waking up and two people were opening their doors. Marcus stepped up on the porch of the post office-general store and found the door still locked. He clasped his hands around his eyes and leaned up against the glass window to see inside. He espied an older man approaching the door after hearing footsteps on his porch. "Hold your horses, hold your horses, I'm a comin'", he yelled in a disgruntled way, but most likely glad he had a customer in those hard times.

He opened the door and welcomed Marcus inside, "What do you need this morning he said as he turned away to start a fire going to a pot-bellied stove.

"Sir, I need to write a letter to Nashville. Do you have that sort of stuff?"

"Of course I do, didn't you see the sign outside? By the way boy, what are you doing running around out there? Why aren't you in the war?"

Marcus told his usual story and showed him his battle scar, then asked, "Sir, have the Yankees penetrated this far south? Am I in Confederate territory?"

"Right now we're under the Confederates. General Nathan Bedford Forest runs this area and makes a nuisance of himself on the Yankees when they come down here."

"Can I mail a letter back to Nashville? I need to contact a friend back there and tell him I am safe."

"Well young man, some of the mail goes through and some of the mail comes south, but when we get it from the North it has been opened and read by 'lookers' I call them. People snooping to see if you are sending secrets about the war, I guess."

"You say General Forest runs this area?"

"Yes sir! When he's around. Matter of fact, old Will Coulter; he's an old man lives east of here, 'spected he saw the gen'ral about a week ago pass by with a bunch of riders. Somebody said he was down around Decatur now, but they say he don't stay around long. He's always on the move. There's lots of Yankees around here, too."

"Well then, is there another Confederate officer around here that I could talk to? I have some important information I need to tell him."

"You're gonna have to get farther south before you'll be safe from running into Yankees. You might have to go as far as Birmingham before you would find a large force of our men."

"In that case, let me have an envelope and a piece of paper so I can write my letter." Marcus took the paper and sat down at a table near the stove and labeled the envelope. He remembered Maggie so he addressed the envelope: Misses Maggie, The River Roost, Nashville, Tennessee. Fearing the letter would also be read by Federal authorities, he wrote:

"Dear Mrs. Maggie, I don't want to scare you none, but yore uncle John and Mr. James is dead. They was killed by bandits on the road to Alabama. This are the truth. I did not get killed 'cause I stopped to water my mules. I hope you remember me since I only saw you onest. I am the Yankee spy you talked to in yore inn. My name is Marcus, and I left with them to deliver a load of chicken eggs. You know'd the ones he was taking south. I found the wagon after they had been robbed. The eggs wern't broke, and I hope to sell them in Mobile."

He stopped and asked the clerk how to spell "sincerely", then printed his name. He thought a minute and added a comma next to his name, and then printed "the Yankee spy." He laughed and uttered out loud, "She should remember me now!"

"What's that boy?"

"Oh, it's nothing, I was just talking to myself." He read the letter again. "That should do," Marcus said as he folded the letter and slipped it inside the envelope. The old man took a bottle of glue and sealed the envelope; Marcus purchased a stamp and asked the clerk to mail it for him. Before he left and while he had the chance, he purchased more flour, sugar, peanuts, and filled the back of his wagon with unshelled corn for his animals.

"I normally don't have that corn due to the war. The Army usually confiscates it before I can get it," the clerk related as he totaled Marcus's bill. Marcus paid up and thanked him for his service and the information about the Yankees in the area. As Marcus walked out the door the old man followed him and looked at his wagon and horses. "Boy, if I were you, I'd go on down south about five miles, and take the right fork in the road. That's an old curvy road that is almost abandoned since we have a straighter road now."

"Why should I do that?"

"It will be safer. Rumor has it there are Confederate deserters that are robbing and killing people. Yesterday, I saw four rough-looking characters pass through here going north. You may have passed them."

"Yeah I passed them alright, but I have a hunch they won't be bothering anybody anymore."

"How's that?"

"They're all dead beside the road. Somebody shot all four of them. Where do you think I got those extra horses and mules?" Marcus took his hat off and scratched his head, "Whoever shot them must have killed them last night and didn't see their horses tied back in the woods. I wad'nt gonna leave those fine animals to starve, so I gathered up their stuff and put it in my wagon. I don't think they'll need it in hell."

As Marcus spoke, it was obvious from the delight on the clerk's face, he was glad the four deserters, who had apparently terrorized the area, were dead. "Young man, thank you for killing those ruffians; we will all be safer now."

Marcus turned, "Wait a minute, sir, I just found them. I didn't kill them. You might have to worry about whoever did kill those men. I just took advantage of the situation and took their horses and stuff." Marcus turned to his wagon to go, then hesitated and turned back, "If you're interested, them dead men are several miles back up the road there. I pulled their bodies off road out into a field. Wait a day or two, and I imagine you will smell them." He mounted the wagon and thanked the old man again for his advice, supplies, and letter.

Before he left, the elderly clerk walked out beside Marcus and added quietly, almost in a whisper as if someone was listening, "Boy, I would take the right fork in the road and go the back way. Like I mentioned, the road is curvy and grown up, and It will take you longer, but with horses and mules in short supply, it will be safer and less likely to run into trouble. Right now, we have all kinds of Yankees, deserters, and Rebels going up and down this road, any of whom may take your animals. To be honest, I doubt you would make it the next fifty miles. The bandits will steal them, the Yankees could confiscate them, and the Confederates would seize them and pay you with worthless Confederate money."

"Then I think I'll take the right fork. None of the other choices sound too good to me." With that Marcus bid him goodbye and headed south again.

Before he arrived at the split in the road, he passed two different horsemen and one man walking. When they saw the horses tied to the back of his wagon, they all stopped him and questioned him about their sale. Marcus said he was taking them home to do the spring plowing soon. When he came to the fork in the road, he stopped and looked down the narrow wooded lane. Since its lack of use, the road had small trees knee-high coming up and limbs filling the pathway, making it appear difficult to pass, but on closer inspection, he saw old wheel marks that indicated wagons had recently traveled the road.

Still being in a dangerous "no man's land," and after thinking about his choices, Marcus came to a decision and turned his mules to take the more difficult, but hopefully safer route.

The road twisted and turned and crossed steep ravines. The woods were thick, and Marcus reckoned in another year the small saplings would be too large for a wagon to pass over them. Several times, he had to stop and remove an old dead tree or limb that had fallen in his path, but he steadily proceeded forward. By the end of the day, he had not seen another soul, only passing several abandoned homesteads along the road. Once, he heard a man popping a whip and yelling commands as if he were driving oxen. Another time, he heard the rumble of many horsemen passing to the east. Marcus concluded the new road ran east of him, sometimes close, and sometimes far away. When he heard the horsemen, Marcus was thankful he had taken the old road. Three times that day before dark, he came upon other roads that crossed his path, some small and some busy, but at each intersection he saw his road continuing on ahead of him. An hour before dark, he came to a beautiful flowing stream. Selected rocks had been carefully placed in the road to pave the stream bed to make a safer crossing. The gurgling sound of the water seemed to ask Marcus to stop there for the night. Having seen nobody all day, Marcus felt safe and decided to camp there. By the time he bedded down under his wagon for the night, he had eaten well, the animals were fed and watered, and with four pistols loaded, he was feeling secure.

Usually, after a long day, Marcus was sleepy. He was that night, but he couldn't sleep. He kept remembering and seeing pictures of himself killing the four deserters. He did not remember the event from his own eyes, but he sensed he was watching himself shoot them, as if he was not the shooter, but a bystander. He could not distinguish whether it was a dream, or what he was really thinking. After an hour or so of this anguish, he eventually fell asleep. Over the next few weeks, this memory plagued his slumber.

The next morning Marcus was awakened by his horses neighing, snorting, and stamping their feet. That meant something was astir.

He threw his cover back to see a grizzly old man with shabby clothes and a long graying beard standing above him silhouetted against the sky. Very startled, Marcus reached for a pistol in his belt.

"Whoa, boy, whoa, I ain't here to hurt you. If I intended to kill you, I'd a done it 'fore you woke up." His words and calm behavior caused Marcus to relax and take his hand off his pistol. The old man turned and spit tobacco juice on the ground as he turned and sat down on the front wagon wheel, placing the butt of his rifle on the ground with both hands gripping the barrel, obvious showing Marcus he was a friend.

"Marcus crawled from under the wagon. "Sorry for reaching for my gun, but you scared me."

"Yeah, I guess I might scare anybody. What you doing on this old road? It's a lot smoother and easier 'bout a mile east of here."

"To save my hide, sir. I stopped in a little country store yesterday, and a man told me that road over there was dangerous. He told me about this old road, and until I saw you, I haven't seen nary a soul. What are you doing out this morning?"

"Looking at you right now."

"Where do you stay?"

The old man yawned revealing few teeth, "I lives on the side of a knoll about two hills over. I come over that hill thar," pointing back behind him, "And I smelt your far' smoke from last night. I know'd somebody was around here, and then I heard a mule. I eased down here to see who was in the woods. I guess I scared the mules a little. He reached behind him and pulled out a dead squirrel by the tail from an old worn, blood-stained hunting sack, the bulge in the knapsack indicating there was more game inside. "I was huntin' squirrels this morning, nearly killed a deer, but didn't take the shot, too fer away. It's getting hard for me to get powder for my rifle, so I have to be sure before I shoot. My eyes aren't as good as they use' to be."

Knowing the old man was friendly and just going about his business, Marcus welcomed him to camp as he came out from under the wagon and put the top hat on his head.

"That's a fine hat thar' you are a wear'in. I'd swap you a half dozen squirrels fer it. I never saw a bird feather like that 'fore."

Marcus took it off and stroked the feather in the brim, "Yeah it is rare, but this hat belonged to a friend of mine. He got killed by Rebel deserters a few days ago." Marcus looked up from the hat and changed the subject, "Are you hungry?"

"I am always huntin' for something to eat," he said as he grinned and started laughing. "Don't you git it, huntin', I am always out here in the woods huntin' for something to eat," proud of his play on words.

Marcus laughed, "Yes, I get it, that's funny. Then stay around, and I'll get those coals stirred up and we'll eat some of them eggs and bacon I bought at the store yesterday. I even have some coffee I got in Nashville."

"You got coffee? I hadn't tasted that brew in more than a year. I can't git it no more. The war stopped that, but here, let me skin one of these tree rats. I got plenty this morning. Seemed like every tree had a dozen in it; save your bacon." In a few minutes, the two new friends were helping each other, and soon, a good breakfast was prepared. They sat on the ground eating and swigging the hot coffee, Marcus listening to tales about bear hunting, and the old-timer learning about the war. Marcus could see the old man just needed someone to spend some time with.

After breakfast, the old hunter helped Marcus pack and stow his gear. He told Marcus if he would wait there, while he delivered his squirrels to a widow and her family, he would return and lead him through the hills and get him on a road to Birmingham. Marcus agreed and after a short while, he soon saw the old man running back through the woods, as if he were a youngster again, getting to do something fun. He jumped up on the wagon seat beside Marcus and the two set forth. Marcus felt he had met a true friend and was glad to have him along. He hoped his new friend, however, would not meet the fate of his other travelers.

Marcus had indicated to the old-timer to keep him off the beaten path as much as possible until they were in Confederate-controlled territory. Sometimes they traveled a good road, and at other times, the old woodsman directed him through narrow ravines, next to steep drop-offs cut out of a hillside, and through swamps. Once, while crossing a bog, the wagon got stuck and it took the extra horses and mules to pull it out of the mire. The belly of the wagon was dragging the mud, and Marcus hoped the detonators stayed dry. That would be a tragedy to go through all the aches and pains to finally deliver the bombs and they were ruined because of water.

At last, after another four days in the deep woods and mountainous area they emerged on a well-traveled road. The old man looked at Marcus, "It's been nice travelin' with ya, boy. This is where I get off. You turn left here and go down thar about five miles, I'm a gessin', and you'll find a little town. Go straight through town and you'll be on the way to Birmingham."

"Where are you going?"

"Home, boy, I imagine Widow Smith's about to run out of them squirrels by now."

"You got a long walk ahead of your sir."

"Not as long as you think. We had to go around curves and out of our way sometimes in the wagon, but I'll be home in two days. I'll go over some of those hills and go twis't as fast. It want take me long. Have a good day, now." He thought a second, "Are you sure you won't swap something for that hat?"

"Naw, I can't do that, but wait, I've got something for you." Marcus jumped down and looked in his leather saddle-bag and pulled out a bag of black powder and some lead bullets. "I remember you said you couldn't buy powder and lead. I can spare a little, so I hope this will help keep you in ammunition for a while." In addition, Marcus gave him $25 in Confederate money and thanked him for his help. With that done, Marcus turned his wagon south and started for Birmingham. He soon found the small town and stopped briefly to buy some grain for his animals. His supplies were holding up and he wanted to get out of town as soon as possible.

Marcus did not want the job he was doing now. He was tired of torpedoes. He wanted to go home. How many more bullets could he dodge? How long would his angels protect him? As he proceeded south, he came up with a plan. He would stop the first Confederate authority he met and turn the detonators over to them. He wanted to turn east now and head for Buckhead. The farther south he went, the longer it would take him to get home. He wanted to find Bonnie and he was beginning to get homesick again.

As he traveled south to Birmingham, he noticed the traffic on the road picked up. He passed many wagons, mounted riders, walkers, and hog-herders as he got closer to Birmingham. Outside the large city, he came upon what he wanted to see, hundreds if not thousands of white tents pitched in neat orderly rows with men parading and marching, and officers on steeds watching and directing the columns dressed in gray. There was a large Confederate flag next to a tent with brigade flags close by. Marcus was excited now, that his adventure was almost over.

He was disappointed though he wouldn't be a hero and have a statue in the park, knowing the only two men who knew about his exploits were rotting in a field somewhere behind him. But he would forgo the hero status until later. His urge to go home was overwhelming his patriotic duty as he drove his mules up to the perimeter of the camp headquarters. There was a group of soldiers milling around the edge of the camp, apparently on guard. As he approached, two of the guards in tattered gray coats stepped into the road. One of the soldiers had on blue pants, obviously the pants of a Union soldier. They looked similar to the deserters he had killed earlier.

"Halt, sir, what's your business?"

"I have some important information to tell your commanding officer. I must see the commanding general, not a low officer. What I have to tell is very important."

"Pull your wagon over here out of the way until I can get an officer out here."

"I need to see the general I said, not an officer."

"I'm sorry, but you will have to work your way up to a general. He's not going to come out here and talk to some kid who rides up in a shabby, broken down wagon."

Marcus, having been in the Army, knew what he had to deal with and apologized to the private, "I understand; sorry I got so loud, but make sure you stress how important this is." The private walked over and entered a tent. In a few minutes, a young lieutenant exited the tent, adjusting his hat and pulling on his coat to make sure he made a proper presentation. Then he followed the private back to Marcus.

"Good morning boy, what kind of information do you need to tell me?"

"Sir, I do not mean to demean your rank, but I need to speak with a general. The outcome of the war may depend on this information."

The officer said nothing, but instead, walked around the wagon, horses and mules, surveying the dilapidated wagon in front of him and wondered about the menagerie. "Where did you come from? Do you live around here?"

"No sir, I have come from Louisville. I must see a higher officer before I tell you more. Please! Let me speak to your captain or Major. What I am going to tell them must be kept secret."

The officer stepped close to the wagon and looked in. "Are you bringing the Army some saddles and horses? Is that why you've stopped?"

"No sir, it is more important than that. I do have something in my wagon, but what I have in my head, what I know, that's whats so valuable to our cause."

"Very well, let me climb up with you, and we will go over to Captain Kent's tent and see what he says." He dismissed the guards and rode with Marcus about a quarter mile to another large tent. On the way, Marcus told him he was a private in Hood's Division and had traveled all the way from Maryland and continued to present his case to see a general and speak with him in private. The lieutenant pointed where to park the wagon and jumped out. "Stay here. I'll talk to him on your behalf." Knowing now Marcus was a soldier, he turned and saluted; Marcus saluted back.

Marcus waited a half hour and finally the lieutenant returned, "He wants you to come in. He will hear what you have to say."

"Sir, can you get someone to watch the wagon while I am inside? It is important that you do this, believe me."

He looked at the wagon, "This old pile of sticks? No one's gonna steal this rolling junk in an Army camp."

"Please, you will find out later why I am asking you to do this."

He looked at the old wagon, took his hat off and scratched his head, turned and ordered a private nearby to watch the wagon while they were inside. The two men entered the tent and saluted. Marcus removed his strange hat and held it by his side, still standing at attention. The captain, without standing, returned the salute, "At ease, now, private, what do you have to tell me."

"Sir, like I told the lieutenant, I don't want to demean your rank, but what I have to say is so valuable I must tell a higher officer. I cannot trust anyone lower in rank than general."

The captain was incensed. He jumped out of his chair, "What do you mean you can't trust me, private? How dare you question my patriotism? You will tell me now, or I will throw you in the stockade for insubordination."

Marcus understood he had come to the end of the road and had to reveal now what he knew. "Very well, sir, but I must talk to you in private. What I know is top secret. It was told to me by a secret agent on the Ohio River who got his orders from Jefferson Davis."

"Very well, you're dismissed lieutenant. I will talk to you later."

Marcus had ruffled the captain's feathers and tried to express regret for not trusting the captain. In a few moments, the gray haired veteran calmed down and, in a manner, defended his temporary outburst of anger. "I have been in the Army all of my life, even fought in the Mexican War, and resent anyone who might question my discipline. Sit down; tell me what you have to say."

"Sir, after you hear what I am going to tell you, I feel you will understand why I thought only a general would do."

He scooted his canvas camp chair closer to the small table in front of the captain and motioned him close so only he would hear what he was going to say. "Sir, I fought and was captured at Sharpsburg but managed to escape."

"I hear that was a terrible scrape."

"Yes, it was; I can verify that. But I eventually made my way to Pittsburgh and from there down the Ohio River floating on a small boat. I hoped to make it to Louisville and then on down to Nashville and eventually home to Georgia."

"Did you steal the boat?"

"No sir, I convinced a man in Pittsburgh that I was a Union soldier trying to get home. Like you, he was a veteran of the Mexican War and felt sorry for me. Anyway, while on the way down, I met a Confederate agent smuggling detonators into the South using the river. After he learned I was a Confederate soldier, he revealed how his operation worked and asked me to journey with him, and if he got killed, he asked me if I would finish the mission."

"I see, tell me more."

Hoping to get his statue in the park back, Marcus related their destruction of the Union gunboats. The captain leaned back in his chair, "Yeah, we heard about that all the way down here. So that was you?"

"Yes sir, but let me go on."

"No, this is getting interesting; let me get Colonel Rutherford over here. I want him to hear this. I hope you aren't making a fool out of me."

"No, I swear, every word I've spoken is true."

The captain hollered through the canvas tent for the lieutenant to come back inside. "Go get the Colonel and bring him over here. Tell him to hurry. I want him to hear what this man has done, or at least, what he says he's done." In a few minutes they heard two horses gallop up and a Confederate Colonel came in. After the proper salutes, introductions, and a short review of the story, Marcus continued.

"After Cincinnati, we continued on southwest. Unfortunately on a severely cold night, the Professor froze to death. I shot him in the back of the head to convince the authorities I had killed the man who had sunk the gunboats. I told them we had met up on the river, he was alone, and one night when he was drunk, he bragged about his accomplishment. When I got the chance, I shot him in the head.

They believed my story. They stopped searching for him then, and I was free to float on down to Louisville."

Both officers kept adjusting their chairs, moving closer to Marcus's soft voice. "In Louisville, I delivered the boat to a Mr. McKenzie as I was instructed. However, I didn't know Mr. McKenzie was a Federal spy and was expecting me. At that time I had the Professor's detonators in my boat. Mr. McKenzie informed me that he was a Confederate agent in on the smuggling operation and would get me a wagon to take them south to Nashville, which he did. Later that day I became suspicious and discovered they had switched the detonators with decoys that wouldn't work. Knowing their plan, later that night I got them back and escaped with the real detonators instead of the boxes of fakes they wanted me to take. Thinking I had left earlier in the day they were never aware of my ruse. I was lucky to have gotten out of there alive.

After several other mishaps, I finally got down to Nashville. The Professor told me if he died, I would find his contact at 'The River Roost,' a tavern on the edge of the river. He would be wearing this hat." Marcus reached down and picked up the odd looking hat with the red tipped feather. "I found this man and delivered the detonators. They encouraged me to finish the mission with them, but I had done my duty, and I wanted to go home. However, they were going my way, so I traveled on with them to the Tennessee River where we secretly crossed at night. The next day, I was slow to arouse, and they went on ahead. Near noon, when I caught up with them, I found they had been murdered. The killers had abandoned the wagon, but took the mules and this hat worn by John Gibbons. The detonators were still hidden in the wagon, so I hooked up my two mules and pulled the wagon off the road. It wasn't long until I saw Army deserters ride by, one of which, had on this hat. They did not see me, so I followed them until they camped. That night I killed them. That's why I have the four saddles and two extra mules."

"Do you have the detonators?"

"Yes, I do. The wagon you are going to see looks like it's about done its last duty, but the people in Nashville built it to look that way so nobody would want it. It has a false bottom in it. There are about 160 detonators under the floor behind the seat."

"I've got to see this," the Colonel said as he stood up and went outside with the Captain close behind and Marcus following. Marcus said they would have to tear the wagon apart to find them, but he told them if they looked close and measured, they could see there was a hiding place under the floor.

After both officers determined there could be a space there, they turned to Marcus and asked where they were to go. Marcus told him they had not told him who they were going to meet, but he knew they were taking them to Mobile. Marcus added, "One night when we were eating, they mentioned a naval officer; I don't remember his rank, but I remember his name."

"What name do you remember?"

"It was a silly name similar to mine. My name is Mills and the officer's name was Milligan. He had the same name as my Sunday school teacher back in my Baptist Church. When I was little, I thought her name sounded funny. That's why I remembered it, I guess."

The officers looked at each other; finally the Colonel said, "I think we should take this man to General O'Malley."

Marcus grinned, "That's what I was trying to tell you when I came into camp. Let me see a general."

In less than half an hour, Marcus and the two officers along with a dozen cavalry guards, were escorting the wagon to General O'Malley's home near the center of Birmingham. The story was told again. However, after the story, the wagon was pulled to a secure enclosed shed. Marcus told them to dismantle the seat and they could see the detonators they had so carefully packed. The last board was pried away and there they were, nearly 160 of them. The general reached in and retrieved one. He unwrapped and examined it. "Where did you say they came from?"

"England, sir. The Professor told me they had been made in England, and sent to Canada. They were smuggled across Pennsylvania to the Ohio River. The old Professor picked them up there and brought them down the Ohio. After he died on the river, I took them down to here." Marcus turned to the Captain and Colonel, "That's why I told you I needed to see a general."

"That's right! Why didn't your officers bring him to me immediately? This is of major importance. Here, put this back in the wagon and repair the wagon. Colonel, have the Captain ready to leave for Mobile in the morning at sunrise. Take a dozen cavalry with you and don't let this wagon get out of your site." He looked at its pitiful appearance, "Are you sure it will get there?"

Marcus spoke up, "Yes, General, it looks worn out, but John and Colonel James said it was very strong."

"Very well, then. I think the detonators should stay in the wagon hidden like they are. If by some miracle, the Yankees captured the old wagon they would pay it no mind, never knowing what was inside, and most likely leave it be. If the old gal got them this far, I imagine she'll get them to Mobile. When you arrive there, find the naval headquarters and ask for an officer named Milligan. If you can't find him, then talk to the highest naval officer you can find. Is that clear?"

Both officers saluted and came to attention and by coincidence, answered in unison, "Yes general." The general saluted back and dismissed them to go do their duty.

Before the group broke up, Marcus asked the general if he might speak with him alone. He and the general went in a private office at his house. "As I told you, I was wounded in the war and have endured much pain and suffering to deliver these detonators. Several times I wanted to give up, but my patriotic duty drove me on. I finished the mission. By chance, I have secured four horses and four mules and that wagon. Would you be so kind as to let me keep those animals and take them home? My folks are having a hard time and need to plant a crop next spring."

The General studied the look on Marcus's kind boyish face. "Marcus, all the South is bleeding right now. We could use those animals in the war."

"Please sir, besides what I endured in the war, I nearly froze to death, I was nearly hung, I helped blow up two ships, and caused much chaos at Sharpsburg. I also stayed with this mission to get the detonators to you. You know, sir, eight animals won't make a difference in the war, but eight animals back home can be used to feed lots of folks who are hungry right now."

"All right, Marcus, you can have your property. I will write a certificate giving you the rights and ownership of these animals, but you must do one more thing."

"Yes sir, what's that?"

"Finish this mission. There's more knowledge in your head about this operation than anyone else has. No one can do this but you. If you will do that for me, I will give you what you want, and I will also give you an honorable discharge from the Army so they can't enlist you again. How's that deal?"

Marcus thought a moment, then looked up and smiled, "That's a deal. Thank you sir; my family will appreciate what you have done for me." He reached in his jacket and handed him the photograph of Bonnie, "She will appreciate it, too. She's given me a reason to endure what I have done. I've gotta get to Texas though, and find her, after crops are in next summer."

The general gazed at the picture, nodding his head, "She's a beautiful girl. I understand why you wish to get back home." He looked up with a look of praise in his eyes, "I also want to admire and thank you for what you have accomplished. You are a real hero."

"Thank you sir; I'm proud of what I've done." He saluted and the general dismissed him. Marcus left and climbed up on the wagon and secured the reins. Before they left, the general came to the door and ordered his officers back inside. He told them Marcus would take the detonators to Mobile and would retain ownership of the horses and mules, wagon, and any belongings inside. He also ordered them to get the proper papers together that gave him an honorable discharge. "And one last thing, make sure the boy gets a bath and clean quarters tonight. Dismissed."

44

All was well the next morning when Marcus clicked his tongue to move his mules forward. The mules leaned into their harness and the wagon moved forward. He was refreshed, bathed, and rested, had eaten a good breakfast and was ready for the long trip to Mobile. The Colonel and a dozen cavalry were ready to escort and guard their valuable cargo. The soldiers calculated it would take ten to fourteen days to get to Mobile, depending on the road conditions and the speed of the wagon.

At last, Marcus felt safe riding along amid the horse soldiers ahead and behind him. Sometimes the Colonel would ride on the wagon with Marcus. Each night they bivouacked in a town. Marcus, although still a private in the Army, was treated with great respect, more like an officer, and at night given good quarters in an inn. Half way to Mobile it began to rain, and they sloshed along in the drizzle for two days. They lost a day when they had to wait for a swollen stream to go down after the heavy rains had washed a bridge out, forcing the caravan to go upstream ten miles to a larger bridge. But after two weeks, the entourage entered the outskirts of Mobile with additional horsemen that had been sent out to meet them.

Before they had left Birmingham, the General had wired the commanding naval officer and asked about an officer or agent named Milligan. The Navy wired back that no such officer by that name could be found, but on their arrival, they should bring the cargo to the naval facility next to the bay.

On the outskirts of the city, they were met by a dozen horsemen clad in gray and were escorted to naval headquarters on the west side of Mobile Bay. There, they secured Marcus's animals and belongings in a stable at the facility and attached a new pair of mules to the wagon. From there, the wagon was escorted to a large wooden warehouse built on a large pier. As the mules entered the building, the clopping sound made by their hoofs on the wooden floor mixed with the sounds of hammers hitting steel and the roar of furnaces. The building was filled with craftsmen working on a variety of projects. Marcus noticed sparks flying from a large iron ship being constructed, similar to the ones he had sunk. After they entered the building, the doors were shut behind them.

The cavalry waited outside and were replaced by sailors who came inside with the wagon. Marcus was ordered to park the wagon near some windows overlooking the pier and bay. Although rather cool outside, the building was warm due to the furnaces inside. At that time a naval officer, an admiral in the Confederate Navy, came out of an office at the front of the building, followed by an aide. The Colonel who accompanied Marcus dismounted, and the two officers exchanged salutes. The two officers mumbled to each other, then the naval officer slapped the colonel on the back and smiles broke the formal gathering. The two officers returned to the admiral's office and closed the door. After half an hour they emerged, and Marcus heard the admiral ask, "Let me see what you have. These must be the little iron devils we've been waiting for. We were beginning to wonder if they made the journey south or not."

The Colonel introduced Marcus, who jumped down from the wagon and saluted. "This is the man who got involved in this mission, the boy I was telling you about. Yes, indeed, he is a hero. As I was saying, Marcus here came on board this mission after he met the

Professor one cold night on the river. Without his hard work and sacrifice we would have lost these weapons. I want you to hear his story. He should be rewarded for completing the mission."

"Yes, indeed, I must hear his story," but anxious to see his deadly cargo, turned toward the wagon. "Now, let's see what we have here."

The Colonel asked Marcus how to open the wagon. Marcus asked for a pry bar and hammer, and soon they were pulling the little deadly eggs from their wrappings. The naval officer picked one up and admired and inspected the little deadly gem. He held it up in front of his eyes and rotated it around, "These seem to be different from the last load, but I am sure we will figure them out." He ordered his men to unload the rest and take them to the corner of the building where a metal shop occupied the space. There were steel tables with anvils and vices. Cabinets and shelves occupied the walls in the corner that were filled with files, hammers, and many other tools Marcus had never seen.

A steel-wheeled cart was rolled out and the detonators were gently placed in a box filled with wood shavings and rolled over to other tables near the workshop. There were furnaces in the building, but the detonators, containing the explosive black powder never came near them. The small bombs were secured in an isolated area away from the fires, locked safely in a metal cabinet.

The Colonel, who had escorted Marcus to Mobile, turned to Marcus, "Private, you have delivered the eggs. I thank you again for your service to your country. Your duty is done. However, I want you to stay around a day or two so we can get more detailed information about your journey, people you met, things like that. After those interrogations, I see no reason you can't take your belongings and head home." As he finished the statement, he reached inside his coat pocket and pulled out an envelope. "These are the papers you requested the other day concerning your belongings. This letter gives you permission to keep the wagon and all of your animals. Also included is your honorable discharge."

Marcus reached and took the papers and saluted, "Thank you, Colonel. I appreciate that."

"You're welcome. It has been a privilege to meet you." Showing much admiration, he stood and gazed at Marcus a moment, then added, "Oh yes, one more thing, the Admiral is hosting a party in your honor Saturday night at his house. He wants the other officers to meet a real hero of this war and hear your story. I wish I could attend, but my horsemen and I are going back to Birmingham tomorrow morning."

"The Admiral has invited me to his house? Oh, I can't do that. I'm just a poor country boy who never spoke in front of a group. I appreciate what you are trying to do for me, but I need to get started for home." The Admiral, standing by listening, interrupted, "Marcus, don't be afraid. Even though we wear gold stripes, most of us are just country boys, too. Please accept, before I ask the Colonel to order you to attend." Seeing no way out, he agreed.

Marcus was ordered then to take the wagon to the livery stable on the naval base and leave it with his other belongings. The Colonel appointed a sergeant to secure a new Army uniform for Marcus. After all, he was still a private in the Army and needed a uniform to wear to the party. As Marcus drove the wagon out of the barn, he was both happy and sad, mostly disappointed he could not immediately leave for home. He looked up at the sky and made a comment to his guardian angel, "You finally let me down. You know, I may die of fright if I have to speak to all those people at that party."

As Marcus drove away in the wagon, a small man stood by the door watching. Dressed in civilian clothes, he looked more like a riverboat gambler than a secret agent in the Confederate Navy. The guard, not recognizing the little man, questioned him at the door. The little man removed a leather wallet from his coat and removed a paper for the guard to read. The guard saluted, and the small stranger ambled slowly over to an empty chair, sat down, and removed his hat; a tall hat with a red band and a red tipped-feather, and placed it on a table.

Marcus drove the wagon to the stables and corrals where the cavalry horses, mules, and army wagons were kept and repaired. One of the officers who rode with Marcus in the wagon gave the attendants orders to grease the wagon and feed the mules. The orderly removed his hat and scratched his head, looking at the old wagon, and wondered why it wasn't scrapped instead. The officer noticed his look of disgust at having to grease an old crate like that, "Sergeant, don't question why. Just have this ready in the morning. In addition, repair the reins and harness where necessary. It looks as if it has been cut in several places." Marcus was appreciative they were giving him the old wagon.

Another sergeant asked Marcus to follow him, and they would find him a uniform. Soldiers could be seen in all directions practicing the various army routines. It was a long walk to the commissary, most likely a half mile. After his long journey floating in boats, riding horses and wagons, but seldom walking; his legs were tired as they entered the store. The sergeant opened the door and hurried to enter as three soldiers came out; the first soldier was talking to someone behind him and did not see Marcus and bumped him accidently. He quickly turned around and saw Marcus. He stared directly into Marcus's face with a startled look on his with his mouth agape. Forgetting he had just purchased a pack of tobacco, he dropped it on the floor and grabbed Marcus on the sides of his arms and screamed, "Marcus, Marcus, is that you?"

Marcus instantly recognized the uniformed soldier, "Wendell, you're Wendell Cade from Buckhead, Georgia! What are you doing down here?"

Wendell was a friend who grew up on a small farm close to Marcus in Buckhead. Wendell did not join the Army when Marcus entered, instead stayed home to help his father work a crop. Except for a letter or two, the best friends had not seen each other since. No two friends could have been closer, and the two hugged and slapped each other as if they were long-lost brothers. There was a bench on the porch, and Wendell told him to have a seat so they catch up on lost times. The sergeant, realizing Marcus would be busy for a while, went on inside to find a uniform.

With tears of excitement in his eyes Marcus asked, "Have you been home lately? How's my mother?"

"Yes, I was home just the other day. I just got back here about a week ago, and your mother, she's fine, everyone's fine. I stopped by there to see if they had heard from you." He stopped smiling a moment, "But they think you've been killed. They got a letter saying you were killed on the battlefield at Sharpsburg."

"I nearly was, but here I am." Then he anxiously asked, "What about Bonnie? Have they heard from Bonnie?" Marcus reached in his coat and pulled the worn picture of Bonnie out and held it for him to see. "She sent me this right before Sharpsburg. She said they were going to Texas."

"Not anymore! She's back home in Buckhead. After they got to Texas, her mother got sick, bad sick. From what I heard, she had a nervous breakdown. Bonnie's father decided to come back home. He figured she would have a better chance to get well back in Georgia. They are staying in that old house down on her Uncle David's place."

"Did you see her? You say she's in Buckhead?"

"Yes, Marcus I saw her." He looked at her picture again, "She's pretty. She's the prettiest girl I ever saw. When they told me you were dead, I thought about courtin' her when I got home."

"No, Wendell, don't you dare; she's my girl, you know that."

"Don't worry, I understand; I'm just glad you're alive," as he gave Marcus a big bear hug again.

"Did you see Fetch?"

"Oh yeah, he remembered me. Your Pa said he really missed you and sat out by the front gate everyday waiting for you to come down the road. He said after you left, the dog wouldn't eat for a long time."

"Ah, old Fetch. I can't wait to get home and hug his old hide." Marcus focused back on Wendell, "When did you enlist? I remember we tried to get you to go with us that day we left, but you stayed home to help your Pa."

"Yeah, Pa and me got that crop in that fall, but after the harvest I got a letter that said I must enlist." Marcus learned Wendell had been sent west rather than to Virginia when he had enlisted. For the most part, he had seen no combat. When they were young lads, he had broken an ankle when Marcus dared him to jump off the barn, and ever since, he had walked with a slight limp. Not realizing it at the time, the broken ankle proved to be a blessing now, and as a result, Wendell had been assigned to the Army post near Mobile and spent most of his time doing guard duty and clerking, rather than risking his life on a bloody battlefield. However, on other occasions, his company was used for other duties, from guarding prisoners of war to burial detail and even to firing squads.

The other two soldiers with Wendell also took a seat and listened to the childhood friends recall their most exciting adventures. After a few minutes, Wendell introduced his army pals to Marcus. Marcus told Wendell about his big adventure and how his journey was ending in Mobile. He told them he was to be honored later in the week at the Admiral's house for what he had done. Wendell and the two soldiers congratulated him and slapped him on the back. "You are a brave man. I didn't know you had it in you?"

"Frankly, I didn't either. I often prayed, when we went into battle, I wouldn't run. My guardian angels have kept me safe on more than one occasion." As the two friends laughed and swapped stories about the past, the other two soldiers soon joined in, and when the sergeant returned with a uniform, he sensed the four soldiers had known each other all of their lives. They were throwing their heads back with their mouths wide open with laughter, slapping their knees, and sometimes pointing at each other and giggling, like school boys playing jokes on each other. Marcus had not enjoyed laughter like this since the war started. He was so relieved his family was well and Bonnie was home and he would be going to see them soon. At last, all was well.

When Marcus saw the sergeant standing at the door, he stood up and saluted, as did the other men. The sergeant came on the porch, "I hate to end the fun, but here, take this Marcus." He pushed a package into his hands. "It might not fit you perfectly, but I never saw a Confederate uniform that did. There's some other under garments you will need, too."

Marcus turned to his new friends, "I must go with him now. I'm going home in a few days and need a place to stay." Wendell stepped forward. "Sergeant, since we are guards and never leave this place, we stay in permanent wooden quarters and not a tent. We even have an extra cot in our quarters since Quincy left. Let him stay with us tonight. He'll be more comfortable than in a tent."

Another soldier added, "And he can get a bath over there, too."

The sergeant grinned, "I am sure the Admiral will appreciate that." The other soldiers also pleaded to let him stay, like children asking their mother to let a friend spend the night. The sergeant thought a moment and then nodded, "Yes that will be good. I'll get the captain to temporarily assign him to your company and squad. He will be easier to find there than out there in all those tents. I will send your sergeant the proper papers to transfer him to your squad." He turned to walk away, then stopped, and informed Marcus, "The Colonel told me to tell you to be sure and wear that funny hat with the red-tipped feather Saturday night. He wants you to wear it when you tell your story."

Marcus got a "goose-feather feeling" again about having to tell his story in front of a crowd. "Sergeant, please tell the Admiral, I can't do that. I might die. I'd rather be back at Sharpsburg than have to go to that banquet and talk in front of those people," he pleaded, not really believing that, but stressing the point to the sergeant. Marcus now, just wanted "a good lettin' alone."

"Marcus, what are you afraid of? There won't be a crowd, just an Admiral and some officers with their wives, sitting at a long table; it will be simple. Just tell them what happened, that's all. They are people, just like you and me. Just pretend you're sittin' around your own dinner table telling your story to your folks back home. Can't you do that?"

Marcus looked down and kicked the ground, then looked back at the sergeant, "I guess I can do it."

Wendell jumped in, "Of course you can, come on, let's get you cleaned up. It's still early. When we finish, we can continue our talking. I just can't believe I ran into you like this. Come on." He grabbed Marcus by the arm and yelled back at the sergeant, "Sarge, don't worry, we'll take good care of him."

The three men herded Marcus to the barracks where he washed and shaved. "This is the second bath I've had in two days. I don't believe I've ever been any cleaner than this." Marcus dressed in his baggy uniform and placed the tall unusual hat on his head. Still in a jovial mood, Wendell laughed, "Where did you get a hat like that? I never saw a chicken feather with a red tip. Where did you find a chicken like that?"

"I didn't, stupid, it's painted on there," he laughed back remembering what the Professor had told him. At that point they all sat down around a table, and Marcus related the story about the hat, which led to his entire adventure since he left Sharpsburg. After a half hour, the three soldiers were amazed at what Marcus had done.

Spellbound and in awe with what he heard, Wendell suddenly stood up to show esteem for his friend. "That's amazing, Marcus! You're a hero. No wonder the Admiral wants to give you a party. I doubt one single man has done more to win the war for us."

Marcus grinned back, "Yeah, that's what they say. Colonel James told me he would recommend they build a statue in the park for me, but he was one of the officers I found killed by the wagon. I think my statue died when he did." The three soldiers were silent as his story sunk in. Suddenly, the door opened and their sergeant came in and told them to get their arms immediately. There was a train coming into Mobile with some Union prisoners, and they needed some extra guards at the station until the train left town.

He looked at Marcus, "Who is this, a new recruit?"

"Yes and no, sergeant, he has been assigned to us until Saturday. You'll be getting the paperwork on him soon. He is a friend of mine from Buckhead, Georgia, and a hero."

"Hero or recruit, it don't matter, you guys get ready for guard duty. There will be a wagon here in a quarter hour to pick you up. They need six men."

The men were disappointed they had to leave Marcus. His personality, storytelling, and big toothy grin had gained their respect. Then Wendell remarked, "He's one of us now; he can go with us to guard the train. Come on Marcus, come with us."

"Naw, I can't do that. As you know, I had my experience with a train."

"Ah come on, It won't take long. The train usually stops just long enough to feed the prisoners. I doubt they'll be here more than two hours. Come on and go."

Marcus pondered their request. "How about this instead? How about me just riding along with you, and when we get to the depot, let me just wander around. Since I was a little kid, I always wanted to see Mobile."

His new friends looked at each other, "Yeah, I think that'll work. We'll tell the sergeant. He'll agree to that." So arrangements were made, and Marcus rode the wagon into town. The men had done this duty many times and took their positions so they could cover the front and rear of the train, discouraging any prisoners who might try to stray down the tracks.

They learned the train would be delayed a half hour. Marcus told his friends he wanted to walk downtown and would be back in an hour or so. Marcus was feeling good. He had a little money, a few horses and mules, a wagon, and his beautiful girl waiting for him back home. Things could not be better. He was completely relaxed.

He saw a barber shop. He hadn't had a haircut since Pittsburgh and looked rather shaggy. He had just had a bath and his hair was clean, so he stopped and got trimmed up. While he sat in the chair, he saw his old shoes, the same shoes Miss Lydia gave him back at Shepherdstown. They were falling apart. The Confederate commissary had no shoes, so he had kept what he had. He asked the barber where he might buy a pair of new shoes. The barber said a shoe store could be found in the next block. Marcus paid for his haircut and sought the shoe store. As he strolled down the street, a sparkle caught his eye from a shop window as he passed by. He stopped and noticed the sparkle came from the window of a jewelry store.

"Bonnie; Bonnie is home now, and she's going to be my wife. I need a ring." He left the display and ran inside. An older man in a leather apron was repairing a beautiful necklace. He looked up at Marcus, "Young man, may I be of service?" as he put his small hammer down, rose, and came forward to greet Marcus."

"Yes, I think so. I will be discharged from the Army Saturday and can go home. My girl is waiting for me back home, and I want to give her a wedding ring as soon as I get there." He gave his friendly smile, "She's so pretty, I hope nobody steals her 'fore I get home."

The elderly man questioned what price Marcus wanted to pay for the ring. Marcus estimated he could spend $75 cash in Confederate money and had it in his pocket. The jeweler took the tray of rings from a drawer behind the counter and showed Marcus his choices for that amount of money. Marcus soon selected a flat, shiny gold band from the tray. "I like this one, but how do I know if this will fit her finger?"

"Son, that's no problem. Any jeweler knows how to make a ring larger or smaller."

Marcus looked at the ring and held it to catch the light from the window. "This here is real gold?"

"Not entirely, there's some silver mixed in to make it harder. Pure gold is rather soft."

"Can you write 'Marcus loves Bonnie' on the outside of the ring?"

"Yes indeed, boy, I can do that for a minimal charge."

Marcus continued to stare at the ring. "I want that written so that when she sees the ring, no matter where I am, she will always know I love her." He looked up, "Even if I was dead, she would know I still love her."

"That's nice, young man. You mentioned you have been discharged from the Army. Were you wounded?"

"Yes sir, I was wounded earlier in the war, but since Sharpsburg," the old man interrupted, "You were at Sharpsburg?"

"Yes sir, like I said, after Sharpsburg I have been on a secret mission to get some Navy stuff down here from the North. It's a long story."

"Young man, if you want that ring, I'll put the writing on it for no charge. From what I read, I admire any soldier who went through that fracas. I will be honored to engrave those words for you."

"Then I'll take it. I will be here 'til Saturday. Can you have it ready Saturday morning?"

"It will be ready Saturday morning." Marcus paid the man in Confederate money and continued to the shoe store where he selected a pair of high-top leather shoes for eight dollars. They smelled of new leather and each shoe was made for the proper foot, unlike the Shoddy shoes he had worn after Sharpsburg. Although a little stiff at first, they felt comfortable with his clean stockings.

He made his way back to the station. While he was in the barbershop, he had heard a train whistle several times and expected the train had arrived. When he got to the railroad, he found Wendell standing guard at the end of the tracks. He showed him his new shoes and told him about the ring, and they talked as he watched the prisoners coming out of the closed boxcars. They were herded into an area that was under a roof with open sides. There was an iron fence around the enclosure, and there were soldiers stationed behind the closed gates. There were also many gray clad-guards who had come off the train, too. Marcus estimated there were 400 prisoners to be watched and fed.

Marcus told Wendell he wanted to get a closer look at the prisoners. "Who knows, I figure I shot at some of them," he laughed. He made his way around the depot and came up behind the guards next to the gate. The men had been fed in groups of fifty and then herded under some trees to stretch and relax before being placed on the train again. As he came up to the fence he saw the last group get up and walk back to the nearby train.

Suddenly, he thought he saw the side of a familiar face, but before he could be sure, the man turned away, and Marcus could only see the back of his head. Marcus moved up close to the fence trying to get a closer view, and the men made a left turn to walk parallel with the cars. Marcus had not taken his eye off of the man he had first seen. Then, he got a good look at the other side of his face for a brief moment before another man blocked his view. The man looked like Edward, the man who betrayed him and turned him in. Marcus stayed outside the iron fence and walked parallel with the path of the prisoners. Again he saw Edward. Edward, it had to be Edward. Then Marcus yelled out, "Edward, Edward." The man stopped and turned for a moment, as if someone had gotten his attention, but was pushed on by the men behind him.

Marcus yelled again, and the dark-haired man turned, and Marcus got a good look. It was Edward! At that moment, the man came to the large door of the train car. Marcus yelled again, and the man seemed to react and look for someone in the crowd he recognized. He wanted to hesitate and turn around, but the Confederate guards were urging the men inside. When the man jumped up into the boxcar, he stopped and turned, grabbing the side of the door to hold him there so he could see out. From his higher position, he heard the voice behind the fence cry, "Edward," and caught sight of the face making the noise and tried to raise his hand to wave. Marcus saw a brief smile on the man's face before he was forced back into the shadows of the car. Marcus saw his hand clinging to the door, but as more prisoners jumped up and entered, the hand disappeared.

After what Edward had done to him, he didn't know why he wanted to save his one-time friend. Marcus ran back down to the gates and told the guards to let him through; he needed to talk to a prisoner inside. They said he couldn't enter until the train had gone. "Please, I saw a friend, a Yankee friend who saved my life. Just let me talk to him. Let me in," Marcus insisted as he tried to move the guards aside and push his way in.

Two of the guards grabbed him and roughly pushed him back, "Boy, what's wrong with you? This is a prison train. You'll get yore'self shot acting like a fool around this train. Calm down boy, or we'll put you in the stockade. Marcus stepped back and watched the guards shut and lock the doors. The train began to move causing loud jerks as the slack in the cars tightened. Marcus watched the train leave with the last image of Edward frozen in his mind. He turned to a guard, now standing aside to let Marcus enter, "Where is this train headed?"

"Andersonville."

Marcus did not know about Andersonville. Marcus entered the enclosure and walked out on the tracks where he had last seen Edward and watched the train grow smaller, until it disappeared except for dark smoke that hung in the sky. His faraway stare at the empty track was broken as he saw Wendell and three others guards come into view walking back to their friend. They approached him as the rest of the squad came up from the rear.

When they came close, they could sense something had disturbed Marcus, as he had not moved since they first saw him. His body was there, but it appeared his mind had gone off somewhere far away. "Marcus, are you alright?"

Marcus moved his eyes and looked at Wendell. "I saw a man I once knew on that train. He was the Yankee soldier I thought I had killed at Sharpsburg. Later, by coincidence, I met his mother. I even went back into the Union Army dressed as a civilian to tell him his mother needed him at home." Tears were visible in his eyes. "I could have been shot as a spy after he betrayed me, and for a long time I hated him and swore I would go back and kill him after the war." He hesitated again as the soldiers came nearer to hear his soft voice. "But when I saw him, I felt sorry for him instead. I wanted to save him. I even called to him; I know it was him 'cause he heard his name and looked around. Then he saw me, and I think he tried to wave, but he was pushed inside." Marcus looked at his new friends huddled near him, "A half hour ago I would have killed him, but when I saw him on the train, I wanted to save his life. Why is that? Is there something wrong with me? I escaped from my train. I hope he can escape from his."

Seeing their comrade feeling low, they tried to ease his worry, "I doubt you know that man. It would be a miracle if you saw him again. These men were captured in the west, not back east."

Marcus turned and looked at Wendell, "You don't understand; I've been seeing miracles ever since I left Sharpsburg. I know for sure now that guardian angels are real; 'cause I got one." He hung his head, "You're probably right. I guess I was just seeing things." Then he looked up, "But I will never forget that face. It had to be Edward."

One of the men grabbed Marcus by the shoulder and turned him back toward the depot. The soldiers climbed in and sat down in the floor of the wagon, and they went back to their quarters. By the time the men arrived back at the barracks, Marcus had cheered up and agreed he had not seen Edward, but probably just an unfortunate look- alike soldier headed for prison camp.

The next three days were enjoyed by Marcus. Although food wasn't the greatest due to the shortages of most everything caused by the war, he enjoyed his new friends as he bided his time until the banquet and his discharge from the Army. He became a beloved member of the group, and all the soldiers sensed they had known him all of their life.

45

Saturday finally came, and Marcus tried to relax lying and resting on his cot fearing the night's event. In his head, he pictured a huge banquet hall with hundreds of eyes looking at him, but in reality, like his friend said, "Just imagine you are home sitting around the kitchen table telling what happened on this miraculous and heroic journey."

An iron stove kept the barracks reasonably warm. Marcus lay on his Army bed thinking about what to say. All of the soldiers around Marcus had heard his story. The past few days had enabled Marcus to rehearse, as he was called upon to tell his gallant tale many times. As he rested on the cot and pondered his impending fear, his new friends encouraged him not to worry about his upcoming talk and wished him the best.

Finally, the hour came for him to go. The sergeant who issued him a uniform came in and insured he was properly attired and he had his top hat instead of the forage cap issued to all soldiers. "You look good and smell much better than you did the other day. Come with me." The sergeant had a wagon pulled by a single horse tied outside. "The Colonel told me to do this proper, so rather than walk, I borrowed a wagon from the commissary." As the two men left the barracks, they were cheered by his friends and other comrades who gathered around to wish him well.

To get to the Admiral's house, they left the army base and traveled down a main street to the wealthier part of town. Wealthy merchants, manufacturers, and plantation owners had their houses in the area. The Admiral's home stood out from the others that night by the number of horses and carriages tied to hitching posts next to the street. Marcus had a touch of "goose-feather" fear as the wagon stopped and he saw the massive house in front of him. There were guards protecting the area who saluted as he jumped from the wagon. Marcus eyed the large estate and imagined to himself, "If God lived in a house, it would have to be one like this."

The sergeant pushed Marcus forward bringing him out of his momentary stare. As he approached the door, the guards came to attention as Marcus climbed up the high steps to go inside. Never in his life, not since he was baptized at home in the creek, had he ever received such honor and respect. The sergeant escorted Marcus inside where he was greeted by a servant and escorted further into a large room, where the room was brought to attention. All the well-dressed ladies and men in gray uniforms turned to meet their new hero. The servant announced for all people present to meet and greet Private Marcus Mills from Buckhead, Georgia. Everyone clapped and both a general and an admiral came forward and stood beside Marcus.

Marcus had removed his hat when he had entered the house, but the Admiral insisted he put it back on. "Ladies and gentlemen, gather here," the Admiral spoke out. "You are in the presence of a real hero. You could almost say a one-man army. The feats this man has performed since September 17th are remarkable. With brave men like Private Mills, we will never lose the war. I have asked him to tell his story after we dine. You will be very impressed with what you hear, as I was." People cheered and the two dozen attendees moved forward to greet Marcus. Marcus shook both men's and women's hands, not aware to kiss the ladies' hands. Officers, already knowing about his survival at Sharpsburg, asked Marcus questions about his journey. Some asked him about how he had survived Sharpsburg and was it as bad as had been written. In a half an hour it was announced dinner was served, and the group, still enthralled with the handsome young man with the heartwarming smile, moved into the formal dining room where everyone found their assigned seats.

Marcus had never eaten a formal meal. He was ignorant about what to do, how to hold a fork, or how to act, but he sat down where they told him. He watched the others and mimicked what the other guests did. There were twenty-four people at the table. Marcus had never seen such a long table. The table was adorned with flowers, and Marcus wondered where they picked the petals this time of year. Formally dressed men came out of the kitchen, and people turned up their long stemmed crystal glasses to be served. When everyone's glass was full, they raised their glasses and gave a toast to their guest. When the server had offered Marcus wine, he declined saying his mother didn't approve. A lady sitting next to him motioned for the server to return and held up Marcus's glass to be filled. Marcus, in the midst of the toasts, still refused to drink the wine, but smiled and nodded, thanking everyone for their kindness. He grinned and said, "If I drink the wine I won't be able to tell my story." Everyone laughed and gave Marcus a hurrah.

Marcus's smile was the sort that welcomed a stranger to be his friend, dimples forming in his cheek when he did so and showing part of his upper front teeth. He also had the kindest soft blue eyes. If he had a sister, people thought, she must be a beautiful girl. Marcus had worn his hat during his introduction, the general wanting his guests to see the memento from his journey.

People sipped the wine, and shortly after, dinner was served. The plates of food were brought out on trays and placed in front of the guests. They served roasts, potatoes, carrots, peas, with fresh tomatoes, along with peaches that had been canned earlier in the year. In addition to wine, water, tea, and coffee were served. Marcus did not say much while he ate. Not having good food everyday made him really appreciate what he ate. He kept asking his server for more beef, until people sitting next to him felt he was turning into a pig.

His lack of table manners clearly showed in the way he chowed down the food.

When the guests finished, the plates and silverware were removed and apple cobbler was brought forth with whipped cream on top. Marcus dug in and remarked that it rated right up there with his mother's cooking. He finished the first helping quickly and asked for another bowl which he quickly consumed. As he held the spoon with his hand, rather than his fingers, and scrapped the last bit of cream and cobbler into his spoon, Marcus looked up from his bent-over position to see everyone looking at him quietly. Even the man at the far end of the table was peeking around the flowers to see. Marcus put the last bit of pie in his mouth, dropped his spoon in the crystal dish, causing a rather loud clink in the room, now all quiet, in awe watching Marcus, who immediately straightened up in his seat.

With the room quiet the Admiral stood up. "At this time, I would now like to introduce to General Alfred P. Lyons, the commanding general at our army base here in Mobile. With that, the General stood up. "Tonight we have been impressed with a young man who has shown great courage and bravery on the battlefield and off. He went beyond the call of duty. His love for his country," he hesitated, "and I must say, too, his love for apple cobbler, have been demonstrated here tonight." People giggled slightly and Marcus felt embarrassed, knowing what he was talking about. "But after talking with my colleagues, we have all agreed to make you an honorary Captain in the Confederate Army." With that statement, everyone at the table, and the servers standing by, cheered and clapped for Marcus, who remained seated. "Arrangements are being made also for Marcus to be given the proper medals of valor for what he has accomplished. "Stand up, brave soldier, and come forward to receive this certificate indicating your new rank while I pin these bars on your lapel."

Marcus was stunned by the honor. He was overwhelmed and never dreamed an honor so great would be given him. This was better than a statue in the park. Marcus rose up from the table and started toward the other end. "Don't forget your hat; I want you to wear it when you tell your story." He picked up his hat and walked up to the

General, who handed him a piece of parchment rolled up in a scroll with a red ribbon tied around it. He took the scroll and saluted the general. The general then reached out and shook his hand and gave him a hug. "People, please meet Captain Mills!" Again they cheered and clapped. After a few moments, the noise crowd quieted hoping to finally hear Marcus speak, but the General continued, "The other morning, I heard the story you are going to hear now. I was absolutely amazed at what this young man has done. I hosted this dinner tonight so that you, my friends and fellow officers, could hear what I heard. I have asked Marcus to tell the story again for all of you to hear. Marcus, don't be afraid. As you know, we all love and salute you. Sit down in my seat and tell your story. I will go down and sit in your chair and listen, please begin."

Marcus, obviously nervous and excited, took a seat in the General's chair. "I ain't set in no general's chair," he began in his soft boyish voice on the verge of changing into a man's. In the next half hour, Marcus told his story to the intent listeners. Having told the story so many times, he knew what episodes in his story drew the most interest and what to omit, thus leaving an exciting story to tell. He began the story telling about his enlistment, the early battles and his wound. He told about the horrors of Sharpsburg and his destruction of the Union wagons and his escape. He told how he and the old man blew up the Union ironclads, his encounters, including his near hanging. In particular, he held up the top hat and told about the death of his two friends. He stressed the anger he felt as he listened to their killers that night by the fire, and finally his arrival in Mobile and the kindness he had received. He then thanked the Admiral for his banquet and admitted how fearful he had been when the Admiral wanted him to tell his story. With a humble remark, Marcus ended his story, "And that's all there is. I just want to go home now." His listeners pushed back their chairs and stood up and started clapping, too awed to cheer. Marcus stood up and gave everyone a slight bow, still wearing his red- tipped feather hat. Everyone knew why he had worn it during his chat.

Before everyone started discussing what they had just heard, a short man adorned by the same red-tipped feather hat walked up behind Marcus and stood above him and put his hand on his shoulder. "That is truly an amazing story, but I am afraid it is not true. Unfortunately, the man you are looking at is a fraud, a traitor, and a Union spy planted in our spy network to shut off the needed weapons coming from Canada."

The Admiral immediately stood up, visibly upset and shaken by what he heard, "How can you say such things?"

The Army General also rose and demanded who this infiltrator was and who gave him the authority to say such awful condemnations against their new hero.

"Sir, my name is Milligan, Morris Milligan. I am a secret agent who was to receive the detonators from Colonel James; the original owner of the hat that's on your speaker's head. What he said about his hat was unfortunately true."

"How did you get in here? Who let you in?"

"I informed the guard outside I needed to speak with you about a traitor in your midst."

The Admiral yelled for the guards outside to enter the room and arrest this man. Before they could grab him he yelled back, "Admiral, hear me out. In a moment you will know I am telling the truth."

Two of the guards grabbed him, and the little man resisted; the admiral raised his hand, "Stop, let him go. Now, sir, give me a reason for not arresting you."

He jerked his arms from the soldiers, now a bit ruffled, dusted his sleeves as if the soldiers were filthy and he was something special. He looked at the officers at the table, "Did you notice our hats are the same; the same peculiar white and red feather? These odd looking hats are known and worn by our secret agents up and down the river; they are signs that enable us to recognize each other. We are also known by a letter of the alphabet, rather than our names, so if a letter is intercepted, no one will know who we really are. I only knew the agents code letters, not their names. In case I am captured and tortured, I am still unable to reveal their names." He approached

Marcus and removed his hat and examined it. "Professor Jennings had a hat like this."

Marcus had remained silent, stunned at what he heard, but he stood up, "Yes, he told me about the hats, but he said he had lost his on the river shortly after he left Pittsburg."

"He probably lost it after you shot him in the back of the head, like you mentioned in your story, while he was still alive. From what we have found out, sometime on this leg of the journey, this young man killed the Professor. He then took on the role of the young boy selling fish that attached the torpedoes to the ships."

The admiral still standing, "But sir, how do you know this is not the same boy who abetted the Professor?'

"Let me finish. After he arrived in Mobile, and I was told his story, I believed him too. However, when we examined the detonators, we found they had been tampered with. Someone had taken each detonator and removed some essential parts that made them useless."

The admiral and Colonel sat down, "Go on with your story," as they turned to look at Marcus.

"We knew then, the real devices had been switched or altered sometime after the Professor's death. Marcus or whoever he really is… is a Union spy."

It was dawning on Marcus this man was involving him in a plot he knew nothing about, and yelled, "I did not switch anything. The man in Louisville, the boat owner, McKenzie, there's your traitor. Matter of fact, he even told me he was a double agent. He told me the Yankees thought he worked for them, but he told me he was a Confederate spy. From the first time I saw him, there was something about the man I didn't trust. Yes, I found out they had swapped the real detonators on me, but I took them back on the night I left Louisville. At some point, when I wasn't watching they must have switched the detonators on me again." Marcus stopped talking and thought a moment, "Yes, it must have been Matthew, one of the workman there who I trusted; he must have told McKenzie I had not gone with him to get the wagon, but stayed and watched them remove the detonators. From then on they knew what I was up to. I thought

I had them fooled, but somehow, some way, they let me return and steal the fake detonators that night and get away."

Marcus lowered his head and recalled, "They wanted me to get to Nashville so they could uncover the other Confederate agents and bring the damaged detonators to you. McKenzie even offered to let me take *Bonnie,* my boat, to Nashville if I wanted, but I was tired of the river." He hesitated, then added, "As I traveled, I kept running into cavalrymen up and down the road, you remember in my story, how they were nearby and saved my life when I almost got hung.....and yes, when I was crossing the bridge coming into Nashville, I saw the same Yankee officer that I had seen up the road a ways. They were watching me all of the time."

Interesting story Marcus, but you know it is all a lie. The little man turned back to the hat he held in his hand. "Where did you get this hat if is not the Professor's?"

"It was Colonel James. I saw it before they nearly beat me to death in Nashville."

He looked down at Marcus's hatless head. "Hmmm, I don't seem to see any scars if you got a beating like you say."

"That was a long time ago. I was bruised mostly and they have healed."

"Or is it you are making up the story about John Gibbons and Colonel James. I didn't even know their names. Since we used letters instead of names, how did you get to know their names? I, myself, was to meet two agents identified only as X and E."

"Yes, the Professor told me about Mr. 'X'. I was to meet him at 'The Roost' if the Professor died, and I did. Colonel James is Agent 'X'."

Maybe you were the one who killed X and E?" He held the hat up. "Why are you wearing one their hats? Explain that."

"After they were killed, as I told in my story, I saw the killers ride by and I saw Colonel James' hat. That's how I knew they did it along with seeing the stolen mules. Later I found their pistols."

"Why did you take this hat?"

"Just to remember Colonel James."

"Or to find me and make sure I got the false weapons, maybe." He hesitated, "Maybe he didn't kill our two agents, but what I am going to show and tell you now, is proof, without a doubt, that he is a Union spy." He reached in his pocket and pulled out a letter and showed Marcus the envelope. "Did you address this envelope?"

Marcus looked at the envelope. "Yes, that's the letter I wrote to John Gibbons' wife, Maggie."

The complainant opened the envelope and unfolded the letter and showed Marcus the writing. "Did you write this letter?"

Marcus leaned forward and looked again closely. When he read the words he had written, trying to identify who he was to Maggie, telling her he was a Union spy; Marcus knew his goose was cooked and didn't say anything.

"Boy, answer me; I asked you a question," he said loudly. "Answer me!"

Marcus looked at the people around the dimly lit table, "Yes, sir, I wrote it, but it does not mean what it says. I was trying to…"

The little man cut him off. "I rest my case. Let me read to you what this letter says.

"*Dear Mrs. Maggie, I don't want to scare you but yore uncle John and Mr. James is dead. They was killed by bandits on the road to Alabama. This are the truth. I did not get killed 'cause I stopped to water my mules. I hope you remember me since I only saw you onest. I am the man who was the Yankee spy you talked to in yore inn. My name is Marcus and I left with them to deliver a load of chicken eggs. You know the ones he was taking south. I found the wagon after they had been robbed. The eggs were not broke and I hope to sell them in Mobile, sincerely Marcus, the Yankee spy.*"

There! How plain can it be?" he claimed looking at his shocked audience, as if he was an attorney in a trial. "Ladies and gentlemen, he not only admits to being a Yankee spy once, he writes it twice. If that is not a written confession to what we suspect, then tell me what it is?"

The General demanded to read the letter for himself. He put on his spectacles and held the letter up closer to the light, then handed it to the Admiral with a stern look on his face.

Seeing the crowd turn against him and trying to explain, Marcus yelled out, "I can tell you why I wrote it," but before he could tell more, the General motioned to the guards, "Seize that man and place him in the guardhouse. I cannot believe what this man has done to us. He should be shot as a traitor."

The Admiral, quite embarrassed added, "And I was such a fool to host a banquet for the scoundrel." He looked at the General, "I am going to convene a court martial tomorrow, no not tomorrow, it's Sunday. We will meet on Monday at ten o'clock sharp; no, I need Monday to get everything ready. Yes then, we will meet Tuesday at ten o'clock."

Marcus was seized, and with a guard holding on to each arm, he was marched out of his finest hour to the wagon he had arrived in, and left in disgrace and was thrown in the camp stockade. The General ordered and informed an officer to double the usual number of guards there, and "If this man escapes, I will put all of you in front of the firing squad, including you!"

Many of Marcus's new friends were waiting in the barracks for his triumphant return. As they played cards and talked by candlelight, they heard a horseman gallop up in the night. He dismounted and came and asked to see the sergeant. Most of the soldiers imagined another prison train had arrived and they wanted them to get ready for guard duty. They soon located their sergeant and they all found out about Marcus. "It seems your hero has been thrown in the brig. At his party they discovered he was not a hero, but a traitor. He's over at the stockade, and I need a dozen soldiers to watch him. The Admiral said if he gets away, he'll execute all of us. Come on, get ready, grab your guns and let's go. Immediately the entire squad jumped up to secure their gear. "Wait," the sergeant screamed, "The lieutenant only needs a dozen of us. The sergeant quickly counted out twelve of the closest men and sent them to guard the brig.

Wendell had been almost asleep on his cot when he heard the awful news. He sat up as if what he heard had been a dream, but he saw the men scurrying for their guns and gear. One of the men not picked came back to Wendell, knowing he had grown up with Marcus and knew him better than anyone. "Wendell, did you hear what the sergeant said about Marcus. "He's a traitor."

Wendell, not believing what he heard, got up and walked over to a table by the warm iron stove and sat down, placing his elbows on the table and cradling his chin in his hands, obviously disgusted by the news. He was soon joined by the other soldiers who gathered around him waiting to hear what he might say. Then he looked up, "Men, I don't know what happened over there at the Admiral's house since I wasn't there, but there is one thing I know for sure, Marcus is no traitor."

Before he could continue, they heard footsteps on the wooden stoop outside, and immediately an exhausted guard came in and approached the group, still holding his rifle. "They're gonna shoot Marcus. I had guard duty at the Admiral's house tonight. I was standing guard out by the street when I heard some shouting inside and then two guards from another squad came out holding Marcus by the arm. They put him in the wagon and took him to the brig. I heard the Admiral say he was going to execute Marcus."

"I don't care what happened. I know deep in my heart and would risk my life to prove Marcus did not do whatever they said he did to be shot. I grew up with him and know him better than I know myself. He's the kindest, gentlest, person I know, and I also know he loved the Confederacy; you all know he did."

All the other soldiers agreed. All of them, except for Wendell, had only known him for a few days, but Marcus had gained their trust and friendship and they knew from what they had seen, he was not a traitor. As the night wore on, more information came in about what happened. They eventually talked with the two guards who were in the room, who heard Marcus's story, and how a short little man had appeared and accused Marcus of being a Union spy. He denied what Marcus had told them was true and told another version of his trip. If what he said was true, Marcus would most likely be shot in a day or two, or shortly after they had a military court martial. "I know one thing, the Admiral and General were awfully mad, said one of the guards."

Slowly the discussion about Marcus went to bed as each soldier eventually left the group. Wendell had stayed until the last man was gone, trying to convince his comrades that Marcus was innocent.

46

The next day, after morning drills, Wendell was sitting with Marcus in his cell discussing the matter. After a half hour, the guard told him he had to leave. When Wendell left, he knew without a doubt Marcus had been framed by the circumstantial evidence. This was a case where the evidence in the story looked different in the eyes of two different people.

On Tuesday, the Admiral had convened his officers along with the General and many of his captains. Mr. Milligan also attended with his condemning letter and Colonel James's hat. The officers learned that Mr. Milligan, although a small man, carried much weight in Richmond. Matter of fact, he was the second in command in the Confederate spy network.

The smuggling of the detonators had been of such importance to the Confederacy that they had sent Milligan to take personal charge, and he was the one who had arranged the network, the contacts, and who had hand selected the secret agents when the war began. He had known the Professor before the war, both university lecturers at Lexington, Virginia. He had a high regard for the Professor and wanted justice done for his murderer, and the killer in his mind was

Marcus Mills. In a written confession, he had proof Marcus was a Yankee spy.

After lunch, they interrogated Marcus, but Marcus stuck to the story he had told from the beginning. He insisted if he favored the Union, why he not saved the Union gunboats. "Since I planted the torpedoes, I could have easily dropped them in the river and saved the ships. The Professor would then believe the bombs got wet and didn't work." Nothing Marcus said swayed the Confederates to believe Marcus's story. After two days of discussion, the board determined that Marcus had been captured like he said, but somewhere during this capture, he switched sides and became a Union spy. He was planted along the Ohio River to watch and detect any suspicious behavior. Because of his innocent looks and kind demeanor, he could be anybody's friend in a matter of moments. He was the type person you immediately trusted. The Union authorities, they surmised, probably promised Marcus a large sum of money and land after the war.

After much discussion and debate and heavy pressure from Richmond, they determined Marcus was guilty of treason, and since he was out of uniform when he came on base, they sentenced him to death at noon on Friday. It seemed Marcus's guardian angel had abandoned him, and Marcus wished he had gone home instead when he had told John Gibbons and Colonel James, "No, I thank you for considering me for the job, but I have extended my luck too long. If I keep doing this I will eventually meet the bullet that I can't dodge or a chain I cannot escape." This time his luck had run out, and he would not escape the firing squad that would kill him Friday.

Wendell appealed and pleaded with any high officer who would listen that Marcus was innocent, no matter if the evidence indicted him. Many officers wanted to believe him. One of the Colonels convinced the Admiral to meet with Wendell and hear him out. This would be Marcus's last chance to be saved.

Wendell went before the Admiral and stood at attention and begged the Admiral to understand that although the evidence could possibly link Marcus to Milligan's accusations, the evidence could also equally point to his innocence and his status as a hero. "Sir, how could you sleep at night knowing you may have killed the bravest man in the Confederate army?"

"I understand your point of view, but what about the letter? If I had not read the message, I might see your side, but as Milligan said, that was written proof of his guilt."

"I know that looks bad for him, but did you listen why he wrote the letter. It was the only way for sure John Gibbon's widow would know who he was. And sir, being surrounded by Yankees he told her in the inn he was a Yankee to protect himself. Even, then he got a terrible beating from our side for saying that."

"But there seemed to be no evidence of a thrashing. I had my personal doctor look him over for any evidence of a beating, and the doctor told me he only found an old bruise on his back that he could have gotten almost anywhere." Wendell continued to beg and plead with the Admiral. Finally the naval officer said, "If I were the only judge in the matter, I could see your point, maybe. However, it is out of my hands now. I have received orders from Richmond to execute this man. If this man was imprisoned instead and escaped, he could compromise our spy network. I even suggested we lock him up rather than kill him. When we win the war, we can then interrogate the Yankees and find out for sure if he was guilty or not, but the authorities in Richmond would have none of it because of the letter."

Wendell continued to talk to the Admiral and stress he was killing a good man. When Wendell faced the fact Marcus would be killed, he asked, "Then please excuse me from the firing squad, a duty I have done before. I cannot shoot my best friend. Appoint me, sir, to the burial detail, so I can be sure he gets a proper burial."

"I haven't thought about that. I will get with your sergeant and work out the details. Help me with that. I know while he was here, he stayed with your squad. If you will, find and select the soldiers in your squad who did not know him so being on his firing squad will not bother them." After half an hour, Wendell left the Admiral's office knowing that it was now a matter of time before Marcus would face the firing squad.

Wendell visited Marcus every day. Marcus wrote one letter to Bonnie and one to his family. In the letter to Bonnie he wrote,

> *"My beloved Bonnie,*
>
> *I learned this week from Wendell that you are home now and feared I was dead. I am not dead. I will be dead in two days though. They are going to shoot me. They think I am a spy and turncoat. When you get this letter, I will be gone, but always remember, I did not turn against my people. A man I did not know told lies about me. That's why I am going to be shot. Please get Fetch and go visit Sandy Creek for me. I will talk to God when I see Him and see if He will let me be there. God knows I am not guilty. If I can, I will shake a bush so you will know I am there. From then on, when you say a prayer, tell God when you are going to Sandy Creek so He can tell me to meet you down there. Please remember, I will always love you even from Heaven. Wendell told me when he thought I had been killed he started having sweets on you too. Then, I think it will be good if you can't marry me, then you should marry him. I don't think I will be jealous in Heaven. One last thing I want to tell you, thank you for being my girl. I will see you some day when you get here.*
>
> *Love you forever, Marcus."*

When Marcus had finished his two letters, Wendell mailed them for him. Marcus told Wendell he had given his permission for him to marry Bonnie, and made Wendell promise he would take care of her and never harm, hurt, or betray her. Marcus made Wendell raise his hand and promise before God he would keep those promises to Marcus.

On the morning of Marcus's execution, he was given his last meal. Marcus requested fried eggs, ham, and toast with blackberry jelly and butter. He made the comment, "You know, when you're gonna go on a long journey, you need to get some hearty food inside you."

A chaplain visited with Marcus until the guards came with a wagon to carry him to the place of execution. There was a coffin on the back of the wagon. Wendell, as he requested, had been assigned to the burial detail and drove the wagon sitting next to one of Marcus's new friends. Four other soldiers sat in the front of the wagon with their picks and shovels.

Marcus had irons on his feet and was helped into the wagon and was asked to sit on the back of the coffin. The Admiral and General did not attend. They both insisted the execution be private. They were embarrassed they had wined and dined a traitor and did not want the public to know. The sooner this matter was swept under the rug, the better for the two high ranking officers. If the local newspapers heard about this story, they would ridicule the officers for their blunder that allowed a spy to infiltrate their security. The ten executioners marched behind the wagon as if marching in a parade. Following them were a dozen cavalry soldiers, the entire entourage ruled over by a captain.

A secluded wooded site was chosen for the execution, south of the base. A rather thin wooden post had been set in the ground to secure Marcus. Wendell's eyes were obviously red and wet as he talked with Marcus for the last time from his driver's seat. He rubbed his eyes to try and suppress his tears. After a short trip, the small train of soldiers rode and marched into the site of the execution. Wendell stopped the wagon a short distance from the pole sticking ominously out of the ground. A freshly dug grave could be seen about twenty yards away next to some small wooden placards that indicated this spot was a graveyard.

Wendell and the five other riders helped Marcus down from the wagon and removed his leg irons and led Marcus to the pole. Wendell had a black sack to place over Marcus's face. Marcus was calm and showed no signs of fear as he walked up and faced the riflemen taking their place in front of him. Wendell asked him if he had anything to say before he put the mask over his face.

Marcus said he would like to make one last statement. "You people that are about to shoot me; I want you to know you are killing an innocent man. I am not a traitor. I did what I could for my country. I hope all of you who kill me know you murdered a man who loved his country. May you all remember this day and what you did to me." The captain noticed a slight rustle among his men, slightly disturbed by what Marcus told them. The rifles had been loaded and given to each soldier. To ease the stress on the executioners, one of the rifles was empty, thus each soldier could assume he had fired the empty gun and was not guilty of killing a man.

Before Wendell placed the hood over Marcus's head, he moved in close and gave Marcus a big bear hug and whispered a final goodbye. They hugged for several seconds, and Wendell stepped back and Marcus nodded and took a last look at the beautiful sky and woods around him. Wendell pulled the black hood down slowly over his face and noticed Marcus was staring directly in his eyes, but noticed a quick smile appeared before the mask came further down. There were two strings on the mask that secured it around his neck. Wendell tied the two strings and with that final act, Wendell stepped back and said, "God speed, Marcus." With that last statement Wendell did a military turn and went back to the wagon.

The captain, mounted on a horse, came up behind the executioners who were standing at attention with their guns beside them. The men noticed Marcus had put his hands together over his chest in a gesture similar to a prayer, but it appeared he clasped something, most likely a cross. The captain then yelled to the men to prepare to fire on his command. "Arms up, ready, aim, fire!"

The blasts of black smoke exiting the rifles obscured Marcus temporarily, but they saw his body jerk from the bullets entering his chest and the blood splash as Marcus slumped to the ground never moving another muscle, not even a twitch.

The soldiers put down their arms; the Captain gave the orders to turn, march, and retreat back to the base. The cavalry waited until the soldiers marched by; then they too, turned and fell in line. The captain ordered Wendell to proceed with the burial detail. Wendell and the other five men pulled the coffin from the wagon and carried it over next to Marcus. The captain walked his horse over to Marcus to make sure he was dead. He looked down at Marcus and saw the ripped shirt and a bloody mess covering his chest as he lay on his back with his arms outstretched, but with both legs bent. The officer saw the new shoes Marcus had purchased. "What a shame, what a shame," Wendell heard the captain say as he rode away to catch up with his detail.

Wendell took a wet rag he had brought from the wagon, removed the black mask, and started wiping Marcus's face and hands as the others straightened his legs and folded his arms on his chest. While they were tending to Marcus, they watched the captain of the squad disappear into the woods with the soldiers marching first, the cavalry next, and the captain walking along behind them on his horse. Wendell noticed the captain take one final look before he disappeared into the woods.

"Marcus, he's almost gone. Stay still just a little longer. We're gonna put you over in the coffin just in case he's looking. Are you alright?"

"Yeah, I'm fine. How did I do? Did you like my final speech?"

"You bet, that was great." All the men on the burial detail were smiling as they knew they had pulled off a great deception. Every soldier in their outfit knew Marcus was innocent, and they had all taken part in the scam. Given permission to arrange the execution, Wendell selected his friends that he was sure would help and volunteer to be an executioner and those that would be on burial detail. They had loaded all the guns with extra powder but no bullet to create more smoke so Marcus would have time to squeeze a hog bladder and squirt the blood on to his shirt. They had torn the bullet holes in the shirt the night before, but carefully ironed them with starch to hold them secure until Marcus wet them with the hog blood they had secured fresh from a butcher that morning. When the rifles were fired, Marcus crushed the hog bladder full of blood on his chest and as he fell he scratched his chest to tear open the starched holes and make them appear as if they had been made by the bullets tearing into his body.

This great deception had been instigated by Wendell after he had talked to the Admiral a few days before. On his way back to the barracks, he came up with an idea that might possibly save Marcus's life. His squad had been on countless burial details, had participated in three firing squads, and was aware of the protocol the military went through to execute a man. When he had learned the major officers wanted this execution kept quiet and hidden from a public investigation, it had made it even easier to undertake.

Wendell had entered his barracks and discussed the ominous matter with two of his closest and most trusted friends, both had expressed to him the Navy was executing an innocent man. With their help, he soon had a burial detail and a firing squad that would work with Wendell and keep the plot to save Marcus a big secret. Even their sergeant became involved and reported to his officer, who reported to the Admiral, that all was ready for Marcus's execution.

The Admiral asked his sergeant how the men felt about the execution. The sergeant assured him the men were outraged that Marcus, the lad they had trusted and who shared their barracks, had betrayed them. He felt the entire squad would volunteer to kill Marcus if asked, and they would not have to leave a bullet out of one of the guns. That pleased the Admiral that the men would not hold his death against him.

Back at the grave, the burial detail figured they were safe now, but they insisted Marcus stay still and play the part of a corpse, a role he had played before on the battlefield at Antietam. They placed his limp body into the coffin and moved it over by the open grave. Suddenly they heard a horse galloping toward them, not visible yet, but definitely coming their way. "Marcus, somebody's coming, keep playing dead. We are going to put the lid on the coffin just in case the captain is coming back."

"Get me out of here as quick as you can. It's kind of scary in here."

A horseman emerged from the woods as Wendell adjusted the top and drove a nail, purposely missing the side, thus not securing the top. It was one of the riders who had stood behind the soldiers and watched the execution. The rider rode up and reined in his horse, as if he had a most important message for the group and maybe the war depended on whether he delivered it. He was very young and appeared to be a new recruit. Excitedly he informed them they were to immediately get back to town when their duty was finished and not to waste time. The captain had been informed by a courier that a large prison train would be coming in soon and the Army needed all the guards at the post.

As Wendell and the other men deduced, he was a new recruit and wet behind the ears when he said, "Sir, would you mind removing the lid so I can see what a dead man looks like? I haven't been in battle yet. I didn't get a close look at him from where I sat on my horse. I saw him alive, but if you don't mind, could I see him dead?"

Wendell and the other men wanted to laugh. What a ghoulish thought, but since he only had one nail in the coffin, Wendell didn't say anything, but pivoted the top aside so the man could see Marcus lying inside. Wendell hoped Marcus had heard the rider's request and would remain still. Never leaving his horse, the young lad leaned over and stared down at the supposed corpse. After a few moments, he thanked them and said, "I guess that's the way we will all end up someday." With that last statement he galloped off to catch the others.

Wendell took his hammer and pounded the edge of the coffin pretending to nail the top back on. They watched him disappear into the small woods that hid the execution site. They waited another minute or two until they were sure the rider was gone. Marcus complained about being in the box. "Get me out of here; I've had all of this I can stand. I know why they wait until you are dead before they bury you."

"Just another minute or two and we'll get you out of there. We can't take any chances now. Stay in there a little longer." As the sound of the lone rider faded out, they were immediately replaced by the sound of several horses and riders coming their way. "Marcus, I can't let you out yet. There are more riders coming this way. Stay put; I need to nail the lid. Don't worry; as soon as they're gone, we'll let you out. Maybe the riders will pass by," but as they watched and listened, the sounds of the hoofs got louder. The top was not nailed shut, so Wendell quickly lifted up the top to refresh the air inside. Then began nailing the top back on as seven riders came down the lane that split the woods. "Be quiet and stay still. They are coming this way."

The group rode up and stopped. The burial detail stopped their work and saluted the officer. "At ease men, carry on with your duty. The Admiral sent us out to make sure that traitor was in the ground. Take off the lid. He told me to make sure he is dead."

"Sir, he is dead. I assure you."

"Pry up the lid. I want to see for myself." Wendell took the claw of the hammer and pried up the lid of the crudely made coffin and pulled it off. Marcus lay still with his eyes just barely open. The captain rode up close, and like the previous rider looked down. He then drew his pistol and aimed it at Marcus.

"What are you doing sir? The man is dead, don't waste your bullet." Wendell walked between the officer and Marcus, stooped down and picked up a shovel and with the handled poked Marcus in the chest. The jabs appeared to be hard, but Wendell pulled back on the shovel just as he touched Marcus's body. Marcus didn't move a muscle and endured the light jabs. "See, Captain, he's dead. There's no reason to put a hole or two in his last resting place. This man was a friend of mine, and I volunteered for his burial detail so I could insure he would rest in peace for eternity."

The captain un-cocked his pistol and holstered it. "Very well, then, get on about your business. Wendell bent down and replaced Marcus's hands above his chest and straightened his shirt. He took his hand and lifted his head to wipe his hair back. He stood up and said a last goodbye, "Marcus, why did you betray us? I am sorry you are dead, but you got what you deserve." The captain was impressed with what he said. Wendell and the men stood a moment expecting the captain to ride away, but he continued to wait, leaning over and crossing his arms on the saddle horn, letting Wendell know he was going to be there a while. Wendell knew now Marcus had only a limited amount of air so he wanted to cover him quickly, hoping the captain would be satisfied he was buried and leave, then giving the men time to uncover Marcus before he smothered to death. "Men, let's get busy." The lid was nailed back on. They fetched two ropes from the wagon and laid them across the ground and lifted the coffin up and placed it across the ropes. They then used the ropes to pick up the coffin and carry it over above the grave and slowly lowered it down.

Marcus heard the words that gave him a severe "goose-feather feeling." He knew he was going to be buried. He wanted to beat on the lid and demand to get out, but knew he would be instantly shot. He had to trust Wendell to save his life. The cracks in the lid of the coffin let in a little light that dimmed as he was lowered into the grave. Then he heard the shovels of dirt hitting on top of the coffin and cutting off his last light. The shovels full of dirt kept hitting the top. In a moment, he was in total blackness. He reached up with the back of his hands and felt the top of his coffin a few inches above his nose. "I can't stand this," he thought. He could still hear the thumps made by the clumps of dirt hitting the lid. Slowly that faded as he was covered deeper. He pushed against the top but there was no give. He realized exerting himself would use more air, so he tried to completely relax and breathe slowly, almost trying to not breathe at all.

Outside, the captain and his men watched as the coffin was covered. When the hole was nearly full, the captain suddenly jerked the reins of his horse and ordered, "Let's go men. We are done here." He then turned to Wendell, "You do know to hurry and finish here and get back to town. There's a large prison train coming in, and we need every man." Wendell saluted and the soldiers continued to fill the grave.

They continued to move their shovels as if they were filling the grave, but their shovels were empty as the officer rode way. Wendell watched the riders merge into the woods. The burial detail had worked fast and the grave was nearly level with the surface of the ground when the officer left. Wendell knew his friend needed air, but he could not rush the excavation until he was sure it was safe to dig Marcus from his tomb. At last, hoping the soldiers would not return and catch them in the act, he ordered the men on the burial detail to rapidly remove the dirt.

Inside the coffin, the air was getting heavy. Marcus found himself having to breathe faster and harder, and he began to feel he was suffocating, as if someone had a pillow over his head, but there was no pillow. He only had a few more minutes at the most, and then he heard a slight thump. Then it was louder; he knew they were coming. He had to hold out now. He was almost to the point of panic, but he dared not use up precious air. He began to hear his friends frantically urging each other to dig faster. Then he heard the shovels scraping the lid wiping away the dirt and then the prying of the lid. He took his last strength to help push up the top and the cool air burst in on his face as he took deep gasps of precious air. He was saved as he saw Wendell pull off the top and reach down to help him up.

"That was close Marcus. I thought you were a goner for sure."

Still gasping for air, Marcus rose up, "What took you so long? It was getting stuffy in there. I never want to go through that again. The fear of a battlefield is nothing compared to being in there."

"Hurry on out of there. We need to get this covered in a hurry. All of a sudden it seems everybody at the base wants to come out here. The four men helped him up out of the hole, Marcus still a little weak from his lack of oxygen. "You look a little shaky. Are you doing all right?"

Continuing to take large gulps of air, "Yes, I feel much better now."

Wendell pointed at some thick green vines and small brush at the edge of the field. "Get over there and hide while we get this hole covered. We have someone coming with your wagon and mules. Just stay right there and don't move. I think we have pulled this off, and you will be going home soon." Those were the words that Marcus feared he would never hear as he staggered toward the brush. The men quickly replaced the coffin lid and filled the hole. They took the back of their shovels and tamped down the soil and drove a placard with Marcus's name on it at the head of the grave. It was done; Marcus Mills, the traitor, had been planted.

Marcus had made it to the woods and lay down under the thick brush. He lay on his back and looked up through the heavy green winter foliage and caught a glimpse of the blue sky, a sight, a few moments before, he feared he would never see again. His guardian angel had saved him once again. Marcus said a prayer thanking God for his deliverance from the grave. He prayed his trials would be over now and he would travel home safely. Marcus rolled over and from beneath the brush he watched his friends finish their work.

With no danger in sight, Wendell came over and told Marcus to stay hidden until he came back. Their plans had been temporarily delayed due to the prison train, but as soon as it left and Wendell was relieved from duty, he would return with Marcus's wagon and all of his animals. The Admiral did not know about the papers the Colonel had written that gave Marcus possession of his belongings and his honorable discharge. When he finished the guard duty at the train, he would go by and get the wagon and animals and come back out here with his official documents. The execution had been kept secret and the officer at the livery stable knew nothing about Marcus and his belongings. Later that day, after their guard duty, several of the men in on the ruse rode the wagon with Wendell out to bid Marcus farewell.

Marcus was relieved to see the wagon and his friends come down the lane shortly before dark. The wagon came over by the brush and stopped, and Marcus crawled from his hiding place, feeling it was safe now. All of his friends huddled around him. Marcus asked if they had water and something to eat, and to his surprise, he saw that his comrades had filled the wagon with supplies and water that would help him on his way to Georgia. His canvas bags had been filled with horse feed, and he still had his saddles and arms. He had lost his money when they had arrested him that night after the party, but Wendell had passed the hat around among his friends and had gathered over a hundred dollars in Confederate money.

Tears welled in Marcus's eyes as he watched the kindness pour out on him. He stood up on the wagon and said a final goodbye. "Friends, I cannot thank you enough for my life, and how you risked your lives to free me. You know they would have shot you if they had found out about this plot. I also want you to know, I am no traitor or spy. I did what I had to do and things just happened to make me look guilty. I am sorry that I did not get the detonators down here, but I did help sink two Yankee gunboats and blow up a Yankee wagon train."

Turning to Wendell as he stepped from the wagon, "Wendell, I can't thank you enough." He smiled at him a moment and then gave Wendell a big hug. "It won't be long, but I expect to see you back in Buckhead where we can fish, hunt, and grow old together."

Wendell hugged him back and slapped him on the back. "Oh brother, I am just so glad you are alive." Then he hesitated and stepped back holding Marcus by the shoulders, then he grabbed Marcus by the arm and pulled him away from the group. "Pardon me men, but I have to tell Marcus something that I only want him to hear." With that he walked Marcus away, then turned with his eyes red and large tears flowing down his face, "Marcus I must confess something to you."

Seeing his friend so visibly upset, Marcus tried to calm him down, Wendell, Wendell what's wrong? Everything is right, I am alive. I will always forever be indebted to you."

"You don't understand Marcus; when you were in that grave over there, the Devil entered my head and spoke to me. He said, 'let your friend die and you can have Bonnie.' I was tempted Marcus, oh how I was tempted, but then I said, 'Get behind me, Satan, and I was so ashamed that such an evil idea had entered my head I dug harder and faster than I ever thought I could. Please forgive me."

"I forgive you. I can understand. If our roles were reversed, I would have probably thought the same."

"And Marcus, when I get home, trust me in what I am telling you, in that moment out there in this field, after I denied the Devil, I sensed my desire for Bonnie was gone. Please believe me."

"I believe you, and if Bonnie will marry me, you will always be welcome on my front porch. We will always be friends, just as before."

With his confession, the two returned to the group with their arms on each other's shoulders. They could see both young men had expressed sincere emotions as they both wiped tears from their eyes. After some final goodbyes and directions, Marcus climbed in his wagon and headed north into the fading light. Marcus was safe, but the hero who had come into town with such glory, was buried in a lonely field near Mobile, and an innocent young unknown lad headed for home.

47

Night had fallen, and Marcus followed the directions to get out of the town that almost killed him. He continued to thank God for his safety and continued to pray for a safe trip home. He drank water and nibbled on peanuts as he traveled north. Outside of Mobile, he found a wagon yard where people parked and rested. Trying to appear to be a stranger passing in the night hunting a place to sleep, he drove his mules to an open place and parked the wagon.

He unhitched the mules in the light provided by many small fires of the campers. He tethered the animals to the wagon wheels and fed them, then in pairs, he walked them a short ways to a water trough. As he watched the mules drink, he thought about the events of the day. He owed so much now to Wendell and his friends who freed him. When the animals were fed and watered, Marcus sliced some pork from a cured ham the soldiers gave him, lay back in the wagon, pulled the canvas tarp over himself and slept that night with no fear or obligation to finish a mission.

Just before the morning light appeared in the east, the camp came alive as people built fires and cooked, hitched up wagons, and broke camp to continue wherever they were going. A family parked next to Marcus invited him to share their fire, as wood was hard to find. He used a pan to fry some eggs and bacon. He learned the family had left their farm north of Richmond fearing for their safety where the war had been so intense. The husband told Marcus they were going to live with his brother in Mississippi until the war was over.

Marcus took the opportunity to question the man about the conditions, in the South, he had traveled through. He indicated after they got north of Richmond, they found food ample but not plentiful, and there were no Yankees. He assured Marcus he should have no trouble getting back home to Georgia. Another traveler suggested Marcus go due east and take advantage of the warm weather blowing off the Gulf of Mexico, and then turn northeast. He also learned if he could make twenty miles a day, he could be home in three weeks. That sounded like an eternity to Marcus, a little discouraging, but he felt more comfortable now than at any other time since he left Sharpsburg. Knowing he was going directly home, three weeks in the wagon would be easy compared to what he had endured.

For ten days Marcus traveled east. The number of rivers and bogs he crossed determined the amount of miles he made each day. He often was delayed so his animals could graze on dried grasses where available to save his corn reserve. Several days he calculated he had gone farther than twenty miles, but once he was delayed two days by heavy rains which canceled any gains he had made earlier. However, since crossing the river, he had made good time as he slowly turned northeast.

On one cold evening, Marcus stayed on the road to reach a small town he knew was ahead. As he came into town, he passed a small white church. He could hear the folks singing hymns. He pulled on the reins and stopped the tired mules to listen for a few moments. The orange light from the four fogged windows brought the sound of singing and silhouettes that reminded him of home.

He wanted to go inside and sing, but from past encounters, it seemed those meetings brought more trouble than not, so he decided to stay in the wagon and listen. He knew the hymns and quietly sang along trying to harmonize with the women and their high squeaky voices that seemed to penetrate the night more than the lower voices of the men. His voice was changing, and occasionally cracked, but overall he thought he sounded good. Using a little imagination, he pretended to see Bonnie sitting with his family.

Suddenly, the singing reminded him of Christmas. Due to the past dangers and the traumas he had endured, he had lost track of the days. He tried to calculate how long it had been since Sharpsburg. After a few minutes, he figured Christmas had most likely passed a few weeks before. Yes, he reasoned, Christmas had passed and he had missed his mother's cooked pies and cakes and the two large baked hens with dressing. Because her dressing was so good, all the relatives came to her house where they celebrated Christmas. Everyone brought food. He thought about Aunt Laura Mae's peach cobbler, made so sweet and chewy, and Aunt Nell's candied yams, which always tasted so good. They sang songs and Uncle Bill played his fiddle. Outside they had a shooting contest, but before the contest started, everyone knew Uncle Jack would win it. He was a deadly shot. If he wasn't too old, Uncle Jack was probably in the Army now. If he was, no telling how many Yankees he had killed. The young'uns ran foot races and climbed trees. However, due to the war, he wondered if they even had a Christmas.

While another hymn started inside, Marcus wondered what his family and friends felt when they received his last letter informing them he would be shot as a spy. Then he sat up, "I am not dead, and I will be home in ten days." Overcome with joy and erasing his depressing thoughts, he hollered out a long loud "yehaaaa," and with a new smile on his face, clicked his mules to continue. He was headed home.

Every mile that rolled under the wagon brought him nearer to what he had missed for so long. It had been two years since he left. Not wanting to go an extra mile out of the way to arrive home, he sought and followed the best opinions about roads and routes.

One man estimated he was seven days from home barring no bridges had washed away or his wagon broke down. Seven, six, four, then another man in an old wagon said six again. Two days passed with no trouble. Another cold wet day and night passed, Marcus sleeping under his canvas-covered wagon on a cot provided by his soldier friends. He woke up and set off again, five days from home now. Another two days and forty miles went by he figured, each step of the mules pulling him closer.

He clicked his tongue to urge his mules onward and watched the familiar pine forests slip by. His mules were healthy and well fed. Having two teams of mules enabled him to alternate their work days and start the day with a fresh set of animals. Marcus had purchased food when available and kept the canvas bags nearly full of corn.

Another day elapsed. Two more days and he would roll up to his family farm. Finally, at last, he joined the road leading out of Atlanta that led to Buckhead. He had been down this road many times during his life with his father, and he recognized the familiar landmarks. He thought about pushing himself and the mules to ride all night, but his better judgment intervened. He would camp one last night.

So many times on his long trek, when it all seemed right, it went wrong. To take no chances, he found a campground that he camped in with his father when they went to Atlanta. He wanted to be near other folks so he would have a sense of security. That night as he lay down in the wagon covered by a tarp, he could hardly sleep, excited about getting home tomorrow and worried about what might go wrong, fearing someone might kill him for his horses and mules. But finally, he dozed off and slept soundly until the stir of the morning camp woke him. All was well. His mules and property were intact and he was alive. What a great day this would be.

Marcus did not take time to cook, but bought some cornbread and bacon from a nearby camper. Marcus was glad to get the food, and the man was glad to get the money. He rapidly hitched up his mules and tied the rest of his animals to the back of the wagon, and he left camp with a big grin on his face. Like a prewritten play, the stage lights were turned on and a bright sunny day presented itself. As the morning passed, Marcus saw the familiar sights that he had missed so much. He was getting close to Sandy Creek now, a few miles from Buckhead. To go there would take him a couple of miles out of his way.

When Marcus came to the fork in the road that would take him to town or Sandy Creek, he stopped the wagon to decide which fork to take. He debated the two roads. If he went on straight he would be at his home in less than half hour, but on the other hand, he had dreamed about Sandy Creek so much during his journey. Sandy Creek won the debate when he decided he needed a bath and clean up before he met Bonnie. The day was warm and the water would be cold, but he had endured much worse. A few moments of icy water getting the road dust and camp smoke off of him would be worth it.

He urged his mules down the secluded road that led him to a clearing above the creek. He knew the road crossed the creek a few rock throws further down from the deeper water and the large rock on which he and Bonnie and spent so many wonderful moments. Down there, he could water and tether his animals while he stood in the shallow water and bathed himself. He looked down at the site that he had waited for and dreamed about on so many cold nights. He wanted to pinch himself. This couldn't be real. He should be dead, but there it was, the sun glistening off the water and a few puddles that collected in the small dimples of the large outcropping.

He clicked his mules on down past the rock and stopped the wagon so all of his animals could drink. He untied the horses and tethered them along the creek so they could drink and eat the green briars that grew next to the creek. The water above and below the rocky road crossing was too shallow to bathe in.

Marcus unpacked some clean clothes and walked back up to the deeper water that he swam in during the summer next to the rock. He eased down to the edge of the water below the rock and removed his clothes. The water was ice cold as he waded into the water. Wanting to get cold and wet all at once, he plunged on down in the water. It nearly took his breath away, but he endured. He took the sand and used it as soap to scrub his hide and get rid of the filth he had gathered since his last bath before the banquet. He scrubbed his hair the best he could and rinsed it in clean water not disturbed by his movements. The hurt from the first shock of the cold had subsided and the cold was uncomfortable but bearable now. He noticed the huge goose bumps on his arms as he waded out of the water and begin to shiver with his teeth chattering. He did not have a towel and used his old clothes to dry. He soon had on the civilian clothes his soldier friends had packed for him, and his hair was drying quickly as he put on his new shoes.

While he finished his grooming, he heard a dog bark and looked up the road above the creek and saw a buggy beginning to appear in the gaps between the trees. He feared his wagon parked in the middle of the stream could block the buggy's path across the creek. He hurried and pulled on his last new shoe. He glanced back up at the road and saw the dog come into view, running ahead of the buggy now emerging from the trees. Marcus's mouth opened in surprise. It was a dog that looked like Fetch. He wiped his wet hair and looked again. He squinted to see the dog clearer. Yes, yes, that had to be Fetch. He now recognized his bark. He was so excited, but who was in the buggy?

Marcus moved closer to the rock to hide himself. He wanted to holler at Fetch, but before he could yell he was elevated to a level of excitement he hadn't felt in two years. There she was, the love and beauty of his life. His mouth silently opened in awe; he swallowed hard, as he watched her approach, the lovely young lady who gave him reason to endure the fear, pain, cold, and hunger to get back home and find her. As Wendell had said, she was not in Texas; she was approaching him in a buggy pulled by a single horse. The sunlight sparkled from her silver combs.

He remembered his last letter. He remembered writing her that he would be at Sandy Creek and would shake a bush to show her he was there if God would let him go there. There was no bush near his hiding place to shake, but instead he would still hide and surprise her.

The dog had slowed up and waited for Bonnie to turn into the clearing and park the buggy close to the rock. Fetch went back toward Bonnie with his tongue hanging out and panting heavily after the run from his home. He came up next to Bonnie with his tail wagging as she lifted her skirt, climbed from the buggy, and petted Fetch. It was a warm and sunny day, a perfect day to visit nature and maybe sun on a rock. She nor the dog could see Marcus from the top of the rock.

Marcus could see her if he peeked from around the rock, but risked being seen himself. Marcus had not been on the rock and had not left a scent the dog could smell.

Marcus did not risk being seen, staying hidden, and gave her time to walk out on top of the rock. If she got near the edge, she possibly could see him if she looked down, so he leaned closer and hid below a slight ledge that stuck out near the top that they used in the summer as a diving board.

As Marcus hid under the ledge with his back against the rock, he heard the most beautiful word he ever heard or would ever hear in his life. In a long soft call that echoed out over the pond he heard, "Mar...cus..., Mar...cus..., are you here?"

Marcus waited, hoping she would call one more time. "Mar...cus..., I am here. Please answer me," the words called out slowly causing the echoes to reverberate back on themselves.

Marcus was so happy. He wanted to laugh but smiled instead. He waited a moment then called back to her in the highest ghostly voice he could make, also stretching the syllables to linger over the pond, "Bon...nieeeee..., I hear you. Where are you...?" There was silence.

Marcus heard nothing for a moment, then he heard a loud shout of surprise, "Marcus! Marcus! Is that you? Are you really there? Are you dead?" Fetch, not recognizing his master's voice yet, started barking and spinning around not knowing where the sound had echoed from.

"I am here. I have come a long way to see you. I have not been in Heaven. I have been in hell."

Bonnie could not believe the words she heard. She was confused. "Oh no Marcus, don't tell me that. I don't believe it. You were too good of a person to be down there," the shocking news causing her to sob.

"Not down there but here on earth, but now I am in Heaven. You are my heaven." Marcus could not hide his ruse any longer. He left his hideout and ran up to the top of the rock to find his girl in a kneeling position, sobbing, with her face in her hands, obviously overcome by what she heard. Fetch was standing close to her whimpering, pawing his feet up in down, disturbed she was crying, and trying to find a way to help her. Then the dog saw Marcus emerging from below the rock. He immediately knew his master; he turned and barked, causing Bonnie to look up and see Marcus standing a few feet away. Bonnie could not believe her eyes. Still not expecting to see anyone, she wondered if she was seeing a ghost or dreaming.

Marcus started walking toward Bonnie. "The hell I was talking about was the war. I am home now, and I will never go to hell again, and they can kill me no more!" he shouted as he came up next to Bonnie with his hands extended." Old Fetch was going crazy, barking with happiness, spinning in a circle and rapidly whipping both of them with his tail. Surprised and confused by what she saw, she hesitated, and then slowly rose to her feet and softly asked, "Marcus, is that really you? Am I dreaming?"

With both arms extended, he took the last step of his long journey and fulfilled his dream and gave Bonnie a big hug, lifting her off the ground. He then gave her a big long kiss, "I can't believe it's you Bonnie; are you really here, too? Are you really in my arms? You won't believe what I have been through."

She pushed him back a bit so she could see his face, "Marcus, you are supposed to be dead!" She reached in her dress pocket and pulled out the letter he had written the day before his execution. "You said you were going to be shot. That's why I'm down here this morning, to see if you really talked to God or not, and whether He let you come out of Heaven to see me. Mother said you were dead and God didn't let dead people talk to live people, and I was wasting my time."

Marcus kissed her again, "I guess he did better than that. He let me get out of hell and come see you for real. Not only that, I got four horses, four mules, a wagon, and some money," then he remembered something else. "Oh, please excuse me; I left something in the wagon. It's right down there below the pond. I'll be right back."

"No Marcus, don't go. I'm still not sure you aren't a ghost. Please stay here."

"Oh, you can bet I'm not a ghost, but I thank you're gonna like what I'm gonna show you."

"Let me go with you."

"No, stay here, I'll be right back."

She clasped her hands and placed them over her mouth, revealing her fear that he was a ghost and would soon be gone as she watched him and Fetch run away down the hill to get the wagon. "And I have something for you, too," as she turned and went back to her buggy.

Marcus retrieved his animals and tied them to the back of the wagon and drove the wagon back up the road and pulled in next to Bonnie's buggy. "Nice, buggy, where did you get that?"

"I borrowed it from Uncle Joe. He's sick; I use it often to help him out." She had returned and spread a quilt out on the rock, avoiding the wet crevices that held water. Marcus saw an item he had seen many times before when they had visited here. It was a picnic basket. "I didn't think if you were here that you would be able to eat fried chicken. I didn't bring much, but we can share what I have."

Marcus walked up and sat down and nestled close to her. "Now, what do you have to show me?" she asked.

He reached in his pocket and pulled out her crinkled photograph. "Remember this? I imagine I would be dead if you had not sent this. I got this the morning of the day I was nearly killed at Sharpsburg. I cannot tell you the misery I've been through. When I was at my lowest, wanting to give up, I would look at your beautiful face and know, whatever it took, I must get home. I must also say, I had the greatest guardian angel who helped me escape situations that were impossible to escape, but I did." He kissed her on the cheek again, "But this is what I want to show you," he added as he reached in his pocket and pulled out the gold ring.

Suddenly, her mouth opened and she put her hands on her cheek, "Oh Marcus, is this for me?" She reached out to get the ring.

He pulled it back, "Not yet, there's something else." He reached in his pocket and gave her a wrinkled piece of brown paper. She unrolled it and started reading.

"Stop, read it; read it so I can hear you."

She looked down, "Dear Bonnie, Will you take my ring and marry me? I will always be your husband and will take care of you.

Please say yes." She looked up at Marcus and then back down at the paper. Reading slowly, she finished, "I love you," she paused, and then added, "Marcus."

She looked back at him and then kissed him, "Yes, Marcus, I will marry you and I will be your wife forever, too."

Marcus then handed her the ring. "Read what it says inside the ring."

She was in awe as she took the beautiful gold ring. She turned it back and forth until she could read, "Marcus loves Bonnie." Marcus reached down and grabbed her hand and gently took the ring and slipped it on her finger. It was a little loose. He grinned, "You know, I think that is about the finest thing I have every looked at."

She looked up at Marcus, "I think so, too." They kissed again and again. "I sure hope your papa agrees with this. You know I didn't have a chance to ask him for your hand. I didn't expect to run into you out here, but when I saw you, I had to go ahead and ask you now."

She held her hand out admiring her beautiful ring. "We won't tell him about it. We can pretend you gave me the ring after you ask him. I already know he'll say yes. He wants you in the family. He told me one time you'll be a good farmer one day."

"Shucks, look at those mules and horses over there. I plan to grow a crop this spring. I even have a written discharge from the Army signed by a colonel."

"Oh! I almost forgot, let's eat." She opened the basket and pulled out two pieces of chicken and a sweet potato, still in its peel, and a piece of cornbread. She also had a teapot full of sassafras tea she had brewed from the roots of a sassafras tree earlier that morning. She only had a small ceramic mug that they shared drinking the tea. "If I had known you were here, I would have brought the whole chicken," she said as they started to share what little they had. Marcus peeled the skin from a piece of chicken and gave it to Fetch, who appeared to ask, "Where is my piece?"

They stayed on their favorite rock with Fetch snuggled against them the rest of the afternoon. Marcus told her his adventures and how he escaped death so many times. He told her about Antietam,

Edward, the kind boatyard owner, his boat named 'Bonnie,' the professor, how they sank the gunboats, and how Wendell had helped him escape. He also told her about the white red tipped feather hat, his beating in Nashville, his many escapes, and the murder of his two comrades.

He had held back the one part of his adventure that he did not want to tell, fearing she would hold it against him, but he did not want to keep any skeletons in the closet that might haunt their relationship later. "Bonnie, there is one more story I regret to tell. Remember when I told you how I found my two friends murdered by the Rebel deserters?"

She nodded.

"I didn't tell you the other part. I still don't want to tell you this, but I have to, so I can clear my head. I want you to see what I have been through, all the things I endured, and living with what I'm going to tell you has haunted me ever since. I didn't want to do it, but I had to do what I had to do."

He then told her how he tracked down the four deserters and killed them. "They were drunk and most likely on their way to hell. I hoped to give them a chance to repent, but due to circumstances, I had to kill them all in a matter of seconds." He looked in her eyes, "Bonnie, I sent four people to hell. I am sure they deserved it, but the Bible says we are to save men's souls." He looked down sadly, "But I sent four men to hell. Of all the things that happened to me, that killing bothers me most."

She leaned over against him, "Don't let it worry you. They would have killed you, too, that morning if you had been there. From their behavior, they were going there anyway; you just got them there faster. You probably did a good deed. How many other people would they have killed if it hadn't been for you?"

"I guess you're right. I know the man at the store the next day appreciated they were dead."

"See Marcus; close this matter in your head. Don't let it bother you ever again. I admire you for the fact that you revenged your friends' deaths. That took a lot of bravery on your part. No, I won't hold it against you; I'll always admire you for it and feel safe when I am snuggled up asleep beside you."

Hearing Bonnie's words made him feel better and helped ease his feelings about the killing. "Bonnie, you are going to be a wonderful wife. You just solved a problem that has been haunting me ever since it happened."

Marcus asked Bonnie to tell him about her trip to Texas. She said her mother almost died. Her father then thought it was best to get back to their roots so they would be around family. She said on their return her mother had gotten well.

The entire afternoon the isolated road had seen no traffic, but late in the afternoon they heard a galloping horse approaching. They watched, and they saw a lone rider coming fast, his image, like Bonnie's, appeared between the trees, then came into view. Bonnie stood up, "Oh, that's Johnnie, you know my kid brother. Since I hadn't returned when I said I would, I guess Ma or Pa sent him out here to find me." When he came out of the woods and into the clearing that led to the pond, he saw Bonnie and reined in his horse. He hesitated a moment, not knowing the stranger, then he gave out a loud yell, spurred his horse and came galloping forward, yelling, "Marcus, Marcus, you're dead! No, you're home." He dismounted before the horse was stopped and ran beside the slowing horse, so excited and elated with who he recognized. "You're supposed to be dead. Bonnie read us the letter you had been executed. How'd you get loose?" Then he thought a minute. "You're not a ghost are you?"

Standing up and greeting him, "No Johnnie, it's really me. It's a long story, but I'm here. I'll tell you about it sometime."

Bonnie raised her hand showing off her ring, "Look, Marcus asked me to marry him, and I said I would, but don't tell Daddy until Marcus asks for my hand."

"He don't have to do that. You know Pa wants you to marry Marcus. He always has."

"I know, but Marcus wants to do this marrying right. It is just proper for a man to ask her father if he can marry his daughter. I want it, too."

"It don't matter, now, but Pa was worried why you hadn't come home. He told me to go find you and make sure you wasn't over at Kevin Hayes' place." Johnnie quickly put his hand over his mouth, knowing he said something he shouldn't.

Marcus looked at Bonnie, and she had a surprised look, as if a secret had been told. Marcus knew Kevin well and never liked him since the first time he saw him in primary school. His father was a wealthy plantation owner and paid a bounty that released his son from being drafted into the Army. His wealth enabled him to buy and bully his way in town. Not many people appreciated his attitude. Marcus looked at Bonnie, who would not look him in the eye but stared down at the back of her hand that had the ring. "Bonnie, you don't have to say anything, it has already been said. Were you seeing Kevin Hayes while I was gone?"

Bonnie looked at Marcus and her eyes misted, "Yes Marcus, but I only saw him twice, twice after I thought you had been killed. I love you, Marcus, and always have. Since I thought you were gone, and men are hard to find now, so many have been killed, I felt I had to get a man while I was still young. I didn't want to grow old by myself."

"But Bonnie, I told you to wait for me. I was coming home. I have been around the world to get back here and see you."

"Nothing's changed. It is the same as it was the day we said goodbye. Can't you see? I thought you were dead? First your Ma and Pa got a letter from the Army that said you was killed up in Maryland, and then yesterday, I got this letter from you that said you were getting shot. Why do you think I'm out here? I came to find you. Even though I know in my heart you were dead, and my Mama told me not to waste my time, I still came out here. Even if it was just one chance in a thousand or even ten thousand, I still had to come and find out for sure. You said in the letter you would be here."

Marcus looked at her glassy wet eyes.

"Please Marcus," she begged, "Believe me. I love you and always have."

Marcus could see and feel she was telling the truth. He raised his arms for her to come to him, indicating she was forgiven. Without waiting a second, she rushed to him and hugged him tightly twisting back and forth. "I know you do. It just scared me for a moment. I guess the jealous bull in me showed his ugly head. Please forgive me."

Marcus knew for sure now there had been nothing to Kevin's two visits with her. After a few more wet tears and hugs the three got on and in their modes of transport and headed toward town. They went first to Bonnie's home. Marcus told Bonnie and Johnnie he wanted to talk to their Pa.

Concerned about the delay of his daughter, Bonnie's father waited on the front porch for her return. The three saw him stand up and come off the porch to greet them as they neared the house. He saw his children and old Fetch, then a stranger coming down the road. Not seeing well, Marcus was nearly in the yard before he recognized Marcus; then he ran forward not believing who he saw. Like the others he said, "Boy, you're supposed to be killed. The whole town thinks you're dead." He stuck his hand out to shake Marcus's hand. "You're a mite taller than when you left, a little meaner looking, too."

Marcus shook his hand. "I don't know about that, sir, but I want to ask you a question." Marcus had wasted no time in getting down to business.

Her father continued, "Come on in the house. Connie will be glad to know you're alive." They all entered the house with a fire in the hearth. Bonnie yelled to her mother, "Mother, come in here quick. I wasn't wasting my time today. Look who's here." His wife came from the kitchen and threw her hands in the air and let out a scream of surprise. She wiped her hands on her apron and ran over and gave Marcus a big hug and another welcome home. Then she went to the back door and called for the rest of the family to come in the house and see who came to see them. As the rest of the kids entered the room, they were all surprised to see a walking dead man. The youngest boy, who came in last started crying when he saw Marcus. "He's dead, Mama. Ya'll said he was dead." He was eight years old and remembered Marcus before he left for the war, but it took a few moments of convincing before he would shake hands with Marcus.

The Staples family insisted he stay for supper, but Marcus told them he had not seen his family, but before he left, he asked Mr. Staples to come with him to his wagon. The others wanted to follow them, but Marcus told them he had an important question to ask Mr. Staples, and they needed to be alone. Mr. Staples grabbed his hat, and Marcus escorted him to his wagon and showed him his new wealth. Mr. Staples appreciated the fine horses and mules, but he did not think much of the wagon and was awed by the fact it had come from Nashville. Marcus quickly told him the story about the wagon and the hidden box that carried the detonators.

Marcus removed his hat. "But why I asked you to come outside, sir, is I to see if you will give me your permission to marry your daughter, Bonnie."

Mr. Staples took his hat off, too, and scratched his head as if he had asked him to solve a very difficult problem that needed a considerable amount of figuring. "Well Marcus, I figured that's why you wanted me out here by ourselves. Yes, with one condition."

"What's that Mr. Staples?"

"That you promise me you will take care of her until death do you part."

Before he said more, they heard squeals from the house. Marcus knew she had showed her mother and sisters the gold ring.

Mr. Staples looked back at the house, "Wonder what that's all about," then he finished his statement, "and that means providing her a warm house, a place to eat, providing for her needs, having lots of children, not getting drunk, never leaving her or being mean to her, and taking her and the children to church each Sunday."

Marcus quickly grabbed and shook his hand. "That's a deal. That's exactly what I wanted for her, too."

"Then you can ask her to marry you."

"Mr. Staples, I hope you don't get mad, but I already have. I even gave her a gold ring I bought in Mobile before I thought I was gonna be shot. Please forgive me, but when I saw her out at Sandy Creek today, I knew I couldn't wait. I love her so much, and she is so beautiful."

"I understand Marcus. To tell you the truth, I hoped you would be the boy around here she would choose. I always liked your family, and I could see a spark in you that told me you would make something of yourself. You were one of the reasons I hated to leave for Texas, but I thought things would be better there. It's been hard around here."

"Don't worry now, I'm home and have a permanent discharge from the Army. This spring, me and you and Pa, using my four mules, we're gonna put in a fine crop of cotton and grow a big garden, a garden big enough to feed all our family, raise and grow some hogs and chickens, too, and of course have a milk cow."

The two returned to the house and Bonnie asked her father, "Did he ask you a question about me Pa?"

Always having a good sense of humor and wanting to have some fun with his daughter, he answered, "No," keeping a stern face, "He wanted to lease my bottom so he could put in a crop next year. What was he supposed to ask me?"

Startled at first, she looked at Marcus with a disappointed face. "You didn't ask him? I thought that's why you wanted to see him?" Before she could think about crying, Marcus and her father began laughing, and when he asked to see the ring, she knew Marcus had done his job. With that question settled and knowing he would soon be new kinfolk, Marcus hugged everyone one more time and bid Bonnie a special farewell. He wanted to go home now, a place he had been seeking for almost two years. Marcus gave everyone a final wave, hollered at Fetch to jump up in the wagon, and the two left for the final destination that would end his adventure.

His homestead was two places over from the Staples's rent property. The sun was going below the horizon creating beautiful abstract patterns on the western sky. It didn't take him long to travel the mile between their homes. Marcus remembered the fun he had surprising Bonnie at the pond. He tied his animals a short distance from the house. He hushed Fetch and eased up to the house to see if anyone was about. He stared at the sight he had dreamed about in so many horrible places. His mind flashed back to the battlefield where he was stranded amid the bullets striking around him. He thought about his near hanging, the torture he endured in the coffin, and the other times he felt he would never see this view again.

He looked around. They still had Clara, their old milk cow; smoke came out of smokehouse, and the chickens were going to roost in their henhouse. The scene was as normal as the day he had gone away. Then, he knew at this time of day, his father, Calvin, and mother, Sarah, and his sister, Evelyn were eating supper back in the kitchen. After they finished supper, his mother would wash the dishes. His father would pack his pipe with tobacco, amble to the fireplace room to stoke the fire and light his pipe with a small twig snatched from the flames. After he puffed on the pipe to get it started, he would light a lantern, and then sit in front of the fire staring at the flames waiting for his wife to join him. His sister would sit down and begin sewing by candle light, mending clothes or darning socks, or if caught up on her chores, read.

They would sit and talk, a term used to discuss the happenings each had faced that day. Before they went to bed, Calvin would pull the lantern close to him, reach over on the nearby table and grab the Holy Bible. He had a place marked where he had ended his reading the night before. He would then read a chapter, and they would discuss its contents a few minutes. During his life, Marcus had heard the entire Bible read four or five times. With that done, his Father would stretch his arms up in the air and say, "I'm getting sleeping. How about you? It's gonna be a big day tomorrow. Let's get our rest." Without saying anything, his mother would rise with him, and they would go to bed. Evelyn would go to a small room near the kitchen. In bed, his parents would grab hands and Calvin would say a short evening prayer, loud enough for all to hear in the house. Then they would all say, "Good night." This was a nightly routine that had been performed thousands of times since Marcus was a boy.

He had lain on the floor and listened to his father read the Bible. He remembered when he was young, he disliked the nightly Bible readings when he had to leave his friends and come inside to hear the dull words his father spoke. He wanted to stay outside and play rather than to worry about his soul. He never thought he would ever see the day he wanted to hear those words again, but tonight, however, he couldn't wait.

Marcus hushed Fetch again and made him follow behind him. He opened the front gate and went to the back door. He knew they were eating in the dining room near the kitchen. He stepped up on the wooden porch, aware the sound of his shoes, like the rumble of a bass drum, could be heard inside. He pushed the unlocked door open, the hinges giving a long slow creak. He knew they had stopped eating now, most likely holding their next bite above the plate, hesitating to see who would enter the room. They would not be afraid. It would always be a neighbor or a friend who stopped by to say hello or leave or pick up something on their way home, never something to worry about.

The couple were holding their forks just as Marcus imagined, both looking to see who was coming when he stepped into the door. "I'm home." They both dropped their forks. At once the somber look on their faces brightened up and both rose, his mother shouting; "Marcus," and his father yelling "Son." Her emotions caught up with her and she had to sit down and regain her shocked senses. His father ran toward him, but when he saw his wife sit down, he turned to her fearing she was fainting. Marcus ran to his mother, "What's wrong Mother. Don't get sick. I've come home."

She reached up and put her arms around his neck. "Marcus, Marcus, I don't believe what I am seeing. God answered our prayers."

His father was aware of whom he saw but was speechless for a few minutes and just hugged and cheerfully shook his son. Finally, he pushed him back away, holding him at arm's length, looking at the prize of his life. "Son, we got the last letter you wrote before they shot you. How did you save your life?" He looked at his wife, "God did answer our prayers. When all hope seemed gone, we still prayed that God would use a miracle and bring you back to us."

"Believe me, Pa; He used lots of miracles to bring me home." They continued to hug each other and thank God their son was home. They looked Marcus over and discussed how he had grown and his voice had changed. There was not a happier place to be on the entire earth than the Mills home at that moment.

"Where's Evelyn? Did something happen to her?"

"Oh no, Marcus, she's over at Aunt Ellen and Uncle Billy's place. They are having a quilting bee. She'll be home in a couple of days. Like all of us did, she thinks you've been executed."

Before they could talk more, his mother, dedicated to her job, immediately headed for the kitchen. "I know you're hungry. I'm going to scramble you some ham and eggs. Ya'll sit down and talk. I can't believe you are here. Thank you, Lord!"

Marcus remembered his animals tied to the wagon. He asked his father to follow him; he had something to show him. As they left the house, Marcus heard his Mother still thanking God for the miracle she had just witnessed. When they came to the front porch, his father didn't see anything. "What is it you want to show me? You got a horse; where is it?"

"It's better than that. You won't believe it." When they walked into the road, his father could see the wagon and animals. "I have five horses and four mules, five saddles, two pistols, two rifles, and some Confederate money. I have been discharged from the Army and don't have to go back. I stopped at the Staples's place on the way home. I asked Bonnie to marry me, and since I will soon be in their family and them in ours, I told him, me, you and him would put in a big cotton crop and garden this spring." They walked to the wagon, his father questioning the condition of the wagon, still fulfilling its purpose to look dilapidated.

They climbed aboard and rode the short distance to the barn where they parked the wagon and turned the animals into the feed lot. The animals seemed pleased to be rid of their bridles, rope halters, and bits. Marcus poured some corn in a trough and hung up the saddles inside the barn. He secured his weapons and returned to consume a feast his mother had so proudly cooked.

After supper, the three actors assumed their old roles on the stage. His father smoked a pipe and lit the lantern. That night they had something finally to really talk about. Marcus told of his daring moments and his dances with death. He did not tell them about killing the deserters. They talked way into the night. Marcus looked at his father, "Read the Bible. I want to lie down on the floor and listen to you read. When I was a child I couldn't wait to grow up so I didn't have to hear you read this Book every night, but now I wouldn't swap anything for this moment." He got down on the floor with a pillow and lay back with his hands clasped behind his head. "Read Pa, I've waited a long time for this moment."

His father reached over and grabbed the Bible and opened it. He suddenly looked up, astonished with his mouth open and his eyes wide open. "This is a miracle."

"What's wrong Pa?"

"Why nothing, but this is miraculous." He looked back down at the Bible. Tonight I am reading from Luke, the fifteenth chapter of Luke," he hesitated and looked at them both again. "This is the story of the Prodigal Son." Is this a coincidence or a sign from God? This is the day our son came home." He smiled, "Tomorrow, we will kill the fatted calf." Then he thought a moment, "On second thought, we can't kill Clara, I guess we'll have to kill a fatted chicken or hog instead." They laughed. He read the famous story, and they all sensed how the father and the son really felt in the Bible story.

When he finished, he informed his wife that tonight, he would say their evening prayer before going to bed. They all stood up and stood close, holding each other's hands. Calvin Mills thanked the Lord for the miracle that had taken place and told Him how grateful they were for their son. They all said Amen, and then Calvin stretched his arms as he acted out the last lines of the nightly play. Marcus's bed had always been in the fireplace room. His mother gave him his old pajamas and he was soon ready for bed. He threw the covers back and crawled in the deep feather bed. In a few moments he heard his father say "Good night, Marcus." Marcus lay down that night feeling more secure and safe than he had ever felt in his life. His war was over.

48

The house came alive early the next morning with more excitement inside than it had seen in several years. Sarah was cooking early and Calvin was stoking the fires. Marcus woke up and looked around, a little confused about where he was, as if he was still on the Ohio River and just dreaming of being home. But this was for real; he remembered, he had come home.

Marcus learned times were hard for his family. Most every family had a man or two in the Army, many of whom had been killed. Because of hogs, chickens, corn, and peas most people had made do, learning to appreciate every bite of food for them and their animals.

They finished breakfast, and Marcus helped his father do his morning chores around the place. They fed the animals, and his father asked him if he still remembered how to milk Clara. Marcus grabbed a bucket and stool and soon brought the pail of milk to his mother.

Word spread through the community that Marcus was home, and it was not long until friends and family arrived to welcome him back, all amazed to see him alive. They were all pleased to learn he was going to marry Bonnie Staples....all but one that is.

By noon, plans had been made to host a proper welcome party in the community hall on Saturday. His homecoming seemed to enliven the community with good news rather than the dire reports of another defeat or letters informing one of their own boys had been killed. Calvin sent word for Evelyn to come home at once; Marcus was at home. Soon Evelyn arrived and hugged her brother not believing it was really him. Everyone would bring food, tables would be set up in the hall, and a dance would be held, not realizing at first there were not enough boys around for all the single girls to dance with. Many young female hearts were broken when they learned Marcus was getting married.

The day of the party, women cooked early, people dressed in their finest clothes, families rode in their best buggy or wagon, and single men rode on their best horse. Many families arrived early so the men could talk and the women could arrange and set out the food. There was fried chicken, rabbit, pork chops, and squirrel with dumplings, fish, collard greens, potatoes, carrots, peas, turnips, biscuits, corn and cornbread, along with pies, cakes, and cookies. Everyone should go home having had plenty to eat.

Although Marcus knew his wagon was sound, it looked decrepit and he was ashamed to take Bonnie in it, so he saddled Red and rode to Bonnie's house. He then escorted Bonnie and her family to the big party in their one horse buggy. Cheers were heard when the people saw Marcus ride up on his magnificent red steed. Marcus took his hat off and waved it in the air to show all he was glad to be home.

As Marcus looked down at the people coming forward to greet him, he thought about the last party given in his honor, and how he had been dishonored before it was over. He hoped this event would have a better outcome. He dismounted, and people cheered louder, as if getting off a horse was a heroic deed. As he pushed his way through the people, he shook hands and people slapped him on the back. When he got to the buggy, he helped Bonnie from the wagon and gave her a quick kiss on the cheek. Everyone cheered again. As the couple arrived at the steps to the town hall, people began yelling, "Speech, speech!"

Marcus wondered why everyone was treating him with such distinction. Outside of Bonnie and his family, no one had heard of his brave accomplishments. It had to be they thought of him as a Lazarus- type character, a man who had been brought back to life after for sure being dead. For many months rumor had it he had been killed at Sharpsburg, and recently they had heard he had been executed by his own Army. Maybe they just needed something to cheer about.

"Tell us why you're alive." "How did you survive?" "Why were they gonna shoot ya?" These were all questions people wondered about. Marcus motioned with his arms for people to quiet down so he could say a word or two. Bonnie stood next to Marcus with both arms around his arm, pulling him close. When the crowd got quiet, Marcus spoke, "Friends, thank you for coming to welcome me home. Bonnie and I will always remember this. However, I know there is some hot food inside waiting to be eaten. Let's go eat before it gets cold. Then, I promise to tell you what has happened to me since I left home. I am sure you will think I'm a liar when you hear it. Thank you all for coming; let's go and eat." Everyone cheered and they went inside, agreeing it was a good idea.

They assembled around the tables, and the local pastor of the Baptist Church was asked to say grace. After the long prayer, thanking God for Marcus's return, the stacks of plates were filled with good country cooking as people grazed from one table to another choosing from the bountiful buffet. Some were able to sit at a table while others stood. Others went outside and sat on the steps, while others used a wagon as a table. Times were hard but for that day, people had been generous and donated their "fatted chickens." Everyone was happy, and they forgot their hardships for a couple of hours. Everyone laughed, ate, and visited.

There were apple cobblers and cakes, cookies, and homemade candy, all washed down with milk or tea. As they finished, un-appointed disciplined women took charge of the cleanup, and volunteered their daughters to wash and dry the dishes. Many men walked outside to smoke and discuss the war, but volunteered their young boys to fold up the tables and straighten the chairs. As the cleanup ended, several country fiddlers and musicians gathered at the front of the hall and began playing. The music summoned everyone to gather back inside. When they had assembled in front of the musical group, the mayor hailed for everyone to pay attention. He began quieting the people by whistling and clapping his hands.

The crowd of several hundred or so quieted down. "Before we begin the dance, let's call Marcus back up here and get him to tell the story he promised us." They all looked over at Marcus and Bonnie and motioned for them to come forward. They walked out in front of the musicians. He had told his story many times now, and being among friends, he proudly stepped forward with no stage fright among friends. He told everyone he wouldn't be like the Sunday preacher and talk all afternoon, but he would make it quick so the party could begin. The people cheered.

Marcus cleared his throat and began the tale he had experienced the last few months. They all cheered when he had blown up the powder train and when the Union ships went down. He told his story stressing how his guardian angel had saved him on the occasions when all hope had been lost. He explained why the Army thought he was a spy. He finished hailing his friend Wendell as a hero. "He knew I wasn't a spy. Being a true friend in a time of my need, he risked his life to save mine. When he gets home, I want to give him a get-together. If it hadn't been for Wendell, I would be in a pauper's grave in Mobile. Matter of fact, I was in that grave for a short while." He then finished the story expressing the fear of being buried alive. When he finished, the hall was absolutely dead still and quiet.

Suddenly a man yelled out. "Marcus is a hero. Let's build a statue in his honor outside our town hall." Everyone cheered and hollered. Their town needed a hero, and a statue would be good. Not knowing at the time the cost of a bronze statue, everyone agreed. Then Marcus quieted them down.

"I must add one last thing, maybe a sad piece of this story. There are two Marcus Mills now, one that is lying in a grave in Mobile. The other is standing before you. If the Army ever finds out I'm not in that coffin, I fear they'll come after me. Please, no statue in the park. I hope you will keep my secret in this town. You all know I am not a traitor, but I will always fear that knock on the door, wondering if they found me. That's all I have to say."

Everyone cheered. They all knew what he said was the truth, that he was not a traitor or a spy. However, one person in the room had not cheered, but sat off to himself, burning with jealousy as he saw his future wife standing next to Marcus. She was his girl. As the roar of the crowd continued, Kevin Hayes looked down at the floor and grinned, knowing she would come back to him when Marcus was taken off and shot by the Army, and he would be the one who would tell them. All of a sudden, he decided to enjoy the party and be the friendliest man there. He would go and tell Bonnie how proud he was that she would marry such an honorable man. That would put him in good stead after Marcus was gone.

Marcus finished his story and stepped back and hugged Bonnie. The mayor came forward and announced for the dance to begin. Kevin made his way to Marcus and Bonnie to wish them the best. When Marcus saw him standing in front of him, his resentment boiled forth and he wanted to slap him down to the ground. He had the same feelings for Kevin as he did a snake. Nobody in the town liked Kevin. Although he was a handsome man, his bullying and crude behavior had isolated him somewhat in the community. Marcus wondered, as he looked at him, how his dear Bonnie could ever see anything of worth in him.

Kevin approached smiling. They both sensed, however, he was not faking his happiness when he expressed his regards for their upcoming marriage. "Bonnie, you are marrying a true hero." He looked Marcus in the eye, stuck out his hand to shake, "And Marcus, I wish you and Bonnie the best of life. I hope someday we can build a statue in your honor. After hearing your story, you deserve it." Kevin then turned and disappeared in the crowd. Next to Marcus, he appeared to be the happiest man in the place. Marcus should not have mentioned he was still sought by the Confederate Army, but these people were his friends and knew he was not a traitor and would keep his secret until the war was over and the Confederacy dismantled. Then he would be safe.

Most of the younger people danced; the older folks sat around the edge of the hall and watched, clapped, or talked. Cake and cookies were snacked on until they were all consumed. Men eased out to their horses or wagons and occasionally had a sip of alcohol. Because of the strong spirits, a few women took their husbands home when they began to act too cute or begin to get a little mean. Kevin had hit his bottle several times and was beginning to feel brave, and he too, talked too much.

On one of his trips to his horse to get a sip, he was joined by a young lad who worked for his father, too young for the Army and too young to drink, and asked Kevin for a nip. "Let me have a little of that stuff. I need a little loosening up."

Kevin handed him the bottle, the cheer had gone from his face. Hatred had overcome his mind. "Did you see Bonnie in there?"

"Yes, I did," he said as he turned the bottle up and took a big swig. "Her shore is priddy ain't she?"

Kevin grabbed him around the collar before all the whiskey went down, almost choking him. "Don't talk about my wife like that."

He pushed Kevin back, "That ain't yore wife, Kevin, Marcus is gonna marry that girl."

Kevin grabbed him around the neck again and pulled the young lad up under his chin, his alcoholic breath on his face. "No she's not; she's gonna marry me. I'm gonna tell the Confederate Army there's a traitor living here in Buckhead. Don't you get it now? They'll come and take him off somewhere and shoot him. Then she'll come back to me." He pushed the young kid back, grabbed his bottle and stuck it back in his saddlebag. "Just remember, Kevin always gets his way. I always have and always will. I wondered how I was going to get Bonnie back, but after he told me the secret, it will be easy now." He turned and walked back into the party.

The party lasted longer than expected and the band continued to play until dark. Due to a lack of young men, the boys and single men who were there had plenty of dance partners, some girls never being asked to dance. Many older people had been taken home, and others left to tend to their farms before dark. Marcus and Bonnie had the time of their life. They had danced to nearly every song, shook hands with everyone there, and had eaten their fill. Finally the music stopped and like all good times came to an end.

The last of the stragglers went to their horses and buggies including Marcus and Bonnie. They thanked the last of the people as they slowly strolled to their horse, taking time to face each other and practice a new dance step they had just learned. Both wanted the night not to end. The Staples had left earlier, knowing Bonnie knew how to ride sidesaddle and would ride home behind Marcus. When they got to Red, Marcus lifted his future bride with pride and sat her down behind the saddle. He mounted up, and they turned the horse for home, wanting to take their time and try to make the night live on.

To make it easy for Bonnie to hold on, he walked Red slowly, just clip clopping along. After a few minutes, they heard a rider coming up from behind. They turned to see a galloping horse coming closer. Then they could see the image of a young boy racing toward them in the moonlight, but beginning to slow down as he rode up within shouting distance. "Marcus, stop," they heard from a young voice. The young boy came up alongside, "Mr. Mills, you don't know me, but I have something important you would like to know I'm sure."

"What is it, boy?"

"You don't know me. I'm one of the Smith boys who live east of Buckhead. My name is Alexander, my friends call me Alex."

"Yes, I've worked for your Pa. What do you have to tell me?"

"I've been worrying about what I heard back there at the party."

"Well, what is it. Maybe I can help."

"It's not whether you can help me, but whether you can help yourself."

"What do you mean?"

"Kevin, I know Kevin Hayes. He's kind of a friend of mine. This evening I saw him go to his horse and take a swig of whiskey." He stopped and looked at Bonnie, "I don't want to scare you. Maybe I should just tell you, sir."

"No, tell us both. What about Kevin?"

"Sir, I know you have given everything to the war. You are a hero, but his daddy paid his way out of the war."

"We know that. Come on, boy, tell us about Kevin?"

"Well, when I saw him get his liquor, I walked over to him hoping he would give me a sip. I could tell he was a bit liquored up. He gave me a swig. When I said how priddy Bonnie was, he grabbed me by the throat and nearly choked me."

"Go ahead, what happened next?"

"If he knew I told you this he would kill me. You know he killed that Cheatham boy who lived down there in the bottom. Nobody ever knew what happened to him but me."

Bonnie spoke up, "Yes, that was big talk around the town," she looked at Marcus, "You had already gone off to war. Go ahead, boy, what happened?"

The boy continued, nervously watching the road as if someone would see them talking. "I was out still hunting one morning; I'd been there since daybreak, but fell asleep in the deep grass. I woke up to hear two people arguing. I hunkered down and stayed hid. As they got nearer I heard Kevin's voice. He was angry with Charles. That was the kid's name, Charles Cheatham. He shouted at him, 'If you tell anyone I will kill you!' The kid answered back and said he was going to go right then and tell Kevin's father what he had done."

"What had he done?"

"I never heard about that. I saw Charles turn his horse and start galloping away. Kevin lifted his rifle and shot him in the back before he got very far." Now beginning to get teary-eyed, the young boy yelled louder, "He shot him in the back. Charles never had a chance. He kilt him, and I saw it." The young boy hesitated, thinking back to the awful event, and fearing now, maybe he should just go home and not get involved with Marcus and Kevin.

"Why haven't you told somebody, the sheriff, or your father?"

"I did. I told my father. He told me not ever to tell anyone, just to keep my mouth shut. Accusing a plantation owner's son of murder would just bring our family a bunch of trouble. He said no one would believe what a tow-headed kid like me would say in court. So I kept my mouth shut. Besides that, Daddy owes him money for our land."

"What does his killing have to do with me?"

"Let me finish. The next summer, our little crop of corn burned up. We needed to get some corn before winter. My father heard Mr. Hayes was looking for some local kid to work and train some horses for him. Somebody told him about me, and I was hired. I started working over there and got to know Kevin priddy good. Of course, I never told him what I had seen. To tell you the truth, I was skeered of him, but over time he was friendly to me. He would steal his Pa's liquor and give me some sometimes. That's why I asked him for some whiskey tonight down at the party."

"Still, you haven't told me how it concerns me."

"He told me that he was going to marry Bonnie, and," before he could go on he was interrupted.

"You mean, he once was going to marry Bonnie, but not anymore. I am going to marry Bonnie."

"No, he intends to marry Bonnie after you've gone."

"Where am I going?"

"That's what I am trying to tell you. He said he was going to tell the Army that you were not killed back in Mobile, but were hiding up here in Buckhead. He said, they'd come and get you, take you back down thar somewhere and shoot you." Turning to Bonnie, "Then you would marry him, with Marcus gone and all."

"I would never marry him if he was the last man in Georgia. I will only marry Marcus."

"When did he say he was gonna tell the Army?"

"He didn't say. That's all I know, but I had to let you know. He's gotten by with one foul deed in his life. He shouldn't get by with another."

Marcus reached over to shake the boy's hand. "Thank you boy, I can never thank you enough for what you have just told me. Don't mention what you said to anyone, not even your father. I will take up the matter tomorrow."

Bonnie looked at Marcus, and with emotion in her voice, "What are you going to do Marcus? Tell me, what are you going to do?"

"Don't worry your little heart. Tomorrow I am going to pay Kevin a little visit. When I finish with him, he will not tell anyone anything."

The boy spoke up, "If I'd been braver, I might have killed him myself. If anybody needs killing he shore does. Wouldn't bother me a bit either, after I had done it."

Bonnie almost screamed, "Marcus, don't kill him. It will just bring us more trouble."

"I didn't say I was going to kill him, I just said I was going to pay him a little visit." He looked at the boy and thanked him again for the information. "Now, run along home, boy; I'll handle this matter now. Remember, forget about what you said or saw tonight."

He reined his horse for home, "I won't say a word, Mr. Marcus." With that he spurred his horse and galloped down the road and disappeared in the dark.

On their way home, Marcus soothed and calmed Bonnie as they walked the horse through the night. He assured her that he had other ways he had learned in the Army that would convince Kevin to keep his mouth shut without killing him. "Remember my friend, Wendell?"

"Yes, I know him. I talked to him a couple of months ago. He asked about you when he was home."

"You know from what I told you, he is a true friend who would do anything for me and proved it by risking his life for me in Mobile."

"Yes, what about it?"

"I will simply tell Kevin that if ever a hair on my head is damaged by the army, Wendell will make him curse his mother and wish he had never been born."

"But Wendell will be arrested, too, and probably shot for helping you escape."

"Don't worry; Kevin doesn't know how many friends both of us have here in Buckhead. I will remind him there are many Wendell's here in Buckhead who would enjoy carrying out any orders we might ask of them. Also, I will remind him that if I am arrested, I will tell them what I saw while still hunting one morning. That should shut him up."

"I feel better now. I thought you were gonna kill him."

The two arrived at the Staples's house and kissed goodnight. Marcus got home in time to hear his father read the Bible, say the nightly prayer, and hear everyone say goodnight to each other, including his sister, even though it was a little later than normal. Marcus would talk to Kevin after he took care of his morning chores.

49

The next morning, Marcus was delayed getting started. A neighbor had come by and asked if he would help him round up a sow that had gotten out during the night. When they had captured the hog, he put a pistol in his belt and told his folks he was going to town.

He had to pass through Buckhead to get to the large Hayes plantation. Kevin lived in a new house his father had built for him on the edge of his large estate. He had never been to Kevin's house but had heard where it was. As he passed through town, he noticed people had gathered near the sheriff's office, all abuzz with news about a killing.

He rode up and was greeted by the men. "Have you heard, Kevin Hayes was killed this morning?"

"What did you say? Kevin Hayes was killed?"

"Yes, it seems he killed his 'self. Shot his 'self in the head. Why would a rich kid like that shoot his 'self?"

"I can't imagine. He seemed to have so much fun last night."

There was a commotion down the street and they saw the sheriff approaching the jail. He was riding a large black horse and was escorting a wagon holding Kevin's body. They stopped in front of the jail and pulled back the blanket covering his body. The Sheriff dismounted and explained what he thought happened. "At first we thought he killed himself. We found his gun beside his body, and one chamber had been fired. His father verified it was his gun. But instead of suicide, it appears he came to the front door and somebody shot him in the heart. Needless to say, plenty of people didn't like him much. Matter of fact, I felt like shooting him a time or two myself." The people laughed relating to the fact most of them had reasons to shoot him too.

The Sheriff continued; Marcus listened from his horse. "We found no tracks. He had a brick walk. He scratched his head, "I expect we are looking at a murder case. We talked to a slave who lived close by, and he reported hearing two shots an hour before daylight. At least he thought it was two; one woke him up, and then he heard another one a few seconds later. Since two shots were fired, if the slave was correct, and we only found one gun with an empty chamber, then someone else shot him. It's that simple. Kevin must have fired before or after he was shot."

"Sheriff," someone asked, "Have you got any suspects or any idea who done it?"

"Yes I do, Jed, I think you did it," but before Jed could deny the accusation, the Sheriff then pointed at Marcus, "He may be guilty, too." He laughed, "The entire town now is suspect. Like I said, thinking back, most everyone is town may have had a reason they would like him shot. I'll just start asking people who might want him shot the worst and arrest the man with the best reason for killing him." The Sheriff then told one of his deputies to go get the undertaker. The people stood around and discussed the matter for a few minutes, then dispersed going about their morning business.

Marcus turned his horse and rode out of town, relieved that Kevin had been killed. He would not have to confront Kevin and threaten him not to tell the Army about his secret. As he trotted back to the farm, he wondered who, other than himself, had a reason to kill him. Kevin's lifelong evil ways and behavior caused many people to hate him, but who would want to kill him that bad or want to kill him besides himself.

Then it hit him like a bolt of lightning, giving him a major "goose-feather feeling." "Ah, no, no!" he thought, "Did Bonnie shoot him?" She had been so fearful the night before when the youngster told them about Kevin. He reined his horse and galloped toward Bonnie's home. He passed people on the road who waved at him, but he was so intense to find her, he did not notice and wave back. When Marcus rode up to the house and entered the yard, he saw Bonnie standing behind the house hanging clothes on the line to dry.

He walked quickly, and Bonnie could detect something was wrong. As he came closer, she could see his worried look as he stared her directly in the eye. "What's wrong Marcus? What's happened? Did you talk to Kevin?"

"No!" Marcus answered in a manner she had not seen before.

"Then why are you so angry? You are safe now. We will always be together now."

Before he could answer, Marcus noticed one of her silver combs she always wore was gone. "Where's your comb. One of your combs is missing."

"Oh, I guess it fell out over by the wash pot when I was scrubbing these clothes. I'll find it later."

He came up and grabbed her by the shoulders and gave her a quick kiss. "Nothing's wrong with me, but there is certainly something wrong with Kevin Hayes."

"What are you talking about?"

"He's dead; somebody killed him during the night."

She put her hand over her mouth and gasped, "He's dead? Who did it, how can that be? We saw him last night."

"Well, he got sick and died suddenly. That's what happens when you're shot in the heart."

"Do they know who killed him?" she said in a quivering voice.

"No. I was going to see him this morning and discuss the matter we talked about last night."

Before he could continue, she yelled, "Did you kill him? Ohhh, you killed him didn't you."

"No, absolutely not; I was going to his place this morning when I heard the news. What I'm worried about," he hesitated, not wanting to utter his next words, "I thought it may have been you that went over there and shot him. I know how upset you were last night."

"Me? Marcus Mills, how could you think of such a horrible thing? I get upset when I have to ring a chicken's neck. I remember how sweet they were when they were little."

"Well then, if I didn't kill him and you didn't kill him, who did?'

Bonnie thought back, "If it wasn't one of us, then it had to be the kid, what's his name, the kid that told us about Kevin?"

"Alex… Alex Smith?"

"Yes, he even said he needed killing and might even do it himself, but for sure, Marcus I didn't kill him. You can ask Pa. I was home all night."

"That relieves my mind. I was so scared you went out of your head and killed him 'fore he could tell our secret. Well, get on about your business. I need to go tell the Sheriff about Alex and that Charles kid's killing. I'll see you later today." Marcus apologized to her for thinking that she could have done such a thing and gave her a quick kiss and left to go tell the Sheriff what he knew.

Marcus rode back to town and stopped at the Sheriff's office. He entered the office to find the Sheriff behind his desk drinking a cup of hot sassafras tea with his boots on the desk. "Come in Marcus and sit down. That sure was a great dance last night. How have you been since you got home?"

Marcus reached over the desk and shook hands, "Sheriff Duncan, it couldn't be better. If we could win the war and end this mess, I would feel even better. You might be able to have some coffee, too, instead of homemade tea," he said as he pointed to the light colored tea in the cup."

"Yeah, coffee prices are too high, but there's plenty of sassafras roots. The blockade has just about cut off all our coffee." He took a sip of tea and offered Marcus a cup. "I know you didn't come here though for a cup of tea. What can I do for you, Marcus?"

"It's about Kevin's killing."

"What about it. You know who did it?"

"Not exactly, but I know who killed Charles Cheatham."

"Did you do it?" he smiled, but after thinking a moment added, "No you couldn't have done it; that happened after you went to the Army." He took his feet off the desk, tilted the cup up to finish his tea, leaned forward and in a quiet voice asked, "Then tell me who killed Charlie."

"Kevin Hayes. He killed him."

"How do you know that?"

"Alexander Smith told me."

"How does Alexander know?"

"He told me last night after the party he saw Kevin shoot him."

"Why didn't he tell me this earlier?"

"He was scared. He told his pa and his pa told him it would be better for him to keep his mouth shut, knowing how Mr. Hayes nearly owned the town. Mr. Hayes could have made it hard on the Smith family."

"Huh, that's interesting," the Sheriff answered leaning back in his chair scratching his head, thinking about further complications in Kevin's death. "Kevin must not have known Alex saw him kill Charlie. If he had, I imagine Alexander would be dead now," the Sheriff reasoned.

"From what I know of Kevin, I would imagine that's so," Marcus agreed.

"I'll send out for Alexander and get him to tell me what he saw."

"No Sheriff, I wouldn't do that. I know what Alex told me was the truth. Somebody gave Kevin his just reward, and he is gone. It took a lot of courage for that kid to tell me what he saw. If Mr. Hayes learned about Alex's story, I imagine the Smith's would have to leave town."

"I suspect that's a good idea. I will stop Alex when I see him in town and find out what he saw, for the records you know, but I will not mention his name." The Sheriff wrote down a note on a sheet of paper, and then he looked up at Marcus, "By the way, why did he tell you about that murder. That's kind of a coincidence that he told you about the murder several hours before Kevin was killed. Do you think Alex killed Kevin?"

Marcus shut his eyes and grimaced as if in pain, knowing he should have kept his mouth shut. He knew what he was going to say could possibly implicate him as a suspect in Kevin's murder. "No Sheriff, I don't think so. Let me explain what I know."

"Yes, go ahead."

"When the party was over last night, Bonnie and I were riding home in the moonlight. We then heard a rider coming up fast from behind us, and Alex came up in the dark. He told me that Kevin was going to tell the Army authorities that I had not been executed but escaped using my friends in the Army."

"Why would he do that to you?"

"Well, sir, while I was at war, as you know, the rumor spread that I had been killed at Sharpsburg. Kevin decided he would get sweet with Bonnie since I was now gone forever. I learned that he had courted her twice. When I came back, he realized Bonnie loved me instead. Telling the army about my whereabouts was how he could get rid of me again. He knew I would be executed, but what's worse, my friends that got me free would be involved and executed too. You know most of those boys who grew up here."

"I see." He looked up at Marcus. "Unfortunately, this makes you a possible suspect in this murder, also."

"Yes it does. As a matter of fact, it makes Bonnie a suspect in Kevin's killing, too. Sheriff, I hesitated about telling you this, but I always knew since I was a little boy, and as long as you have been the boss around here, you treated everybody in a fair way. If I had been guilty of Kevin's murder, I wouldn't have told you this story."

"Don't worry, I feel for certain you are not the culprit." He leaned farther back in his chair and cocked his head slightly, a sign that he was going to ask Marcus a tough question.

"Marcus, when I went out to Kevin's place this morning, I found his body. In the dirt beside the walk Kevin had written the letter "P" in the sand, and then died."

"What do you think that means?"

"Oh, maybe he was trying to write out the name of his killer. What troubles me with this is what I found out there in the sand next to the brick walk."

"What was it?" Marcus fearfully asked.

The Sheriff leaned forward and opened the top desk drawer. "This." With the simple answer, he held up a silver comb that matched Bonnie's missing shiny comb. "I think you know whose comb this is as well as me and everyone in town."

Marcus's face turned pale as he stood up straight as if he was facing a severe punishment, similar to his stature when his father would punish him with a belt. His father always added, "Stand up and take it like a man."

The Sheriff studied Marcus observing every clue that Marcus might emit determining whether Marcus had told him the truth. The Sheriff scooted his chair closer to his desk and took a pencil and wrote the letter 'P' on the back of a used envelope. "You see Marcus, the letter 'P' could be the beginning of the letter 'B' and 'B' followed by and 'O', then an 'N' followed by another 'N', and finally an 'I' and an 'E.'" The old lawman, with years of knowledge on his face, looked Marcus squarely in the eyes, "Marcus, you know as well as I do, it looks bad for Bonnie."

Marcus folded his arms in disgust and squeezed his lips together knowing what he said was true. "Sheriff, I just got back from Bonnie's house. When I heard this morning Kevin had been shot, I thought the same thing and galloped over there to ask her if she killed him, and she said she couldn't ring a chicken's neck, and I believed her. I still believe her. I know it looks bad Sheriff, but I know she is innocent," his eyes beginning to shine with tears and knowing what he had suffered to get home might be lost and his dreams shattered like his beloved Dixie and the finger of guilt pointed directly at her.

"Do you think she loved you enough that she would kill to save her future husband?" the sheriff continued.

"That's a cutting question Sheriff. I think she loves me very much, but whether she would kill for me, I couldn't say."

"Let me change the subject. Did you notice if one of her silver combs was missing?"

Marcus paused as if he was remembering. He knew the answer, and the answer would certainly seal her guilt. He hesitated longer trying to use his mind that had saved his life so many times to see if he could conjure up a satisfactory response. He was sure Bonnie was innocent, and there had to be another answer to this riddle, but rather than lie and say no and possibly taint any future testimony, Marcus hesitated, looked at the ceiling, then at the Sheriff and sadly replied, "Yes, I noticed one of her combs was missing."

"Well Marcus, I hate to have to do this, but I must go out to the Staples's place and bring Bonnie back here to jail. Instead of me doing that, why don't you go out and bring her down here. Talk to her and help her gather some things together. I hate to mention this, Marcus, but she may never go home again. I'll see to it she is comfortable and have a lady sit with her at night to keep her company during her trial."

Marcus swallowed the dire event and promised the Sheriff he would return with Bonnie later in the day. Marcus, visibly upset, shook hands with the Sheriff and walked to his horse followed by the Sheriff. "Don't fear Marcus, she will have a fair trial, and most likely if she didn't kill him, the truth will be known."

Marcus mounted his horse and reined her away from the Sheriff and trotted down the road. Marcus, for the first time felt sorry for himself. It seemed God was continuing to place horrible situations in is life. Marcus slightly kicked his horse to a trot to hurry and get out of town. The brave hero's eyes moistened with tears again as he felt like a young child who needed his strong father to talk to and reinforce his grit and say, "Son, don't worry. Everything's alright." Suddenly, out of the blue, a strong gush of wind slapped Marcus in the face and brought Marcus out of his despair. Marcus looked up at the wonderful cold sky and understood he had a Father who had made things alright many times in the last two years, and He would continue to be his Father and things would be alright. Reinforced by his faith in God, Marcus urged his horse into a gallop and raced toward Bonnie's house.

Marcus galloped up to the Staples's gray unpainted house. Smoke was coming out of two chimneys, one for warming and one for cooking. He knew it was going to be a difficult task to face the Staples family and tell them what he was sent to do. He knocked on the front door and Mr. Staples greeted him at the door. He led Marcus to the kitchen where Bonnie and her mother were cooking and baking. Bonnie ran to Marcus and gave him a kiss, "You got here just in time for dinner."

Rather than cause an interruption before dinner, he decided to wait until after they ate to pronounce the real reason for his presence. Everyone seemed happy and Bonnie didn't show any sign that she had ever killed anyone. Marcus was convinced she was innocent.

When done with dining, the table of food was covered with a tablecloth until supper, and Marcus pitched in and helped wash the dishes. When they finished, Bonnie hung up her apron, and at Marcus's request walked with him outside to stroll through the woods. After a few minutes, Marcus stopped, faced Bonnie, and put his hands on her shoulders. "Bonnie, I need to ask you something, the hardest thing I had to ask anybody in my life. Where did you go last night after the party?"

"Like I said, I came home and went to bed like I always do."

Marcus held her tighter and slightly shook her and in a slightly louder voice, "Bonnie, you know that's not true. You went to Kevin's house last night! Don't lie to me."

Bonnie jerked back, rebelling against what he said. "Why do you question me?" speaking back, loudly confronting Marcus in a tone of voice Marcus had never heard.

"Bonnie, where is your other comb?"

"I already told you; why? What are you getting at? Are you trying to say I killed Kevin?"

"No, I'm not saying that, but the Sheriff is! I went to see him this morning, and he has your missing comb in his desk drawer that he found beside Kevin's body. He showed it to me!"

Bonnie gasped placing her hands over her mouth, hesitated, then stepped forward and wrapped her hands around Marcus, realizing her falsehood had been revealed and began sobbing, "Yes, Marcus I went over there last night to ask Kevin not to tell the Confederate Army where you were. That was my intention."

"Now, tell me all you remember about what happened last night. If you didn't do it, then I can find out the truth and get us out of this situation. I have a Friend that has helped me before."

"Who is that, Marcus? Do I know him?"

"Yes, by all means you know Him. It's God. When I thought my world was over, He worked a miracle and my life was saved. I know He will stand by us now. Let's pray and hope that everything will be resolved. I do understand He answers prayers."

She hugged Marcus, "Marcus, please believe me, I did not kill him."

"Bow you head and I will say a prayer." Marcus pulled Bonnie closer and remembered back when he was next to the Potomac River looking at Bonnie's photograph wanting to be closer to her. "God we need your help. You helped me so many times I might not have any miracles left, but Bonnie hasn't used any of hers, so please help her with this falsehood against her. I, Bonnie, and You know she is innocent so move your mighty hand and make things right for her. Help her in the coming days to overcome this tragedy. Amen."

"Thank you, Marcus. That was a good prayer."

Marcus now had to find out what Bonnie knew about the events of the night and inform her why he was there. "Bonnie, the reason I came back today was not to have dinner, but to bring you back to the Sheriff. He wants to talk to you and ask you some questions."

"I don't mind, I'll tell him everything I saw."

"But Bonnie you don't quite understand. He is going to keep you in jail. He found your comb, and he also found where Kevin had written the letter "P" with his finger in the sand before he died."

"Then that proves I am innocent. My name doesn't begin with a "P".

Marcus picked up a stick and kicked a smooth spot in the dirt and wrote the letter "P" and then added the curve to make a "B". "You see, he was trying to write the word *Bonnie*; that's what the Sheriff is thinking, so tell me everything you saw over at Kevin's last night. Don't leave out anything. Let's sit down here on the ground, and you tell me your story."

Bonnie was obviously shocked with what she heard Marcus utter. She quietly let go of Marcus and sat down on the ground as Marcus gently held her and eased her to the ground. Marcus sat down next to her to listen intently to what she said.

"Yes, I went over there." Then in a stern voice she added, "I was not going to let that cur ruin our lives. I was going to tell him in no uncertain words I would never marry him if he told the Army about you and I would hate him forever. I was also going to tell him if he told on you, I would tell the Sheriff what Alex had said."

"Oh, you didn't tell him about Alex." Then Marcus thought, "I guess it doesn't matter now whether you told him about Alex or not; Kevin is dead now. Go ahead with your story."

"I had to wait until Pa was asleep. I slipped out to the barn and got the bridle and went to the pasture and caught old Pete and rode over to Kevin's place. The moon was out, and I could see clearly in the dark. I saw nobody until I got to Kevin's house. There was a lantern in the front room, so I tied Pete to the fence, opened the front gate, and walked quietly up on the porch. To my surprise, I heard someone snoring in a chair on the front porch. It scared me for a moment, and I stopped. Then, as I got closer, I saw it was Kevin. There was a whiskey bottle by his chair. I saw the reflection of the window light on the bottle. I eased down the porch until I was standing in front of him. He was still asleep. Then I kicked him on the leg to awaken him. At first he didn't move and I had to kick and shake him several times to bring him to. When he opened his eyes, he must have thought he was dreaming and started talking out of his head. In a deep voice he tried to say words, but I couldn't understand him. Finally, I yelled, "Kevin, wake up, this is Bonnie; I want to talk to you." He seemed to fall back to sleep. I had backed up after I had yelled at him, so I moved forward again when he lunged forward, grabbing me and pushing me back down the porch toward the steps. I twisted and turned to get away, and finally both of us fell down the steps, and I rolled on the ground away from him. The smell of whiskey was awful."

"Did you get hurt?" Marcus asked.

"No, I seemed alright and jumped up as fast as I could. Being drunk, he tried to stand, but kept stumbling and falling down. Standing then, I stepped back realizing I was looking at a wild man. After falling several times, he seemed to regain his balance and started yelling, 'Bonnie! Bonnie! You've come back to me. I knew you would.'

I immediately told him he better not tell the Army about your whereabouts. I told him I would never marry him whether you were living or dead and to forever forget about that notion. I also told him I knew he had killed Charles, and if he told on you, I was going to tell the Sheriff about him. He started walking toward me, and I started backing up telling him to stay away. At that time, I tripped on something; maybe it was a whiskey bottle, and I fell backward on the ground."

"Where was Kevin?"

"He stumbled forward and stopped, standing above me. Then he reached inside his belt and pulled out his pistol and aimed it at my head." Bonnie began to sob, "I can see his silhouette against the moon as he aimed the pistol at me. He said I wasn't telling nobody anything and I could join Charles in Calhoun's well."

"Are you talking about the old abandoned well on the Calhoun place?"

"I don't know what he was talking about," Bonnie now sobbed, tears flowing down her face. "I noticed his hand holding the pistol was moving back and forth, and he would lose his balance and catch himself with his foot. I heard him cock the pistol, and I knew he was going to kill me at that moment, so I rolled over; I don't know what caused me to do that, but I did."

Marcus smiled and thought to himself, "I know who made you move."

"When I rolled on my side, I heard the pistol shot. It was so loud, but I didn't hurt nowhere. I heard him cock the pistol, and then I heard another shot, but it sounded farther away. Suddenly, Kevin collapsed on me and starting writhing around on the ground. I was scared then. All I knew was Kevin was hurt, and I wanted to go home. Before I could get up, he grabbed my hair. That must have been when I lost my comb. I jumped up, lifted my skirt, and ran for old Pete. I didn't know if I would be shot or what was happening. I had ridden sidesaddle on the horse riding over, but I lifted my skirt and straddled old Pete and we raced for the house. All I reckoned was I was safe and not hurt anywhere. While I galloped home, I wondered who shot Kevin, and whether they saved my life or would shoot me next. Before I got to the house, I slowed to a walk, dismounted, and led Pete into the pasture, unbridled him, and slipped back in the house. I was so upset I couldn't sleep. All I could think about was Kevin silhouetted against the moon and how lucky I was to be alive."

Marcus realized Bonnie's story could be proved. He told Bonnie not to fear going to the Sheriff. What she had told him would prove what she said was true, and she wouldn't spend any time in jail. As they walked back to the house Marcus looked up in the sky, "I told you I had a Friend who could help us and He just did. Let's go talk to the Sheriff."

Marcus harnessed Pete to the buggy, and the two lovers rode into town and stopped in front of the jail. They entered the front door and Marcus escorted his future wife inside. "Sheriff, here she is like I promised."

"Where are your spare clothes? You know it might be a while before you get to go home."

Marcus smiled and stepped forward, "Sheriff, she will not spend the night in jail."

"You mean you hired a lawyer?"

"No sir, when you hear her story you will dismiss the charges against her."

The Sheriff pulled up two chairs close to his desk and asked her to tell him what she had seen. She told the Sheriff what she related to Marcus with Marcus sometimes inserting a detail she omitted from her first story. When she finished, Marcus leaned back and stretched his arms out, "I think if we take Bonnie back to Kevin's place and let her show us where she was on the ground we can find that bullet in the sand. That should prove what she told us was true, but if you are not convinced, there's one more thing; Kevin told her where he hid Charlie's body. Why would he tell her that if he wasn't fixing to kill her? We can go get Jacob, the well digger, and go clean out Calhoun's well and see if he can find Charlie's bones in there. If the bones are there, then Bonnie has told you the truth, and she is innocent of Kevin's murder."

"I'll agree to that," the Sheriff added. "Let's go to Kevin's front walk. Maybe we can also find out who shot Kevin. Whoever it was they saved Bonnie's life and I won't arrest him."

Bonnie hesitated, "I'm afraid. I don't want to go back there. In my mind, I can still see Kevin trying to kill me. It's so real."

"Have no fear girl. If what we suspect is true, this will be the finest trip you'll ever make."

The Sheriff gathered up several locals hanging around the small town to get their shovels and follow them to Kevin's place. They soon arrived. They could tell Bonnie was nervous as she stepped down from the wagon. The Sheriff encouraged her to reenact the story from the time she tied her horse. Step by step she carefully walked through the scene, constantly using her handkerchief to wipe her nose and eyes. She was visibly upset, and her voice quivered as she told what happened as best she could remember. She quietly retraced her steps up the stairs and down the porch to Kevin's empty chair. The whiskey bottle was on the floor beside Kevin's chair. "He was sleeping right there," she pointed. She recalled her struggle with him as she was pushed back to the stairs. Finally she arrived at the spot and estimated where Kevin was standing and pointed to the ground where her head had lain. The wind had blown Kevin's letter written in the sand and it was almost gone, but it was very close to where Bonnie had fallen.

The men did not have a screen to sift the dirt, but they carefully took each shovel full of soil and placed it on the hard pavement of the walk and slowly moved it back and forth with their fingers until all of it was gone. A small coin was soon found, along with two rusty square nails. In the fourth scoop of dirt a flattened shiny lead bullet was found. "I guess this is proof you were telling the truth," the Sheriff said as he took the flattened bullet from one of the diggers.

Bonnie and Marcus were elated. She would not spend the night in jail nor be on trial for murder, and Kevin would never tell the Army about Marcus. Next, the Sheriff picked up Jacob, the local well digger, along with his other laborers and went out to the Calhoun place. They erected a heavy wooden tripod over the well entrance that supported a pulley with a long rope attached to a wooden seat that enabled Jacob to be lowered down into the well. Soon the skeletal remains of Charles were brought out of the well in a bucket. It was a gruesome sight as the dingy white bones and skull wrapped in tattered rags were raised from the well. When their work was done the Sheriff ordered the men to bring a couple of mules with a slip, a device for moving dirt, and fill in the well. He shook his head as he got on the wagon and looked at the men, "I don't think I would want to drink water from that well. Would you?" The Sheriff returned to town with Charles's remains and proof that Bonnie had told the truth. However, the mystery was not yet solved; who shot Kevin?

Marcus and Bonnie had stayed in town while the well was searched. It was midafternoon when the Sheriff returned with all the facts in the case that fit perfectly. Word quickly spread, and soon a crowd of rubberneckers gathered to gawk at Charles, or what was left of him. Comments were heard from various people. "I always wondered what happened to that boy." Another quoted as he nodded his head up and down, "I know'd it all the time that the Hayes kid had something to do with it."

The Sheriff stood up in the wagon and announced he had solved a murder that day, and Kevin Hayes would spend an eternity in Hell's fire for what he had done. "But if anyone of you knows anything about who shot Kevin, I need to know. Come to my office and tell me." He looked down at Bonnie. "Bonnie, what we found in the Calhoun well proves without any reservations that what you told me was true. Now, both of you go home. I'm done with you, thank the Lord."

Marcus grasped Bonnie and kissed her gently. "Let's go home and get married." With that said he lifted his future bride into the buggy and turned Pete toward home. The horrible ordeal was over.

The undertaker came and took the bones. The large crowd began to disperse, and the Sheriff entered his office knowing that solving the Cheatham case was a feather in his hat. He went inside with a deputy to have some tea, rest, and read his local paper on how the war was going. The deputy prepared his hot tea, and the two lawmen discussed the day's events. It wasn't long until the Sheriff heard the latch on his front door clink and the door slowly open. The Sheriff looked up to see a young boy peeking through the slightly released door.

"Come on in son. Don't be afraid. What can I do for you?" When the door opened wider, the Sheriff could see it was Daniel Smith's boy, Alexander. The Sheriff knew most of the families in his county. The lad entered the room without saying a word and walked up to the Sheriff's desk. In a trembling voice he stated, "Sheriff, I have something to tell you. I was outside and heard you say if anyone knew who killed Kevin Hayes to come and tell you."

That sentence caught the Sheriff by surprise, and he laid down the newspaper. "You know who shot Kevin?"

"Yes sir, I do." He began to tremble in front of the Sheriff, as if he were in front of a king. He was silent and stared down at the floor, and the Sheriff could see he was dreadfully frightened.

"Go ahead, son, tell me what you know. Nothing is going to happen to you if you tell the truth."

He looked into the Sheriff's eyes as his own began to fill up with tears. "I shot Kevin!" he cried out. "I had to. I didn't want to, but I saw everything," he sobbed aloud.

The Sheriff stood up and looked at his deputy who was as surprised as he was. He walked around to Alex and sat him down in a chair while he pulled up another. He watched for a moment as the boy continued to cry. "Young man, you did the right thing coming to tell me this. Don't be afraid for saving a woman's life from an evil man. Now, tell me what you saw."

Alex sat down and wiped his eyes with his dusty fingers, leaving a little teary mud streaked on his face. "Well, it all started with 'Bear,' you know, 'Bear' Hastings, the black boy. Anyway, I had just come home from the big party when Bear came by. He wanted me to go fishing with him in the creek. I was tired and all, but he was a friend, so I decided to go. The fish were really biting good, and we soon had a bucket full of perch, so we brought them home and was scaling them next to where I stay at the end of the barn."

"Do you live at Kevin's place?"

"Yes sir, I help train his horses. I'm pretty good at that."

"That's why you were at Kevin's house?"

"Yes. We was about done when we heard a shot nearby. Didn't thank too much of it; probably just Mr. Hayes shootin' at a varmint or something like that. The moon was out and we could see pretty well. Then we heard another loud shot. I told 'Bear' that sounded like it came from the front of Kevin's house. We got curious and I told him to sneak up thar and see what the shootin' was all about. After a while he came running back grinning. He said Kevin was drankin' whiskey and was real drunk, but he had gone back on his porch and sat down in his chair and most likely went to sleep."

"Boy, what you tell me sounds as if you are telling me the truth. Go ahead and finish."

Alex was getting control of his tears and continued. "When we were done cleaning the fish we put them in two buckets and we started up toward the road past Kevin's yard. About the time we got even with his house and could see Kevin on the porch, we heard a galloping horse coming toward the house. I waved at 'Bear' to hide, and we lay down behind the plank fence around Kevin's yard. In the moonlight, I could soon see it was Bonnie. She got off her horse and tied it to the front gate and came in the yard. She walked to the porch and saw Kevin asleep. She walked up to him and kicked him to wake him up, but he was drunk. After a good shaking he came to and started wrestling with her. They both fell down the steps and that's when I saw Kevin get up and raise his pistol. I couldn't believe he was gonna shoot her. That's when I grabbed my musket and stood up."

"What were you doing with your rifle?"

"I had it when we were fishing. You know, Sheriff, I might have run into something in the dark that I might kill and bring home, something that was tastier than fish, like a big fat coon."

"Yes, yes, I see, go ahead."

"But when he raised his pistol to kill Bonnie I had to do something. I stood up and aimed at him, but he fired before I did. When I saw he had missed, and when I heard his pistol cock to shoot her again, I fired my rifle and killed him. When I saw him fall and Bonnie get up and run back to her horse, I looked at 'Bear' and told him never to tell anyone what I had done or what he had seen. I was so scared. I know'd I had erred terribly. I know'd what I did saved her life, and I guess I am proud of that, but when Kevin's Pa finds out I killed his son, he will kill me. You know how mean he is to everybody. He'll run my daddy and mama off our land. Daddy still owes him lots of money for our farm."

"No, after what you have told me, you and your family will be safe; I will protect you and your folks. What did you and 'Bear' do next?"

"We skedaddled to where we stays. I went back home and left Kevin's place. I been thar ever since until Mama sent me to town to see if I could find any flour. That's when I saw the crowd and came over to see what was happening. I figured it had something to do with Kevin."

"Indeed it did, and because you told Marcus you had seen Kevin kill Charles, Bonnie will not go on trial. Everything has worked out well. I just wish you had told me about Charles right after it happened."

"I didn't 'cause I was skeered of Mr. Hayes."

"Don't worry about what you did. You done the right thing. I am going out and ask 'Bear' what he saw, and if he matches what you said the case will be closed, and I mean closed." The Sheriff looked over at his deputy as he continued to talk to Alex, "And Alex, don't you tell a sole what you have told me today. Deputy Carter and I are the only people who have heard your story, and we know the truth now.

We will tell people Kevin was shot by one of the many people that he had mistreated during his life, so don't worry about Mr. Hayes. You go home and act like nothing has happened. For your safety, we will keep what you did a secret."

Alex smiled and exited the jail, got on his pony and traveled back to his home. 'Bear' confirmed what Alex had told him, and after a long discussion about the matter, the two lawmen decided there was no need to start a feud in this town over an innocent boy doing the right thing and killing a wrongdoer. He explained to the people that apparently Kevin had been killed by one of the many folks he had cheated or tormented during his life. In that regard, Mr. Hayes could not seek revenge on anyone.

Marcus and Bonnie rode home that day, their life problems completely erased. The war was over for Marcus, and Bonnie could not be accused of killing anyone, and soon the Civil War would be over for everyone. As they rode home sitting close to each other in the bouncy buggy, Bonnie suggested they stop at her house so she could fry some pork sausage and bake some biscuits and gather a few of her mother's cookies and celebrate this day relaxing on their favorite rock down by the creek. Some of their best memories were spent there, and this day had to be one of those.

In the next few months Marcus and Bonnie wed, and his father gave him a piece of the farm to work. The Confederate Army would never bother Marcus again. The Army concluded Marcus had been executed back in Mobile, and the one who would reveal his whereabouts was lying in a cemetery. It wasn't long until Marcus and Bonnie had their first of seven children, who in time all helped to make their farm a success. They prospered well until Marcus was too old to work and handed the farm over to his oldest son.

One day, Marcus was in town with two of his granddaughters. The town had recently erected a statue in memory of the local Georgian soldiers who had fought and died in the war. All the veterans' names had been cut in marble at the base of the statue. Although the local people knew Marcus was a hero, he had refused to discuss his war experiences with his children or family, not wanting to be troubled by the horrible memories he had encountered.

"What is that new statue for?" one of his granddaughters asked.

"It's a statue honoring all the soldiers who fought in The War Between the States."

"Grandpa, did you fight in the war?"

Marcus hesitated for a moment, recalling his near suffocation in the coffin. He breathed deeply, but admitted, "Yes, I did."

"Then let's go over and see if your name is on the statue. You never told us you fought in the war."

"I know, darling, there's some recalls in a battle you want to forget. It is a terrible place to be."

When they walked up to the tall statue of a Confederate soldier holding a rifle by his side one of the girls asked, "Did you look like that man?"

"Yes, that could be me."

"Let's find your name."

After a moment or two of searching, one of his granddaughters squealed out with excitement, "Here it is, Grandpa." Both girls started jumping up and down with enjoyment. Suddenly their farmer grandfather had turned into a hero.

"Tell us about the war, Grandpa! You never mentioned you were a soldier." Marcus looked over at his young granddaughters, patted the closest child softly on her head, and smiled, "My little darlings, if that's what you would like to know about, bring a pencil and paper over to Grandpa's house this evening and we can sit in the swing, and I will tell you what *I did in the war.*"

THE END

Lightning Source UK Ltd.
Milton Keynes UK
UKHW022107210921
390987UK00002B/274